NO DENIAL TO DESIRE

Alec crushed his mouth on Mira's, his body pressing her back against the wall even as she tried to shrink away. He forced her lips open, plundering her hungrily. She tried not to respond, tearing her mouth away from his and gasping frantically. "You're mine," he said, his lips hot against her throat, "—how can you deny it, when even I can't? Don't lie to me . . . dammit, don't turn away from me. . . ."

She fought him until his mouth found her once more, and then, suddenly, she was flooded with warmth, and she gave a helpless sob . . . she was born for this . . . for him . . . and she lifted her head and gave herself to his mouth . . . his hands . . . his body . . . his hunger and his love. . . .

PUBLISHER'S NOTE

This book is a work of fiction. Names, characters, places, and incidents either are the product of the author's imagination or are used fictitiously, and any resemblance to actual persons, living or dead, events, or locales is entirely coincidental.

NAL BOOKS ARE AVAILABLE AT QUANTITY DISCOUNTS
WHEN USED TO PROMOTE PRODUCTS OR SERVICES.
FOR INFORMATION PLEASE WRITE TO PREMIUM MARKETING DIVISION,
NEW AMERICAN LIBRARY, 1633 BROADWAY,
NEW YORK, NEW YORK 10019.

Copyright © 1988 by Lisa Kleypas

Onyx is a trademark of New American Library.

SIGNET, SIGNET CLASSIC, MENTOR, ONYX, PLUME, MERIDIAN
and NAL BOOKS are published by NAL PENGUIN INC.,
1633 Broadway, New York, New York 10019

First Printing, December, 1988

1 2 3 4 5 6 7 8 9

PRINTED IN THE UNITED STATES OF AMERICA

*To Daddy, for his love and support,
and to Ki, for being my friend
as well as my brother*

1

*H*er full name was Mireille Germain, but no one at Sackville Manor knew it. For that matter, no one in England knew it. It would have invited much unwanted trouble to use her real name. Another lifetime was attached to Mireille Germain, one she had sought to escape by leaving her native country for good. In France she had been Mireille. Here she was Mira, and she much preferred her new identity over her old one.

Leaning her elbows against the sill of the turret window, she looked outside and enjoyed the breeze and the splendid view that the lofty height of her bedchamber afforded her. It amused Mira to watch the arrivals of Lord Sackville's guests. The wealthy lords and ladies were all occupied with constant preening, a habit which Mira had once jeered at and mocked openly, until she had been taken under Sackville's wing. Now she had been taught better manners . . . but despite the rigorous tutelage she had received, she found that many of her old beliefs and attitudes were too deeply ingrained to change. She had been brought up in a world vastly different from this, in which the polite affectations of the gentry were looked on with contempt.

Another carriage approached the manor, having made the mile-long journey through the carefully wooded drive from the gate. The colors of the carriage were royal blue and black. According to Sackville's gossip about the guests that would attend his hunting party, blue and black were the Falkner colors. As the elegant pair of bays pulled the vehicle to a halt in front of the portico, Mira leaned a little further out the window, her coffee-brown eyes focusing on the figure of Alexander Falkner, Duke of Stafford, as he stepped into view.

He looked much younger than she had expected, and he was very handsome, with tanned skin and black hair that had been cropped short at the back of his neck. There was unconscious arrogance in the way he straightened his coat and walked to the front of the carriage. In a smaller man that stride could have been called a swagger, Mira thought, and smiled slowly as she stared at him. Around him there was an air of vitality and health that she found very appealing. Currently the vogue for men was to adopt the romantic pallor that Byron had made so popular. Most of the fashionable young bucks tried to look indolent and melancholy, as if they were pining with hopeless longing . . . but here was one man who seemed to have no such pretensions.

Mira rested her chin on her hands as she watched him extend a brown hand to one of the horses and stroke its neck in an absentminded gesture. He grinned at something the coachman said, his teeth gleaming white against his skin. Was Lord Falkner really the man who had reputedly suffered so terribly over the death of his cousin? It did not seem likely. He did not look as if he had recently been bereaved. Sackville had said that Falkner had grieved a long time over the murder of his cousin, but Mira decided that this must have been one of Sackville's typical exaggerations. In her short lifetime she had often seen death and the shadows it left behind, but there were no signs of grief on Lord Falkner's face.

Two of Sackville's footmen appeared in all their pompous grandeur, powdered, wigged, and curled, bowing to Falkner and holding the doors open for him. After he went inside the manor, more carriages arrived to discharge their entertaining assortment of richly garbed strangers, but Mira watched only half-heartedly now, her mind still occupied with thoughts of the black-haired stranger.

Alec walked into the library and found William Sackville waiting for him with a drink and a pleased smile. That expression of quiet pleasure and good humor was one that Sackville wore often . . . and why not? Except for a wife and heirs to carry on his name, he had everything a man could want: a well-run home, many friends, financial stability, and the respect of all who knew him. His main interests, namely politics and hunting, were well-known to his friends. These interests were conveniently seasonal: each spring he went to London to represent Hampshire at Parliament sessions, and each fall he retired to the Sackville estate to hunt. He was unquestionably more skilled at the former pursuit. Sackville possessed the true essence of political genius, being able to keep from committing himself fully to any one loyalty. No one ever knew what stand he would take on a given issue, but everyone knew that he would manage to end up on the winning side. Having lived with him for more than two years, Mira had discovered the simple truth about Sackville that his closest friends had only guessed at: he was desperately afraid of being ridiculed. His image and his reputation were paramount to everything else, and his fear of censure sometimes drove him to irrational extremes.

Sackville's exact ancestry beyond his father was unknown; he had paid to have a distinctive pedigree created in order to mask the less admirable elements of his family's history. Pride had robbed him of a sense of humor, for although Sackville enjoyed teasing his friends and ribbing them in a friendly way, he did not receive such treatment from others in good spirit.

And it seemed that pride had inhibited his romantic life as well; it was rumored that the reason he had never married was that he had never found a woman to suit the high standards he desired in a wife.

"You're here earlier than usual, Falkner," he commented, handing Alec a brandy and sitting on the corner of the dark mahogany desk. His blue eyes twinkled. "Eager for the hunt this year?"

"Bored with London," Alec replied, curling an arm around the neck of a bust of a Sackville ancestor and taking an appreciative swallow of the fine brandy. "Tea and sympathy have always been tiresome to me, but never more so than the past few months."

"Oh . . . yes," Sackville muttered. "But have a tolerance, man, for those who wish to comfort you and those who feel the loss just as keenly as you—"

"No one felt the loss as keenly as I did," Alec interrupted bluntly, "though it's fashionable to pretend so." His face was expressionless, but something in his eyes led Sackville to believe that the statement was one not of self-pity but of cynicism.

"Holt was a well-liked man," Sackville said quietly. "I had considered canceling the hunt this year for fear that it would be overshadowed by the memories of him in the midst of this same gathering only last September."

"Have no fear. Give our distinguished assemblage a few bottles . . ." Alec paused and took another swallow of brandy, ". . . a few baubles, some music, and a dance or two—they'll forget him soon enough."

"Falkner," Sackville said, his lightly lined face creasing in worry, "I don't like the sound of this. Granted, you have never been the most tenderhearted of souls, but I don't want you turnin' into a hard-hearted fellow."

"What would you rather have me do?" Alec inquired mockingly. "Cry in my cups?"

"I'm not one for tellin' you what to do, 'cause God knows you'd be inclined to do the opposite. But it's been more than half a year, Falkner, and soon your friends will stop excusing your coldness because of Holt and start drifting away. Oh, you'll still have the hangers-on . . . the ones who are after your money and all you can do for them . . . but once your real friends start to turn away, it's hard to get 'em back."

Alec stared at him silently, inscrutably, and then he smiled.

"This isn't like you, Sackville—a lecture before I even get 'hello' and 'how are you.' "

"I only lecture you when I know you need it."

"Which is what makes you a valuable friend," Alec replied, splaying one large hand over the bust's scalp and drumming his fingers on the smooth marble brow. "Well, then . . . lecture more, if you please. Tell me of a curative for cynicism. Tell me how to look beyond simpers, insincerity, and hypocrisy—for, God help me, that's all I can see in every face I look at."

"A change of scene," Sackville suggested. "That's what you need. Italy, France—"

"I've tried that already. Same faces, same paintings, same food . . . same boredom."

"A new horse—"

"I have too many horses as it is."

"Perhaps," Sackville said hopefully, "you could try to find comfort in the company of your family."

Alec grinned, shaking his head. "I have too many relatives as it is. And every last one of them is intolerable."

"Then try a woman."

"I have—"

"Not one of your rented doxies," Sackville interrupted. "A real woman. The same woman, for at least a few months. Someone to be comfortable with, someone who knows what you like to drink and how to tie your cravat. By God, have you ever tried having a steady woman? It's wonderful, and I recommend it thoroughly."

"You're damned enthusiastic about it, aren't you?" Alec remarked thoughtfully. "Does this attitude have anything to do with the rumors I've heard about you? Is is true that you've got a mistress living with you here in the manor?"

Sackville smiled widely. "The most exquisite creature you'll ever rest eyes upon," he admitted. "Warm, passionate . . . she's taken an empty life and made it paradise on earth."

"God." Alec looked at him, one corner of his mouth turning up wryly. "How are you going to handle all of . . . this . . . with her here?"

"You mean the hunt?" Sackville inquired, waving his hand around in a dismissive gesture. "She'll stay out of sight most of the time, reading and so forth in her room. She's not much for socializing with this sort of crowd. She prefers . . . er . . ."

"She prefers one thing and probably does it quite well," Alec finished for him, smiling ruefully. "Does she have a sister?"

"I'm afraid not. She's one of a kind, Falkner . . . and I don't share."

Their companionable conversation continued as they left the library and walked upstairs, where the groom of the chambers had prepared the rooms for the guests. They always had a great deal to discuss, for despite the disparities in their ages, Alec being twenty-eight and Sackville almost thirty years older, they had much in common. Each had inherited a title and fortune in his schoolroom years, and all the problems associated with having too much power at too young an age.

Somewhere in Alec's mind had always lurked the resentment of having been forced to take on the responsibilities of family, land, and tenants when he was still in his teens. The death of his father had forced Alec to become a man overnight, robbing him of the carelessness and the frolicking that his peers were enjoying. He had come to rely on his cousin for companionship and laughter. Wild, reckless Holt had lured him into many unsavory adventures, never failing to provide a break from the monotony of responsibility and work. Sneaking women up to Alec's rooms and leaving them there as a surprise . . . sending messages in the middle of the night that begged clownishly for companionship at a disreputable bar . . . mischievous, lively Holt, who had fallen in and out of love once a week and had coaxed Alec to join him in drinking to the ficklenesss of women. "You need me around," Holt had often told him, "because everyone else takes you too damned seriously." Now that Holt was gone, Alec knew just how true that had been.

After seeing him to the room, Sackville left to welcome his other guests. Alec wandered about aimlessly, reacquainting himself with the manor. The interior of Sackville Manor was as comfortable as the exterior was captivating. There was a fire in every room, a bounty of artwork and books to peruse, plenty of deep, well-upholstered chairs and plush, richly draped beds. At Sackville's annual hunting parties some of these luxurious beds were used far more than others, for this was an occasion of great indulgence in many areas.

The outside of the manor was sturdy and fortresslike, yet so picturesque that the eye jumped from place to place in agreeable fascination. The walls and rooftops were edged with crenellation and the gables were stepped, giving it the appearance of a castle. Of particular note were the tall, square turrets that bordered the corners of the building, for they appeared to be the kind in which fairy-tale princesses were destined to be locked up and held captive.

Alec's room was located at the end of the hallways, near the entrance to one of the square towers. He paused at the small stairway, leaning against the wall and contemplating what might be stored in the turret. Perhaps it was used as an attic or a garret for some of the servants. Suddenly his musings were interrupted by the sound of small feet on the stairs.

Mira came down from her bedroom to go to the kitchen. The cook and the housekeeper were busy preparing for the guests and Mira knew that her help would be appreciated. Lord Sackville was incensed whenever he heard that she lifted a finger to help, but Mira was no stranger to work. She liked to feel useful, and in her present capacity she felt as if there was no opportunity for her to be useful to anyone. She stopped short on the second-to-last step as she realized that there was a man standing in front of her, a very tall man. She recognized his coal-black hair at once and stared at him with unabashed curiosity.

His eyes were the light gray of rainwater, crystalline and framed with spiky black eyelashes. His brows, strongly drawn and faintly slanted, were velvet black. It was an unnerving effect . . . those shrewd and brilliant silver eyes set in that dark face, narrowed slightly as if he could see every secret written in her heart. His mouth was wide and expressive, one corner lifted just enough to reveal that a sardonic wit lay behind those wantonly handsome features. Immediately she wanted to take a few steps backward. That aura of physical strength that she had sensed from far away was overpowering up close. Every line of his body was perfect, from the taut thighs encased in buff pantaloons to the wide shoulders and lean torso covered in blue coat and conservatively striped waistcoat.

"Hello," Alec said, his face wiped clean of all expression as he stared at her. Then his eyes darkened intently, seeming to drink in every detail of her appearance. He noticed the agitated movement of her fingers as she curled them into the folds of her dress. "I hope I haven't startled you," he said, his voice low and oddly hushed.

"Oh, you haven't," Mira replied, her long lashes sweeping down to her cheeks. Then she dared to smile at him, and Alec was enchanted by the dance of laughter in her eyes. "You're Lord Falkner, aren't you?" He nodded, looking up and down the hallway before replying. It was time for a watchful chaperon to come in search of her charge, for a girl with her looks would not be left alone and unguarded for long. As she correctly interpreted his glance, Mira's smile faded. "I was just on my way to—" she began, and took a step forward without remembering that she was still on the steps. Pitching forward, she stretched out her arms instinctively to brace herself, anticipating the shock of her body hitting the floor. In a quick reflex Alec reached out and caught her, absorbing the momentum of her fall as she stumbled fully against him. His arms closed around her, strong and steady, protective.

Momentarily stunned, Mira looked up at him, her heart hammering and seeming to rise up high in her chest. An indescribably pleasant fragrance clung to him, a subtle mixture of male skin, clean linen, and the faintest touch of bay rum. His gray eyes were very close as they met hers, and she couldn't help noticing how beautiful they were.

"Oh, how clumsy I am," she said breathlessly, her voice muffled by his coat.

"No, not at all. Anyone could have—"

"I'm glad you were so quick, or I might have been—"

"—yes, the floor is very—"

"—I don't know how to thank you for . . ." As she looked up at him, they both became still. He was still holding her close, much too close against his body, and Mira knew somehow that he was as acutely aware of her as she was of him . . . but a man like him was forbidden to her, would always be forbidden. "You . . . you may let me go now," she said reluctantly.

His arms did not loosen. "Are you steady on your feet yet?" he asked gently.

"Yes, I think so."

"You should be more careful," he murmured, still

holding her. "I wouldn't want you to get hurt." Her body was so soft and yielding against his that Alec found himself unwilling to release her. Dozens of questions ran through his mind. He wondered who in the hell she was, why he hadn't seen her before . . . he wondered why she stared up at him so uneasily and what she would do if he kissed her. What a temptation she presented! Her velvety brown eyes were dark and filled with secrets, and she seemed so eager to fly away that his hold tightened on her. "What is your name?" he asked, his dark head lowering slightly.

"My lord, please." She pulled away from him in a startled movement.

Alec let her go reluctantly, beginning to smile as she flushed and averted her gaze from his.

"I'm sorry," he said, his eyes gleaming with warm amusement. "It seems we've both made a misstep. I'm usually much better mannered."

"And I'm usually very surefooted," she said.

"I believe that."

"Thank you for . . . catching me. I must be going downstairs now—"

"Wait," he said, making an impulsive move as if to take her arm, and then his hand fell by his side. "What is your name? Are you one of Sackville's guests?"

Mira wanted to shrink away from him in sudden discomfiture. So he didn't have any idea of who she was. She knew what was coming next, and yet her pride would not let her run from him.

"My name is Mira," she said stiffly. "Yes, I'm one of Lord Sackville's guests, more or less a permanent one. I live here, in the turret."

Alec could not believe his ears at first. She was Sackville's mistress? His silver gaze turned to ice as it traveled from her head to her toes, noting her smoothly confined hair and the beautiful garment she wore, the well-outlined shape of her body and the pristine paleness of her skin.

"I was just talking to him about you," he said, his voice noticeably cooler. "Somehow I had imagined you to be much older."

"It seems you were mistaken."

"It seems I was very mistaken," he agreed softly.

"I must be going," she said, turning away, until his voice stopped her.

"I've heard that you tend to hide away up here."

"Yes," she replied without looking at him.

"Why?"

"Because I like to be alone."

She could feel his eyes lingering on the wide boat-shaped neckline of her gown and the smooth swell of her breasts. His gaze had previously held the warmth of admiration; now it contained a searing insolence.

"I can't help wondering about something," he murmured. "What were you before?"

"Before?" she repeated warily.

"Before you became Sackville's mistress. A girl from the village who was willing to sell herself for fine clothes and a room at the manor? Or an impetuous merchant's daughter, hoping to entice Sackville into marrying you but ending up as his—"

"Neither," Mira interrupted, favoring him with a disdainful smile. So it seemed that Falkner was the same as the rest of his peers, eager to pass judgment on other people, contemptuous of the lower classes . . . so certain that he himself was above reproach. "Please excuse me, my lord. I would not soil your immaculate presence with my company any longer."

She left him there while he stared after her, his mouth set and his handsome face cold.

Alec adopted a mask of charm and agreeability that night as he and the sixty-odd guests of Lord Sackville sat at the immense table in the eating room. His mood was only superficially pleasant, for inwardly he still brooded about the girl in the rose gown . . . Mira . . . and he became more disgusted by the entire situation as he thought about it. How could she have agreed to become the mistress of William Sackville, a man more than twice her age? Could she actually cherish some tender feeling for the older man, or was it entirely a financial arrangement? It must be for the money, he decided savagely, remembering the expensive cut of her gown and the delicate beading on the bodice and sleeves. Yes, she was mercenary, as all women were at heart.

Despite his intention to enjoy the meal, he chewed and swallowed without much concentration on its delicate flavors. To him the truffled roast chickens were tasteless, the fresh river trout cooked in Bordeaux wine was uninteresting, as were the braised goose and glazed vegetables. The dinner conversation seemed interminable. On his left sat Lady Clara Ellesmere, the greatest bedhopper in London. On his right, Lady Caroline Lamb, vivacious and vaguely unbalanced. Alec could barely wait for the hunt to begin on the morrow, for at least that reduced life to more basic and less-complicated terms—predator and prey, the chase and the victory. He liked hunting because it was fast-paced, and on the field he could forget about such meaningless, nagging matters as Sackville and his woman.

The difficulty of hunting on the Sackville estate was the quantity of subdivided fields; the vast number of fences and hedges that the riders had to jump over made the sport more hazardous but also more exciting. In order to save the horses from the weary pace of a prolonged chase, each rider possessed two or more mounts, which were exchanged as frequently as necessary. Alec had brought three horses with him, his favorite being the chestnut named Sovereign, a skittish and spirited animal that required a hard ride before the main event began in late morning.

An hour or so after the sun rose, Alec was out riding Sovereign alone. Later in the day he would have to change into appropriate hunting attire, including a top hat and red coat. For now he was dressed casually in a pleated white shirt, tan pantaloons, and cuffed topboots. The morning coolness clung to his clothes and dusted his coal-black hair with sparkling dampness as he rode through the woods. The horse was more nervous than usual and Alec grinned as he decided to give the animal a freer rein.

"All right, boy, we'll work some of the energy out of you," he said, touching his spurless heels to the animal's sides, and they catapulted through the woods at a breakneck pace. The clean, fresh air seared through his lungs, filling his senses with exhilaration. In these few minutes Alec was aware of being completely alive. There was freedom in not having to think, in letting the power of muscle, motion, and reflex take hold of him. They soared over a hedge, the straining urgency of galloping removed for the second that they were airborne, light as a breeze. Then sharp, fleet hooves dug into the ground again and the mad flight continued. Another hedge followed, but just after taking it, Alec saw another fence loom directly in front of him. It was too late to refuse the jump and they were not going fast enough to clear it. He had no time to react before the horse's front hooves clattered against the top rail.

Mira walked through the woods leisurely, swinging a cloth bag as she made her way carefully over the ground. She spent a great part of each morning outside, picking herbs and digging up roots to use in powders and salves. Her dress was a simple and old one, its pale blue color reduced by vigorous washings to a nondescript gray. The hem was cropped to a point between her knees and ankles, almost up to her pantaloons, revealing more of her legs than any respectable woman would ever show. She took care that no one ever saw her in this outlandish outfit. It made moving much easier, not tangling around her legs as longer skirts tended to do.

Pausing at the distant thunder of hooves, she listened until the sounds stopped abruptly, and she wondered if someone had been thrown. Considerations of her appearance kept her from going immediately in the direction of the hoofbeats. She had no desire to invite ridicule or even worse attentions from whoever might have fallen. But neither could she ignore the possibility that someone had been hurt. After walking for a few minutes, Mira came across a riderless horse, its eyes wild and its sides quivering. The veins in its muzzle and neck were distended and pulsing. The horse stood there as she approached it in a gentle manner, her voice soft.

"Poor animal . . . my poor one, I won't hurt you. *Qu'est-ce que c'est le problème?*" Instinctively she reverted to French, for it was more fluid and calming than the staccato sound of English. *"Où est ton maître?"* Cautiously she took hold of the reins and wound them around a branch before moving in the direction that the horse had come from.

Alec dragged himself against the papery trunk of a tree, his breath hissing through his teeth. His arm, sticking out at an odd angle, had been either broken or dislocated. He felt as if some giant hand had wrenched the limb backward from deep inside his shoulder. The brilliant pain of it caused points of light to dance in front of his eyes, and Alec began to wonder hazily if he should allow himself to pass out. He retained a feeble hold on his consciousness, looking at the broken fence through slitted eyes. Slowly he became aware of an approaching figure. It was her . . . Mira. Mira in some kind of strange dress, her dark hair gathered in a thick braid that fell to her waist, her expression tinged with an emotion he couldn't identify. How or why she was there, he did not question.

"Go . . . get someone . . ." Alec gasped, sweat trickling from his brow into his eyes.

"Your arm—"

"I think it's dislocated . . . it'll have to be set . . . dammit, go!" He could not stand the acute pain much longer, and in his belly gnawed the dread of having the bone set. He had seen men howl before at the process, and now he knew exactly what they had been howling about.

Mira walked toward him, her eyes moving over him in quick analysis.

"I think I can help you. Around here they come to me for heal—"

"I told you to leave," he snarled.

"Can you move your fingers?" she persisted quietly, and Alec leaned his head against the tree trunk, regarding her through cloudy eyes.

"If you're thinking . . . of getting back at me . . . for yesterday," he muttered, "forget it. I'm still capable of . . ." He blinked hard in an effort to focus on her. "I can still—"

"I understand," Mira said wryly, feeling an unwanted flicker of sympathy for him, the bad-tempered brute. "But I assure you, I paid little attention to what you said yesterday." She began to draw closer to him, keeping her voice low and gentle. "Of course I will go to fetch someone, just as you asked. The pain is only in your shoulder? If you'll just let me make you more comfortable . . ." Slowly she approached him, wondering if Falkner had fallen unconscious, for his eyes were closed and his face was pale.

She was close enough now to see the damp strands of ebony hair that clung to his forehead, the taut clenching of the muscles in his jaw. The black lashes lifted as he looked at her, and his gaze caused a flare of anxiety in her stomach. Despite his weakened condition, she could not help but sense his considerable physical power. The wisest thing to do would be to leave him and go back to the manor—although he might have a thought or two about the damage she could do to him, she had much the same thought in reverse!

But there was no one who could help him as well as she could. The local physician was inept and clumsy, a drunkard. And although there was no reason in the world why she should feel any compassion for Alec Falkner, she did not like the idea of him suffering needlessly. Kneeling beside him, Mira stroked the hair off his forehead.

"Let me make you more comfortable," she said, and before Alec could make a sound, her fingers brushed over his injured shoulder in an exploratory touch. "Ah . . . I see what the problem is. It's not bad at all . . . I don't think it's broken."

Alec's good hand flew to Mira's waist, biting into the soft flesh hard enough to make her wince.

"Don't touch it—" he began hoarsely, and she took hold of his shoulder with one firm hand, his upper arm with the other.

"Let me."

"No . . . it's not . . ."

"Shhh—I know what to do," she murmured.

"Damn you, don't touch . . ."

Alec's protest died away, and he gasped as he felt her rotate his arm gently into place, her hands seeming to have some intricate knowledge of how the muscle, bone, and nerves were all connected. He winced, his fingers splayed in midair as the shoulder snapped into place. Suddenly the pain, the nauseating pain, abated rapidly. His eyes opened slowly, the pupils dilated until the gray was nearly consumed by unrelieved black. Alec stared at the intent face so near his, his lips parted in amazement. At first he was numb . . . then tiny needles of sensation pierced his arm. A shiver raced through his body at the onslaught of relief.

"Relax," Mira said, her hands slipping through the open neck of his shirt to the tightly knit surface of his shoulder. "You could still do damage if you move." Her fingertips sought the ravaged nerves deep inside his flesh, massaging with a surprisingly confident touch, soothing. He would not have expected her small hands to be so strong. Sighing, Alec loosened his hand and let it rest on her back, his eyes closing.

"How did you do that?" he whispered, a flood of lassitude sweeping through him.

"I've always been good at this kind of thing," Mira said, working on his shoulder with an engrossed expression. His skin was smooth, stretched tightly over well-exercised muscles. Black hair was spread over his chest extravagantly, like luxuriant fur. Now I know, she thought wryly, how it feels to take a thorn out of a lion's paw . . . in such a situation, one's compassion was overridden by doubts about one's own wisdom. "More because of necessity than real talent," she continued, "but I do have—"

"According to Sackville, you have a greal deal of talent," he interrupted. "Although at the time we were not discussing the art of healing." Her fingers loosened, and his arm tightened around her waist. Immediately his tone became beguiling. "No . . . don't stop."

"For someone who needs my help, you're very arrogant," Mira observed, resuming her probing massage.

"You'll receive my thanks when I get up from here in one piece," Alec said, his eyes still closed in bliss. It felt too damned natural for his arm to be fitted around her waist. The warmth of her breath caressed his cheek as she leaned closer, the silken length of her braid brushing against the uncovered area of his chest. Why did she have to feel so good? Why did she have hands that were pure magic against his skin? Why did he have to want her when he knew that he couldn't have her? She's Sackville's mistress, Alec tried to tell himself . . . she belongs to another man . . . she's not mine. "Your voice . . ." he murmured. "Your accent. Just a hint of some foreign—"

"French," she said, and as if the personal remark had either frightened or annoyed her, she made a small move to pull away. "I think you'll be fine now."

Alec's eyes opened, the pale hue of them almost startling Mira.

"Not yet," he said huskily. "My neck is still sore."

"Here?" Her fingers moved higher up his shoulders.

"No, more in the back . . . right over . . . God, yes." Bliss descended upon Alec in an unprecedented measure. Suddenly he seemed like a great purring cat, and Mira felt a stab of uneasiness as his hand splayed out over her back.

"Racing through the woods like that," she said reprovingly, "it's no wonder you were thrown. It's surprising that I didn't have to run around the forest picking one part of you up here and another part there."

"Just as long as you picked up all of the essential parts."

"You didn't make good use of the head on your shoulders, my lord . . . not if you have so little sense that you ride like a demon through the—"

"Now that my arm is better," Alec interrupted, ignoring her criticism, "can you do something for a headache?"

Mira laughed softly, her fingertips accidentally brushing against the thick ebony hair that curled against the nape of his neck. "No. Really, I am not a witch, Lord Falkner. I cannot pull out a wand and recite some magic charm to make headaches disappear."

"Your hands are magic," Alec said huskily.

Abruptly the movements of her fingers stopped. Mira realized in flustered confusion that he had wound her long hair around his wrist and that he was pulling her head closer to his.

"Let me go," she said, going stiff and cold all at once. He stopped urging her forward but did not relinquish his grip on her braid. Their lips were just an inch apart. Mira could not smother the trembles that took hold of her. She felt surrounded by him, dominated by him.

Alec swallowed, so tempted by the delicious feel of her in his arms that he could barely keep himself from drawing her completely against him. It would be the most natural and effortless thing he had ever done to kiss her. What was wrong with him? He could not kiss her, he could not let her go. The feminine smell of her was a potent aphrodisiac, causing him to respond like any rutting bull in heat, and he either had to have her or find some way of getting rid of his desire for her.

"I suppose," he said in a low voice, "that you'd prefer to be paid for it first."

Mira's eyes widened. Then she slapped him, instantly gaining her freedom as she left a streak of fire against the side of his face. His head was turned with the force of her blow, and then his brooding gaze returned to hers.

"Your manner of showing gratitude leaves much to be desired, my lord." She stood up and backed away from him.

Alec smiled bitterly as he regarded her. Her beautiful face was flushed, her eyes gleaming with a dark flame. Was this how she looked as Sackville made love to her?

"I don't particularly wish to feel grateful to you." He sneered. "And your overwhelming show of mercy this morning doesn't change what you are or what I think of you."

She stared at him in disbelief, then turned and fled from his jeering smile, her slim legs showing in a pale, lovely glimmer as she ran.

*　　*　　*

It took all of Alec's concentration to be civil to Sackville, who noticed that something was wrong but declined to ask what. Luckily Sackville's private pack of hounds kept the chase fast and aggressive, robbing the hunters of the necessity of making conversation. Alec's shoulder ached slightly but gave him no real trouble. Every time he became aware of it, he could not help thinking of Mira's hands slipping underneath his shirt, and the thoughts of her threatened to undo the cords of his sanity.

None of the women had decided to hunt today, a fortunate circumstance in that the hearty flavor of the chase was undiluted by any sight of feminine feathers or bobbing curls and bows. Whenever a woman was along, no matter how skillful, the men's enjoyment of the hunt was diminished by constant awareness of her and concern for her safety. The ladies were back at the manor preparing to go for a country drive or pay visits to neighboring estates. They gossiped and played cards, dividing themselves into groups that the members would seldom stray outside of. Some groups were livelier, brewing mischief among themselves and casting aspersions on those not present to defend themselves. Others talked quietly of books and poetry, and more rarely of politics. Some talked of fashion, others of romantic interludes and adventures. The entire hunting party, now numbering about ninety, all included, would meet again in the evening for dinner. Afterward they would dance, put on small vignettes, sing or play instruments, and engage each other in games such as charades, chess, and cards. And so the pattern would be repeated each day for three weeks, until the men tired of the hunting and the women tired of the monotony, and they would all disperse to seek new parties and new activities.

Mira kept herself well-separated from everyone except the servants of the manor. She had managed to charm her way into a multitude of friendships with the maids, the cook and housekeeper, the footmen, and even the stableboys. They all knew how she had originally come to Sackville Manor two years ago, and she suspected that they were kind to her because they suspected the real reasons for her position as Sackville's mistress.

The guests of the hunting party and the servants they had brought with them were not so kind. She knew that Lord Sackville gossiped about her often, making certain that everyone was aware of her role at the manor. He did not mind that she seldom appeared in front of anyone; the element of mystery about her only intrigued the women and aroused the envy of the men that much more. And Mira did not mind Sackville's gossip, for that was part of the bargain they had struck with each other. Part of his pleasure in her was the image that her presence in his house created.

She reveled in the hours of solitude granted her. Mira read voraciously from the well-stocked library. She had a liberal amount of time each day to take a perfumed bath and dress with care. Sackville had insisted on outfitting her with luxurious clothes, stipulating only that she please herself in the choices of design and materials. Mira had not settled on the fashionable style of dress, the washed-out pastels and icy colors that were all the rage—lavender, gray, yellow, pink. Instead she picked out vivid, exotic hues that suited her taste and coloring—brilliant red, peacock blue, emerald, violet, and even a black velvet gown that played up her dark eyes and the exotic cast of her features. She went on rides and walks by herself, occasionally accompanying Sackville on trips to the village and making him laugh with the tales of her adventures in France.

Most of her meals were taken in her turret room, a place so airy and exquisitely decorated that Mira sometimes felt as if she were living among the clouds. She had been happy for the past two years, her pride undamaged by her label as Sackville's woman. Until now.

Perhaps, Mira thought reflectively, I have let myself become too vulnerable. Perhaps I am not meant to find happiness in one place for too long. All of her life she had wanted to belong somewhere. Life had been constant change, constant moving. She had never sunk down roots anywhere. But now she had been here for the longest period of stability she had ever experienced. There was joy to be found in becoming familiar with one place and the people that surrounded her. There was peace in forming habits, in knowing when she would eat and sleep, in being protected. Of course, she was not completely happy—Mira could not deny that sometimes she was lonely. And today, after Alec Falkner had thrown those contemptuous words at her, she had been unexpectedly disturbed. But wasn't security always bought at a price? And wasn't the contempt of one arrogant man worth the safety of being Sackville's mistress? What have I done, she asked herself in confusion, to make Falkner hate me so?

Puzzled and upset, Mira made her way downstairs to the small music room and found that it was empty. Closing the door to muffle any sounds, she sat down at the pianoforte and began to play. In the past two years she had taken enough lessons to be proficient at a few simple melodies. Her fingers moved nimbly over the keys as she sang quietly. The song was from Touraine, one of her favorite places in France, and it usually lifted her spirits the moment after she struck the first note. But today it failed to bring her any pleasure. She was not aware as she played that the door opened, or that her performance was being observed.

"How entertaining," a woman's voice echoed slightly in the room, and Mira turned with a start to see someone in the doorway. She was very beautiful, her hair pale blond and her skin milky white, her age somewhere between twenty-five and thirty. The woman was sumptuously dressed in a mint silk gown with black braiding, a sophisticated gown that suited her well. "So you're Sackville's . . . little treasure. All my husband has spoken of for the past day and night are the stories that Sackville has told about you, my dear." Her voice was silky and sweetly pitched.

"I'm sorry," Mira said, shooting up from the tiny bench and taking a few steps back as if to flee. There was no way out of the room except the doorway the woman occupied. "I did not intend to disturb anyone. I thought no one would hear among all the—"

"Do finish, please. Among all the gossip?" the blond woman inquired, and laughed huskily. "You did not disturb anyone. I was passing by and heard your performance. I am Lady Ellesmere, my dear, and I am simply enchanted by you. I can certainly see why Sackville is so taken with you."

Mira did not like the strange contrast between Lady Ellesmere's kind words and cool eyes.

"I must go," she said, edging closer to the doorway and averting her gaze from the hard, beautiful face.

"But why?" Clara Ellesmere inquired, turning with a mocking smile to watch Mira slip through the door. Her light laughter burned Mira's ears. "Do you think you are too good for my company? Or are you embarrassed because of your relationship with Sackville? You shouldn't be . . . you're very fortunate to have him. How did you manage to catch him? You must be a very clever girl."

Mira ran as the woman's laughter followed her down the hallway, her cheeks tingling with the heat of shame. Lady Ellesmere's voice had been filled with ridicule. It should not have hurt Mira, and yet it did. Inexplicably a picture of Falkner's handsome, sarcastic face shot through her mind, and she felt the pressure of tears build behind her eyes.

*　　*　　*

"And so ends the hours spent in pursuit of 'the noble science' of hunting," Sackville said, clapping Alec on the back.

"Noble science," Alec repeated curtly. "More like an efficient way to founder a good horse."

"You're still thinking of Stamford's mount? Well, just write it down as aggressive riding—"

"Aggressiveness is one thing, irresponsibility is another. He should have changed horses more often."

"You could have told him more gently, Falkner—"

"Was he gentle with the damned horse?" Alec inquired tersely. "He rode the animal into the ground!"

There was a short silence.

"He knows that now," Sackville said. "Try to forget it, my boy. You know accidents happen during every hunt."

Alec sighed. "I know."

"You've been unusually quiet today," Sackville said, giving him a conciliatory smile. "Tired? What the deuce, it's been a long day, hmmn?"

"Yes, it has.'"

Alec wore a morose expression as he shrugged out of his red coat and headed up the ornately balustraded staircase to his room. For some reason Sackville tagged along after him, continuing to prattle.

"We'll catch a brace of foxes by the weekend if our luck holds out . . . but wait until Berkeley arrives with his private pack. Best foxhounds in the country, and everyone knows it."

"Berkeley's coming to the hunt?"

"The third week."

Alec's interest was stirred despite his foul mood. The Earl of Berkeley and his wife, Rosalie, lived in Warwick, not far from his own estates in Staffordshire. The couple was a popular one, for the earl's ready wit was matched by his wife's charm, and their presence would enliven the gathering at Sackville Manor considerably.

"Lady Berkeley," Alec said slowly, his gray eyes narrowing thoughtfully as they climbed the stairs. "Now, there's an ideal woman. Beautiful, charming, and above all, a *lady*." He thought of Mira and scowled as he continued. "A faithful wife. Gently bred and—"

"Many of us would be grateful if she were a sight less faithful," Sackville interrupted, chuckling.

"I wouldn't think you'd have any reason to look outside Sackville Manor for your pleasure."

"True, true," Sackville admitted, his grin broadening. "Mira is all I could desire in a woman."

As they proceeded upstairs, Sackville did not notice the long, measured glance that Alec gave him. For the first time Alec noticed his old friend's slight paunch and thinning pale red hair. Sackville was not in the best of physical condition, nor did he possess the vigor of youth any longer. Undoubtedly he was generous and benevolent to his mistress, but could he truly satisfy her in bed? Though Alec was mildly disgusted at the turn his own thoughts were taking, he could not help but continue asking the silent questions. Sackville's skin was soft and slightly wrinkled with the advent of late middle age, and his body had lost the edge of toughness and strength it had once possessed. Wouldn't Mira, a young woman of twenty, prefer a man closer to her own age? Wouldn't she prefer a man with a full measure of vigor and passion, a man with a talent for pleasuring women?

Immediately a vision appeared in Alec's mind, of her slim, naked body writhing under his own, her mouth seeking his, her thighs opening to his hands, her hips arching up to him. Her hair, the rich, deep brown-black length of it, falling silkily over his body, her sweet voice crooning in his ear as he brought her to fulfillment over and over again. . . .

"Damn," he breathed, furious with himself as he struggled to overcome the rising heat in his loins. She had put a spell on him, one that he was determined to resist. But the hunt would last nearly three weeks more. Could he endure three weeks of wanting her, knowing that she was nearby, knowing that he could not have her?

"Did you say something?" Sackville inquired.

"I . . . no, I didn't." They reached his room, and Alec managed to smile at his friend. "Well, until supper . . ."

"I'll see you then," Sackville responded, his round face creasing with a cheerful expression. As Alec watched, Sackville started the climb up to the room at the top of the turret steps. To visit Mira. "I'll try not to be late," the older man murmured confidentially, and winked before continuing up to Mira's room.

Alec went inside his bedchamber and flung himself on the canopied bed, his hands behind his head as he stared at the clock. Alone with his brooding thoughts, he waited, giving a string of soft, meaningful curses as each quarter-hour passed. Finally an hour had gone by, and then Alec heard the sound of Sackville's shuffling feet on the turret steps.

An hour, he thought bleakly. He had spent an hour up there with her.

He wondered how she looked right now. Probably tumbled and tangled in the sheets. Her fair skin rosy, marked by another man's caresses, her hair falling in a black-brown cascade over the pillows. Were her eyes filled with satisfaction or wistful longing? Had she wanted to be held after making love, had she wanted to be caressed and kissed? He thought of how she had felt in his arms that morning, trembling, shy, outraged. He wanted to hold her again.

Feeling the need of companionship, Mira ate supper downstairs that night at the upper servants' table. The most significant members of Lord Sackville's household sat at this table, which was presided over by the housekeeper. Although the atmosphere was much warmer and congenial than that of the guests in the main eating room, dinner at the upper servants' table was conducted with all the rules and graces of proper etiquette. The cook, the butler, the valet, and the menservants were seated according to rank, while Mrs. Daniel, the housekeeper, took the head of the table. Mira sat to Mrs. Daniel's left, her brown eyes darting curiously to the doorway as the more boisterous noise of those who ate in the servants' hall floated into the room. Most of Lord Sackville's guests had brought their personal servants with them, and none of Sackville's staff particularly liked such an invasion.

"An unruly lot, the visiting help are," Mrs. Daniel remarked, casting her twinkling blue eyes upward in feigned dismay. Her plump, jolly face was ruddy with good health and good humor. "Thank the Lord we don't have to share our table with them."

"Yes, I'm glad o't," Joseph, the groom of the chambers, replied gruffly. "The livery that the Duke of Bedford brought wi'im . . . a snottier lot o' daffodils you never seen, I assure 'ee."

They all chuckled softly, partaking of the hot, steaming meal with pleasure and enthusiasm. There were roast beef, chickens and sausages, root vegetables, pudding steamed in a round-shaped mold, and thick slices of bread. Mira lifted a glass of watered-down wine to her lips, peering over the rim inquiringly as one of the footmen turned his head to cough harshly. It was Pauly, a tall man of about thirty-five, who had been tormented by a long-lasting chest cold.

"Pauly, I did not know your cough was still with you," Mira said, setting down her glass and looking at him in concern. "Did those coltsfoot lozenges do any good at all?"

"Best-tastin' one y'iver made," Pauly replied, pausing to suppress another rattling cough with his napkin. "It's no use worreting more about it, the cough'll go when it's gone, and none sooner."

"I should have known to make them stronger," Mira said, sighing and then looking at him impishly. "The better-tasting my concoctions are, the less effective."

"I'd sooner take your remedies before the physician's, Mira," Mrs. Daniel commented, and there was an agreeing murmur heard around the table. There was not one of them who hadn't been helped in one way or another by Mira's cures; they went to her whenever an ailment struck them. She was unquestionably more popular than the local physician, a quack who insisted on haphazard potions and bleeding his patients as a standard remedy for everything from wasp stings to fever. Mira's compassion and her natural ability to help those in pain were the reasons why they had all come to accept her so readily into the small community. Ordinarily the lord's mistress would earn nothing but scorn from any one of them.

"I'll make you some calamint tea after supper, Pauly, and that will clear it up if nothing else will," Mira said.

He nodded in thanks, his face turning red as he sought to prevent the cough from further disturbing the conversation.

"It's the September chill," remarked Percy, Lord Sackville's valet. Percy, an older gentleman with gray hair at the temples, had always been extraordinarily gentle and kind to Mira. She knew that he understood her relationship with Sackville, and although he was not entirely approving of it, Percy treated her with the deferential respect that was usually shown only to the highest-born ladies. "The beginning of winter's creeping up on us."

"Another winter," Mrs. Comfit said glumly. "I can hardly bear the thought, not when last spring was so long in coming and the summer so short."

"My third winter here," Mira murmured, putting down her bread slowly. Three winters at Sackville Manor. Would she wake up one morning and find that instead of twenty she would be twenty-five, or thirty? Would the next seasons slip by even faster than the last ones? Mira cast a look around the table at the familiar faces, bewildered by the sense of loneliness that had come over her so suddenly. Why was she unhappy when they all seemed so contented with their lives? Perhaps I should dose myself with some of my own medicines, she mused wryly. With all the herbs in her bag—confrey, coriander, flax, basil, and the rest— didn't she have something for this nameless affliction?

2

After a dream-ravaged sleep, Alec woke up with difficulty and found to his surprise that it was still early morning. Dressed in cream-colored pantaloons, a matching shirt, a chocolate-brown coat, and well-worn boots, he made his way downstairs and sat down to breakfast. In stark contrast to the scene in the eating room the night before, there were few people at the table. Lord Palmerston, the Earl of Bridgewater, Sir John Waide, and Squire Bentinck were all nursing either a cup of coffee or a stiff drink in their hands, while Sackville munched contentedly on liberally buttered oatcakes. They were all quiet in the face of a communal hangover. A few murmured greetings reached his ear as he joined the subdued group, and Alec inquired idly if any of them wished to join him on a ride.

"A ride?" Sackville repeated, wiping his mouth with a linen napkin to erase a smear of berry preserves. "When we're going hunting in a few hours?"

"The morning air might clear up your—" Alec began, and Sackville interrupted hastily.

"Falkner, I have no interest in anything the morning air might do for me. I'll rest here and send you off with good wishes for an invigorating ride."

"My thanks," Alec murmured, grinning briefly and setting his cup of half-finished coffee on the table before leaving.

The morning light was unblurred by any clouds. It

promised to be a warm day; there was an absence of the mist that had collected on the forest floor yesterday morning. Alec rode Sovereign in the same direction that he had taken once before, keeping the horse under stringent control. The aches and tightness of the night's tossing and turning gradually left his body. Alec enjoyed the morning, the daylight, the quietness and the concentration of solitary exercise, but the peace he had hoped for still eluded him. Finally he admitted unwillingly that he was looking for Mira, hoping that she would be walking outside in the forest again, and though he called himself a fool, he continued searching for her.

It was not long before he saw her; she was sitting in the crook of the trunk of a fallen tree, a muted ray of sun striking off her black-brown hair. Alec sat astride Sovereign and almost caught his breath at the sight of her. She was tousled and disheveled, and so beautiful that she did not seem real. He shook his head slightly, suddenly engaged in a silent battle with himself. The fact was that he could not allow himself to want her for many reasons . . . including that of his own honor. It was part of the code he lived by; a gentleman did not poach on a friend's property or take his woman.

Mira looked up from the pages of the book she had been reading, her bare toes curling into the bark of the log she was perched on. As she realized that someone was watching her, she drew her legs underneath her faded, shortened skirt, but not before his gray eyes had swept over the bare curves of her calves. They stared at each other in silence, the rustle of the forest and the nicker of the horse filling the wordless pause.

Her face was strangely arresting. There was a look of good blood and refinement about her—perhaps even a look of aristocracy—but there were also the strong features of a much sturdier stock. She did not possess the wan delicacy of a pure blueblood but rather a blooming hardiness that betrayed a mixed parentage. Dressed as she was, she might have easily been mistaken for a lovely peasant girl. But her eyes . . . the dark autumn depths of them contained a wealth of knowledge that no one as young as she should have possessed. Her heavily lashed eyes were mysterious and unfathomable, and Alec could only guess at all that she might have seen with that bittersweet gaze.

"Do you intend to ride by here every morning?" she asked, her voice low and terse, tinged with the unexpected precisions and rhythms of a foreign accent. He liked the way she spoke; although she pronounced the words almost perfectly, she tended to stress the wrong syllables, giving the language a more flowing sound than usual. In respone to her question, Alec glanced around the charming little clearing in the forest.

"It's an attractive path. Yes, I believe I will."

"Then I will find some other part of the forest to occupy until you're gone."

Alec laughed, his smile an attractive white slash in his dark face. "Do you sit out here every day?"

"I enjoy the privacy," Mira said pointedly, closing her book with a firm snap.

His eyes traveled over the book cover assessingly, then returned to her face.

"Jane Austen . . . *Northanger Abbey* . . . surprising."

"Why is it surprising?"

"I would have expected," Alec said softly, "something more along the lines of *Bewildered Affections* or *The Beggar Girl and Her Benefactors.*"

It was a remark calculated to annoy Mira, since those were absurd and sensational romantic novels currently popular among many of the foolish women who were attending the hunt. She smiled reluctantly, saw the teasing glint in his eyes, and then laughed.

"No," she said, "but I will confess that a copy of *Manners of the Day* was recently pressed on me with firm admonitions to read it carefully."

Alec grinned. "Really? I can't imagine why."

"Perhaps you would like to borrow it after I'm finished?" Mira suggested.

"Ah . . . what a kind offer," he responded with exquisite politeness. "But I'm afraid that I'm far too set in my ways to change—"

"What a pity."

"Yes." Alec's eyes lost some of their glinting coolness as he looked at her. "You like to read?"

"Constantly. I like almost anything. But Jane Austen is my favorite author."

"Why?"

Mira's expression became distant. She thought back to those long, lazy summer days in the little French village of Anjou . . . when she was fifteen, and Rosalie Belleau had taught her the nasal and complex sounds of the English language. They had pored over poetry, newspapers, and the novels of Defoe and Addison, studying and reading until the laughter or the glare of the sun on the pages overcame them. Rosalie had taken Mira's rudimentary knowledge of reading and writing and doubled it . . . and Mira, eager to please, eager to learn, had soaked up the lessons quickly. Five years ago, when she had been Mireille Germain, a girl in love with life, a girl who had loved her brother devotedly, unaware of his plans to betray them all . . . Mira, Rosalie, and Rand Berkeley.

"I read her books when I was in France," she said finally. "They gave me a sense of what the English might be like."

"Superficial?" Alec asked. "Materialistic . . . pleasure-seeking?"

Mira sensed that he was trying to trap her in some way. She did not know what he was trying to make her admit, but she chose her words carefully as she answered him.

"I discovered after spending some time here that her works were less reality than satire," she said quietly. "But her portrayal of the English seems to be very accurate at times. The English are very odd sometimes, and difficult to understand. You are seldom a straightforward people."

"And the French are?"

"The French I knew were."

"And what kind of people did you associate with in France?"

"I think you already know," she said, meeting his gray eyes squarely. "It is obvious that I'm not *pur sang*. It is obvious that my background is very different from yours and that I am not highborn as you are."

"Not so obvious," he replied slowly. "You have a certain air of pride that I wouldn't expect from a mere rustic."

Mira laughed suddenly. "A *rustic* . . . how snobbish you sound."

Alec's expression went blank with surprise. Impudent little wench! Hardly anyone ever dared to criticize him to his face, especially not a woman in her position. Yet she sat there and taunted him with a mischievous sparkle in her eyes. "Why do you look so amazed?" she asked innocently. "Aren't rustics allowed a little pride?"

"I suppose they are," he said, his handsome face shadowed with a dawning scowl.

"I think we rustics are more entitled to pride than you are," she said, smiling flippantly and daring to annoy him further, finding an unaccountable enjoyment in provoking him. "There is more merit in the struggle to raise a family than in attending endless parties. There is more value in the hunt to find food for the table than in the chasing of a small fox."

"You seem to have experienced life among the virtuous poor as well as the decadent rich," Alec murmured. "Yet it is obvious whose company you prefer."

His dart was sharp and superbly accurate. All of a

sudden Mira's enjoyment fled. Oh, she should have known better than to cross swords with someone like Alec Falkner. What was the matter with her, that she would try to taunt him so? She bent her head, unable to look at him.

"I do not prefer *your* company," she said huskily. "Will you leave or shall I?"

Alec turned Sovereign before she had even finished the sentence.

"I'll be looking forward to a continuation of our conversation," he said, and rode off gracefully, his powerful thighs gripping the sides of the horse.

Mira went to a different part of the forest the next day, but somehow she was not surprised when she heard the prancing horse's feet and a lazy masculine voice interrupted her labors.

"Do they feed you so poorly that you are compelled to go picking roots and weeds to supplement your diet?"

Mira turned around with a reluctant smile, an oddly shaped root in her hand and a smudge of dirt on her delicate cheek. She looked like an impish child who had been playing in the mud, and Alec could not resist smiling at the sight she made. Her maturity, however, was well attested to by the firm curves of her breasts under the sagging, faded gown and the shapely legs revealed by the cropped hem of the garment. Rich, dark curls escaped from her thick braid and edged her face softly, curls that tempted a man to wind his fingers in them and tilt her face upward for a kiss.

"I am beginning to suspect that you are following me."

"Small forest," Alec replied, swinging lightly off the horse and ignoring the strong impulse to go over and wipe the smudge off her face. "It's impossible to avoid you."

Mira turned hurriedly and focused her attention on

a nearby plant as Alec came nearer. He became more attractive each time she saw him, and even though she disliked him, she could not ignore the peculiar effect he seemed to have on her. She was strangely drawn to him. Perhaps it was because he reminded her in some ways of the Englishman she had known five years ago, big, healthy, and excessively male—though Alec was not in any part as gentle or kind as Rand Berkeley had been. "What's that?" he asked, stopping a few feet away from her.

"Something for Lord Sackville," she said, then could have bitten her tongue off for the slip she had made. Her fingers tightened around the root.

"Oh?" Alec's voice sharpened. "What is it?"

"Nothing."

"I think I've seen something like that before. It's a mandrake root, isn't it?"

"Do you come here merely to torment me?" Mira exploded, trying to sidetrack him with an irritated spate of words. "It's . . . it's merely for good health. I'm the only one around here who dares to dig it up because everyone else is so superstitious."

"Why? Is it bad luck to dig it up?"

"Yes. It's supposed to be dragged out by a black dog, so unless you can change into one, you're not needed here!"

Alec's next words were threaded with laughter.

"The mandrake. If I'm not mistaken, the Gypsies call it the 'two-legged man plant.' If you insist on ripping those out of the ground, it will not bode well for your reputation."

"If there is one thing that is useless to worry over, it's my reputation," Mira said. "It's well-shredded by now—"

" 'Pulverized' would be a more accurate term."

"*Yours* is hardly puncture-free," she pointed out.

"Bad reputations are a family characteristic," Alec replied, leaning against a sturdy slanting tree trunk and crossing his long legs idly. "I would hardly be a Falkner without one. Everyone has a blighted character, even my mother." Especially his mother, Juliana Penrhyn Falkner, who had informed him pertly before he had left Hamiltonshire that she hoped to be hearing his name soon in connection with a scandal or two. "You've been quiet for far too long since your cousin's passing," she had said to him sternly. "I've always encouraged my boys to be rowdy and troublesome . . . healthier that way. I didn't raise you to brood, and I won't begin to tolerate it now." Sharp-tongued, wise, and aggressive, his mother, with a heart that he suspected was soft, but had never been quite certain of it.

"You have a large family?" Mira asked, fingering a pink-flowered sprig of coriander and glancing at him out of the corners of her eyes.

"Very large. Very eccentric."

Mira laughed, the sound free and natural, so unlike the well-practiced and self-conscious giggles that Alec was accustomed to hearing from women.

"Eccentric in what way?"

"I suppose we span the usual variety of faults."

"And what is your fault?" she asked, her coffee-colored eyes daring him to answer honestly.

Alec smiled slightly and pushed himself away from the tree, walking back toward Sovereign. Mira waited in silence, wondering if he was going to reply or not. In a lithe movement Alec swung himself lightly into the saddle, the sunlight playing lovingly over his raven hair as he inclined his dark head to look at her.

"I never ask for permission."

"Oh. I suppose . . . that would tend to earn trouble for you, wouldn't it?"

"Where you're concerned, I suspect it will," he said softly, and touched his heels to the horse's sides. Flustered, Mira could not bring herself to say good-bye as he left.

* * *

The fourth morning Mira was exasperated with herself to find that she was unconsciously waiting for him to appear. Before going out she had spent several minutes debating with herself in front of the mirror, wanting to arrange her hair in a more elaborate and becoming style than the simple braid, and then cursing herself for even daring to think of such a thing. You are learning new things about yourself, she thought wryly. I did not know that your vanity was so great that you would want to make yourself more attractive for a man you dislike! And you probably won't even see him today! Gritting her teeth, she plaited her lustrous hair into its customary braid and tromped out to the woods.

It was becoming cooler every day, all the more reason for Mira to enjoy her mornings out before the weather began to inhibit her walks. The forest that bordered the fine gardens and lawns of Sackville Manor was lush and mysterious, inviting her most fantastic thoughts to come to life. Lush ferns and spicy golden pine needles carpeted the ground, while trailing moss and small, bright flowers permeated the air with an earthy scent. It was dim, the air shadowed by the brawny trees, but in some places the sunlight shone through to dapple the ground. Sighing in contentment, Mira sat on a huge rock and hooked her arms around her bent knees.

As Alec approached her, he wished that he had not given in to the urge to find her again. He had to find some way of dispelling his damned fascination with her. Ever since he first met her, thoughts of her disturbed his sleep; unconsciously he compared her with all of the women that were available for his pleasure, and he wanted only her. To his dismay, he was beginning to realize that his desire for her might not be merely a temporary thing. Dismounting from his horse, Alec wrapped the reins around a tender sapling and approached Mira slowly. She appeared not to notice him, then spoke with her eyes fastened on some distant point in the woods.

"I heard that the fox was not taken yesterday," she said.

"We ran him to ground."

"Lord Sackville said that many of the men wanted to dig the fox out of its hole but that you convinced them otherwise."

"Yes," Alec answered, leaning one solid shoulder against a tree and looking at her with that strange rain-gray gaze, which caused a faint flush of awareness to spread across her cheeks. "It's unsporting to dig a fox once he's found a place to hide."

"Coming from you, that was an unexpected show of mercy," Mira remarked thoughtfully.

"From the way you look at me, it's obvious that your sympathies lie with the fox," he said, his mouth quirking with amusement. She nodded silently. "No books today?" he asked.

"No."

"No strange roots or little flowers?"

Mira chuckled at his teasing. "No. I'm fully stocked with everything I might need."

"Where did you learn about such things?"

"I've always been interested in how to cure sickness," she replied, a smile tugging at her soft mouth. "When I was in France, traveling from place to place, I committed many bits of knowledge of natural medicine to memory." She paused and her eyes twinkled as she added, "I have an excellent memory. I rarely forget anything that I've seen or that's been said to me."

"Then somewhere in the realm of such a remarkable mind," Alec said, ignoring her last sentence, "is information about where you come from. Pray tell, where is home to you, aside from Sackville Manor?"

Even as he asked the question, he knew that she would not answer it.

"Home is everywhere," Mira said softly, the lost, burning expression in her eyes giving Alec an odd sensation. "I come from nowhere. I belong to no one." Her expression was sincere and mischievous all at once, as if she took a particular delight in avoiding his questions with such nonsense. He was exasperated by her vagueness; he wanted to *know* about her, he *needed* to know who she was, and he had no idea of how to force the answers out of her.

"You belong to whoever pays your price," Alec replied coldly.

"Do I?" she asked, unperturbed by his growing temper. "Do I belong to Sackville?"

"I suppose that depends on your own sense of loyalty."

"I have a very strong sense of loyalty . . . so I suppose I do belong to him. Ah, you are frowning . . . but isn't that the answer you wanted? Surely you can appreciate it, since loyalty is something you're quite familiar with. You are so loyal to the rules of hunting that you wouldn't dig up a fox, no matter how much the hounds and your companions long for blood . . . you are so loyal to a friend that you would not try to take his woman away from him . . . though I think you might want her for yourself."

Alec's mouth hardened into a straight line, his eyes flaring with silver light.

"I don't want you," he muttered. "Though I might enjoy turning you over my knee and spanking the disrespectful hell out of you, you little imp of Satan."

"What's stopping you?" she asked gently.

It was a contest to see who would lose control first. Alec muttered something under his breath. He looked into her face and she smiled engagingly at him, with the expression of a child who had lit a Roman candle and was waiting for the explosion. Suddenly he grinned, folding his arms across his broad chest, his anger fading away.

"It amazes me," he said, "that you haven't given Sackville apoplexy yet."

"Lord Sackville finds my conversation very soothing."

"Then I've underestimated him unforgivably."

Mira laughed helplessly, hiding her face against her knees, and the sound of Alec's soft chuckle fell on her ears with delicious lightness.

"I think I've underestimated you, my lord," she said, her voice muffled, and then she lifted her head to stare at him with a bright, penetrating gaze.

"How so?"

"Until now I thought you were merely a pompous, judgmental boor."

"And now?" he asked.

"You are not pompous. And you are not a boor."

He was adept at concealing his emotions; she could read nothing in his expression. As the silence ripened Mira wondered if she had dared to tread too far. Perhaps he had become angry with her. His temper was unpredictable and quick-flashing . . . she sensed that he was not used to someone purposely trying his patience.

"But you think I'm judgmental?" he finally inquired.

"Aren't you?" she countered. "You like to form your opinions very quickly—and once you have, you don't like to change them." He was the kind of man, she was certain, who would defend those he loved without hesitation . . . and would fight his enemies until there was no breath left in his body. "It's a dangerous fault, I think . . . since you may someday risk losing something very important—just because it doesn't fit into your scheme of things."

"Why do you say that?" he whispered, looking so wary and angry that Mira knew she had hit a vulnerable spot. She backed down immediately, her voice faltering.

"I . . . I don't know. I . . . just thought . . ."

"Someone once said almost those exact words to me."

"Who?"

"My cousin."

"The one who . . . who died in a duel?" Mira asked timidly.

He pinned her with a splintered-crystal stare, something so raw in his gaze that she wished she had kept her mouth shut.

"It was not a duel. I found him in an alley, beaten to death." Alec closed his eyes, unable to repress the memory from filling his mind with darkness—Holt, nearly the mirror image of him, the same black hair and well-defined Falkner features. Since boyhood they had pulled each other out of scrapes and trusted each other more than they had trusted their own brothers. Holt had been more likable than Alec, less sarcastic in speech, more carefree, more tender with people. He was the only one who could make Alec laugh right in the middle of an awe-inspiring storm of rage . . . yes, that had been Holt's talent—seeing the ironies of life and the weakness of human nature, and caring for people in spite of their faults. He and Alec would have died for each other, their bond fast and deep because they were Falkners and because they understood each other.

After Holt had failed to show up one night at the Rummer, a popular London tavern where they had agreed to meet, Alec began to search for him, rounding up his friends to scour the web of shadowy streets and alleys. Alec had been the first to find him . . . oh God, the sight of his long, broken body sprawled on the ground . . . *Holt!* . . . he had buried his face in the rough linen waistcoat, his mind reeling with the bruises, the blood everywhere, Holt's hands curled in a frozen spasm. Alec had turned into a stranger to himself, vicious and howling with grief, unable to stop even after becoming aware that his friends were trying to pull him away from the mangled body. Some of those friends would still not meet his eyes, even now, so many months after it had happened. Sinking into utter moroseness, Alec had hated the entire world for months after that, especially himself. If only he had known . . . if only he had been able to help Holt. But even after facing what had happened and understanding that he had to go on, Alec found that the unanswered questions kept plaguing him. Who had beaten Holt to death, and for what reason? *Why*, for God's sake, hadn't Holt's money or valuables been taken? His possessions had been left there, even the round gold Falkner medallion that he had always worn around his neck. Holt's death had been all that the unknown assassin had required.

Suddenly Alec understood why he was so unwillingly drawn to Sackville's mistress. She laughed at him in the same way Holt had, unafraid to tease him, unafraid to test his anger. How you would laugh, Holt, he thought to himself grimly. I've finally met the woman who could be the perfect match, and she has an angel's face, and she's more seductive than sin . . . and she already belongs to another man.

"I've got to leave," he said, and Mira nodded slowly.

He's a man of little moderation, she thought, watching him ride away as if the devil were in pursuit.

The drawing room was packed with guests, the air scented with coffee, tea, and perfume. It was eleven o'clock at night, the men and women all reunited after a day of hunting and social calls, having just shared a splendorous supper together. Privately Alec considered the room the least preferable of all to spend the post-meal hours in, for it was decorated in shades of red so brilliant as to affront the eyes. The dark, ornate scheme of crimson and gold swirled in endless patterns over the ceiling and carpet, rococo curves that connected intricately in confusing proliferation. It was a large room, the windows and the red draperies at least fourteen feet high. Cavorting angels pranced through the rampant designs of the elaborately painted and carved ceiling. The drawing room was a vision of overabundance unrelieved by any tasteful simplicity.

As they all sat down to relax and enjoy an evening's entertainment, Alec winced as he realized that Clara Ellesmere had managed to procure the seat next to his. She was completely amoral, indifferent to the needs and desires of anyone but herself . . . a hungry woman who enjoyed physical pleasure in all its various forms. Perhaps if she cared for anyone's opinion, it was that of her husband, who appeared to be indifferent to Clara and her reprehensible habits. Sometimes she would interrupt her flirtations to glance at Lord Ellesmere's resigned countenance in a taunting manner, but he never displayed any reaction to her activities. It was generally hoped that someday Ellesmere would take his wife in hand and either take a whip to her or confine her on a leash. Her public displays ranged from amusing to exasperating. It was entirely likely that she had slept with more than half the men present in the room—no small feat, considering the large number of the gathering. Alec only regretted that he had been one of them.

It had been a mistake to sleep with Clara that one night two years ago. She had been entertaining in bed, but Alec had found that all of her sophisticated sexual tricks were curiously one-dimensional, exciting the body but not the mind. He had experienced no further desire for her after that night, though she still professed to wanting him. She was a beautiful woman without a conscience . . . a lonely, lusty woman who used men and was used by them. She had nothing to offer except her well-groomed body—a poor substitute for a real woman with honest emotions.

"Have you enjoyed your hunting so far?" she asked silkily.

"Have you?" Alec countered.

She laughed lightly. "I have heard that you've had considerable success, Lord Falkner."

"Perhaps success—but little satisfaction," he replied, his gray eyes fixed on the piano as the Countess of Shrewsbury began to play.

"How ironic," Clara said, her red mouth curving enticingly. "I feel the same way." Her voice lowered conspiratorially. "But I never forget a good souce of satsifaction, Alec . . . and you're *very* satisfying." She leaned closer and began to whisper, each syllable cloying and sweet. "Do you recall that night we shared? It could happen again . . . perhaps even tonight. I remember everything, everything you did to me, and each time I look at you the memory becomes—"

"I'm sure you have many such memories," he drawled. "Are you certain that you're not confusing me with someone else?"

"Not you . . . I would never forget you, Alec," she said, rising in a sinuous movement to leave the room. "Excuse me, *mon cher* . . . I'll return soon."

Lord Sackville, who was seated on Alec's left, tapped him on the shoulder as Clara disappeared.

"Is Lady Ellesmere retiring for the night?" Sackville asked.

"Unfortunately not . . . and when she does, it won't be with me."

"Poor fellow . . . when I advised you to find a woman, I didn't mean her kind."

"I know exactly which kind I want," Alec assured him dryly.

"I propose," Squire Osbaldeston said amid the half-hearted applause for Lady Shrewsbury's performance, his face flushed with too much wine, "that my wife, Lady Osbaldeston, follow her recital with a song!"

Alec groaned inwardly, settling lower into his seat.

*   *   *

Mira heard the inept crooning of yet another would-be songstress as she came from the kitchen. Grinning, she slowed her pace and went to the closed drawing-room doors to hear better. This assemblage might contain some of the wealthiest, most elegant aristocrats in England, but talented they were not. The voice that emanated from inside the room was reedy and wavering, as someone sang a recent poem of Byron's that had been put to music.

"Poor lamb . . . what are you doing out here?" Mira spun around to see Lada Clara Ellesmere directly behind her. Mira's smile disappeared instantly. Lady Ellesmere leaned closer to the door, tilting her sleek blond head to hear the dreadful strains of the singer's final verse. "Ah, not a very inspiring performance, is it?" Lady Ellesmere asked. "But not many people are as talented as *you*, my pet."

"My lady," Mira began, "if you'll excuse me—"

"But why are you listening all alone?" Lady Ellesmere inquired kindly. "You should be in there with the rest of us, lending your support to the efforts of the entertainers."

"No, I must—" Mira stopped speaking with a gasp as she found her wrist held in a tight, clawlike grip. "Ouch—what are you doing?"

The applause for the song came in a muffled clatter through the doors.

"Come, I will escort you in," Lady Ellesmere said, her eyes glowing with malice.

"No!" Mira answered in rapidly growing panic, tugging at her wrist. The other woman was surprisingly strong; her long-nailed grip was unyielding. "Let me go!"

Clara flung open the doors, pushing them hard enough so that they swung against the walls and alerted everyone's attention. Mira began to shake as a sea of heads turned toward them. She had never seen so many faces, so many eyes, and they were all focused on her.

"Come in, lamb," Lady Ellesmere purred, dragging her further into the room. As the crowd began to realize who she was, a multitude of murmurs and whispers slid around Mira, suffocating her. She felt all the blood drain out of her face. Then all sound shriveled away, and the silence was worse than the noise had been. "Lord Sackville," Lady Ellesmere said, her red mouth tilting upward in a sweet smile, "I believe this is one guest we have not made the acquaintance of. But she was listening outside the door like a deprived little waif, when I am certain you would wish her to be included in the evening's festivities."

Lord Sackville stood up slowly, while Caroline Lamb and a few of the other women tittered behind their hands. How scandalous! Only Clara Ellesmere would dare to drag Sackville's mysterious mistress into the middle of a respectable society gathering, and only Clara would do it with such wicked glee.

The haze in front of Mira's eyes disappeared as she heard the women's snickering. Her dark brown eyes traveled around the room slowly, from face to face. She saw contempt, interest, mockery. Deep in the pit of her stomach she felt icy anger collect, a cold anger that vanquished the heat of shame. Lord Sackville, she noticed, looked mildly annoyed . . . a man fiercely protective of his own pride, he wished above all else to avoid being made a fool of. Next to him sat Alec Falkner, whose face was unreadable and his mouth harshly set. Mira met his gray eyes, feeling a strange, lightning-hot sensation as he stared at her. She knew instinctively that if she made one sign of appeal to him he would help her. But Mira would not bring herself to ask for his help, not his or anyone else's.

"Don't you think she should be allowed to perform?" Lady Ellesmere inquired of Lord Sackville.

"She is such an entertaining creature." The gathering was deathly still. The situation was growing to absurd proportions; surely it had not been suggested that they sit there to be entertained by Sackville's mistress! Mira looked at Lord Sackville expressionlessly, while his own expression turned thoughtful. She had often played for him privately, and he knew that she was proficient. Mira could almost see the inner workings of his mind as he calculated how best to resolve the situation in his own favor. After a long moment he nodded to her.

"Why don't you play something for my guests, Mira?"

White-faced, Mira inclined her head. "It will be my pleasure, my lord . . . as soon as Lady Ellesmere releases my wrist."

There was a sudden flicker of laughter among the crowd. Clara let go of her immediately, her red-lipped smile faltering for a split second as she realized that she was in danger of looking like the villainess of the piece.

Unable to restrain himself any longer, Alec stood up. "My God, William!" he hissed in Sackville's ear. "Stop this immediately. Have you no consideration for her feelings? She's not a possession to be displayed in such a manner!"

Sackville turned affronted blue eyes to him.

"Are you telling me how to treat my mistress, Falkner?" he rebuked. "If you're so concerned about her feelings, sit down before you make the scene worse for her."

Slowly Alec lowered himself back into the chair, every muscle in his body taut with the control he imposed on himself. The smothering silence of the room did not ease, and the rustle of Mira's skirts was audible as she walked to the piano. She moved with straight-backed grace, her slender figure riveting every eye. She wore a black velvet gown, its softness skimming the lines of her figure in stark simplicity. The sleeves were puffed and slashed in the Elizabethan style, a row of tiny buttons fastening the bodice in front. The firm curves of her breasts and the line of her throat were resplendent, emphasized by the black velvet in a classically pure contrast. Her dark hair was pulled away from her face by a ribbon, and it fell down her back in long curls. She looked young and painfully vulnerable, not at all what one would have expected of Sackville's mistress.

A glitter of admiration lightened Alec's eyes as Mira sat down to the piano without assistance. She smiled a little in a disparaging manner as she looked around the room while several women peered at her and giggled together behind their fans.

Mira had a right to be contemptuous, Alec mused, his mouth twisting cynically. Most of the women present lived by the very lowest standard of morality. Adultery was a way of life to them; they knew nothing of loyalty or modesty. If Mira could be called a whore, then the others had been as well, for much longer and with a lesser degree of discrimination. *Are you making excuses for her now?* an inner voice questioned silkily, and his jaw hardened with self-disgust.

Mira's dark lashes lowered as she hesitated before the piano keys. Then she placed her small hands on the instrument and played a French ballad. The melody was haunting and plaintive, and no one moved or made a sound as she sang in her native language. Her voice was unexpectedly low, and while it lacked vibrato, it was pure and resonant. The unashamed emotion that colored her song was clear and stirring. Alec watched her with narrowed eyes, sensing that she was absolutely aware of the reactions that her looks and her music were producing. The little cat, he thought wryly; she meant to make them all ill-at-ease, and she was succeeding. It was not an appropriate performance—something light and pleasant would have ended the situation gracefully—but she had chosen a piece so passionate and bittersweet that it made the worldly-wise crowd uncomfortable. Her hands flickered over the keys, the gentle touches eliciting sounds of longing. Then the last note hung in the air, lengthening until the sound disappeared into a whisper, and as the piece finished, she looked down at her hands.

The applause was quiet and subdued, serving to break Mira's concentration. She stood up and looked at them all, her gaze blank as she saw that Caroline Lamb and some of her contemporaries were whispering behind their fans and handkerchiefs, no longer giggling. Mira smiled grimly. Lord Sackville stood up and went to her with a smile. He lifted her cold fingers to his lips, entirely pleased with the way the evening had turned out.

"Every man here envies me, my dear. Well done—I only wish I had planned this! Well done."

She nodded and let her hand slip from his. As she made her way out of the room, she paused at Lady Ellesmere's chair. Her eyes met those of the older woman, and suddenly Mira swept into a low curtsy, a deferential and mocking gesture.

"I hope you were pleased with the performance, my lady."

Clara Ellesmere inclined her head frostily.

Calmly Mira left the room, hearing a burst of excited murmurs erupt as she closed the doors.

Her knees were weak. It took a long time for her to climb the stairs. She had never felt so drained and numb. Now that the ordeal was over and the tension past, she found that she was weary with the effort it had taken to face Sackville's guests. Why had Lady Ellesmere attempted to crucify her in front of all those people? How cruel, how terribly cruel to make sport of someone in such manner. Tiredly Mira walked to her room, wanting to crawl into bed and never come out. When she reached the turret stairs she heard footsteps behind her, and she turned around abruptly to face him. "Lord Sackville—"

"Congratulations." It was not Sackville, but Alec Falkner, who paused a few feet away from her and leaned against the wall in a casual attitude. He was in a dark shadow and she could not read the expression on his face. "You were quite impressive."

"I've taken a few lessons," she murmured, shrugging her shoulders dismissively.

"I wasn't referring to your musical abilities."

"Then I don't know what you mean," she replied sharply, raising a trembling hand to her forehead in order to ease a pounding headache. She was tired of the verbal battles with him, she was tired of constantly having to defend herself. Something inside her seemed to break . . . because of *him* . . . he had the power to hurt her when that entire room of people had not.

"I'm complimenting your courage. You don't lack mettle, whatever else you may—"

"I felt like a trained monkey on display," she interrupted harshly. "I despise the lot of you. None of you are fit to judge me. Tell me, why should my sharing Sackville's bed make me a person without feelings? Why should I be forced to entertain you all at the whim of some shallow woman, as if I've sold my mind and my soul as well as my body?" Her eyes blazing, she stepped closer to him, clenching her fists. "Why are you here?" Her breath rasped in her throat. "Why did you come after me? Not to compliment me. Go on, say anything you like—sneer if that's what you came for! I don't care about anything that you have to say, not you"—she struck his chest with her fist—"or anyone else!" She hit him again, her wrist half-numbed by the blow against the steely surface of his chest. "I don't care!"

And then suddenly she was in his arms, her body racked with trembling. She tried to pull away, but she could not stop shaking, and she let him draw her into the shelter of his powerful form. Instinctively she clung to him, her face pressed against the velvet collar of his coat until she moved her cheek and felt the warmth of his skin through the material of his shirt.

Alec sat down on the deeply shadowed turret steps, cradling her in his arms. "This is why I came after you," he murmured, his dark head bending over her as she shuddered and moved her arms around his neck. She closed her eyes tightly as he murmured incomprehensible phrases into her hair—his tone was soothing, low and gentle, inconceivably tender.

"Don't mock me," she whispered dazedly, unable to believe that he had changed into this soft-voiced stranger.

"No, I won't hurt you . . . shhh . . ."

"I don't need you to—"

"I know you don't . . . just shut up for a minute and let me hold you."

She obeyed him, letting the warmth of his body seep into her skin, into her flesh, into her very bones, until the trembling stopped. His brutal strength was no longer something she had to contend against . . . no, all at once it had become her protection, bent around her in a shield. The familiar fragrance of him surrounded her . . . the clean masculine scent of his skin, the smell of expensive clothes, the faintest touch of bay rum . . . she breathed deeply of it. She would never be this close to him again and she wanted to remember . . . she had never felt so safe, comforted, protected.

"They were all laughing at me," she whispered, her teeth chattering.

"No, they weren't. They would have if you had been afraid of them—"

"I was."

"No one could see that. Not even me."

"I would have run away if I could have."

"It's all right now . . . it's all right."

Giving a broken sigh, she rested her head on his shoulder while his broad chest rose and fell steadily

beneath her. She did not know how much time passed
by as she relaxed against him, but gradually it seemed
that she had floated into the middle of the sweetest
dream imaginable. His lips touched her forehead, sending an exciting chill down her spine, and his muscled
arm tightened under the back of her neck as he eased
her head higher.

Mira kept her eyes tightly closed, afraid that soon
she would wake up. But for now her world was secure,
filled with shadowy darkness and pleasant scents and
with the warmth of Alec's body engulfing hers. Pleasure crept through her body, pleasure more potent
than an addictive drug. It made her helpless with
desire, eager to yield to him, craving his touch, wanting his lips on hers. She felt his hot, moist breath
against the softness of her neck . . . his seeking mouth
brushed her skin, then moved lazily across her throat.
Weakly Mira turned her face against his shoulder as
Alec's raven head lowered over her, his tongue flickering against the most sensitive parts of her neck.

"Mira . . ." he muttered, his mouth moving over
her skin hungrily. "I want you . . . I want to make you
feel things you've never dreamed about . . ." Her eyes
fluttered open, and he became lost in the bewildered
darkness of her gaze. "You don't belong to Sackville,"
he said thickly.

"I promised him—"

"To hell with whatever you promised him. It's not
right for you to be his. He doesn't want you as I do.
You can't say he satisfies you, not when you respond
to me like this. You're starving for a man who will
take the time to please you in bed, someone who will
see to your needs as well as his own. A strong, young
man in his prime—"

"He does please me," she choked, trying to twist
out of his lap.

"Like hell he does. Look at you—you're panting
and I haven't even kissed you. If you don't have the

look of an unsatisfied woman, then I've never seen one before."

Outrage cleared Mira's mind with a wintry blast. She tried to slap him but the motion was stopped in midair as his large hand closed around her slim wrist. "Don't lie to me," Alec said quietly. Mortified, Mira made an effort to calm herself.

"I'm not lying to anyone. Let go of me."

"Look at me and tell me honestly that you don't want me to—"

"Let me go," she interrupted, breathing hard with anger, "you prinking, conceited cloak-twitcher of a—"

The barrage of invective might have continued for some time had Alec not heard approaching footsteps.

"Quiet. Someone's coming," he said, dumping her out of his lap, clapping a hand over her mouth, and dragging her across the hallway into his room. Mira struggled in his grasp, pulling at his wrist as the door closed behind them. "Stop squirming and listen," he hissed into her ear. Mira relaxed slowly as she heard footsteps pass by the door. Her eyes widened as the heavy feet went up the turret steps. "Sackville," Alec muttered grimly. "Come to take up where I've left off, no doubt."

"I've got to get out of here!" Mira said tightly. "He'll ask about what I've been doing."

"Don't worry—you can tell him you were in the middle of considering an interesting proposition."

She tried to pull away from him, her confused flurry grinding to a halt as his arms locked around her waist.

"Let me out before he starts to look for me!"

"When I'm finished with you. I want to know how you came to be Sackville's mistress. Obviously it wasn't because of the physical attraction he holds for you. So tell me how and why—"

"No!" As Mira found that her glare was met by impervious gray eyes, she tried to soften her answer. "There . . . there isn't time."

"You have all the time you need," Alec purred. "I'm not going anywhere."

"Oh, do stop this!" she said desperately, pushing at his chest.

"Can't wait to get up there with him? My, my . . . perhaps he should thank me for having stirred you up like this."

"You're detestable!"

"The clock is ticking. And you're not going anywhere until you tell me how your arrangement with Sackville came to be."

"Name of Satan!" she exclaimed, her eyes on the door. "All right, I'll tell you this much. I've been his for . . . I've been here for two years. Since I was eighteen. I met him after I left France and came to England."

"Alone?"

"Yes, alone. I had no money and no employment, and I was well on the way to starving to death. It was September, a very cold one. I caught a fever and became too sick to look for work or find food. I curled up in the back of a hay wagon in Dover to sleep—and I suppose I fell unconscious, because the next thing I remember is waking up here. Lord Sackville is a very compassionate man. He took me in, paid money out of his own pocket to keep me fed and clothed and taken care of until I was well again."

Alec waited for her to continue, arching a black eyebrow as she remained stubbornly silent. "So you ended up in his bed out of gratitude?" he asked.

"I became fond of him."

"As well as his money and living on his estate."

"Yes," she snapped. "Now is your curiosity satisfied?"

"No. Why did you leave France in the first place?"

Exasperated, Mira let out a stream of smothered curses, her face so animated and her tone so venomous that Alec's expression became less harsh, his eyes starting to twinkle with amusement.

"Either you let me leave this room *now*," she threatened, "or I will sprinkle powdered rhubarb in your wine and steal your chamberpot!"

Alec gave a muffled laugh, reluctantly withdrawing his arms from around her.

"Since you ask so charmingly, I can hardly refuse," he said, giving her a small bow and opening the door with a flourish. As Mira skittered away indignantly, Alec closed the door. "Good Lord. I've been threatened with knives, bullets, fists, swords, and good hands of cards—but never rhubarb," he mused, and began to laugh again.

Mira went up to her room, smiling guilelessly as she saw that Lord Sackville was still there.

"Hello, my lord," she said.

"Where have you been?"

She was a convincing liar when she had to be. "I've been conversing with Mrs. Daniel in the kitchen. Have you been waiting long?"

"No, not long at all," Sackville said, refusing to meet her eyes. "I came up here to . . . well, inquire if you were in any way distressed by this evening. You took it very well, but still I wanted to be certain . . ."

He looks like a guilty little boy, Mira thought, and she smiled, feeling a reluctant twinge of fondness for him. She knew that he had not meant to cause her so much distress. The William Sackville she had come to know would never voluntarily hurt a soul. If not for him she would have died of fever and chills that September two years ago. She would never forget his kindness to her.

"I must admit," she said carefully, "I was rather taken aback by the whole thing."

"I could not see any way to end the situation gracefully," Sackville said in a rush. "And then I thought: Damn your ears, old boy, she plays well enough.

What the deuce—let her at it! And you did a capital job, Mira—a wonderful job!"

"I would rather consign the whole thing to the past," she replied. "And, my lord . . . I would rather not have to do something like that again."

"Of course, of course!" Relieved, Sackville pulled out a handkerchief and patted his damp brow. "So glad you're being sensible about this—can't stand to have a woman peeved with me, you know."

"I know," she said, giving him a small smile. She turned to her gilded dressing table and pulled out a knotted cloth. "As long as you're up here, I found another mandrake root for you. Just take a little at a time—"

"I know the dosage by now," he said, taking the cloth eagerly and stuffing it in his pocket. "I think it's helping, truly I do."

"I hope it does," she replied, tilting her head and regarding him quizzically.

"You've never told anyone about this, have you?" he demanded, his blue eyes squinting anxiously. He asked the same question every time she found another root for him.

In a flashing second Mira remembered her slip in front of Alec Falkner—but he wouldn't remember, would he? "No . . . our secret is safe, my lord."

"Walter," Alec inquired absently, drumming his fingers on the side of the porcelain tub, "do you know anything about herbs or plants?" Alec's hair was as wet and shining as the coat of a sleek seal, drops of water from the bath clinging to his eyelashes, his tanned face wearing a mild frown.

Walter, his faithful valet for the past five years, paused in the midst of straightening up Alec's room. He was the ultimate gentleman's gentleman—hardworking, well-mannered, discreet, a well-hidden but dry sense of humor occasionally surfacing . . . and at forty-four years of age he was old enough to give advice when requested but young enough to survive the rigors of accompanying someone as restless and travel-oriented as Alec.

"Milord," Walter replied evenly, "as far as gardening goes, I don't know a clod of earth from a horse dropping."

"Dammit." Alec sighed, his expression brooding. "Get me a towel, will you?"

"However," Walter said, handing him a huge length of huckaback, a stout linen with a rough surface used for toweling, "I do have odd bits of information stored here and there—would you care to ask the question anyway?"

"Why not?" Alec wrapped the rectangle around his lean hips and reached for another towel as he stepped out of the tub. "What exactly is a mandrake root used for?"

Suddenly Walter began to choke, his round fuzz-topped head reddening. Usually he prided himself on the fact that he seldom laughed or even cracked a smile unless it was absolutely unavoidable. Alec scowled at Walter's uncharacteristic fit of snickering. Finally the valet regained control over himself, his slight form straightening as he settled back into his perfect posture.

"Has someone told you recently that you needed one?" he inquired blandly, his mouth twitching at the corners.

"No. It was a . . . reference I heard the other day . . . and I'd never heard much about it before." His expression darkened as he added sardonically, "Until now I had never suspected such vital knowledge had been omitted from my education."

"You would be the last man in England to hear about it, my lord, for the simple reason that you have no need of the effects of the mandrake root."

"Well, stop standing there with that prissy smirk on your face. Out with it, Walter!"

"It is usually given to a man for certain reasons, all pertaining to the . . . reproductive organs. It can enhance fertility . . ."

Oh God, Alec thought, he wants her to have his child.

". . . or, more frequently," Walter continued, "it is taken by a man in the hopes that it will cure impotence."

Not a muscle in Alec's face moved.

"Just . . . just to get things straight," he managed to ask after a few seconds, "we're talking about the commonly understood sense of the word 'impotence'?"

Walter nodded matter-of-factly before resuming his tasks about the room.

"Thanks," Alec said, frowning thoughtfully before rubbing his head roughly with the towel. What kind of game was Mira playing? Was it possible that for all his manly talk, Sackville was impotent? Or was it just that Mira was a scheming little mischief-maker?

3

Mira took great pains to avoid Alec for the next few days. She did not venture out in the mornings any longer, though that activity would soon be curtailed by the decreasing temperatures of the autumn days. Staying in the kitchen, finding a solitary spot in the garden, or curling up in the sitting room when they were empty, she managed to put a measure of physical distance between herself and the man who had the power to fluster her so easily. Unfortunately she could not keep her thoughts from dwelling on him constantly.

It would not be difficult to fall in love with Alec Falkner—that was a truth that she could not ignore. He appealed to her in every way . . . she did not even mind his temper, having discovered that it was coupled with a wry sense of humor. Though he had a temper, he could also be gentle. The thought that he wanted her filled her with excitement and a peculiar kind of dismay. She knew that he was attracted to her in spite of himself and that he would not have chosen to want her, if such a thing were merely a matter of choice. She thought often of the minutes on the turret steps when he had cradled her in his arms, and she wondered if he thought of it too. Unable to dispel her obsession with him, she began to ferret out information about him, even questioning Sackville discreetly.

"How did I meet him?" Sackville repeated as she poured tea for him and handed him a plate of his favorite biscuits. The firelight shone cozily around the two of them as they sat alone in a small parlor. Sackville's face was red from a long day of hunting, and he stretched his legs before the fire appreciatively. He loved to chat idly and relax with a cup of brandy-laced tea after a great deal of exertion. "It was about seven years ago during a hunt . . . black-haired young devil . . . he was the kind that I like to take down a peg or two when I can. By himself he was a tolerable sort, quiet and polite, but whenever that cousin of his was around—Holt, the one who's gone now—he was the most unruly rake I'd ever seen."

"Why was he different around his cousin?" Mira prompted, her voice deliberately casual.

"Holt kept urging him on, you see . . ." Sackville chuckled and shook his head reminiscently. "They looked so much alike that there were many jests—Holt was the worse half of the pair, while Alec was the one with the conscience. Put together, they comple-mented each other perfectly."

"But you had more of a liking for Lord Falkner?"

"Didn't like either of them at first. Holt preferred chasing women over hunting game. And Alec and I began an argument the first day of the hunt, about whether a double-barreled Westley Richards or a Joe Manton is more effective. We started a bet to see which one would bring down a greater number of birds with his respective firearm."

Mira smiled, picturing a much younger Alec in the middle of a quarrel with Sackville. "Who won?" she asked.

"We compared tallies at the end of the hunt and found that we were exactly even. That was when the friendship began. I discovered soon afterward that he is a talented architect—he redesigned part of the manor for me, did you know that?"

Mira was fascinated by the revelation. An architect . . . did Alec possess a more fanciful nature than she had originally thought? Did his tastes in design run to classical Palladian or picturesque Gothic? When she had pressed for more details about it, Sackville gave her an odd look before murmuring something non-committal about Falkner's designs, causing Mira to wince in the realization that her interest was becoming far too obvious. She was not aware that she had mentioned his name so often in the most casual of conversations. But this disturbing fact was pointed out to her one day while she was taking tea in the kitchen with Mrs. Comfit and two of the housemaids, Lizzie and Tessie.

"This is the randiest group o' gentlemen Lord Sackville's ever 'ad over to the manor," Lizzie exclaimed, her bright red curls bobbing emphatically as she spoke. "Another one tried to 'ave 'is way with me this morning, 'e did!"

"Wa'd 'e do?" Tessie, a timid girl of seventeen, inquired in fascination.

"Looked me up and down as I was carryin' a tray by 'is room—pinched me on the be'ind, 'e did, and chased me down the 'all!"

"Goo!" Tessie exclaimed.

"That's the third one this week," Mira said dryly to Mrs. Comfit, who shook her head with resignation. Mrs. Comfit was a wise and cheery figure, her body solid and round, her expression perpetually elfin, her appearance resembling that of a friendly forest gnome.

"Yes, but that's men for you, Mira," the cook said. "After a week of good food, spirits, and fine hunting, each one starts to feel like twice the man he was when he got here. But I'll agree with Lizzie, this is a randier lot than usual."

"Lizzie," Mira inquired a little too casually, "do you remember which man in particular it was who pinched you this morning?"

"Lor', why d'you ask that, Mira?" The housemaid

stuffed half a buttered scone into her mouth and chewed appreciatively.

"Well, just . . . so that I will know which ones to avoid," Mira said. "Was one of the men who . . . made advances to you . . . young and . . . well, large and rather good-looking? Maybe with dark hair?"

"Lor', no . . . would I complain about *that*? No . . . just the old goats as soft and white as snow, and old enow to be me father."

"Mira," Mrs. Comfit inquired gently, "who in particular are you thinking of?"

"Oh . . ." Mira flushed crimson and took a sip of freshly steeped tea, which nearly burned the roof of her mouth. "Well, one can't help but notice the Duke of Hamilton . . . Lord Falkner . . . he's got a roving eye if I've ever seen one. I thought it might be him. You watch out for him, Lizzie, and you too, Tessie! He is not a very *safe* kind of man to be around, if you know what I—"

"Goo, if you want 'em fer yourself, just say so," Lizzie said generously, reaching for another scone.

"No, that's not what I mean at all!"

"You've mentioned him many times before, Mira," Mrs. Comfit remarked with a thoughtful smile.

"No, I haven't!" Mira denied the accusation, setting down her teacup and regarding them all indignantly. "I haven't . . ." Her voice became smaller as she looked at the three placid countenances on the other side of the table. ". . . have I?"

"You 'ave," Lizzie said flatly, and immediately Tessie chimed in, "Mira's gone sweet on 'im, Mira's got a eye for the Duke—"

"You just close your mouth!" Mira snapped, her eyes gleaming with sudden anger. "I couldn't care less about the conceited wretch! Why don't you both stick your noses in someone else's affairs and leave me alone?" She stopped and clapped a hand to her mouth as she stared at the two startled housemaids. "Oh, I'm sorry . . . what a temper I'm developing. Please forget what I just said." She pressed her fingertips on her temples and closed her eyes. "It's this bloody headache—"

"Girls," Mrs. Comfit said calmly, "it's time for you to 'namel the floors for the dancing this evening. Run along while I have a chat with Mira."

Grabbing the last of the scones and stuffing them into their pockets, Lizzie and Tessie threw Mira forgiving glances and flew out of the room with giggles and whispers.

"Now," Mrs. Comfit said, "Mira, I think you need a talk. I know you usually go to Mrs. Daniel when you need to talk, but she's too busy and I'm near as good at—"

"There's no need for a talk," Mira said, dropping her head wearily into the crook of her arms. Her voice was muffled as she continued. "You'd think the very worst of me if I told you."

Mrs. Comfit chuckled warmly. "I know it has somethin' to do with Lord Falkner, and it isn't a surprise that you have an eye for a handsome man, not with you being twenty . . . you're not the girl you were two years ago, Mira—and a woman needs a man, much trouble as they are. Have you gone to his bed? Is that it?"

Made uncomfortable by the cook's frankness, Mira nearly exploded with defensiveness. "How can you even suggest that? How can you ask that, knowing that I'm Lord Sackville's—"

"Aaaaa . . ." Mrs. Comfit drew out the vowel slowly, her expression both wry and chiding. "You should know by now, Mira, the servants are worse than a family—we know more, we're smarter. Do you think that Percy doesn't know what's gone on for the past year or so? Do you think Mrs. Daniel doesn't? Do you think *I* don't know? Be honest for once, luv, and stop playing your game for a minute."

"What game?" she asked, desperately trying to keep the truth from her face.

"Mira, do you think we've been fooled by Sackville's jaunts up to your room? He's a dear man, but he's a man that's got his problems, and there's no hiding those kinds of problems. And I guess the agreement between the two of you was supposed to be kept secret . . . but it's plain that you and he are only playacting your affair."

"What makes you think that?"

"The sheets, for one thing. You must be an innocent, luv, if you don't know that the sheets give it away every time. Mrs. Daniel collects the sheets from your room and Sackville's room, both sets as clean and sweet as you please . . . and unless you two do it standing up or on the floor—"

"Oh, please!" Mira cried, covering her ears with her hands. "Don't say any more!"

"That's what I thought," Mrs. Comfit said, nodding in a satisfied manner. "Now, out with the rest. You're miserable because of your duke."

Mira sighed, resting her forehead in her hands. "He's not mine. There's nothing to tell. He hates me."

"Luv, there isn't a man alive who could hate you."

"There is," Mira insisted. "And I thought I hated him at first . . . but I think about him all the time, and I imagine all sorts of . . . Oh, it's too embarrassing. When he smiles at me, I have the strangest feelings, hot and cold shivers. He's like some sort of dreadful sickness! And no, I haven't gone to his bed—from the way he acts sometimes, I don't even think he'd allow himself to want me! But . . ." Her voice became a mere whisper. "He's held me . . . close . . . and I forgot about everything but him. And the only thing I can think of to do when I'm around him is to say things that make him so angry . . ." She sighed and the mournful soliloquy ended with the glum observation, "I think I must care for him."

"God bless you," Mrs. Comfit said in the silence of the still kitchen. "You're not the first and you won't be the last, Mira."

"Knowing that doesn't help me. I'm tied to Lord Sackville, and Lord Falkner thinks that I'm his friend's mistress."

"Then untie yourself! Tell me something: what does the future hold for you here? You're at the age to be living life, to be a *real* mistress, or to be a good man's wife, and how are you going to meet any men when you're playacting as Sackville's woman? I'll be one of the sorriest to see you go, Mira . . . but you must leave sometime to find your own life."

"I know that," Mira said glumly. "But it's so hard to leave." She had left so many places before, and she wondered if she would be able to anymore. Had she lost the strength to uproot herself once again? She would have to sooner or later. Sackville would not want her here forever.

"Then don't leave alone," Mrs. Comfit urged, her eyes bright with affection and pity. "Maybe when your duke goes, you should ask him to take you along."

They went shooting on foot one day, aiming for the succulent partridges and pheasants that abounded in the fields. Alec had not hit one bird all morning, causing those who had until now been envious of his phenomenal marksmanship to be more kindly disposed to him. As he took his hat off and wiped the back of his hand across his forehead, a gentle breeze ruffled his hair. He was suddenly irritated with the whole business of hunting. Somehow the thrill of it had dulled for him, and his heart was no longer in the sport. His mind kept wandering back to one absorbing, exasperating subject, and he was completely occupied with thinking of a way to end this maddening situation. Never one to allow a problem to nag at him for long, Alec came to the conclusion that he had to make some sort of decision soon. He would not let his reason be eroded by some little dark-eyed wench with a teasing smile.

But what kind of decision could he make concerning Mira? One by one he examined the beginnings of a list of possibilities. Steal her away from here and take her to his London apartments . . . confront Sackville openly about her . . . seduce her and then settle her at one of the small, convenient estates that numbered among the Falkner possessions . . . or perhaps he should take her abroad for a long stay in France, if that was what she wished. No matter what it took, he would find some way to have her even if it cost his friendship with Sackville, even if he had to sacrifice one of his few remaining virtues, that of loyalty. He did not know how long it would take before his obsession with Mira faded away, but Alec did not intend to go unsatisfied while it lasted. Perhaps he would have been able to play the gentleman and leave Mira alone had she shown signs of being happy with Sackville. But she was not happy or she would not have clung to him so tightly the other night, nor would she have talked to him so eagerly when he passed by her on his morning rides. She was not happy . . . he could see it in her eyes every time he looked at her.

"Falkner, you're jolly well lost in your own world, aren't you, old fellow?"

Kip Sanborn, a high-spirited young man of twenty-four, approached with an overly careful stride. Since the party at Sackville's had begun a week ago, Sanborn had been drinking more heavily each day. This was the lad's first encounter with shooting, and he had been drowning with a liberal amount of alcohol his trepidations about handling a gun. Alec regarded him with narrowed gray eyes, thinking that it would take a good week to dry him out.

"Come to reload," Sanborn said, setting down a small pile of equipment and squinting at the little heap before selecting a steel charger filled with an ounce or two of shot.

"Sanborn," Alec inquired dryly, "I know that Sackville told you—"

"Sackville?" Sanborn interrupted, picking up a flask of powder. "Oh, yes . . . always listen to the Sack. Capital fellow—"

"Undoubtedly. I know he told you to take a sandwich and a glass of brandy each time you were nervous . . . but with all due respect and concern, I'd like to suggest that you keep your sandwich case and your liquor flask closed while you're around me."

"Keeps the nerves steady," Sanborn replied, busily employing a ramrod on the seven-pound gun.

"The nerves don't concern me," Alec said, lazily donning his hat and pulling the brim down on his forehead. "It's the aim I'm worried about."

"Nothing to worry about. Nothing—" Sanborn reassured him enthusiastically, and then his eyes brightened as new game was sprung and a flock of birds soared overhead.

"Wait," Alec snapped, noticing in that instant that Sanborn had not put his powder flask on the ground. "Don't fire, you fool, the powd—"

As he started to run toward the half-drunken man, Alec heard him fire. The powder flask exploded. A violent blast knocked Alec to the ground, a jolt of lightning that rushed through him and caused his ears to ring. Stunned, he lay sprawled on the ground, becoming dimly aware of the cool earth beneath his cheek and the shouts of the other men as they realized what had happened. His black lashes flickered slightly. "Sanborn?" he muttered, his ears roaring so loudly that he could hear no answer, and then a buzzing cloud seemed to surge over him.

Mira bent over her book, her feet curled underneath her body as she sat on a plush sofa in the blue sitting room. She could hear the men coming in from the hunt and the women returning from their outings, their footsteps passing by the closed door. Shifting to a more comfortable position, she paid no heed to their noise, knowing that in their eagerness to go up to their rooms and change for supper, none of Sackville's guests would come in here. Quietly she concentrated on the book she held, reading until more than an hour had passed and she heard the clinking of supper dishes. They were all in the dining room, Mira surmised, and closed the book as she stood up and stretched.

The door to the sitting room opened a crack, the familiar white of a housemaid's cap gleaming as a young woman peeped through the door.

"Tessie?" Mira said curiously, and the small mobcapped head was extended fully into the room.

"Oh, I 'oped you were 'ere!"

"Aren't you supposed to be helping to serve supper?"

"I 'ad to tell you . . . they're all talkin' about it, and I snuck away, fast as I could, when I 'eard o't!"

"Heard of what?"

"They 'ad an accident on the field today, a explosion, a man 'urt, and the hacksaw called in—"

"They called the doctor?" Mira said, her brow wrinkling. "*Dieu*, I'll bet he bled a bowlful out of the poor man."

"Don't know . . . but this is the int'restin' part. Lizzie sent me to tell you that she thinks your duke was the one who got blown up."

The book fell to the floor with a thud. Mira's hand flew to her cheek, and then she brushed by Tessie with an inarticulate sound. She ran up the curving staircase, using the balustrade to pull herself up more quickly as her feet skimmed over the stairs.

"Are you sure you're all right?" Walter asked dubiously as Alec fell across the bedspread with a grateful sound.

"Perfectly fine," came the smothered reply. Alec lifted his face from the pillow to add, "Just tired. I've had a narrow escape."

"From being injured?"

"No, from Clara Ellesmere. As soon as we all came in, she was wrapped around me tighter than skin, offering to 'nurse me back to health.' " He laughed dryly. "Some nurse."

"I can't imagine that she would allow you much sleep," Walter admitted. "And speaking of sleep, how long would you like to rest?"

"Just an hour," Alec said, rolling onto his back and locking his hands beneath his head. "I need the peace and quiet. I have some thinking to do, and they're all down there yapping like poodles—God, what an interminable day. I hope Sanborn is better."

"The physician is seeing to him. Several burns, painful but not serious if cared for properly." Walter smiled sardonically. "I am both relieved and surprised that you were uninjured. Fools and drunks like Sanborn are more dangerous to others than they are to themselves." The valet paused and surveyed him with a doubtful expression. "Are you certain that you don't want to take your bath before resting?"

"Bath and food when I wake up. Right now I couldn't move to save my life."

"However many of them you have left," Walter added dryly, leaving the room.

In the lamplit stillness, nothing moved except the shadow of a moth fluttering against the window. Alec yawned and closed his eyes, the warm yellow light spreading over him like a soothing balm. Sleep stole over him and his body went lax.

Mira arrived at Alec's door and stopped in front of it abruptly, her heart pounding. She was almost afraid to find out if he was the one who had been hurt, for she knew the kinds of accidents that invariably happened on the hunting field—anything from being peppered with shot to blowing off a hand or foot; powder flasks were likely to explode like small bombs, sometimes just because of faulty spring-catches on the lids.

Please don't let it be serious. The small prayer ran through her mind, and she knocked on the door with trepidation. There was no answer. Apprehensively she turned the knob and looked inside, biting her lip as she saw him stretched out on the bed. She had not realized that the sight of him hurt would affect her so.

"Lord Falkner?" she whispered, slipping through the door and rushing to him. He looked younger than he did when awake, his relaxed face erased of its habitual cynicism, his firm, straight mouth gentled, his black eyelashes fanning the ruthlessly drawn lines of his cheekbones. The acrid smell of gunpowder and smoke clung to him, faint black smudges marring his copper skin. Mira could not see any blood or bandages —did that mean the damage might be internal? She realized that she, who never allowed herself to cry, was on the verge of tears. Drinking in the sight of him with haunted eyes, Mira rested a hip on the edge of the bed and leaned over the large masculine form. In the yellow light she could not see if his color was normal or not. *If they've bled him I'll find some way to kill that drunkard of a physician!* she thought grimly, reaching out anxiously to examine the side of his neck.

Alec stirred at her touch, a sleepy sound escaping him. Slowly his eyes squinted open, his wide shoulders tensing in a stretch.

"Mira?"

She pressed her cool fingers over his forehead, measuring his temperature.

"I heard you were in an accident today," she murmured. "Why isn't anyone with you?" Her autumn-shaded eyes were filled with concern, her touch so gentle as she stroked the ruffled waves of hair off his forehead that Alec's first inclination was to believe he was still asleep, in the middle of yet another dream.

"Me?" he asked groggily. "Who told you—?"

"How have you been hurt?"

Despite his sleepy state of mind, it did not take long for Alec to conclude it would be worth any number of agonizing wounds to have her coddle and caress him. The pity of it was that he had nary a scratch to offer for her ministrations.

The enticing scent of her drifted to his appreciative nostrils, and he inhaled deeply. Very carefully he shifted his hand to where the end of her braid rested on the counterpane and inserted his fingers into the heavy plait. "Lord Falkner? Do you have any pain?" she prompted, her eyes fixed on his face.

"Yes . . . God, yes."

"Where?"

"I'm not sure exactly where . . ."

"Has the physician seen to you yet?"

"No."

"Ah . . . then there's still hope for you," she said, concealing her worry with gentle humor. Alec smiled slightly.

"I gather you don't think highly of him?"

"His treatment of his patients is criminal . . . don't let him do *anything* to you, do you understand?"

"Then unless you care to let my wounds fester and my injuries go unattended, you'd better take care of them," he said, making a move to unbutton his shirt. After fumbling with the first button, he fell back with a perfectly timed wince and let his hand drop to the pillow.

"Here, don't move," Mira soothed, her heart skipping a beat as she witnessed his pain. She would have given up a king's ransom for the right to hold and comfort him, kiss his brow and smooth his tumbled hair. Deftly she unfastened each button of his shirt and spread the edges of it open.

The sight that greeted her eyes was not what she had so fearfully expected. No shotholes or cuts . . . no burns . . . not even any dirt! The wide expanse was clean and brown, magnificently trim, the stomach hammered with washboard muscles, his chest lightly furred with coal-black hair. In the course of tending countless wounds she had seen many men's bare chests, but nothing quite so physically superb as this. No man had a right to be so healthy! She lifted her face to look into his bright eyes, which were regarding her with mocking laughter.

"Name of Satan!" she exclaimed in a burst of fury, beating on that invulnerable chest. "You prankish blackguard! You're not hurt at all—you ought to be shot!"

Like a lazy cat sprung into action, Alec caught hold of her rampaging fists and rolled over, pinning her beneath him. She continued to berate him with a flood of the saltiest language he had ever heard from a woman, consigning certain portions of his anatomy to a painful fate . . . swearing at him until they both were choking, she from anger, he from laughter.

"I couldn't help it," Alec said, gasping with amusement as he pinned her hands on either side of her head and tried to still her violent thrashing. "I just couldn't . . . Mira . . . just wait . . . you don't really blame me, admit it."

"You are shameless!" she snapped, struggling against him and attempting to box his ears. "How *dare* you sham Abram when I was . . . You mop-squeezing pimp, you prigging muckworm . . ."

As she made wounding observations about his character and ancestry, a gold medallion on a finely wrought chain hung down from around his neck and rested against her chest. It was warm from his skin, lying in the hollow of her uplifted breasts and burning into her like a brand. Mira paid it no attention, too occupied with her efforts to twist her wrists out of his confining grasp. She glared into his eyes, which were gleaming with deviltry. It had been a long time since anyone had teased her like this, a long time since someone had encouraged her to play. Suddenly a choked laugh escaped from her, a fact which he pounced on immediately.

"There. You just laughed—"

"I did not!" Mira protested hotly, trying to scowl and ruining the effort with another chuckle. She gave up trying to maintain her anger as her shoulders trembled with laughter. "I thought you were on your deathbed! I had no idea you were such a talented actor."

"All the Falkners are good at feigning illness—it was the only way we could get out of our lessons."

"You must have been a terrible little boy."

"Very likely." Alec grinned at her. "But I was my mother's favorite."

She laughed breathlessly, shaking her head at him. "You're impossible." She looked up at him, unable to keep her expression from softening with concern. "But . . . you're not really hurt, are you? What happened today? Your clothes are sooty, and you smell like gunpowder—"

"Sanborn's powder flask exploded and I happened to be nearby. I'm told that the boy is fine, a little singed around the edges, but he's being taken care of."

"Perhaps I should see if I can do something to help him," she said, trying to wriggle off the bed, but Alec pinned her down more securely, his coal-black hair falling down over his forehead. Mira frowned, becoming aware of how easy it was for him to hold her still—she could struggle with all her might to escape and it would make no impression on him.

"I need you more than he does."

"All you need is some rest . . . and a lengthy reacquaintance with soap and water," she said, pulling at her wrists with growing agitation. "It's safe for you to let me go now. I won't hit you again."

"How can I be certain of that?" he purred, and her wrists remained imprisoned. Uneasily she shifted beneath him, realizing for the first time that she was helplessly splayed out under his body.

"Lord Falkner—"

"Alec," he corrected, staring down at her with darkening gray eyes, his face becoming utterly serious.

"I can't call you that."

"I won't let you go until you do."

"Do you always use physical force to get your own way?"

"With you it always seems to be the most convenient thing to do."

"Alec," she said obediently, trying to pull away . . . but still he held her pinned to the bed. Their bodies were entwined far too intimately, his chest pressing against her breasts, one of his tautly muscled thighs impacted between hers. He smelled of sweat, horses, and smoke, a primitive scent that caused a quiver inside her midriff. "Alec, please . . ." she said, turning her face away from him. Her wrists were transferred into one of his hands, while the other grasped her chin and turned her face back. She shivered, closing her eyes in denial even while her heart pounded in anticipation and her skin prickled with heat. "Don't," she protested faintly.

"Do you know why I can't let you go, Mira?" His voice was husky and deep, tickling her ear. Her breath caught in her throat as he kissed the soft spot behind her earlobe . . . she felt the sensation of his mouth all through her body. "You were meant for me," Alec murmured, brushing his lips over her temples and her fragile eyelids. "You belong to me more than you'll ever belong to Sackville . . . I want you more than he ever could. There's something about you that pulls at me, something I can't resist. I don't know what it is, I don't know *why* you do this to me . . . but you feel it too. You know as well as I do that we're going to end up together, no matter how you try to resist it."

His thumb brushed over her lower lip with the lightness of thistledown, stroking in a slow, erotic movement. Moisture began to collect in her mouth and she swallowed, her lips tingling under the touch of his thumb. Alec's glinting silver gaze missed nothing, his mouth tilting slightly at the corners. Slowly his fingers wandered over her chin and down to her neck, caressing her skin with that same soft stroke. He traced a circle across her throat with his fingertips, watching her eyes dilate, staring down at her intently until her breath quickened and her breasts lifted involuntarily against his bare chest.

"I'm a novelty to you," she said, astonished at the throatiness of her voice. "That's why . . . that's the reason you want me."

"I thought so too, at first."

"This is all because I'm your friend's mistress," she said, deliberately trying to provoke his anger. "It excites you, doesn't it, the prospect of having something forbidden to you."

His mouth brushed leisurely against hers, gentle and questing. Mira was completely still beneath him, rigid with confusion and a peculiar panic. Her lips were soft but unresponsive. Unhurriedly Alec tasted her top lip, then the bottom, as patiently as if he planned to spend eternity holding her in his arms, and as his mouth played over hers with coaxing warmth, fire blossomed within her. She moaned and tried to move away from him, but his weight pressed her into the mattress, holding her down. Impossible . . . it was impossible to fight him when she wanted him this much. Gasping, she surrendered to the hot, languid kiss, allowing his lips to urge hers apart.

He let go of her wrists to pull her closer, slipping a supportive hand underneath her head. Her lips softened and clung to his, seeking the warmth and the taste of him. His tongue feathered against hers, and she shivered, answering him timidly as desire overtook her in a dizzying rush and coursed through her veins in a heavy torrent. She wrapped her arms around his neck, unconsciously pulling his head down closer. She had never imagined that such a powerful craving could exist, more biting, more urgent than hunger or thirst.

Lifting his mouth from hers, Alec looked down at her, his drowsy gray eyes filled with smoky promise.

"I've always been able to resist temptation," he whispered, kissing one corner of her mouth and then the other, "before you. Before you . . ." He muffled her small sigh as he kissed her again, his large hand sliding over her body possessively, cupping over the material that covered her breast, stroking until he felt her nipple contract underneath the soft velvet. Mira groaned, pressing up against that knowing touch, her body on fire. The shadows of the room seemed to collect around her, and she was sinking deeper into their darkness . . . and it wasn't a cold darkness, it was hot and vibrant with piercing sensations. Her eyes fluttered open and she saw the deep golden gleam of his skin, her own slender fingers tangled in his black hair . . . her head tilted back as his mouth moved to her throat, and the only thought that remained clear in her mind was that she would die if he stopped. "Alec . . ." she whispered, her hands caressing the breadth of his shoulders, and she felt his muscles flex involuntarily.

"God, what am I doing?" he muttered. Abruptly he tore his mouth away from the fluttering pulse in her throat and took a deep breath, shaking his head as if to clear it. "Not now," he said, seeming to find it difficult to speak. "There's no time . . . dammit, I won't let the first time be rushed."

Blinking in bewilderment, Mira loosened her arms from around his neck, quivering with a kind of frustration she had never felt before. Slowly she came to her senses, realizing what she had let him do—encouraged him to do. She could hardly believe that she had responded to him so wantonly. What kind of dangerous magic did he possess?

"Not ever," she said, her voice shaking. *"Bon Dieu, qu'est-ce que j'ai fait? . . .* How could I have . . . ah, let me *go!"* She rolled away from him and jumped off the bed in a fluid movement, her hands going up to her chest to still her violent gasps. Alec turned onto his side to stare at her, propping himself up on one elbow. His long body stretched out in a sprawl, like a black panther sunning himself.

"You look horrified," he observed calmly. Though his mouth was touched with a satisfied smile, his eyes were still warm with a passionate gleam. "Hasn't it ever been this way for you with Sackville?"

"I am *not* horrified," she said, a pronounced French accent coloring her words heavily. Alec grinned at the sound of it. "I am . . . I'm disgusted," she continued vehemently, "and I want nothing more than to never have to face you again!" She headed for the door, but the sound of his voice stopped her just as she turned the knob.

"Mira."

"What?" she asked stiffly.

"Thank you for your kind ministrations to me in my hour of need. I feel so much better now."

Throwing him a venomous glare, she flounced out of the room in a speechless rage, wanting to slam the door but unwilling to attract the attention of others.

The morning sun made a valiant effort to warm the air and the ground, but all the same a distinct chill caused Mira to pull the edges of her long-sleeved, short-waisted jacket together. The day was cool and dry, puffs of wind stirring up tiny clouds of dust from the ground. For her walk to the village she had dressed in muted colors that would attract little attention and did not show dirt easily. Her gown was pale blue edged with navy ribbons and sprightly sash, her low-heeled boots made of sturdy leather. Since it was an unusually slow morning and there were few people to see her, Mira took her hated poke bonnet off and stuffed it in the sack she carried.

The road was well-kept and smooth, the ruts filled with wood and the holes with large stones. Cattle were driven frequently along this road, nibbling at patches of green along the way, their milk occasionally tainted by the garlic-flavored buckrams that sprang up here and there. Humming a soft tune to herself, Mira was absorbed in her thoughts until she noticed the sound of hooves approaching from behind her. Turning to observe the rider, she lifted a hand to shade her eyes. As the brilliant white horse and its rider came nearer, Mira nearly stumbled, her jaw slackening in surprise. Alec slowed the pace of the white stallion to a slow, prancing gait, his coal-black hair ruffled attractively by the wind as he threw her a lazy smile.

"I don't believe you're . . . What are you doing here?" Mira asked, continuing to walk while looking up at him in a stupefied manner. Clothed in gray pantaloons, a dark blue coat, a soft ruffled shirt, and a low-cut brocaded waistcoat, he looked vital and dashing enough to send the most implacable female into a swoon. She moved her gaze away from him and quickened her pace, determined to remain indifferent to him.

"There is a conspiracy afoot in Sackville Manor," he said, staring down at her with warm gray eyes.

"Indeed?" she questioned coolly.

"To keep me informed of your various plans and whereabouts. This morning two maids stood by my door while conversing just a little too loudly about your schedule for the day, and it was obvious that they—"

"Oh! *C'est un attentat!*" she exclaimed, flushing in irritation. "Lizzie and Tessie—I will make them regret this! They imagine that . . . well, never mind what they imagine! It is wrong!"

"They didn't mean any harm. Besides, I found their information extremely helpful."

"Did they happen to talk about the fact that I am visiting a sick man and his wife, and that any visitors would be an unwelcome nuisance?"

"No . . . only that it was a pity you had planned to walk such a long distance unaccompanied."

"I like to walk! I could have taken a horse or carriage if I had wanted to! It is not a long distance at all. In fact, we are almost at the outskirts of the village now."

"I can take you the rest of the way." Alec extended a brown hand to her, which she resolutely ignored. "Well, as long as you enjoy walking . . ."

The white horse's hooves kept pace perfectly with her stride.

"Don't you have a hunt to attend?" Mira asked pointedly.

"I begged off for today, due to my injuries from yesterday."

"Injuries!" she scoffed, sneezing vigorously as fine dust was kicked up and wafted into her nostrils. "Your injuries would be apparent only to someone with an extraordinary imagination."

"I was in terrible pain."

"I don't believe you."

"It's true. After you left me last night, I ached for hours."

Mira went crimson, no longer feeling the chill of the wind as every inch of her skin glowed with an unwanted flush.

"Only your pride was injured yesterday," she gritted, and lifted a hand to her mouth as she sneezed once more.

"Severely. I've never had a woman so anxious to leave my bed before. God bless you—is the dust bothering you?"

"Yes!" she said, covering her face with her hands and sneezing yet again. "Your horse is kicking it up."

"I don't think it will get any better—"

"It would if you would turn around and go back!"

"—unless you ride up here with me."

"I wouldn't even if you were the last . . ." She lifted a hand to her nose and mouth, warding away the dust. "Oh, please stop it! All right. I surrender. You have your way again, but don't be smug about it."

A slight smile betrayed Alec's satisfaction as he leaned over and held his hand down to her. They grasped each other's wrists in an unbreakable clasp, and then Mira gasped as Alec pulled her up easily, his muscles bunching underneath his clothes. Her buttocks landed on the saddle in front of him, her feet dangling against the horse's side. In a reflex action Mira grasped at his coat lapels to steady herself, and Alec's arm went around her protectively. Immediately aware of the vital strength of his body, Mira turned away from him to face forward, releasing his coat to find something else to hold on to. Accidentally her hand brushed against his taut, well-muscled thigh, and she jumped in confusion, nearly falling off the horse.

"Here, stop wiggling around." Alec's voice was close to her ear, low and shaded with amusement. "I've got you." One of his large arms was braced firmly around her waist, doing little to ease her flustered condition. Mira thought briefly of telling him that she had changed her mind and wanted to get down. But then he curved his other arm around her, and as the huge white horse started forward she was provided with the excuse to lean her back against the solid wall of Alec's chest. Suddenly this seemed like the most delightful place in the world to be, here in the hard shelter of his body with the breeze blowing through her hair.

"Where . . . where is your other horse?" she managed to ask breathlessly. It was hardly an inspired topic of conversation, but it would have to do.

"Sovereign? He's having a peaceful day in the stables. This is Requiem."

"Requiem? What a dreadful name."

She felt Falkner shrug lightly.

"An appropriate one. He's fond of mauling anyone he doesn't like, sometimes a little too roughly."

"And you invited me to ride on him with you?" Mira asked indignantly, her eyes widening.

"Relax," Alec replied, his warm breath caressing her temple. "He's perfectly safe now. Do you think I'd take chances with your pretty neck?" She shivered slightly at the pleasant touch of his breath on her skin, and his arms drew around her more securely. "Cold?" he asked.

"A little," she lied gamely. "The breeze is very cool for September . . . it's a perfect day for the hunt. You shouldn't have missed it."

"The fox can do without my pursuit for one day."

"So could I," she said meaningfully, causing him to chuckle.

"At least admit that you're glad you don't have to walk."

"I admit it," she said ruefully, allowing herself to relax against him. He was so casually tender, his voice so caressing, his arms so warm and irresistible, that Mira felt like a blunt-winged moth that had flown so close to a flame its wings had been irreparably singed. There was no flying away now . . . and worse, she was too enraptured with the attraction she felt to be sorry for the mistake she had made.

"It's the first cottage we'll come to," she said eventually. "Mrs. Daniel is our housekeeper . . . her son has been taken ill with fever and cold."

"Have you always had this interest in tending sickness and learning about—?"

"Yes, especially in France. Wherever we . . . I went, there was something to learn about remedies and cures. Every place has its own traditions and recipes."

"You said 'we' . . . so there was someone else traveling with you in France?"

"No," she said quickly—too quickly. "It was a slip of the tongue."

"What about your family? You had to come from somewhere."

"I have no family."

"Who took care of you when you were younger?"

"Is this why you came riding by? To satisfy your curiosity with prying questions?" Mira demanded.

"Why the devil are you so defensive? You're right, they are prying questions, and I'll be damned if I ask you another one. Be mysterious if you like."

She was silent for a minute, so surprised by his unexpected retreat that she did something she had never anticipated doing. She told him a little about Guillaume.

"My brother took care of me. He and I went all over France, from place to place." At Alec's noncommittal silence, she even dared to say more. "My brother made friends easily . . . but they were always a dangerous kind of people, fighting and . . . I learned how to treat wounds, and how to set bones, and I found that I could *feel* how to make things right sometimes."

"Like you did with my shoulder."

"Yes. Sometimes it is not that easy. But I am able to help often, and it makes me feel useful . . . it is the only way that I have ever been ne . . ."

"Needed?" Alec asked softly, and she shook her head, horrified at the way she kept on making mistakes around him.

"No," she said, shaking her head firmly, "I don't know what I was going to say, I was just rambling."

"But doesn't Sackville need you?" he continued as

if he hadn't heard her. "Doesn't being his woman make you feel useful and needed?"

"Of course it does."

"How could it?" Alec asked, a faintly savage note shading his voice. Mira stiffened, but he pulled her back against him with a slight motion of his arm. "He doesn't really need you, Mira, not like someone else could. He might enjoy you, he might receive pleasure from your delectable little body, but even when he waxes poetic about you, even when he chatters about the two of you together until I'd like to gag him, there is no passion in his voice. Just smugness. Why is that, Mira?"

A violent conflict raged inside her. She was a prisoner, held against him and being forced to listen to words she did not want to hear. He was coming closer and closer to the truth, and it was becoming impossible to continue misleading him. He seemed to be able to see right through her lies and evasions, and his acute perception alarmed her.

"Do you think I would be living with him if he didn't need me?" she asked, countering his questions with a few of her own. "Why do you think I'm staying at the manor for any other reason than that?"

"I don't know why you're living with him," Alec admitted roughly. "But it damn well isn't for the reason that everyone assumes it is. Perhaps it isn't even for the reason that you think it is. Does he ever tell you that he needs you for yourself?"

"All the time."

"Does he tell you that he dreams about you? That when he thinks about you, every other sane thought flies from his head? That when you smile at him, his heart pounds as if he's been running for hours . . . that he was buried alive until he met you, never knowing the taste of real hunger until he became afraid that he couldn't have you? That's how you should be needed, and don't tell me you prefer his milk-and-water passion to real desire, or I'll show you the difference between—"

"We're here," Mira said, her voice trembling. She was so unsettled that she doubted she would be of much use to any member of the Daniel family now. "Mind what you say in front of these people . . . and please, *please* don't talk to me about this anymore. There is so much you don't understand . . ."

Holding the reins, Alec dismounted first and grasped her waist in his hands, staring up at her.

"Then explain it to me," he said huskily. "Soon." Unable to speak, she looked away, and he chose that moment to unseat her, lowering her against his body and then holding her there. Her hands fluttered up to his broad chest in protest, her body molded tightly against the hard, well-knit surface of his. "Soon," he repeated, not letting her go until she looked up at him uncertainly and gave him a tiny nod.

The Daniels, a small farming family, lived in a quaint cottage. Their yard was edged with a hedgerow studded with large, durable elm trees. The earthy scent of a peat fire permeated the air, while the sounds of chortling geese drifted from the grounds in back of the cottage. Mira pulled away from Alec hastily as the door of the small home burst open. Two little girls with curly brown hair and rosy-cheeked round faces ran up to Mira without hesitation, chattering and giggling. Mira dropped to her haunches, setting her bag down on the ground and opening it deftly.

"These are the twins, my lord," she said. "Mary and Kitty . . . oh dear, I never know which one of you is which . . . ah, I know now—Kitty is just a little shy, aren't you, *ma chère*?" Mira beamed at the little girl who stood behind her sister. Alec smiled as the children bent over and stared into the bag that Mira had brought, their brown curls bobbing excitedly. Triumphantly Mira pulled out a bulging paper-wrapped parcel. "*C'est le cadeau*, almond biscuits this time," she said, handing the parcel to Mary. "Now, you must share these with each other while I visit with your parents . . . and while I am inside, you may ask this nice man questions about his handsome horse, but don't tire him or he will not be pleasant company on our journey back." She glanced at Alec's wry expression, and then she stood up with her bag in hand. "I won't be long," she murmured.

"I'll be waiting no matter how long it takes," Alec replied, and Mira gave him a cautious smile before going into the cottage.

It seemed that Rachel Daniel had caught the fever and chest cold that had already afflicted her husband. Her skin was hot and dry, her nose and throat congested . . . and there was little that could be done except wait for the sickness to run its course. Mira pulled out a bag of dried currants and turned toward the hot fire, casting Rachel a sympathetic look.

"I am very sorry you and your husband are ill at this time—is there someone to help you with your land?"

"We have friends who are helping," Rachel said, her young face flushed as she lifted a handkerchief to her mouth and coughed roughly. "I simply pray that this will go away soon."

"Try to rest—"

"There is never time to rest."

"I know," Mira said with a compassionate sigh. After pouring a half-pint of brandy into a small dented pot, she warmed the liquid carefully and added several handfuls of currants.

"That doesn't smell very good," Rachel wheezed, and Mira could not help chuckling.

"When this boils down, it will be a very nasty liquid. But you must force yourselves to take it, because I know of nothing better to help your throats. Oh, and I have a message for you that might make you feel happier. Mrs. Daniel has offered to take her granddaughters for a few days, to give you more time to rest and to lessen the chance that they will become ill."

"Oh, that is wonderful!" Rachel exclaimed, her expression lightening. "Please tell her that we would be so grateful—"

"Then someone will arrive later today to take them to Sackville Manor."

After boiling down the currants, Mira added some herbs, wrinkled her nose at the concoction, and exchanged a resigned smile with the other woman.

"Good-bye. I hope it works."

"I pray that it does," Rachel responded, peering dubiously into the syrup-filled pot.

Mira left a handful of dipped candles on the corner of the table, where they would be found after she had gone.

The quiet tableau that greeted her eyes when she closed the door of the cottage was a surprise. Mary and Kitty were unusually well-mannered, perched on a fence side by side with their eyes fixed on Alec. Their high-pitched voices rose and fell with questions, receiving responses from him that must have been vastly entertaining, for they kept giggling and kicking their feet with glee. Mira smiled and drew closer, making the discovery that Alec was sketching the twins, using a scrap of charcoal and the paper that the biscuits had been wrapped in. Engrossed in the new experience of being the subjects of a portrait, the little girls watched him intently.

"I didn't know you were an artist," Mira said softly. Alec glanced at her briefly, his hair gleaming with black fire in the cold daylight. His mouth twitched with amusement.

"Hardly. But I do well enough with charcoal and brown paper," he said, letting the shard of ashy stone fall to the ground and handing the twins the finished picture. "Obviously I sketch only the most attractive young women." Turning, he helped the twins down from the fence one at a time. It gave Mira a strange feeling to see the miniature hands clutching Alex's brawny arms as he lowered the children to the ground. They were so fragile, so helpless compared to him, yet they seemed to trust him; he was very gentle with them.

Walking over to Mary, Mira looked down at the sketch and smiled. In a few strokes he had captured the essence of the little girls, Mary's impishness, Kitty's shyness, the charm of two children sitting together on a fence, their plump legs dangling and kicking cheerfully.

"You do very well indeed," Mira said, lifting her eyes to Alec's. "You have many talents, my lord."

"Why, Mira," he replied huskily, a taunting grin tugging at his mouth. "I am pleased by your compliment. But it pains me to realize that you are not acquainted with my greatest talent . . . yet."

4

The last few days of the hunting party were inevitably the most spectacular, intended to send all of the guests away with memories of glamour and excitement. There were more than three hundred people seated at supper on Saturday. Chandeliers and candelabra filled the manor with blazing light, while the tables almost swayed under the weight of food and elaborate dinnerware. Crystal basins filled with preserved fruit glittered richly, while fanciful sugar figurines adorned each place setting. It had taken more than fifty people in the kitchen to prepare the meal and an army of servants to see to the comfort of those who dined at the long tables. The wine was more plentiful than water, the air warm with the scents of roasted meats and rich sauces, the conversation profuse and merry as Lord Sackville's guests agreed that this promised to be a highlight of the off-season parties. The meal was similar to the splendorous suppers at Brighton, begun with four different kinds of soup, a variety of fish dishes, and huge platters of ham, poultry, and veal, along with forty side dishes.

The manor was overheated in every room from the excess of light and the multitude of roaring fireplaces. Windows and doors were thrown open to admit the cool evening air, but even taking these measures did little to relieve the stifling atmosphere. The sound of music, conversation, and clinking dishes drifted out into the night, inescapable no matter where Mira went to avoid hearing it. She walked along the empty hall-ways, paused at the open windows, and looked out into the courtyard. The supper scene was clearly visible, the huge glass doors of the eating room folded back to present a perfect view of the sumptuous feast. Biting the inside of her upper lip, Mira scolded herself for giving in to a sudden sense of loneliness. She remembered what Lady Ellesmere had called her—"a poor little waif"—and suddenly it was difficult not to feel like one. Self-pity, she thought wryly, is surely the most unattractive of all human faults! With a sigh, she folded her arms around her waist and continued to peer out the window.

She thought she could see Alec, whose black hair shone like jet under the lights. Was he sitting next to beautiful women, smiling at their sophisticated jests, and pondering over which ones he would dance with after supper?

She had not seen him since yesterday afternoon, when he had brought her back to the manor on Requiem. She had dismounted before they reached the manor, walking the last part of the way by herself in order to keep from being seen with him. Falkner had given her a teasing grin before riding away, as if he had known that for a moment she had been breathless from wondering if he was going to kiss her good-bye. But no kiss, no caress, nothing but that annoyingly superior smile! Mira had tried to pretend to herself that she was relieved at not having to endure a kiss from him . . . *vastly* relieved.

He was annoyingly inconsistent. How could he drop such sly comments about wanting her one minute and then ignore her the next? How could he hold her and whisper sinfully intimate, sweet words into her ear, and then pull away to make a snide remark about her relationship with Sackville? From now on Mira decided that she would not let him throw her into such a dither. She would be cool and terribly composed, a little bit frosty . . . but she would give him a small, indifferent glance every now and then to show him how little he disturbed her.

At these thoughts, Mira was already beginning to feel better. She stared at the crowd across the court-yard and grinned; nearby crouched little Mary and Kitty Daniel, the twins, who had already managed to get into a good deal of trouble since their arrival at the manor last evening. The little girls were hiding in the arched opening of a sitting room that bordered the courtyard, their faces pressed between the spokes of a railed balustrade that framed the small balcony. They had been missing since the supper began, but Mrs. Daniel had been too busy to look for her grandchildren.

"*Pauvres filles*," Mira murmured, leaving the window and walking down the hallway to the sitting room. "They are curious about the party and the music . . . just like me!" Quietly she went through the sitting room and out to the balcony, kneeling behind the children and sliding an arm around each small set of shoulders. "Your *grandmère* has been wondering where you were," she whispered, and the two round faces turned to her with engaging smiles.

"Miss Mira!" Mary whispered back. "We just wanted to watch them. The ladies are so pretty . . ."

"Yes, they are," Mira agreed, wrinkling her nose in a friendly way at the child.

"May we stay until the fireworks are over and the dancing begins?" Kitty asked timidly.

Mira shrugged lightly.

"*Pourquoi pas?*"

"What does that mean?" Mary asked.

"It means 'Why not?' You may stay for a while. I don't think it is too late in the evening yet. And I would like to join you."

The three settled together on the balcony as the music drifted out to them. Mira experienced an unfa-miliar peace as the twins settled on the hem of her outspread skirt. She did not mind if the velvet material was crushed, since no one would see her tonight. Was this how it might feel to have children of her own, to have the small bodies cuddled against hers, to smell their sweet, clean hair and let her hands rest against their plump, sturdy arms? Quietly they all sat together, staring through the railings.

After the sweet wines were served and the meal concluded, the enormous assemblage moved out into the courtyard, the gentlemen gallantly accompanying the ladies to view the fireworks. The show was unquestionably magnificent. Huge bursts of color lit the sky, showers of gold, red, silver, and green blossoming like unearthly flowers. Cheers and choruses greeted each new explosion, so that the voices and the rockets blended together in a strange symphony of rhythm. Unnoticed by the gathering, Mira and the twins stayed on the balcony, their faces lifted to the shimmering sky.

"Look at all those little falling stars . . ." Mira murmured, conscious of the children's excitement, forgetting for a moment to look for Falkner. "Both of you, make a wish on them."

"My star disappeared!" Mary exclaimed.

Mira smiled. "You're allowed another wish, then."

"What are you wishing for?"

"I am not wishing for a 'what,' " Mira said, chuckling. "I am wishing for a 'who.' "

"It sounds like thunder," Kitty said, torn between pleasure and uneasiness at the spectacular noise and vivid colors, inching closer to Mira until she was sitting in her lap.

"Kitty," Mary said, "don't be such a baby."

"I'm not a baby, *you're* a baby—"

"Look over there," Mira interrupted, pointing to a multicolored cloud of sparkles in an effort to distract them, and the twins subsided as they craned their necks.

Alec regarded the fireworks with a blank expression. He had the appearance of a man whose thoughts were a different world away. Lady Alice Hartley, married young, recently widowed, and making up for lost time, was accustomed to receiving far more attention than this from men, and she frowned prettily at him. Her voluptuous figure, golden ringlets, and wide blue eyes were formidable artillery, guaranteed to attract anyone she cared to set her sights on. Why, then, was Falkner evincing so little interest in her?

"Oh! My word, that was so close!" she squeaked as a rocket flew overhead. Clutching his tautly muscled forearm, she feigned a semblance of feminine helplessness, appearing to be overcome by the loud fireworks.

Alec said nothing, his gray eyes flickering down to her and then focusing back on the sky. The theatrics of a brainless flirt like Alice Hartley would have amused him a week or two ago, might even have attracted him enough to visit her bed, as she was so blatantly trying to entice him to do. But when he looked at her he felt a lack of desire that was appalling for a man in his prime—Alec knew that by now he should have dallied with half the women who had attended the hunt. Hell, that was why the women had come here, and most of the men, including their husbands, knew it. Most of Alex's contemporaries were making the rounds from bed to bed, making mental notes of the ladies' performances and exchanging reviews with each other in smug whispers. But so far Alec had not felt a stir of interest for anyone except the one woman that was off-limits to him. Mira . . . innocent, worldly Mira . . . beautiful, tormenting Mira. Mira-of-the-no-last-name. He gave himself a silent, rallying lecture on the matter.

He would forget her. She was nothing more than any of the rest of them—she had eyes, a nose, a mouth, a pair of breasts, the requisite number of fingers and toes . . . there was no reason to want her more than anyone else. She was damned annoying, in

fact . . . a little know-everything with a sharp tongue
and a tarnished background. Mira probably preferred
some doddering father figure like Sackville, who
wouldn't ask anything of her more than to hold still
while he labored on top of her. Furthermore, it would
take far too much time and patience to teach her how
to please him. And on top of all that, she was French
. . . and flighty . . . oh, God only knew why he was
so attracted to her!

But damn, how he wanted her.

As the final fireworks were being shot up into the
sky, Lady Hartley kept on clutching Alec's arm and
making slow-witted exclamations, until it was all he
could do to restrain himself from brushing her away
like a bothersome gnat. A silver sunburst exploded
overhead, and in that moment Alec felt an inner awareness brush delicately along his nerves. Turning his
head, he looked over the heads of the crowd around
him and saw a little balcony tucked away almost out of
sight. The bright light of the explosion illuminated the
courtyard like a bolt of lightning, and Alec saw a
scarlet dress, a slim arm, and neatly confined dark
hair. Mira was sitting on the balcony, and unless he
was mistaken, she was holding the Daniel twins on her
lap as she pointed up at the sky. She did not see him,
nor did anyone else see her. He smiled and then
looked back up at the sky, careful not to stare and
alert anyone else to her presence.

Finally the show was over, and Alec looked down at
Alice Hartley, who was exuding what she obviously
thought to be delightfully helpless confusion.

"It was all so stunning, wasn't it?" she asked. "And
so loud—"

"Yes, it was," Alec agreed, lifting a brown hand to
his forehead and rubbing between his eyes. "In fact, I'm
afraid that the explosions have aggravated the headache I've had ever since that hunting mishap the day
before yesterday."

"Oh dear, what a pity," Lady Hartley said, her expression rapidly becoming dull with disappointment.

"I think that I shall take a headache powder and lie down for a few minutes—"

"I will come with you and bathe your forehead with cool water—"

"No, no . . ." Alec interrupted hastily. "You are too kind, but I would not deprive you of the dancing merely to nurse me. No, I would prefer to be alone, and perhaps I will be able to make it downstairs before the evening is over to claim a waltz with you."

"I certainly hope so," Lady Hartley murmured, and suddenly Alec seemed to look right through her as he smiled, as if his thoughts were wandering somewhere else. Still, the effect of that smile was not lost on her, and she strove to remain unaffected by his blatant handsomeness.

"Thank you for your understanding, Lady Hartley," he said politely. "Until later."

As she watched him walk back inside the manor, leaving her in the company of the other women, Alice Hartley sighed with disgust. "I could simply tear my hair out over him," she commented.

"Alice, dear," Clara Ellesmere said, coming up to her elbow, "if the fish aren't biting, you're simply not using the right bait."

"Unless someone else's hook is already in him. That must be the reason."

"Do you really think so?" Clara asked speculatively, tilting her head to the side. "Well, don't worry about it. That kind of man never belongs to *anyone* for very long. You'll have another chance at him."

"Do you hear that music?" Mira whispered to the children. "It's a waltz, the most wonderful music in the world to dance to."

"Have you danced the waltz before?" Mary inquired, leaning her cheek against Mira's propped-up knee, her eyes fastened dreamily on the scene in the ballroom. Mira smiled, also watching the collage of swirling satin gowns and flashing jewels.

"Yes. Not at a ball like this . . . but I have waltzed before."

"Why aren't you dancing now, at this ball?"

The twins looked at her expectantly. Mira hesitated, uncertain of how to reply. She could not explain to the two little girls that she and they were looking at a world that they would never be able to enter . . . that there were boundaries that could not be trespassed . . . wishes that could never come true.

"Oh, I don't think I would fit in at all," she finally said. "My gown isn't nearly as pretty as those."

The children seemed to consider that a perfectly plausible explanation. Suddenly a soft masculine voice drifted to them from the opening of the sitting room.

"It's an attractive gown, nonetheless, albeit a little rumpled."

All three of them looked around and saw Alec standing there. Mira tried to struggle to her feet, miserably conscious of the disheveled picture she made, especially compared to him. He looked magnificent in formal attire, the scheme of black coat, white pantaloons, white shirt, and starched cravat emphasizing the tan of his skin and the darkness of his hair. His appearance was faultless; she had never seen anyone so handsome. Her heart stopped as he smiled at her.

"My lord," she managed to stammer, dislodging the twins off her lap and standing up to face him, "how did you know we were . . . I was . . . how—?"

"I noticed that you were here during the fireworks."

"He must have been the 'who' you were wishing for," Kitty said pragmatically.

"Was I?" Alec inquired lazily, and Mira flushed.

"No! Kitty and Mary, it is your bedtime. Come, I will take you to—"

"No, you can't leave yet," Alec said. "I have risked

my honor and reputation to come here for a dance with you, resorting to deceit and outright—"

"Hardly new for you," Mira interrupted. She meant to sound sharp and cool, but somehow her voice came out so breathless that Alec laughed.

"One dance. Just the rest of this waltz."

"Oh, do!" Mary exclaimed, as Kitty added, "We want to see you dance!"

"I . . . I can't," Mira said in a low tone, trying to walk by Alec with her head bent. He caught her wrist as she brushed past him, his warm hand closing gently over her arm and sliding down to her hand.

"One dance," he coaxed, stroking his thumb around the backs of her knuckles until her fingers were curved around his. Then his voice was even quieter. "Just one."

Still not looking at him, she allowed him to draw her to the center of the circular balcony while the music fanned over the night and distilled its gentle rhythm through the air. Mary and Kitty stepped out of the way and stood there eyeing the scene with delight. Alec smiled at them and then fixed his gaze on Mira. Her dress was of scarlet velvet, fitting closely to her slender form before flaring out at the hips. The boat-shaped neckline was cut very low, displaying the exquisite swell of her pale breasts, her sleeves full and slashed with black. Her dark, shining hair was covered with a black hairnet studded with pearls, a fringe of bangs escaping to frame her face and highlight her brown eyes.

"It will make things more difficult if you insist on standing so far away," Alec murmured. "This isn't a quadrille."

"I know that," Mira said, and stepped forward reluctantly, feeling painfully awkward.

"Why are you so stiff?" he asked so softly that it was almost a whisper. "I've held you in my arms before."

"This is different. I . . . I'm not comfortable with this. We shouldn't."

"Coward," he said, his eyes caressing her warmly.

"And I can hardly hear the music—"

"You could if you were quiet."

Mira smiled, reaching out to his wide shoulder and placing her hand in his. Alec seemed to sense her shyness, and he waited with unexpected patience for her to draw nearer. Slowly his arm slid around her waist, his hand splaying over the small of her back. As they began to move, Mira stared at the center of his broad chest, concentrating on the crisp whiteness of his shirt. She had never known that following a man could be so easy. Not only was the pressure of his hand on her back firm and explicit as he guided her, but there was some sort of silent understanding between them, as if their bodies knew exactly how to move together.

Alec's breath disturbed the wisps of her bangs. He had a strong urge to nuzzle past her hair and find her forehead with his lips . . . but there were the twins to consider. Turning Mira until her back was to the children, he mouthed silent words to them and winked. The next moment they left, smothering their high-pitched giggles with small hands. Mira lifted her gaze to Alec's face in bewilderment.

"They left. Where did they . . . what did you say to them?"

"You wouldn't continue to dance with me if I told you."

"You've just unleashed two small but destructive storms inside the manor," Mira said. "I wash my hands of all responsibility; whatever they do is your fault." As he grinned at her unrepentantly, she added, "You should be down there with everyone else, Alec."

"Where did you get this remarkable fondness for telling me what to do?"

"*Someone* needs to."

"Heartless creature—you'd actually send me back to the ball if you had your way, condemning me to hours of inane chatter and perfunctory dances."

"It's where you belong."

"And where do you belong?"

"Upstairs, in bed," she replied, and as she saw the devilish gleam in his eyes she added promptly, "by myself."

"But we're each entitled to a few minutes of escape from where we're supposed to be . . . and that's why we're both here."

"What could you have to escape from?" she asked. "A man of your station—"

"—has his own kind of problems," Alec interrupted dryly.

"Very *small* problems. I suppose one of your problems is boredom? Well, that's nearly inexcusable. There's no reason for boredom, not when the world is full of so many things to be done."

"What about loneliness?"

"Loneliness . . . that's more difficult to solve," she said thoughtfully. "But that's not a problem of yours, is it? There are so many people who want to be with you, who want to be your friends, women who want . . ."

"Women who want . . . ?" he repeated quickly. "What about you? Do you want anything from me? I've been trying to find that out for two weeks."

She did not reply as she looked at him and wondered what kind of game he was playing with her. She was too transparent to him; she knew that if she weren't careful he would discover things that she had been afraid to admit even to herself. Her eyes were caught by his, and although she knew that he was seeing far too much, she could not look away.

Her thighs brushed against his as the dance forced them closer; their steps became smaller as their bodies molded to each other. Their palms pressed together until Mira was not certain if it was her pulse or his that she felt beating between them. Again she was filled with that yielding weakness, that awareness of him, and the moment became timeless, a moment to remember for the rest of her life. One by one their fingers laced together, her small hand bound to his large one. She could not speak as she looked up at him, her eyes as black as midnight . . . and she knew that she was beginning to love him. It made her afraid and exhilarated, reckless. The wide, striking lines of his mouth were softer than usual, the brutally clean cut of his features highlighted by the stars and the clear white moon. He was like something out of a dream, his face all silver and shadows as he bent his head and kissed her cheek.

She shivered at the velvet brush of his lips, excitement crackling along her veins and awakening her nerves. She did not resist him, didn't turn her face away as his mouth traveled over her skin and grazed her cheekbone. A slight frown gathered between Alec's brows as he lifted his head to look at her, and it seemed as if he were torn between different impulses. As he stared at the softness of her lips, he swore quietly, and then his mouth sought hers, hot and insistent, urging her to yield to him, demanding that she open to him. Parting her lips, Mira succumbed to the searing magic of his kiss, stumbling against him as they stopped waltzing and simply stood there locked tightly together. Her arms went around his neck, her hands crept up to the back of his head, her fingers weaving through the raven smoothness of his hair.

Clinging to him, she responded to him with abandon, her mouth moving strongly under his, her body pressing sweetly against him as his hands wandered over her. One of his knees parted her legs and he cupped his hands over her buttocks, pulling her upward. She quivered as his hard thigh pressed into the softness between her legs, the firm pressure easing her mounting frustration slightly . . . but it was not enough, not nearly enough. Purring and sighing, Mira writhed against him in an effort to be closer. Her nostrils filled with the intoxicating fragrance of him . . . ah, she was drunk on him, and the night, and the sweetness of the feelings that flowed through her lavishly.

Alec caressed Mira's slim velvet-clad figure, and her passion caused the blood to course through his veins with the speed of mercury. He held her carefully, taking care not to crush her with the force of his need. Her eager response was an admission that she wanted him, and his loins swelled and hardened to aching readiness for her. A slight tremor shook his hand as he fought for control . . . his fingers slid into the hollow between her breasts, tracing along the inside of the neckline until the backs of his knuckles rested against her tender nipple. Gently his knuckles rubbed across the soft peak until it contracted and hardened, and Mira groaned into his mouth, her body shaking. Alec wanted to voice the thoughts that blazed across his mind . . . that she was as soft as silk, that she was beautiful, that he needed her more than he had ever needed a woman, but he could not stop kissing her long enough to say a single word. Greedily he devoured her lips, his tongue meeting hers and engaging in erotic play.

The flames rose higher, burned hotter, until Alec pulled away with a groan, and Mira blinked groggily as cool air touched her lips. Dumbfounded, she wrapped her arms around her middle as Alec turned and went to the balcony railing. Breathing hard, he braced his arms on the balustrade, his face lifted to the fresh, biting evening air. He inhaled and held the coolness of it in his lungs until his desire began to recede.

Mira's legs were wobbly. Bereft of his warm touch, she walked over to him timidly and trailed her fingers across the back of his hand. She opened her mouth to say something but was stopped short as he turned his head and looked at her with narrowed gray eyes.

"Let's go somewhere," he said huskily.

A noiseless pause followed his words while her eyes widened. What was he asking of her? Perhaps neither of them was entirely certain.

"Where do you want to go?" Mira asked, her voice nearly inaudible.

"Do you really care?"

"No," she whispered.

A brilliant fire leapt in his gaze. "If I asked you to come away with me, to leave Sackville, would you—?"

"Yes."

They stared at each other wonderingly, and then Alec took her small face in his hands, dislodging the pearl-studded web that confined her hair. He kissed her firmly, his head moving over hers with slow sureness until a tender sound vibrated from her throat.

"Come on," he said, enveloping her hand in his and pulling her through the sitting room into the hallway. "We're leaving for good, now, before you change your mind." Mira followed him blindly, her heart beating wildly. Somehow she knew that it was right for her to go with him. No matter what part chance had played in causing their paths to cross, the conclusion of their meeting was undeniable: they needed each other, they were good together, they were good for each other. Her hand tightened on his, and he paused to murmur some muffled endearment to her. But just as they stepped out into the hallway, disaster struck.

William Sackville was standing there.

"Falkner," he began, his face wreathed in a pleasant smile. "I was just coming to find you . . ." His voice trailed off into silence as he noticed the smaller figure standing a half-step behind Alec, his eyes becoming round and startled. "Mira," he said, his voice immediately strained. "I thought by now you would have been in your room."

"I . . . I was out on the balcony to watch the fireworks," she said, her hand slipping from Alec's loosened grasp. Sackville's ruddy complexion turned slightly gray as he noticed the tiny movement and realized that their hands had been joined. He turned his face to Alec, whose expression was unreadable.

"I was told that you were ill, Falkner. Something about a headache—"

"It's better now," Alec said dryly, meeting his gaze squarely.

All three of them fell silent. Mira felt her face turning a multitude of different colors as the air became thick with tension. She had to say something to break the silence or she would go mad.

"We happened to meet here . . . and went out to watch . . ." she stammered, and then words failed her. Alec, damn him, was deadly quiet in that provocative, challenging way of his, while Sackville looked so . . . so hurt and desperate. Sackville reached out a hand to Mira in a deceptively casual manner.

"Come here, Mira."

Mira felt Alec stiffen beside her.

Oh, please don't let this be happening, she thought wildly, caught between her desire for one man and her vows of loyalty to the other. She cared desperately about what Alec thought of her . . . but she had made a promise to Sackville, a promise based on her word of honor not to betray him, a promise that she had given to him because he had saved her life. She risked a glance at Alec, who did not return her look, his face turned away as he waited for her to make the next move. *You must know this isn't a choice of one of you over the other!* she wanted to cry out to him. *Don't make it an issue, it isn't significant unless you make it so!* Stiffly she took Sackville's hand, letting him draw her away from Alec to his side. Sackville curved his arm around her shoulders possessively, removing his eyes from Alec's face to look down at Mira.

"Well, I certainly hope you had an enjoyable chat," he said mildly.

Alec's jaw hardened. So this was the way Sackville intended to handle things, pretending ignorance of the situation, ignoring the obvious attraction between his friend and his woman.

"Yes," Mira murmured, not daring to look at Alec's face.

"It's time you went up to your room," Sackville continued, squeezing her affectionately. "And wait up for me—I'll be up there to see you later."

Shocked at his unusual bluntness and the blatant implication of his words, Mira looked up at him in surprise. She started as he lowered his silvery-russet head and kissed her soundly, displaying his possession of her for Alec to take good note of. As his cool, wet mouth covered hers, Mira automatically made a movement to push him away. Then her hands stopped and fell to her sides as she endured his kiss unprotestingly. I owe this to him, she thought grimly, and, by God, I will stand here without a sound if only for the sake of my own honor!

Alec watched them stone-faced, his eyes glittering like ice, something inside him dying and something else burning in deep-felt outrage.

Finally Sackville lifted his head and smiled down at her. Mira tried to force her lips into a quivering imitation of a smile, her cheeks burning as she resisted the impulse to draw the back of her hand across her mouth. Sackville's kiss was so far removed from Alec's as ice was from fire.

"Mira," Sackville said in a satisfied tone, "I'll be upstairs later, my pet."

She nodded her head in a nervous bob, then turned to look at Alec.

"Lord Falkner," she murmured deferentially.

He did not answer, one side of his mouth lifting in one of the nastiest and most cynical smiles she had ever seen. Inwardly anguished, Mira walked away from the two men toward the stairs in the front entrance-way. It took every bit of willpower she had to keep from running.

"A most uncommon woman," Sackville commented.

"Fine for you," Alec replied smoothly. "A little tame for me." Was Sackville deceived by the disdainful words? Probably not. Alec suppressed a grimace as sanity began to infiltrate his bemused senses. He must have gone a little mad a few minutes ago. A mere woman was not worth the sacrifice of a good friendship. How could he have seriously thought about taking her away from a man who had been loyal to him, to whom he had been loyal for so many years? He would have to find a way to avoid her, and all thoughts of her, from now on.

"Yes, you always like them a little wild, don't you?" Sackville said, forcing a hearty chuckle. The two men pretended that nothing out of the ordinary had happened, yet neither was content with the charade they had chosen to play. Perhaps outwardly things would go on as before, but inside they both knew better. Something about the character of their relationship had been changed for good.

"We must talk."

"Yes," Mira replied in a low tone, opening her bedchamber door. Sackville walked inside slowly, his face utterly serious. The dandyish accent he usually affected was gone.

"About tonight. I want to ask you—"

"Nothing happened." Mira closed the door and leaned her back against it as she stared at him miserably. "I'm so sorry, so terribly sorry. I don't know what happened. I'll never—"

"I knew," Sackville said, his face stiff, "—that there would come a time when you would want to end this. You're a healthy young woman with . . . a strong appetite for life. In fact, I have been surprised that you have stayed so long."

"I don't want to end *anything*. Have I imposed on you for too long?" Mira's vision became misty as she felt tears stinging her eyes. She blinked them back with an effort. "You should have told me to go."

"I wanted to keep you as long as you were willing to maintain appearances," Sackville replied, folding his hands behind his back and sighing. "You have done me much good, and you have helped me to retain a semblance of the life that I had . . . before. You have enabled me to maintain my pride, and I will always be grateful for that."

"I have been most content for the past two years—"

"But if you stayed, you would no longer continue to be so." Flinching in the face of his flat statement, Mira knew it to be true. "I have thought of you and me," Sackville continued with a weary smile, "—as two friends who have supported each other when they have most needed it."

"You saved my life," Mira whispered. "I can never repay that."

"You have, my dear, you have. But you cannot help me any longer by staying, and I am not helping you any longer by letting you hide here from the rest of the world. You are . . . How old are you?"

"Twenty."

"Twenty years old," Sackville repeated, his face both sad and ironic. "Twenty years ago I was already almost forty years old."

Mira shook her head, not understanding what her age had to do with anything.

"Believe me, my lord, when I tell you that I have had my share of living."

Sackville laughed shortly. "That I do not doubt, my dear. You've never told me how a little French girl comes to end up half-drowned in the back of a wagon in the south of England, but I imagine it takes a hefty share of living to accomplish that. You never told me why or how, but I could see that the spirit was tired as well as the body—and I've let you recuperate here. I've tried to help you, give you polish, educate you—"

"You have. I'm a different person now. You've helped me so much—"

"Yes. You were a girl. Now you are a woman, and I think you would like to cling to the illusion of security you find here instead of living your life as fate ordained it. Do you understand?"

"All I understand is that you want me to leave."

"For your sake as well as mine," Sackville said. "That is my point."

"When?" she asked, swallowing at the tightness in her throat.

"It might be best if you left after the hunt is finished. One more week. I will give you some money and provisions, and a good reference for respectable employment in London. But I must make one more request."

"Of course," she said, her face drawn with misery.

"Please finish out the charade while my guests are here. Please help me to make them believe what I wish them to believe. My reputation as a man depends on it. I, too, wish to cling to illusions, and this is the only way I can sustain my pride. For my sake, and in appreciation of what I have done for you, grant me this last week."

Mira's hands trembled, and she twined her fingers together. "About Lord Falkner—" she began huskily.

"You must make him believe the illusion as well. I value his friendship, and if he knew about me his respect for me would diminish. He cannot tolerate weakness, having little himself."

Confused, she shook her head slightly. "I would not hold him to be so shallow."

"You don't know a great deal about men like Falkner."

Sackville's tone was pensive. As she met his blue eyes, Mira suddenly understood why he wanted especially to impress their "relationship" upon Alec Falkner. It was not only because Sackville was afraid that Falkner would no longer respect him. It was also because Sackville liked the idea of having something that Falkner wanted. Side by side with his respect for Alec went an unsuspected trace of competitiveness. This was a new side to Sackville, one she had not previously seen or guessed at.

"I will do as you ask," Mira said dully, unwilling to argue the point. After having seen the contempt in his eyes, she knew that Alec would not want her any longer. She had nothing to lose by continuing Sackville's charade for one more week.

"Thank you." Sackville paused to note her expression before he left. "Do not pity me, my dear. In every situation there are always compensations. You will discover how to find them someday."

If Mira could have had her wish, she would have been able to avoid any sight or mention of Alec Falkner for the next week. She would have stayed in her room and not have come out until he and the rest of the guests were gone from the manor. But Sackville saw this final week as some kind of grand finale performance, getting his worth out of her by creating a picture of closeness between them in front of his friends and especially in front of Falkner. Sackville took walks with her in the garden, strolled with her through the portrait gallery, and took tea with her alone in one of the sitting rooms where everyone would notice them. Near the end of the week he asked her to join him in the library for a drink. At his bidding, she sat on the well-upholstered arm of his chair and stared with him into the roaring fireplace, unaware that Sackville had planned to receive a visitor he had not informed her about.

Alec walked through the door, his leisurely stride grinding to a halt as he took in the picture before him. The ripe orange-gold light of the fire played over Mira's small, beautiful features. Her finely sculptured hip pressed against Sackville's shoulder as she sat on the arm of a bulky chair, her blue velvet dress edged with soft white swansdown that accentuated the porcelain softness of her skin. Her eyes shone with a mysterious glow, slanted like those of a cat as she stared at him. Alec hated himself for the jolt of desire he felt immediately upon seeing her, and his teeth clenched together.

"Excuse me," he muttered. "I thought you wanted to meet me here, William."

"I do, I do!" Sackville said, taking a swallow of brandy and patting Mira's hip. "Off you go, my dear. Thank you for an enjoyable evening."

Wordlessly she stood up. For a second her eyes caught with Alec's. He was looking at her as though she were beneath disdain, and mixed with his contempt was an odd sort of rage. Catching her breath, she folded her arms around herself protectively and left the room.

Every time Alec looked at her, he was confronted with more evidence of the close relationship between Mira and Sackville. His previous assumptions about her began to decay. He wondered if all the signs of her innocence had been a game. Had she been amusing herself with him, was she a masterful little actress who was now making sport of him behind his back with Sackville? Resentment and desire intermingled in his blood, making him light-headed whenever he saw her.

After a late night of drinking, he passed by her near the turret steps, and they both stopped in painful confusion. They were alone in the hallway. His expression was indifferent, hers uncertain. Suddenly he seized her shoulders roughly, lifting her so that her feet almost left the floor. He glared into her face.

"What are you trying to do to me?" he demanded harshly, his fingers tightening until she gasped with pain. "I don't want to see you anymore, do you understand? No more well-planned scenarios with Sackville's hands down your dress. No more *accidental* meetings to show me that you're in heat for each other—I get the idea, and you can tell him that I don't have the slightest interest in a promiscuous little—"

His monologue was broken off as she kicked him in the shin.

"Ow! Damn you!" Alec let go of her immediately, massaging his leg and raining a string of heartfelt curses on her head.

"You . . . you big, stupid, blind . . . *barbarian*!" Mira snapped, lifting her hands to her throbbing shoulders. "Don't you *ever* touch me again. You can *think* whatever you want about me, I don't care a single bit, but don't you dare go around with the idea that you have the right to attack a defenseless woman!"

"You're about as defenseless as a python," Alec said coldly, rubbing his bruised shin and scowling at her.

Mira drew herself up with dignity.

"If I am a python, then you're a worse one," she said, her voice cutting. Then she swept up the turret steps in a regal manner, wondering exactly what a python was.

From the nearby château came the sounds of a string quartet rehearsing to perform during supper. Mira had spent hours sitting in the garden on a stone bench, her feet propped up and her arms braced on her knees as she thought. Sighing, she looked around at the peaceful green of the landscape, knowing that she would miss the Sackville garden. It was a place of solitude and beauty, a well-composed scheme of immaculately shaved lawns and clusters of spruce and fir trees, miniature waterfalls and an artfully dug stream.

Across the stream arched a small bridge which led to a fanciful vine-covered pagoda. The design followed the innovative patterns of Capability Brown, a landscape gardener who favored gardens with a natural appearance rather than the overly cultivated ones previously in vogue. Brown had advised Sackville to get rid of the pagoda, but Sackville had fancied the little structure too much to get rid of it.

Listening to the rustle of the falling water and staring absently at the pagoda, Mira wondered what she was going to do in London. She had been in the huge city before, especially the grimy eastern section of London, which was worse than anything she had seen in Paris. In the mornings the sky was black with the sea-coal smoke that burned in thousands of hearths. The streets were filled with garbage and drunkards, and men who stared at her in a frightening way, and women who looked wretchedly tired, and children who did not look like children at all. They were too desperate, too skeletal and animalistic to be children. Mira had been filled with despair at the sight of those little beastlike creatures, and it had not taken long for her to soak up the hopelessness that saturated east London. She had sunk down into the mire of it, becoming one of the scavenging crowd, until she could barely recognize herself. But she had been too vulnerable to survive there and too strong to die easily—and so she had settled for a compromise between surviving and dying, crawling into the back of a hay wagon and casting herself on the mercy of fate.

"How can I go back?" Mira asked herself, stemming a faint shudder. She knew that this time she would have money and references, and she would not have to live so far east, but her dread of London remained unshakable.

Nearby came the crunching of feet on a sanded path. Mira took care to remain still, for she and the wanderers through the garden were separated by a hedge. At the moment she had no wish to be discovered by anyone. She kept quiet. It sounded as if there were only two women walking leisurely along the path.

". . . someone should tell Clara that she's making a fool of herself," one of them was saying indignantly. Her companion's voice was much calmer and a little amused.

"My dear, she's finding that out already. It's plain as day that Falkner doesn't want her. I only hope it's set her down a step or two—"

"Pooh! That won't daunt her for long. Lord Falkner is a handsome devil, but Clara's really just biding her time until the man she really wants comes along."

"Who is that?"

"Why, didn't you know? Clara has always preferred Rand Berkeley over every other man, and he's arriving tomorrow."

"With his wife in tow, I'll wager."

"Probably. Rosalie Berkeley—how that name rankles! —it isn't enough that she actually managed to marry the Earl of Berkeley, but he insists on dragging her around with him like an umbrella—"

"Yes, keeping her within arm's reach and pulling her out whenever one of us tries to approach him!"

"Doesn't he know that it's unfashionable to be seen too much with his own wife?"

The two women giggled lightly.

"Unfashionable or not," one of them concluded, "he'll undoubtedly have Rosalie with him. Do you think that will stop Clara from trying . . . ?"

Their laughter faded as they continued down the path, while Mira sat on the bench feeling as hard and frozen as one of the marble statues in the garden.

"Rand Berkeley," she whispered, her eyes round and unblinking. "Rosalie." Sackville had never mentioned them to her before—she had had no idea that he was even acquainted with them! She could not believe that they would be attending the hunt. The thought of them coming here made her tremble, made her stomach tighten in a sudden cramp. She put a hand to her midriff, her gaze vacant as a horrible scenario appeared before her.

Rosalie would see her and stiffen in shock, her lovely face becoming pale with fear and hatred. "*Mireille. I had prayed never to see you again . . . traitress, liar . . . you deceived me, you took my friendship and tried to destroy me!*"

"I didn't mean to," Mira whispered. "Forgive me."

"*I loathe the sight of you. You don't deserve to be forgiven for the pain you caused us.*"

And then Mira would turn to Rand, only to find the same cold condemnation written on his face.

"*You were not only disloyal,*" he would say, "*you were a coward. You should have stayed to face what you had done, you shouldn't have run away.*"

"I was afraid . . . I didn't know . . ." Mira blinked and shook herself as panic took hold of her. "I've got to leave," she said, one hand fumbling with the neckline of her dress, which had suddenly become too tight. "I've got to get away . . . *mon Dieu* . . . tonight." She began to cry, and put a hand up to her face as tears fell from her eyes. Rand and Rosalie would be here tomorrow. She tried to make plans and could not think. Weeping harshly, Mira bowed her head at the folly of having tried to escape her past. The nightmare of five years ago was upon her again, as fresh as if it had happened yesterday.

Lord Sefton was in a jovial mood, a liberal amount of port having loosened his tongue and mellowed his spirits. Sefton was unusually gossipy, reciting a load of rumors and social tidbits that Alec cared not a whit about, but one of the penalties of attending a hunt this long was that sooner or later one had to endure tedious conversations of this sort. They walked slowly toward the eating room, whiling away the few minutes before supper.

"I say, did you hear about the king's forthcoming visit to Hanover? He's leaving at the end of the month."

"Affairs of state?" Alec inquired.

"No—I hear there are a few Protestant princesses he intends to look over most thoroughly. He wishes to marry again."

"Of course," Alec murmured sardonically. George IV had shown little grief over the death of his wife, Caroline, the year before, despite the fact that they had had so much in common—fat and slovenly, both of them, as well as being loose-moraled and vindictive. The only difference between the two was that Caroline had been coarse while George was pretentious and affected. Now it seemed that the king, whose taste had always been for older women, was turning his eye toward young and lively girls. "I suppose it won't present much of a difficulty for him to marry despite the fact that he already has a wife?"

"You mean Mrs. Fitzherbert? It's never actually been proven that they were legally married, and besides, they have been separated for nine years now—"

"Separated but not divorced."

"Do you really believe that they were married?" Sefton asked.

Having once made the acquaintance of Mrs. Fitzherbert, Alec did believe in the rumored marriage. Maria Fitzherbert was an honorable woman and a loyal one, saying not a word against the king even after he had used her poorly. Had she discarded her pride to weep and beg for the king's favor, she might have retained his affections. Perhaps if she had pandered to his vanity, or perhaps if she had reproached him for the way he had cast her aside, she might still be the king's right-hand companion—but there were some sacrifices that Mrs. Fitzherbert had not been willing to make even for the sake of love, a position which Alec agreed with wholeheartedly.

"It doesn't matter what I believe," he said, his distant tone causing Lord Sefton to look around for a new conversation partner. It was clear that although Falkner was proficient enough at small talk, he hardly relished having to make it.

"There are Squire Bentinck and his lovely wife," Sefton exclaimed, edging toward them in a way that made Alec smile wryly. "Excuse me, Falkner, I must give them my regards."

"Certainly," Alec murmured, watching Sefton make a relieved escape. The other man's eagerness to be away from him was both amusing and disturbing. I can't stand to be around most of them, he thought. Then his amusement disappeared like a puff of smoke. What had happened to his compassion and tolerance for others? Why couldn't he feel something more than indifference for them?

Walking over to a nearby window, he leaned against the sill and stared out at the darkening sky.

It had all gone with Holt. Honestly he acknowledged to himself that he was not the same man he had been before Holt's death. There were so many things he didn't *care* about anymore, so many things that had to be done before his wounds could heal, before he could allow himself to forget. There had been only one small promise of comfort, one chance at happiness . . . but that had been only an illusion.

"Oh, damn," Alec whispered quietly, his troubled musings interrupted by the sight of a small figure outside, a long distance away. A woman was running across the small bridge that led to an odd little pagoda on the far end of the garden. She was too far away for him to see her face clearly but Alec knew that it was Mira. It had to be. She had a long dark braid of hair and was wearing a sapphire-colored dress, and even from here he recognized the trim curves of her figure.

What was she up to? he wondered, inclining his head to watch her. In her rush she fell to her hands and knees. Then Mira picked herself up and continued on her frantic pace to the pagoda. It looked as though she were being chased. More games? Or had someone actually hurt her? Swearing under his breath, Alec stood up and looked down the hall to the gathering crowd in the eating room.

She's not mine, he thought with a scowl. Let Sackville see to her if she needed someone.

"Lord Falkner, are you waiting for someone?" a feminine voice intruded on his thoughts. The Earl and Countess of Shrewsbury stood before him with pleasant expressions, and Alex pasted a thin smile on his face.

"I'm afraid so."

"If you would like to accompany us to supper . . ."

"Thank you, your offer is most kind," he replied amiably, "but I believe I will wait a few more minutes." He exchanged smiles with the pair. After they left, Alec drummed his fingers impatiently on the windowsill and cast another glance outside. Mira had disappeared from sight. There was no one else outside, not Sackville or any of the other guests. "Bloody hell," he muttered, "I'm not going out there . . . I won't, not if I have any damned sense at all."

5

Curled up in the corner of the pagoda, Mira closed her eyes against the sight of the shuttered walls. She had been running all of her life with no destination and no hope of refuge, running without tiring because she had never any other way of life. Until now. Now she was too exhausted to run any longer. Defeated, she made a feeble attempt to gather her thoughts together but lacked the strength to make decisions.

The sight of her reminded Alec of a hunted fox that had dug deep into the ground for refuge. He had not been able to stop himself from coming to find her; she had become an obsession of his, a temptation beyond measure. As he looked at her, he could see that someone or something had frightened her, and he was filled with the self-mocking awareness that he wanted to take her in his arms, shelter her from harm. Fighting against a surge of tenderness, he hardened his expression into one of cool indifference.

"Well, now . . ." he said softly, leaving the tiny door open to admit the dusky glow of twilight into the pagoda. "I thought it was you I saw out here. What for—a pre-supper tryst?"

Her quiet sobbing stopped abruptly. "Get out of here," she said, her voice fringed with a betraying tremor.

Alec sat down across from her, his legs stretched out so that his feet rested on the cushion next to her.

Mira cast his boots a venomous glance before lifting a handkerchief to her nose, blowing loudly, and then resting her forehead on her bent knees.

"What happened?"

"Nothing." She refused to look at him. "Oh God, I don't want to talk to you! Out of pity, *please* go! I can't bear your company right now, and I don't know why you're here, but—"

"Don't you? Perhaps I'm giving rein to my irrepressible curiosity. Or maybe I'm playing Good Samaritan."

"Samaritan?" Mira repeated, suddenly choking on a combination of amusement and disdain. "You? That's ridiculous. I've never met anyone more unsuited to that role. You can be kind when you want to be, but that isn't nearly often enough. And even if you could help me, I wouldn't let you . . . no, because you'd want something back. Your kind always wants something in return for what—"

"Easy, easy . . ." he said, holding up his hands in a gesture of surrender. "I didn't come out here to serve as a target. I only wanted to see what the weather outside was like. I thought I saw a few storm clouds gathering."

"I couldn't tell you anything," she said, undistracted by his teasing. "You wouldn't understand any of it!"

"I understand about being in trouble." Alec settled back against the cushions and regarded her steadily. "I've had a long and sometimes profitable acquaintance with trouble. I've had vast experience at pulling myself out of scrapes . . . hopeless messes, most of them, and occasionally I've learned a thing or two about . . . perspective."

"I couldn't begin to explain it to you."

"Why? Do you think you'd shock me?"

Strangely, it was the mocking tone of his voice that caused Mira to consider telling him. Lifting her head to look at him, she expelled a tight breath. He was little more than a large shadow inside the pagoda, looking vaguely satanic in the darkness. No, she did not think that she could shock him, for if there was one thing that she did know about Alec, it was that he was not shocked easily. In some ways he was one of the most cynical men she had ever met.

"I suppose . . . there is a chance you would understand. I mean . . . you've probably done some unsavory things during your life—"

"—and enjoyed most of them quite shamelessly," he added helpfully.

"I wonder what your motive for listening to my confession would be," she mused, her tone gently acidic. "Is it that you're bored? Would you like me to fill the few minutes before your supper with entertaining anecdotes of my sordid past?"

"As a matter of fact, yes . . . I would. It's not that I don't already have a few suspicions about the kind of trouble you might be in . . . I'd just like to hear your version of it."

"You're a fine one to judge me!"

"Oh, I'm not judging you," he countered wryly. "As you pointed out, I'm the last person qualified for that. I'm merely offering to lend a sympathetic ear."

Looking at him warily, Mira decided that confiding in him—a little bit—was not too great a risk. After all, there wasn't much for her to lose. "I . . . I have to leave tonight," she said, waiting for some sort of reaction from him and hearing none. "I mean *leave*, for good. I found out something today . . . I didn't know about it before, but I can't stay here now . . . you see . . . Rand Berkeley and his wife are arriving here tomorrow."

"Berkeley," Alec said emotionlessly, his gaze locked on her face. "You've made his acquaintance before, I gather?"

"Yes. I first met him in France."

As he calculated what sort of connection Mira might

have had to the Earl of Berkeley, a man universally acknowledged to be one of the most financially powerful and physically attractive men in England, Alec was not pleased with the most obvious answer. "Were you his mistress?" he asked sharply.

She was too annoyed by his blunt question to notice the jealousy that rang out in his voice. "No," she replied stonily. "Believe what you like, but I have not . . . I don't . . ." She sputtered to a halt and closed her mouth with a snap.

"Go on," Alec said, impatiently drumming his fingers on his taut thigh. "Tell me about Berkeley."

"He doesn't know I'm here in England. When he knew me, my name . . . my name was Mireille Germain."

"Mireille," Alec repeated as if savoring the sound. He pronounced it differently from her; his easy drawl was miles away from her pert French syllables. "An attractive name. Why did you change it?"

"Because Mireille was a child who . . . wasn't aware of the wrongs she did. She didn't know enough to be ashamed of what she was."

"But Mira does?"

"Yes." She hid her face and began to weep again. Alec let her cry a minute or two, finding that it took incredible concentration to remain where he was instead of scooping her up and cuddling her close. He focused his attention on the puzzling questions, the mysteries about her. What kind of life had she led? What jumbled mixture of experiences had made her into a creature of such bewildering contradictions? She had the strength of a woman and the vulnerability of a child. Constantly he was torn between rampant desire and an alarming feeling of protectiveness toward her. In that moment Alec would have given a fortune for her to have been anything other than his best friend's mistress. Why couldn't she have been the daughter of a respectable family, untouched by any other man? Or a distant cousin, far removed enough to be eligible for his attentions, delicately raised and nurtured . . . or even the daughter of a merchant? He would have been free to court her in any of those instances, with no doubts and no obstacles in his way.

Mira's tears subsided eventually, and she gathered herself together with a heaving sigh, entirely unaware of the thoughts that lurked in her companion's mind.

"Did Berkeley hurt you?" Alec asked, his voice soft and chilling.

Mira shook her head, drawing the back of her hand across her damp eyelids. "He didn't hurt me. Just the opposite. I hurt him and the woman that he loved. And he would never forgive or forget anyone who hurt Rosalie."

"What in the hell did you do to them?"

"First you must understand about Guillaume, my brother. He had a great deal to do with it. The first time I saw him I was twelve. Our mother had just died, and she was . . ."

Mira stopped suddenly, realizing that she could not tell him. She looked into his alert gray eyes and realized that her every instinct called for her to keep the secret about her mother hidden from him. He would not understand; he and she were at the opposite ends of an impossibly wide spectrum, and the kind of life she had led was entirely foreign to him. Alec Falkner came from a background of wealth and prosperity. His rightful place was in a world of leisure time, opulence, a world of exquisite manners and carefully protected reputations. He had been educated at the best institutions, he wore expensive clothes, he rode only thoroughbred horses, he drank and ate of the finest fare, he associated with the most affluent people in England. He would be revolted by the knowledge that her mother had been a prostitute. After she told him, he would think of her as something unclean. He would no longer be attracted to her in any way . . . he would never want to touch her again.

"Mira," Alec said dryly, "don't turn shy. To be indelicately frank, my expectations concerning your background have never been too high. What were you going to say about your mother?"

"Nothing," Mira whispered.

"What caused your mother to—?"

"Nothing!" she repeated angrily.

Sighing in an exasperated manner, Alec let the subject drop. "All right, then . . . we won't talk about her. What were you going to say about Guillaume?"

"He took care of me after our mother died," Mira said carefully. "He was my only family. We went everywhere together. He earned money here and there, doing different things, and I worked when I could. But it was not enough money to live on, so we had to . . . we had to do dishonest things in order to get more. Guillaume taught me many things. We robbed people, lied to them, and conned them." Guillaume had been pleased that she could make friends so easily, because the more they had liked her, the more easily she had been able to take advantage of them. "I hated it. I always hated what we had to do for money. I hated to hurt people . . . but it's so much worse to be hungry. You wouldn't understand what it's like."

Alec made no reply as he pinned her with a shrewd stare.

"And even if I hadn't been so afraid of being hungry," Mira continued, "I would have done it all to please Guillaume. He was the only person in the world who cared about what happened to me. He loved me—I know he did—and without him I would have been alone. I was afraid of being alone. But everything changed when I was fifteen, when I was working at a hotel in Paris as a chambermaid. Guillaume would leave me for a few weeks at a time."

A young girl, alone in Paris. Working in a hotel. Alec knew that she must have been uncommonly resilient to have survived that. She had to have been exposed often to danger . . . yet she was not asking for pity, merely telling him the facts. Reluctantly he felt a twinge of admiration for her—as he had once said, she did not lack mettle.

"At the hotel," Mira said, "I met Rand Berkeley for the first time. There was a woman with him—they were not married, but they seemed to care for each other. The woman was Rosalie Belleau. She was ill, and I helped to take care of her while they stayed at the hotel. I went with Berkeley and Rosalie when they retired to the country for her to recuperate. During that summer I was her companion, and we became very fond of each other." Mira smiled wistfully. "But there were many things that I did not know about Rosalie, including the controversy that was taking place in England at the time. She was rumored to be the illegitimate daughter of Beau Brummell."

"Ah . . ." Alec nodded thoughtfully. "I remember the scandal now . . . it was in all of the newspapers. The Berkeleys have since covered it up well, but Lady Rosalie has quite a checkered past."

"Yes. Guillaume, my brother, found out about it and followed me to the château where we were all staying. He was involved with a bad crowd of people, an organization that extends from England to France. They convinced him to do terrible things. I did not know what he and they planned, but I knew somehow that Guillaume was making use of my friendship with Lord Berkeley and Rosalie, and that he was going to take advantage of their trust in me. I didn't say anything, blindly hoping that he would not do anything wrong. I was happy for the first time in my life. I had a home and security, and I wanted it to go on forever. Berkeley and Rosalie asked me to come back to England with them. I would have, but then . . . then—"

"Guillaume interfered?"

Mira nodded slowly. "Yes, Guillaume tore it all apart. He arranged to have Rosalie kidnapped, right out from under Berkeley's nose. She was . . . she was sold to someone for a great deal of money, to someone who wanted her because she was Brummell's daughter. And unwittingly I was the one who made it all possible. My friendship with Berkeley and Rosalie nearly ruined their lives." She closed her itching eyes and rubbed them gently. "I ran like a coward when I found out what Guillaume had done. I couldn't face Berkeley; I was afraid he would kill me. I loved Rosalie and I wanted to die when I realized what she might have been suffering. I don't know how Berkeley got her back, but he did. Eventually I found out that things had turned out well for them . . . but I was too overwhelmed with guilt and shame to approach them. During my stay with them I had learned many things, you see . . . I realized how many people I had hurt, how many bad things I had helped Guillaume to do. So I left Guillaume and came here. He followed me, but I kept on running and hiding from him—I didn't want his love anymore."

"And that's why you're so distraught over their arrival tomorrow?" Alec asked when it appeared that she had finished. His tone was dry and faintly ridiculing, as if her fear and shame had been unfounded.

"If not for me, all of those people wouldn't have been hurt, and Rosalie would never have been kidnapped—"

"Wait . . . stop for just a second. You didn't *intentionally* help Guillaume arrange the kidnapping, did you?"

"No, but—"

"Then you have nothing to feel guilty about," he said matter-of-factly.

"But all the other people I stole from—"

"Do you really think *they* give a damn about your pangs of conscience? No. They've forgotten all about the dirty turn that some little French imp did to them once, and they're going on about their lives as usual while you're here stewing and fretting over nothing. Mira, my mixed-up brat, you should put your energy to better use than this."

"I'm not stewing over 'nothing,' " she said half-heartedly, beginning to feel comforted by his practical assessment of the situation. "I'm facing the very real problem of how to leave here."

Suddenly Alec's face hardened.

"Leaving is very simple, m'dear. Choose two or three of your favorite gowns, a change of undergarments, and a good pair of shoes. Throw them into a bag and squeeze a little money out of Sackville before you go. Does that solve your problem? Or is there something that makes it difficult to walk out the door? Perhaps you care for Sackville more than you thought you did? Or do you find that you are reluctant to leave the luxuries behind?"

"Now you're being hateful," Mira said, staring moodily at the open door of the pagoda. What had happened to set off his quicksilver temper? Why had he suddenly decided to goad her now, when he had been almost kind a few minutes ago?

"Why leave at all? Is it that you're afraid of what the Berkeleys will say when they see you?"

"Yes, of course I'm afraid! Only a fool wouldn't be afraid! Rand Berkeley will wring me out like a towel to find out where Guillaume is. And I don't even know. I haven't seen him for years—but Berkeley won't believe that."

"Then tell Sackville to protect you."

Clearly he was mocking her. Mira chewed on the inside of her lower lip in an effort to keep from flying into a rage. Alec knew very well how helpless Sackville would be against someone as powerful as Rand Berkeley! She ground her teeth together as she struggled to find an appropriate reply.

"Perhaps I will," she said, and he snorted derisively. Then Mira railed at him helplessly. "Don't sneer at me! You know already that Sackville would crumble like wet toast! And there's no one else who . . ." She looked at him and paused. "Well, *you* would be able to handle Berkeley. He wouldn't cross someone like you, and he wouldn't do anything to hurt me if *you* were there to . . . But you're not about to help me, are you?"

"I might. If you ask nicely."

Mira regarded him with suspicion. "What would you demand in return for your protection?"

Alec smiled. "You learn very quickly, don't you? Reasonably, the payment should depend upon how much I have to exert myself to keep you in one piece."

"You already owe me a favor," Mira pointed out, thinking rapidly. "Remember what I did for you that morning when you were thrown by Sovereign? Remember all the pain in your shoulder and the way your arm—"

"Yes, I remember," he said smoothly. "But I don't owe you a thing for that. I didn't ask for your help."

"Why, you ungrateful—"

"Be wary of the names you call me, my sweet. Otherwise you'll hurt my feelings, and you can't afford to do that right now."

"You have feelings?" she asked, pretending to be astonished. "Oh, I'm sorry . . . I had no idea."

"I warned you," he said softly. "Just for that, maybe I'll demand my payment now." He looked at her in a different way than before, his eyes flickering, and the enclosed pagoda seemed to shrink to half its original size. "What is my protection worth to you?" he asked, unlocking his long legs and moving to where Mira was sitting. She was disturbed by the slow, predatory way he lowered himself to the cushion she sat on, yet she tried to look unconcerned.

"Do be serious. You're always playing games," she said, jumping as he leaned over her, one hand braced on either side of her hips. She could see the spikiness of the black lashes that framed his gray eyes, and the subtle shadow of masculine stubble that shaded the lower half of his face. Their lips were only inches apart, causing her pulse to rocket and her nerves to dance wildly. "What kind of payment are you going to ask for?" she demanded contemptuously. "A kiss? Or do you think that you might deserve more for condescending to protect me? Perhaps I should let you put your hands on me and let you have whatever it is you want—"

"Whatever it is I want," Alec repeated, almost pressing his words against her mouth. "Do you know what it is I want? Why does Sackville's mistress have a habit of looking at me with such bewildered innocence when I touch her? Why did you kiss me that first time like an untried schoolgirl?" He paused, and then his whisper singed her ears with its heat, "The payment I demand is an answer to one question. Only one, Mira."

"You know everything about me," she said uncertainly. "I told you every—"

"No. I don't know quite everything."

"Then what is your question?"

"Are you really Sackville's mistress?"

She tried to bolt away from him. He caught her around the waist easily, standing up to pull her back against the solid breadth of his chest. As she fought the arm around her middle, Mira's panic increased when Alec bent his head to speak in her ear. "Maybe I should rephrase the question," he purred. "Was Sackville man enough to make you his woman? Have you ever belonged to any man? I think the answer is no."

A small cry broke from her lips.

"Let me go," she gasped, trying to twist out of his steely grip.

"In fact, I'll even go so far as to bet that you've never been bedded before. Perhaps those are long odds . . . but in spite of all that you've done, in spite of all of your misadventures, there have been a few experiences that you've managed to wriggle out of, haven't there? And while you're at it, you might as well tell me how long Sackville has been impotent. He must be—it explains too many things that I've wondered about for a long time."

"Oh, I *hate* you!" she cried, her breath coming in dry sobs. "Stop it! You're wrong about everything. Yes, I've had men before, hundreds of them, hundreds and—"

"Little liar. I'd check myself before taking your word for it."

"Oh, don't!" Mira went stiff as she felt him pull up the material of her skirt, his hand burrowing ruthlessly until he found the fine silkiness of her long-legged pantaloons. "What are you doing? Stop it!"

Alec's fingers curled into the rigid line of her thigh, and suddenly his voice contained what might have been a trace of desperation.

"Mira . . . listen to me—"

"I can't tell you, I can't!"

"I know you made some kind of promise to him. I know you're afraid of breaking it, but God help me, I have to know or I'll go mad. I don't care if you're an innocent or not. I don't care if you *have* had hundreds of men. I just have to know if you're his. Tell me . . . I need the truth." Slowly his hand moved up and down the inside of her thigh in a gentle caress, his touch burning through the thin material. "Are you Sackville's mistress?"

"Alec—" she gasped.

His hand moved further up her leg, venturing near the warm crevice between her thighs. "The truth, Mira."

"I won't—"

"Are you Sackville's mistress?"

"Oh—"

"Are you?" he insisted.

Suddenly Mira sagged in his arms. She could not fight him any longer. "No," she sobbed.

With a relieved groan he turned her around and crushed her against his body. She felt his lips against her hair. It seemed that he held her like that for hours, his arms firm and possessive. Mira gave a shuddering sigh, holding on to him desperately, letting him support her weight, never wanting to move again. She could not deny to herself any longer that she loved Alec Falkner; she would never love anyone else in this way. She loved everything about him, the way he bullied and teased and comforted her, the way he laughed, the way he held her, his anger, his desires . . . she loved his strengths and even his faults.

"Sackville had a riding accident before I came to the manor," she said, nestling against him and burying her face in his neck. "He hurt his back. It took a long time to heal, but he was well by the time I first arrived. He made it a special project to see that I was well taken care of."

"I'll bet he did."

"If it weren't for his kindness I would have died. When I recovered, he told me that he cared for me and . . . and that he wanted to take me as his mistress. I knew that I owed my life to him, and there was nothing else I had to give him. He . . . he came to my bed a few times, but he never . . . he couldn't . . . Do you—?"

"I understand."

"The accident had taken away his ability to . . . make love. But he is such a proud man, and so afraid that someone will find out. Sackville said that I would still be able to help him by pretending that I was his mistress. He is so proud, so afraid of what people think. I promised him that I would never tell anyone and that I would help him to convince you—"

"It's all right." Alec's punishing grip loosened. His hand cupped around the back of her head and tilted her face upward so that he could look directly into her eyes. "You are not going to leave tomorrow," he said quietly. "As far as I can tell, you've always solved your problems by running away. Not any longer."

Mira tried to wriggle away from him. He didn't know all of the truth. He had no idea that her past was too complicated, studded with too many obstacles. It couldn't be solved or put behind her. Sooner or later it would rise up to threaten her again . . . over and over, for the rest of her life. She had to run from it . . . it was the only way.

"I don't want to face them," she said.

"You can't run from the Berkeleys forever. And after you face them there won't be anything more to dread."

She only wished that that were true. But how could she argue when he spoke with such authority, such absolute certainty? Mira nodded halfheartedly, closing her eyes as he dropped a casual kiss on her forehead. His mouth felt very warm and light, stirring her senses pleasantly. Mira remembered that bold clasp of his hand on her thigh . . . suddenly she felt indignant, excited, and nervous all at once.

"Alec?" she asked in a small voice. "Do you . . . have you ever kept a mistress?"

She longed for a third foot to kick herself with as Alec grinned, seeming to know exactly what she had been thinking. His expression was wry and amused as he stared down at her, his free hand coming up to stroke the fragile lines of her throat in a gentle, knowing caress. "One thing at a time, sweet," he murmured. "Let's get you out of this tangle before landing you in another."

"I wasn't asking you—" she began with straight-backed dignity.

"I know what you were asking."

"Well, I don't really care—"

"The answer is no. I've never found a woman who

managed to keep me amused for very long. Setting up a mistress in a grand residence, satisfying her whims, and being seen with her more than a few times all add up to a kind of responsibility that I haven't yet entertained an interest in."

"Heaven help the woman you decide to marry," Mira said gruffly. "One woman will never be enough to satisfy you!"

"Oh, I disagree. I plan to mend my philandering ways after I marry. Since I'll demand absolute fidelity from my wife, it's only fair for me to pledge the same, don't you think?"

"Oh. Yes, I think that's very . . . very . . ."

"Practical," he said as she floundered for the right word. "Much more convenient, not to mention less expensive than keeping a wife *and* a mistress. But it makes the task of finding a suitable match far more difficult."

Mira was disturbed by the turn of the conversation. It's obvious, she thought unhappily, that I'm not the kind of woman that someone like him could marry. But if I were going to be someone's mistress, then . . . it wouldn't be that terrible to be Alec's. It wouldn't be that bad at all.

"I guess your standards are exacting," she commented dully.

"Exacting, but not impossible to uphold. I'm very fair-minded." His smile was taunting. "Why, if it weren't for your temper, your disreputable past, and your habit of scowling at me, you'd probably be high in the running."

Why did he love to bait her so?

"I don't know why I bother talking to you," Mira said shortly.

"I do. Because for the most part, I don't condemn you for what you are. Because I'm cut from the same cloth, and in an odd way the two of us suit each other."

How could he say that? Mira wondered, wanting to

laugh and cry at his words. He did not know what she really was, the daughter of a prostitute. Cut from the same cloth? Even if that were true, there were too many significant distinctions between them. They were opposites in every way. She opened her mouth to tell him so, but he interrupted her.

"Don't bother denying it. You have a quick mind and can see right through the superficial airs of those around you. So can I. You don't genuinely respect many people . . . neither do I."

"You obviously don't respect me or you wouldn't be speaking to me so rudely," Mira replied, her ears burning. "If this is your idea of sympathy, reciting a list of my faults—"

"But they're not faults, my precious brat. I'm complimenting you."

"I wish that you would stop giving me insults and telling me they're compliments, and giving me compliments that are insults in disguise!"

"If my company begins to worry you, you can always leave," Alec suggested, and laughed as she did exactly that.

The clock struck eleven. Mira sat at her dressing table in a small lyre-backed chair, resting her chin in a small palm. The glow from a single candle was reflected in the shield-shaped looking glass, shining on her face and across the mahogany surface of the table. In the looking glass she could see the shadowed images of her surroundings, illuminated by the starlight that shone through her windows. Her turret room was filled with feminine, delicate furniture, woodwork painted white, walls papered with an intricate rose design, frilled curtains and draperies. Gowns and pelisses were stored in the mahogany armoire, gloves and hats in the brass-inlaid cupboard. It was a light and airy room, filled with knickknacks of painted pottery, needlework samplers, china ornaments. There had once been a time when she could never have even imagined a place such as this, when she could never have pictured herself in the midst of such luxury. Thick toweling, polished oak floors, and ivory-handled brushes had once been unknown to her.

Living with Rosalie and Rand Berkeley at the Château d'Angoux had given her the first taste of this kind of life. Rather than being intimidated by such a foreign world, Mira had immediately taken to it. She was curious and possessed a sharp, accurate memory; learning had never presented a problem to her. She soaked up language and knowledge readily, she learned to imitate more gentle manners until they had become second nature to her. Given enough time, Mira could adapt to any situation. It was a necessary talent. If she had not been able to do this, she would never have survived beyond her first few years of life. She had been many things so far: an actress, a chambermaid, a companion, a mistress. What other parts would she have to play in the future? Only time would tell.

Curiously she stared into the mirror, wondering what it was about her face that continuously gave her away to Alec Falkner. Why was he able to read her so easily? As she stared into the wide brown eyes, the reflection dissolved, and all she could see was her brother's face, her brother's eyes. Despite the fact that their fathers had been different, she and Guillaume could have been twins.

Mira closed her eyes and rubbed her temples tiredly, but Guillaume's image remained in front of her. Dark, bittersweet eyes the color of autumn, a flashing smile that could signify friendliness, slyness, or merry good humor, hair so deep brown that it was almost black, curling slightly over his forehead. Mira did believe that he had truly loved her. But how strange, when they had parted years ago . . . how strange it had been for her to find that the brother who had always seemed to be so wise and knowing had the capability of being so brutal in his greed, so cruel in his desperation. She understood his hunger for the security of money, but she could not forgive what that hunger had prompted him to do. Hurting other people was bad enough, and she was guilty of that to the same degree that he was. But destroying them intentionally was unforgivable . . . and Guillaume had known just as well as Mira that to separate Rand Berkeley and Rosalie for good would have destroyed them both in the slowest and most unmerciful way.

"Oh, Guillaume," she said out loud, standing up from the dressing table and blowing out the candle. "What has become of you? Where are you now?" She wished she could stop caring about her missing brother. But even after the things he had done, her feelings were still there, damaged but intact.

Mira had trouble falling asleep. Her eyes remained open and staring through the darkness until the night had aged to pitch blackness. And in her sleep awaited troubled dreams that filled her mind with jarring impressions. She was sitting in an overgrown garden with Rosalie, the air thick with the smell of ferns and roses, the sunshine hot on the backs of their necks as they read together. Rosalie was smiling, her face open and vulnerable, her eyes the most intense shade of blue imaginable. "You're learning so much," Rosalie said warmly, and pointed to a long passage. "Try this one." Mira bent happily over the book. Then she heard a smothered sound and an ominous rustle. As she looked up, Mira found that Rosalie had disappeared. The garden was green, quiet, and eerily empty. *Rosalie! Where are you?* Mira tried to cry out, but no words would come out of her mouth. She struggled to her feet in horrified silence. Guillaume—Guillaume must have taken Rosalie!

She started to run. It was hard to move her feet; they were heavy, as if they had been weighted with bricks. In desperation Mira doubled her efforts to move. As she began to stumble to the ground, a huge pair of hands caught her tightly around the shoulders. "What happened to Rose? Where is she?" a voice snarled in her ear. Mira was looking straight into Rand Berkeley's blunt-featured, golden-eyed face. It was harsh with anger. She shuddered with fear, unable to speak. Berkeley threw her to the ground and she felt herself falling, falling, downward like a stone dropped into a pond, reaching out in panic to grab hold of something. Abruptly the scene changed and she was at the bottom of the towering hill. At the top she saw Berkeley and Guillaume fighting, dueling with swords. As she heard the scissoring sounds of finely tempered metal and saw the flash of bright blades, Mira felt great frightened tears falling down her face and neck. Climbing up the hill, she opened her mouth to call to them. But she could not make a sound, and they ignored her as she approached. In a savage, efficient movement, Guillaume plunged a sword into Berkeley's chest. Berkeley fell, his large body crumpling to the ground. Sobbing with terror and pity, Mira crawled to the prone figure while Guillaume ran away.

Blood ran in tiny rivulets from his chest to the ground, soaking into the earth like dark rain. And then Mira's aching pity turned to utter despair, for she saw that the wounded man was not Rand Berkeley. She cradled his dark head in her lap, her body racked with sobs as she tried to stanch the blood with her hands. His drowsy silver eyes opened slightly and he seemed to smile derisively at her anguished panic. Then his face turned away and his body went limp. Alec Falkner was dying in her arms and she could not help him at all. Cold blackness surrounded them, causing her to clutch at Alec more tightly . . . her voice came back suddenly and a low cry came from her throat.

Jerking up suddenly. Mira shook her head and opened her eyes, her chest heaving with gasps. Her face was wet with tears, her body rigid. Patting a hand to her heart, she tried to still the frantic pounding of it as she looked around the room. It was a dream, she thought. Although she felt relief begin to take hold of her, remaining traces of fear were still congealed inside her.

In a few seconds the door vibrated with two or three decisive raps. Mira stared at it blankly, unable to move. Again someone knocked. This time she flew to the door without even putting on a peignoir over her nightgown, opening the door with trembling fingers. She could not believe that it was him . . . but it was indeed Falkner standing there, looking sleepy and irritated, and vaguely concerned. His robe was made of charcoal-gray silk which gleamed dully in the dimness of the room. How had he known that she needed him? And why had he bothered to come up here?

Alec sighed as he saw that she was all right.

"You must have cried out in your sleep. I was in my room when I heard . . . and I thought . . . Well, it seems that you're all right, so I'll go back to—"

He was interrupted as Mira threw her arms around his neck, shaking and upset, her words a rapid torrent.

"I was dreaming, but I thought it was real, and I couldn't speak at all. It was horrible, horrible . . . Guillaume was there, and it happened all over again. He took Rosalie away—"

"Shhhh . . ." His eyes flashed with sudden sympathy. Alec closed the door and slid his arms around her. She was wearing a thin, high-necked nightgown, a modest garment that flowed around her in chaste folds. He stroked her back gently, his fingertips skimming over the curve of her spine. "It was just a nightmare."

". . . and I couldn't find . . . I couldn't talk, or tell anyone—"

"No matter how real it seemed, it didn't happen. You know that nightmares aren't real—"

"Yes, they are sometimes, they are," she said tearfully, clutching him desperately. Alec picked her up effortlessly, carrying her over to the bed. Mira clung to him, her fingers slipping on the silk that covered his wide shoulders. His body was so large and reassuringly solid, making her feel that nothing could hurt her when he was near, nothing at all. She did not let go of him, even while he slid two pillows behind her back, rearranged her twisted cotton nightgown, and brushed the escaping strands of dark hair away from her damp forehead. His manner was comforting, almost brotherly. She held on to the lapels of his robe as he braced an arm on one side of her, bending his head to listen to her tremulous whisper.

"Thank you. I'm . . . I was afraid to be alone."

"No trouble at all," he said, smiling down at her casually. "I've had a great deal of experience at taking women to bed."

Instead of laughing or becoming annoyed with his provoking comment, she looked at him solemnly, her eyes glittering with unshed tears. "Thank you for checking on me."

"I'd better leave soon." Alec indicated the door with a nod of his head. Now that she was settled in bed and her initial fright had passed, she realized that he was restless, agitated. "I have a feeling there'll be hell to pay if I'm found up here with you," he said.

She was reluctant to let him go. "No one ever comes up here except Sackville, and he never visits at this time of night."

"Close your eyes and go to sleep," Alec murmured, a wry smile curving his mouth. "I must leave now anyway. You see, in some areas I'm a remarkably controlled man. In others I have a marked lack of self-discipline, and I'm beginning to suffer from it." He looked down at her with what was, for him, an uncommon gentleness. Then, as if he could not resist it, he lowered his head and brushed a light platonic kiss across her lips. Blindly Mira wrapped her arms around his neck and pulled him closer, her mouth opening under his. Alec stiffened and then a muffled groan resonated in his throat. He kissed her with scorching heat, his tongue exploring the soft inside of her mouth with a sensual expertise that made her toes curl. And then Mira realized in shock that he had drawn her tongue into his mouth with gentle suction. She shivered as the love play continued, an understanding dawning in the nether recesses of her mind that they were mimicking the act of love with their mouths. A soft, burning glow began deep within her and spread everywhere.

Slowly Alec ended the kiss and took a ragged breath. He tried to pull away from her but her arms were still locked around his neck.

"Don't leave," she said unsteadily. "I'm still afraid—"

"Mira, what do you have to be afraid of?"

"Of being alone. I've never belonged to anyone. I don't belong anywhere. I'm afraid that I don't even exist . . . I need to belong to someone just for now."

"Mira—"

"I don't want to talk, I don't want words, I don't understand what they mean anymore." Her eyes blazed like fire, her voice and hands trembled with excitement, her mouth was soft with passion. "Make love to me. I want you to make love to me."

Alec's pulse beat swiftly in an unsteady percussion . . . he stared at her and caught his breath. He fought to remember that she was upset and didn't know what she was asking of him. "I won't take advantage of—" he began, and she smothered his words with her lips, her hands slipping beneath his robe as she pressed her palms against his smooth hard back. "Brat," he gasped, laughing shakily as he lifted his head to look at her, "Where you're concerned, I don't have a hell of a lot of self-control. And I'm not feeling very noble at the moment. You'd better be prepared to finish what you're trying to start . . ." He paused and swore as he felt her fumbling with the knot of his robe; the laughter faded from his eyes. Catching her slim wrists in one hand, he stopped her clumsy movements and stared down at her. "Just remember when it's over that you asked for it," he said thickly.

Hungrily he parted her lips with his own and kissed her deeply, the taste of his mouth more intoxicating than wine. He let go of her wrists, his hands going to the neck of her gown and unfastening the long row of buttons one by one. Mira quivered as she felt the unhurried movements of his fingers on her clothes, knowing that soon there would be nothing to hinder his possession of her body.

He pulled the hem of her gown up to her waist. Mira stiffened involuntarily as his hand wandered boldly up her smooth leg to her naked hip; then she clasped her arms over her midriff as he tried to pull the gown up further.

"You want it all the way off?" she whispered in confusion. "Is that the usual—?"

"Raise your arms," Alec said, wavering between amusement and white-hot, greedy impatience. The impatience won out, for suddenly he could not get the gown off her fast enough. He found that his raging desire had made him surprisingly awkward at the simple task. Don't be rough with her, he had to warn himself, forcing himself to be patient. He was ready for her right now, his manhood aching and taut with the desire to thrust into her without prelude . . . no, he could not allow himself to do that. He had to make her want him just as much as he wanted her.

As his warm hands slid over her, Mira moaned and shifted involuntarily; she had never felt so vulnerable to another human being in her life. Alec dwarfed the feminine surroundings, the frills and ruffles of the bed hangings, his very presence seeming to be an invasion of the small turret room. He shed his robe, and his broad shoulders blocked out everything in her view as he bent over her.

He pulled her against his body, his hands splaying over her back and pressing her close, his mouth searching the sensitive hollow just beneath her jaw. "Mira," he said with a slight catch in his voice, "I've never wanted anyone this much."

"I want you," she replied softly, nuzzling behind his ear, arching her naked body up to his eagerly, her heart overflowing with love.

"From the moment I first saw you . . . I couldn't believe how beautiful you were . . . and you put me through such hell—"

"I didn't mean to."

"I couldn't bear the thought of anyone else having you."

"No one ever has," she said, and he rolled her onto her back in order to look down at her face.

"What?" he whispered.

"I want you to be the first . . . I want . . ." She couldn't finish what she had been trying to say because his mouth was on hers and he was caressing her with dizzying slowness; sweet, vibrant sensations seemed to spill from his fingers wherever they wandered. His hand cupped over the curve of her breast and rotated in an exquisitely light touch until her nipple contracted firmly in his palm. Mira gasped, her chest lifting up to his hand . . . his thumb rubbed over the hardening peak, and he teased the corners of her mouth with small kisses.

His dark head moved down her neck to the highest curve of her breast, his tongue darting out to taste the fragrant flesh. His deep, irregular breath fanned out over her skin, and then his mouth took custody of the sensitive, aroused nipple, enclosing her in wet heat. Mira was floating in an ocean of pleasure, liquid pleasure that invaded every pore and opening of her body. Impatiently she writhed and groaned his name, straining in the grasp of sensations she had never felt before. She made a weak protest as Alec lifted his head.

"Easy . . ." he said softly, stroking the curve of her waist and hip in a soothing motion. "Patience, sweet . . . let me love you slowly . . . we have enough time." Breathing hard, she forced herself to relax, releasing her tight grip on his shoulders. Slowly his mouth slid back to the throbbing peak of her breast, and she curled her arms around his neck, pressing her face against the silkiness of his raven hair.

"Alec," she sobbed, and his tongue explored the sensitive hardness of her nipple with velvet strokes, tickling, caressing, arousing. He showed her a new kind of communication, with words, soft kisses, slow and exploratory caresses. As the minutes drifted by in a thick haze of pleasure, Mira thought dazedly that Alec knew her better than anyone had ever known her before.

"I'm going to take care of you from now on," he whispered, his dark hands moving over her pale-skinned body like a shadow rippling over the winter snow. "I told you that you'd be mine eventually . . . and you'll never be sorry. I know you, and I know how to make you happy—"

"Don't . . . please don't make any promises," she said, turning her face into the pillow.

"Oh, but I'm going to," he murmured, nibbling along the side of her neck. "You'll have to learn to accept them . . . because I always keep my promises."

"There are things you don't know about me—"

"They don't matter. All that matters is that I want you . . . I did the very first moment I saw you . . . you, with your Gypsy hair and big brown eyes and teasing smile. I wanted to know everything about you, how you tasted, how you felt . . ."

His large hand slid from the base of her neck to the valley between her breasts, his thumb caressing her skin lightly. Mira flushed as his fingers trailed down to her stomach; he touched her as if he owned her, he seemed to know the secrets of her body. She gasped as he brushed through the triangle between her legs, the dark, fine curls tangling around his fingers. He gave the curling strands a light tug, not enough to hurt, only enough to cause a shocking ripple of awareness to course through her body. Her eyes opened wide as she met his, as he slid a thigh between her knees, his hair-roughened limb abrading hers pleasantly.

Mira was paralyzed with a bewildering mixture of dread, desire, and escalating anticipation. Keeping his eyes on her face, Alec ventured lower, his fingers seeking and finding a minute conglomeration of nerves. Softly he touched and stroked her. Her eyes closed, her lips parted, and he felt a rush of fierce satisfaction as he saw the fine mist of perspiration that shone on her skin.

Shivering, she heard her own incoherent whispers sift through the darkness, her voice breaking as she pleaded for him to ease her torment. She was burning with a hunger that would never cease, and yet his sensitive fingertips offered no release from the tumult he had caused.

"Don't struggle for it," Alec said huskily, kneading the tender nerves between her thighs, his mouth burning against her throat. "Don't struggle . . . let me take you there, let me do it. . . ." His index finger flickered against the opening of her body, and then glided gently inside her. He was stunned at how tightly her virgin flesh grasped that questing touch . . . even in the midst of his passion, he could not help smiling into the curve of her neck, his heart skipping a beat from a stab of pure tenderness. Startled by the intimate intrusion, Mira gasped and tried to twist away.

"Oh . . . oh *stop,* Alec."

"I can't stop now," he said hoarsely. "You're almost there . . . almost . . ." Delibertely he caressed her damp, silken warmth, probing inside of her with his finger and urging the palm of his hand against her soft flesh. Suddenly Mira cried out, convulsed by an inner storm, a raging delight that crashed over her in a great wave. Her thighs tightened around his hand, her breath was trapped in her lungs as ecstasy overtook her in a violent deluge. "Yes, that's it . . . ." he crooned, his fingers coaxing another shiver of response from her helpless body, and he whispered softly in her ear. He held her while the fire inside her diminished to quiet embers, and after a long while Mira discovered that she was partially draped over him, her head resting on his shoulder, her body pressed against the sanctuary and shelter of his.

"I can't believe you did that," she whispered, rubbing her cheek against his shoulder.

"I told you I'd make you happy," he murmured, winding his hands in the long, glossy skeins of her hair. "That was just the beginning."

"I want to make *you* happy," she said, playing shyly with the fur on his chest and inching upward to kiss the base of his throat.

"I intend to be." He rolled over with her in a lithe movement, pressing her onto her back. A bright gleam of gold caught Mira's eye as a medallion on a heavy chain hung from Alec's neck. The coin-shaped object fell to the pillow and slid downward to the mattress as Alec's head bent over her. She remembered having seen the medallion around his neck before, and began to ask him about it, when her attention was abruptly diverted. His fingertips were skimming over her body, stirring up new fires, awakening her response once more with sensual artistry. "You're very small," he said, his mouth so close to her that she could feel the whispery touch of his words against her lips. "It's going to hurt . . . hell, I don't want to hurt you."

"I don't care," she said throatily. "I don't care at all . . . I like everything you do . . . *everything* . . ."

He teethed the peaks of her breasts lightly, then lavished them with feathery strokes of his lips and tongue, and Mira's nails dug into the mattress.

"You don't have to be so still," Alec murmured, nuzzling the hollow of her throat. "You can touch me."

"Where should I . . . ?"

"Anywhere you want to. I like everything *you* do."

Carefully she slid her small hands around his back, from his deeply muscled shoulders to his lean waist. His skin was silken to the touch, stretched tautly over hard muscles. "So strong," she said, nearly awed by the power of his body. "You're so handsome . . ."

"I'd hoped you would think so," he replied with a heart-stopping smile. "It makes your seduction that much easier."

"My seduction? I thought *I* was seducing *you*." Curiously her fingers wandered down the firmly indented line in his back, dipping into the slight hollows of his spine.

"You are." Alec shivered and drew a quick, disturbed breath. Encouraged, Mira continued to explore the broad surface of his back, and her oval fingernails scraped delicately across his skin, just under his shoulder blades. "Yes," he said with a betraying tremor in his voice, "if you keep that up, I just might let you have your way with me."

Mira smiled, delighted by her newfound power to arouse him. With growing confidence she caressed him, giving herself liberties to touch him wherever her impulse dictated. She swirled her fingertips through the silky black hair on his chest, brushed her thumbs across the points of his small, flat nipples, let her hands splay across the powerful cage of his ribs and the steely muscles of his abdomen.

Suddenly she paused in indecision. "Is there any place," she asked hesitantly, "that it is not right to touch?"

"No," he said softly, understanding exactly what she was asking. "If you want to . . . here, give me your hand and I'll show you—"

"No, let me touch you . . . on my own . . . let me . . ." Cautiously her hands alighted on the bold thrust of his manhood. She was nervous, and as he felt her cool, trembling fingers gently encircle him, Alec groaned. No sensation of pleasure or pain had ever made his knees go weak and his head spin like this. He was hard and throbbing with agony as she caressed him slowly. Her dainty palm stroked down the length of him, then up again, her fingers touched the velvet tip lightly, and as she lifted her face to his, his mouth covered hers. Groaning her name, he thrust once, twice, against her exquisitely tender hands.

Heady sensations flooded over her: the supple artistry of his lips, the sleek power of his masculinity in her palms, the feverish longing of her own body. Shifting slightly, she felt moist heat gathering between her legs, and she began to shake as he spread her knees wide with his own. Passionately she wound her arms around his neck, her head tilting to accommodate his deep kisses.

Taking care not to crush her, Alec lowered his body to hers, his chest pressing into the fullness of her breasts, his elbows braced on either side of her head. She was surrounded by the massive cage of his arms and chest, her nostrils filled with the virile male scent of him. The searing heat of his manhood nestled in the cradle between her thighs. They both inhaled at the electrifying contact of naked flesh, their abdomens contracting and then pressing together in one simultaneous breath.

"Alec . . ." Mira said, a faint question in her voice. He stared down at her, stroking the straying hair off her forehead with his fingertips.

"What?"

"Don't wait any longer."

His eyes gleamed oddly as he looked at her. "I'll be gentle," he promised huskily.

Mira clenched her hands into small fists that tightened against his back as she felt a hard, insistent pressure between her legs. He eased into her body slowly, but as the languid slide began, she gasped in distress. The fusion of his large form to her slim, delicate one was not easy, and her teeth caught at her lower lip to keep in a small cry of pain. Instinctively she moved to escape the demanding thrust, but the shifting of her hips only helped him to push deeper. Her body struggled to accommodate him, rending, expanding, widening, yet still he thrust further until he was sheathed within her. Alec buried his face in her hair for a moment, stunned by the incredible sweetness of her flesh tightening around him. Aware of her discomfort, he murmured soothing words against her temple.

"Shhhh. Hold still for a moment . . . Mira, my beautiful one . . ." His fingers moved to where their bodies were joined and he touched her intimately, massaging and stroking. "Now you're mine," he said, and eased into her, pulled away, pressed deeply into her again. Slowly her fists opened, her fingertips spread wide over his shoulders. Her sobs lessened, then gradually became helpless moans. Her legs opened, knees flexed. "Relax," Alec breathed, lingering inside her with each thrust. "Move with me . . . oh, that's so damned good . . ."

The rhythm was elemental, a pulse as basic as the beating of their hearts. Through the slight pain of his possession, Mira felt a strange, paralyzing ecstasy creep over her, until finally she arched up against him, still and transfixed with bliss. Alec drove into her with a quiet gasp, his large body shuddering as he too surrendered to the wrenching pleasure of their union.

They subsided in each other's arms, filled with lassitude. A cool breeze fluttered the curtains at the window and drifted into the room. The night air was misty and sweet; Mira breathed deeply of it as she pressed close to the man at her side. He gathered her closer, nuzzling the top of her head as her long hair streamed over his chest in a satin curtain. "Now you're mine," he repeated sleepily, and only when he had relaxed into slumber did she allow the tears to fall from her eyes.

6

*M*ira relaxed in the small, deep tub, her head resting back against the rim. Absently she traced the mint-colored shell pattern that adorned the porcelain, her eyes slitting as she stared at the wafting curls of steam that rose from the water. Her bath was scented with a light floral oil that soaked into her skin, soothing every inch of her body. She welcomed the calming effect that the heated water had on her nerves. After waking up this morning to find Alec gone, she had scarcely known what to think or how to feel.

Her body was vaguely sore this morning, her mind filled with the memories of last night. She had come alive at Alec's touch, and now she was aware of sensations she had never known before. How fortunate she had been to have had one glorious night with the man she loved, to have known his tenderness, his passion. It was more than some women would ever have, and she would not dare to ask for more. Sighing, she sank deeper into the bath, wanting to wriggle with the uneasy pleasure of it all. All the details of what they had shared were still vivid in her mind . . . she would never forget a bit of it. She had awakened several times in the darkness to find herself gathered against Alec's large warm body, her face pillowed against his shoulder, her fingers tangled in the long gold rope chain that draped across his chest.

"What is this?" she had inquired during one of their cozy whispered conversations, holding the medallion up to examine it in the moonlight that had filtered into the room. A savage design was engraved on both sides, a falcon in flight, with pointed wings spread wide and knifelike talons extended. The solid gold piece was adorned with tiny sparkling jewels: rubies for the eyes of the bird, emeralds for the leaves of the holly branches etched above the falcon's head.

"The Falkner crest. The medallion was a gift to my great-grandfather from George II. A reward for training the royal falcons."

"Your great-grandfather was a falcon trainer?"

"A family tradition which died out several years ago." Alec had brushed his fingertips over her wrist and traced the pattern on the medallion. "But we used to keep falcons when I was younger. My cousin Holt and I would sit and watch them for hours . . . while the birds were tethered, of course. See those back talons? Those are what they strike and kill with."

Mira had shivered slightly. "Why are there holly branches over the bird's head?"

"A private jest between my great-grandfather and the king." Alec had smiled wryly. "Holly is a tough and resistant type of wood. Stubborn, little resilience—it will split or break before bending. It seems that King George considered my great-grandfather to be a very obstinate and willful man, and so the king ordered the holly design to be included in the medallion. We've kept it the crest ever since."

"You've also kept the stubbornness," Mira had said, causing Alec to chuckle softly.

"I'm not always stubborn . . . not when I'm approached with the right persuasion." Then he had lowered his mouth to steal a warm kiss from her lips . . . and then another, and another, until the medallion had dropped from her fingers and she had lifted her arms around his neck.

She had woken up to find the chain fastened around her hips, the medallion lying on top of her smooth abdomen. Like a brand. Like a mark of possession. Staring dazedly at the ornament, Mira had felt a strange kind of panic take hold of her until she had discovered how to unfasten the clasp on the gold chain and take the necklace off. Had he meant it as a gift to her? Had he found some obscure humor in enchaining her with it?

The medallion was beautiful, but she was not at all certain that she wanted it. She would never be able to look at it without remembering last night, perhaps the only night of love she would ever know. She did not need or want any visible reminders, though loving him had been worth any price, even that of longing for him every single night for the rest of her life. No one could take the memories away from her, and no one, not even Alec himself, could destroy them. From now on, whether he treated her with kindness or malice, nothing could change last night—the memories were hers to keep.

After rising from her bath and drying herself with a length of toweling, she dressed in a dark chocolate-colored gown trimmed with cream corded silk. The color of it intensified the darkness of her eyes until they appeared almost black. A cream-colored sash was tied in a saucy bow at her side, while elaborately tucked and gathered sleeves tapered to her wrists. The hem was adorned with a band of the same corded silk that edged the bodice. Mira was pleased with her appearance, especially when she added the pearl-studded net to her hair as a finishing touch. It was important that she look her best today; if she was going to face the Berkeleys, she would confront them in a composed manner.

Mira felt a wild flutter of nervousness at the realization that finally she would see Rosalie again. Perhaps Rosalie might forgive her for what had happened five years ago; Mira hoped desperately that she would. Biting the tip of her finger absently, she sat on the edge of her bed, expelling a long sigh. What should I do when they've arrived here? she wondered anxiously. Send a note to their room? It would not be wise simply to appear before them without warning. Maybe she should wait for an opportunity to meet Rosalie alone while Berkeley was out hunting. One thing was certain—she would not go anywhere near the Berkeleys unless Alec was close by to watch out for her. There was no telling what Rand Berkeley might do to her, for although he was not an unjust man, he would never forgive or forget someone who had been instrumental in taking Rosalie away from him.

No pack of foxhounds in the country, not even the royal buckhounds in the Windsor kennels, could equal the Berkeley pack. The Berkeley hounds were bred for incredible speed and indomitable spirit. When it was made known that the pack was being brought for the last few days of the Sackville hunt, the hour of the hunt was delayed considerably, for the Berkeley pack would catch the fox far too quickly in the early-morning hours, later in the day the fox was faster, his belly less full than at daybreak, and therefore he would present more of a challenge to the hounds.

The Earl of Berkeley's general philosophy was to avoid half-measures; he either committed himself fully to an interest or left it alone, and this attitude extended to his treatment of his animals. He demanded frequent and meticulous reports on their care and progress. Unlike the trainers at many notable kennels, those who managed the Berkeley foxhounds were not allowed to practice the traditional customs of bleeding the puppies before cubhunting started or giving them port. Their training was hardly unorthodox, merely conservative and practical. The puppies were walked often . . . in fact, many of the earl's own tenants were paid to walk the spirited animals. Occasionally Berkeley hounds were bred with the flawless Yarborough and Meynell blood, to keep the quality of their speed, endurance, and physical superiority consistent. In anticipation of the Sackville hunt, the hounds had been sent a day early and were already lodged in the kennels.

The eagerly anticipated arrival of Lord and Lady Berkeley would occur in late morning, in plenty of time for them to move into their rooms and prepare for the dance that would be held this night for their benefit. Sackville and many of his guests were preparing in their own way for the appearance of the couple. Sackville was reading the past several issues of the *Times* and other papers in order to know the current political and financial news, for the Earl of Berkeley owned a fast-growing shipping business that would someday provide serious competition for the Dutch East Indies Company. The ladies were all gathering the latest bits of gossip to regale Lady Berkeley with, for she was extremely popular and had of late become a leading fashion figure. The way her hair was dressed and the style of her clothes were always copied down to the last detail, and the women were all eager to see the gowns that she would wear during the coming weekend.

As the preparations at Sackville Manor progressed, an enclosed carriage jostled along the poorly mended roads from Warwick to Hampshire. The livery of the servants and the coachwork were royal blue and crimson, colors which glowed richly against the muted landscape. Its sturdy six-inch-wide wheels plowed steadily through muddied tracks and miry byways. Four immaculately groomed black horses trotted gracefully over the country roads, pulling the vehicle at a sedate pace. Even the coachman was a noteworthy sight, dressed in plush clothes with shining gold buttons, his head ornamented with a flaxen wig and a low-brimmed hat. Two outriders and two grooms clad in equally splendorous finery completed the picture. The curtains at the windows of the carriage were discreetly drawn to afford the two occupants of the vehicle privacy. Privacy which they had made good use of.

"You should be ashamed of yourself," Rosalie said, idly walking her fingers through the gold-tinged hair on her husband's chest. "Because of you I'm abominably disheveled. My buttons are all undone and my hair is in ruins—and we'll probably arrive at Sackville Manor any moment."

Berkeley grinned, his aggressive masculine features temporarily softened in the aftermath of their passion. He was a strong-willed man with a fearsome temper, but Rosalie had learned over the course of their five-year marriage that in the few minutes just after they made love Berkeley was always in an agreeable and good-humored state of mind. At times like this he had agreed to many of her schemes and demands against his better judgment, unable to refuse her anything after he had been so magnificently satisfied. Rosalie sometimes found it privately amusing, for Rand Berkeley could intimidate the most powerful men in England . . . yet she alone had the power to wrap him around her little finger. And that is the way it should be, Rosalie thought contentedly, snuggling against his warm chest.

"I am indeed ashamed," Rand replied, his light hazel eyes caressing her as his fingers toyed with the curled locks that fell down her back in a cascade of sable. "It's been far too long since I made love to you in a carriage." He nibbled at the side of her throat while adding, "Don't worry about arriving too soon— you know I always leave you enough time to restore your appearance."

"The devil you do. I wouldn't give you three blind 'uns and a bolter for the amount of time you allow me," Rosalie rejoined, using the slang phrase for a bad team of horses. "Restore myself? You know that I never look the same after you're through with me."

"No one's opinion matters but mine. And I approve wholeheartedly of your appearance."

She giggled lightly, her fingers tracing over the soft, broad lines of his mouth. He caught her fingers between his even white teeth and flicked his tongue across her fingertips.

"It's just that I have the disconcerting feeling that when they look at me, they all know what we've been doing."

"*Fleur*, of course they do. Never let it be said that I'm the kind of man who doesn't know what to do when he's alone with his wife."

"Heaven forbid," Rosalie said throatily. "I've always been told that the passion between a husband and wife fades after the first few years . . . but you're even more amorous now than you were before we were married. Mind you, I'm not complaining . . . now, why are you suddenly frowning?"

"I just thought about Christian." Berkeley's expression became less complacent and his brows drew together. "I wonder if he's all right."

Rosalie fought to keep her smile from broadening into a grin. She had never dreamed that Rand Berkeley, the former rake and confirmed bachelor, would have turned out to be such a doting father. They had taken their son around the world with them to many exotic and distant places, so that at three years old young Christian was already a seasoned traveler and a singularly independent little boy. Rosalie could see, however, that Rand could hardly bear the thought of leaving him even for a weekend, no matter how nonchalant he tried to appear about it.

"My darling," she said patiently, "we have this conversation every time we go somewhere without him. Christian is perfectly fine, surrounded by a score of people who would do anything to please him. You're turning him into a little maharajah, and although I think he's perfectly wonderful, I must agree with what someone said to me the other day: he is becoming a little spoiled."

"Who told you that my son is spoiled?" Rand asked, scowling.

"That doesn't matter," Rosalie said quickly, knowing that anyone daring to say a word of criticism about golden-haired angel-faced, mischievous little Christian would earn Rand's everlasting antagonism. If ever a father was blind to the faults of his son . . . "The point is, dearest, that he spends more time with you than he does with Nurse, and instead of doing the things that other children do, he's usually with you while you're ordering people around at the shipping office and supervising the tenants. He's learning to imitate you far too well . . . don't you agree that he is becoming just a little too dictatorial for a child his age?"

"And what the deuce should he be doing that the other children do?"

"Well . . . riding his pony, I suppose. Spending time in the garden . . . or playing nice games."

"Nice games," Rand repeated darkly.

"Yes."

He twisted around so that she lay on her back on the cushioned seat. Looking down at her, Rand let his gaze wander slowly over her, to her sweet, earnest face, her enticing bareness, and the wildly twisted, disarranged ruffles of her gown. After five years of marriage their feelings for each other were stronger than ever. Since they had first met, neither of them had had eyes for anyone but each other. Love had reformed him, had filled her life, had made the commonplace seem special and the extraordinary seem possible. Rand caught his breath as his wife smiled up at him. He loved her with a passion that would take a hundred lifetimes to burn itself out.

"I have a nice game in mind for you," he informed her huskily, and she giggled while trying to squirm away from him.

"Rand, don't you dare . . . we don't have enough time."

His hand searched boldly through the myriad of ruffles.

"What about this? You always liked this one . . ."

"Take your hand away from there!"

They engaged in a brief tussle. Rand chuckled at Rosalie's playful attempts to twist away from him. Both of them knew that after a short struggle Rosalie would let him win. She always did.

The library exuded a companionable atmosphere. Alec, Sackville, and Squire Osbaldeston sat with their feet propped up on the mahogany table, enjoying the warmth of the fire and the brilliant light of day that poured in through the windows. Since the hunt was being delayed today, the residents and guests of Sackville Manor were all gathered in small groups throughout the estate, talking idly just as these three were. Alec was in a lazy good mood, his gray eyes warmer and his smile easier than usual. His broad shoulders were relaxed against the back of the deep armchair in an attitude of masculine contentment. He was entirely aware that the reason for this unfamiliar sense of well-being was last night, and his mind kept turning back to the memories of what had transpired in the small turret room.

It had been hell to leave Mira's warm bed this morning, to disentangle himself from her slender body when all he wanted to do was make love to her again. But she had been so exhausted that she had not even stirred when he left her. Alec had decided not to awaken her, for not only did he want to allow her the rest she needed but also he had had no idea of what to say to her this morning. Where Mira was concerned his emotions were frustratingly cloudy. What in God's name was it going to take to untangle the coil he was woven in?

"Falkner, did you hear what I just said?" Squire Osbaldeston demanded, swilling port although it was only eleven in the morning. He was a ruddy, beefy individual in his late forties, popular for his warm, gruff nature and distinctive booming voice. He was impossible to ignore, for his stout girth was matched by a hearty personality that extended itself to everyone within shouting distance.

"Every word," Alec lied, reaching over to the desk and pulling a sheaf of blank white parchment onto his lap. "Hand me that quill, will you?" He concentrated on remembering the most recent snatches of Osbaldeston's monologue. "You said something about the plans for your new manor house—"

"I said that I'm deuced unhappy about it!" the squire boomed. "A demned Grecian palace! Huge columns, statues everywhere. Cold, big, nothing but marble to rest my backside on. All because I let Lady Osbaldeston's grand ideas get in the way of my common sense. I'll put some good words in your ear, my young fellow: never listen to a wife's advice. You'll both be happier that way."

Alec grinned, dipping the tip of the quill into a small pot of ink.

"The Grecian style is very popular, Squire Osbaldeston," he said reasonably. "Classic. Pure. Of course, it's a little more suitable to public buildings than private residences—"

"I want to live in a home, not a shrine," the squire said grimly. "Egad, you architects . . . changing the style every month, as if houses could be bought like hats."

"Falkner," Sackville intervened, "I mentioned to the squire that you're a talented architect. Would you be willin' to do him a favor—come up with some kind of design that'd represent a compromise between his tastes and his wife's? It seems the Lady Osbaldeston prefers the grand classical style, while the squire is interested in a Gothic house . . . rather like this one, in fact."

"Yet another battle in the war of classic against Gothic," Alec commented, a smile tugging at one side of his mouth. "And even worse, the battle occurs between a good man and his wife. Squire Osbaldeston . . . perhaps you would like the front of your house in one style and the back in the other?" His gray eyes were all innocence as he made the suggestion.

Suddenly the squire laughed, his ill humor abating. "Young whelp. No, for once, the house will be designed the way I like it. Something snug and comfortable—like the Regent's York Cottage. Or the Berkeley mansion in Warwick."

"Yes," Alec murmured, his quill scratching busily on the parchment. "I designed that one."

"Oh? That's good, very good," the squire exclaimed, his small blue eyes lighting up. "Except that I want mine spikier than that. Maybe stained-glass windows and perforated ironwork—what do you think?"

"I think you'll feel as if you're living in a church," Alec returned, not looking up from his sketch. The statement disconcerted the squire slightly.

"Oh? Hang it, I didn't think of that."

"Perhaps something a little more fanciful might appeal to you . . . neo-Gothic, picturesque but designed along classical lines. Something that would satisfy your desire for comfort and Lady Osbaldeston's as well. Plenty of windows, lofty chimneys, round turrets . . . a few scenic arches. Simple, romantic, tasteful. It will have all the aesthetic qualities of a Gothic castle without the discomforts."

Intrigued, Osbaldeston stood up and peered over Alec's shoulder at the sketch taking shape.

"By George, that's just the thing!"

Alec smiled, finishing the sketch and handing it to him.

"That's the rough idea of it," he said.

"Sackville, fasten your eyes on this!" Osbaldeston exploded happily.

"You've got a knack, Falkner," Sackville said, nodding admiringly at the sketch.

"So I've been told," Alec replied.

"And outrageous conceit."

"I've been told that too."

"Would you see this thing through for me?" Osbaldeston demanded of Alec, who hesitated before answering.

"If I can't, I'll recommend someone to you who'll do a fine job. Though I would like to design it, I'm afraid time might not permit—"

"Time?" the squire repeated with a frown. "Why wouldn't you have enough time?"

"I have in mind a few new ambitions to devote myself to."

"Such as?" Osbaldeston persisted.

Alec shrugged and smiled enigmatically.

"Possibly finding myself a wife."

"A wife?" the squire said, and Sackville sat up in his chair with a surprised expression. "My good fellow," the squire continued, "that's an inadvisable undertaking until spring. Women are deuced hard to court in the winter, what with the weather and . . . well, take my word for it. Don't look for a wife in the off-season. Wait until spring, when a fresh new batch of pretty maidens is unwrapped and brought out. This year's stock has already been picked over."

"That is sage advice, I am certain," Alec replied politely, a dance of laughter shining in his eyes. "But there are urges a man can't always regulate by the seasons. And suddenly I find myself facing the coming winter with a newfound loathing for cold sheets."

"Then," Sackville inserted with mock gravity, "make certain, Falkner, that the woman you choose is the type who will have a penchant for warming her husband's sheets instead of some other fellow's."

"I will," Alec said gravely, and after that was very quiet.

Mira paused at the library door before knocking. She knew that Sackville had been engaged in conversation the past hour or two. But she had just seen Osbaldeston's heavyset form leave the library and now it was possible that she would have a few moments of privacy to speak to Sackville. After thinking about the subject of the Berkeleys all morning, she had decided to tell him that she might have to leave sooner than she had planned. If her presence proved to be intolerable to the arriving couple, Mira would leave today, for she had no wish to inflict more pain on them. It was only fair to warn Sackville of an early departure, although she did not yet know what reason she would give him for it.

"Come in," she heard Sackville call, and cautiously she opened the door. Immediately Mira realized her mistake. Sackville was not alone. Alec was in the library as well, encased in pale gray pantaloons and short Hessian boots, were crossed and propped on the heavy wooden table, the sleeves of his white shirt billowing and gathered at the wrists in a piratical style. Slowly he lifted his raven head, his gray eyes containing a smoky darkness as he looked at her.

"Forgive me," Mira said to Sackville, already beginning to back out the way she had entered. "I didn't know you were conversing with—"

"Please, don't apologize," Sackville said instantly, catching her by the upper arm and dragging her into the room. "I'm speaking with Falkner. I'm certain he doesn't mind such a pleasant interruption."

"Not at all," Alec said softly.

"After all," Sackville continued, sliding his arm around Mira's waist, "he's an old friend of mine and knows all about the relationship between you and me."

It took all of Mira's acting skill to keep from turning crimson. Her eyes darted to Alec's impassive face, and he shook his head slightly. Mira would have sworn at first that he looked vaguely amused by the unknowing accuracy of Sackville's remark. But as the older man pulled her even closer into his paunched side, she saw Alec's jaw tighten into a rigid line. And as Sackville's thick fingers moved to stroke along her waist, Alec looked like a man completely incapable of amusement. Suddenly Mira sensed an explosive tension in the room. Her forehead creased with uneasiness.

"My lord," she said to Sackville, "I wished to talk to you privately. But there is ample time for us to talk later, so I will leave you to—"

"You are a picture this morning," Sackville declared, warming to his role. "A veritable picture. A beautiful flower." He bent his head to kiss her on the corner of the mouth. Mira stood there, frozen and revolted. It was intolerable to her to be touched by any man but Alec . . . but to have him sitting there watching . . .

"Please, Lord Sackville . . ." she said stiffly. In response to Mira's obvious reticence, Sackville became playful, squeezing her affectionately.

"The perfect woman," he said to Alec. "Knows when to tease and when to be affectionate. A man never gets bored with a woman like this, eh?"

Alec made no reply, his expression unfathomable. Mira tried ineffectually to edge away from Sackville's groping. "Lord Sackville," she said, making a greater effort to pull away from him. His hand continued to caress her waist, brushing perilously close to the curve of her breast. What was he trying to prove? Mira thought wildly.

"There are thoughts going on in that pretty head that you would never suspect." Sackville remarked. He threw a wink at Alec, whose narrowed eyes were now following the movement of that errant hand as it moved up and down Mira's side. "To look at her, you'd never suspect what special talents she has—"

"Please!" Mira cried, flushing as Sackville caressed the curve of her hip.

Alec could stand no more of it. "Like digging up mandrake roots?" he asked. The venomous question was belied by the casual softness of his voice. Alec stood up slowly, heaving an almost unnoticeable sigh as Sackville's hand dropped from Mira's body. The gall rising in his throat from watching her being handled by another man subsided a degree or two, but still Alec had to fight the impulse to snatch her away from Sackville. "It's not necessary to fondle her for my benefit any longer. I know. *I know*."

Both Sackville and Mira stared at him as if they hadn't quite heard what he had said. Then Sackville turned to the woman at his side, his blue eyes faintly dazed. "You told him?"

She forced herself to meet his gaze, feeling like a traitor, wanting to crawl away in shame and regret. "I'm so sorry," she whispered.

"I trusted you!" Sackville said in a rasping voice, his face heavily lined with encroaching pain.

"I know you did. I . . . I don't know what to say—"

"She didn't want to tell me," Alec broke in quietly. "I forced her to."

Sackville did not spare Falkner a glance. He continued to stare at Mira, his face contorting, his breathing irregular. "You told him. You promised you wouldn't tell anyone. You knew how important it was to me that no one know. After all I've done to help you, after taking you in instead of throwing you back out in the streets . . ." His voice had a queer, papery sound. "Disloyal . . . lying . . . You're not good enough for me to . . . to walk upon. You've unmanned me. By God, I should *kill* you."

Mira flinched and dropped her head. On the carpet she saw the shadow of his arm lifted to strike her. She could not move as she watched the shadow begin to fall. Closing her eyes, she waited during that split second for the blow to land and the pain that would ensue.

In a swift movement Alec grabbed Sackville's wrist. His teeth gritted as he exerted the force necessary to counter the power of Sackville's intended blow. Alec was amazed at the strength of Sackville's bulky arm and the momentum that had already gathered behind the meaty fist.

"My God," Alec said, his hand biting into the thick wrist as he stared at Sackville's trembling fist. "You would strike a woman in such a way . . . do you know how much you could have hurt her? She's only a small . . ." His gray eyes were filled with a combination of compassion, wonder, and untrammeled fury. "You could have . . ." He broke off, his eyes flickering to Mira's downbent head and the delicate structure of her jaw. For a moment Alec felt a dry tightness in his throat and he could not speak.

Mira lifted her eyes to his. "How could you?" she asked, her voice shaking. "I never should have told you . . . but never dreamed that you would use it against him . . ." Her voice trailed into nothingness, and she could not keep the hurt and anger from her face as she looked at him.

The charade was over.

What a threesome we make, she thought wretchedly. I betrayed Sackville by telling his secret to Alec. Alec betrayed me by breaking the confidence I had given to him. And Sackville betrayed us both . . . forcing me to help him lie to everyone . . . yes, and he taunted Alec because he sensed what existed between the two of us.

"I am unmanned," Sackville whispered, his voice cracking with strain and confusion. "No one was supposed to know. I am ruined." The locked gaze between Alec and Mira was broken as they looked at the older man. Sackville looked bewildered, frightened. Had something in his mind snapped?

"I'll get him a drink," Alec said tersely, shoving Sackville down into a chair. "Leave, Mira. I'll deal with you later."

Mira fled the room without a thought as to what direction her feet were taking. She ran out the front door and flew down the steps . . . toward the woods, where there were no people, no poisonous words, no hurt. Only peace and blessed aloneness. She needed a place to heal, a place to rest.

As her feet crunched on the gravel drive, Mira stopped in sudden confusion. She found that she stood in the shadow of a newly arrived carriage. Horses' feet stomped impatiently as luggage was unloaded from the vehicle by well-dressed footmen. A tall man with familiar gold-streaked hair faced away from her as he spoke to the wigged coachman. One of the footmen helped a woman out from the carriage, and Mira realized that she had unknowingly stumbled into the woman's path. Somehow she already knew who it was. Trembling with a sense of unreality, Mira stared at the woman's face and met a pair of violet-blue eyes that could have belonged only to one person. Her heart seemed to stop.

It was only now that she fully realized what Rosalie Berkeley had been to her—a sister, a friend . . . perhaps in some ways even a mother. Rosalie had been so very different from her—open and easy to read, vulnerable and loving. Rosalie needed people and was unafraid to show it, encouraging them to need her with the same openness. Even Guillaume had been charmed by her, as much as he had been capable of being charmed. Rosalie was the kind of woman that seemed incapable of harboring an unkind thought about anyone. Rosalie was everything that Mira had longed to be.

She had remembered Rosalie as a girl of unusual prettiness, quick to smile, quicker still to blush, her face serene, her manner unpolished and artless. But the slender woman in front of her was strikingly beautiful, a glamorous creature who radiated both confidence and self-possession. She wore a gown of sea-green and white silk, with puffed sleeves showing through oversleeves of gauze. The bodice was green, the skirt pure white. Her rich brown hair was pulled back with gauze ribbons to reveal a perfect oval face with cheekbones that had not been so well-defined five years ago. Rosalie looked more womanly and sophisticated, yet still the innate sweetness shone on her face as she tried to suppress gathering tears.

"I remember a little girl . . ." Rosalie said, holding out her hand, "about this tall." Then she brushed at the tears under her eyes. "Mireille . . . I can't believe it's you. How have you come to be in England?"

Mira's tormented gaze faltered, then returned uncertainly to Rosalie's face. "I . . ." Mira stopped at the thin sound of her own voice and then resumed with effort. "I came to see if Monsieur de Berkeley had found you. I was so . . . I was so happy to find out that you and he had married."

Rosalie held a hand to the side of her own face, turning her forehead into the cup of her fingers in a helpless gesture for just a second before looking back at Mira. "We've had people looking for you for five years. Why didn't you try to find us?"

"I didn't think you would want to see me."

Rosalie gave a choked laugh, shaking her head violently. "We've tried to discover your whereabouts ever since it happened. I was frantic every time I thought of you."

"But Guillaume . . . what he did . . . I knew you would hate me for what I helped him to do."

"You were just a child, a frightened child. Rand and I both understood that it wasn't your fault. We never blamed you, Mireille. You were such a good friend to us, especially to me." Her voice broke, and her face seemed to crumple. "We never blamed you at all."

Mira burst into tears as Rosalie moved toward her and hugged her. Feeling like the child she had been five years ago, Mira dropped her head wearily on the fragrant silk-clad shoulder and let herself cry helplessly. Rosalie had been the only good part of the past. There was no home, no family, no other friend that Mira could look back to . . . but suddenly the Berkeleys were here, they were real as nothing else from her past life was real to her.

"Mireille," Rosalie said, patting her back gently as she became aware that Mira was weeping not from joy but from confusion and misery. "Please don't cry so hard . . . there, now . . . there's no reason to cry. You're safe and well, what could possibly be so heartbreaking?"

"Everything is wrong," Mira sobbed, past reason, past the point where she could control herself. She thought of Alec and her tears seemed to scald her cheeks. "I've made everything so *wrong*. There is nothing I can do now—"

"Don't cry," Rosalie soothed, her voice filled with motherly reassurance. "Nothing is worth getting yourself in such a state. We'll fix whatever it is."

"No one could," Mira sniffled, about to explain further, when she looked up and saw Rand Berkeley's dark golden face. His hazel eyes were as barbaric and oddly piercing as ever. She quivered with fright, freezing like a startled doe. "*Monsieur*," she said hoarsely, expecting a cloud of anger to descend over his attractive masculine features. But he didn't appear to be angry. In fact, his expression was kind as he spoke in the gentle, resonant voice she remembered so well.

"Mireille Germain. I'll be damned." A huge hand descended on her shoulder, his touch strong and warm. Then, seeing that Mira was in no condition to converse rationally, he patted her upper arm briefly before turning to his wife. Ever mindful of Rosalie's welfare, Rand decided to remove the women from the stares of the liveried servants and the increasing number of onlookers. "Rose, why don't the two of you talk inside the carriage?" he suggested, whispering in Rosalie's ear. "First of all, find out what the devil she'd doing at Sackville Manor. And more important— ask her where—"

"I'll ask her about Guillaume later," Rosalie murmured. "Something is terribly wrong, Rand, and we want to help her, not quiz her. We'll have plenty of time later to ask about her brother."

Berkeley was about to dispute the issue, since his immediate and overwhelming interest was in the whereabouts of Guillaume Germain, but the sight of Rosalie's tear-drenched eyes was too much for him. Muttering under his breath, he nodded and helped the pair into the carriage. As he turned to cast an assessing glance at the front of the manor, Rand saw the dark, nearly indistinguishable figure of a man at one of the ground-floor windows, a man who watched the scene on the drive intently, his fingers curved against a glass panel like talons.

Rosalie emerged from the carriage several minutes later. She took her husband's hand as he helped her out, smiling at him, although her expression was anxious. Their thoughts and emotions were attuned almost perfectly, and they each knew from a glance at the other that a private discussion was in order. Slowly they walked a few feet away from the vehicle.

"I don't believe it," Rosalie said, whispering so that Berkeley had to duck his head to hear her. "After five years we've finally found her."

"A more accurate statement would be that she found us," Rand murmured. Rosalie shrugged impatiently.

"This is not a time to examine rhetoric, Rand."

"And hardly the place, my love. I dislike standing in the middle of the drive and airing our private life for the amusement of Sackville's guests. Wouldn't we be more comfortable if we moved this conversation into a quiet sitting room in the manor?"

"Not just yet," Rosalie replied, slipping her arm through his and looking up at him worriedly. "Everything is a little confused. *I'm* a little confused by all that has happened in the last half-hour. It is so very odd to look into that young woman's face and see Mireille's eyes. Do you realize that she is the age that I was when you and I met?"

Berkeley shook his head absently. "Somehow I kept picturing her as a child."

"You'll never know how many times during the past years I have stopped in the middle of something to think about her and wonder where she was."

"I've done much the same concerning her brother," Berkeley informed his wife grimly. "Where did she say he—?"

"Darling, we did not talk about Guillaume. She is so overwrought that I could hardly understand any of what she said." Rosalie held his arm more tightly, and he slipped his free hand around her back in an automatic gesture. "I don't know quite what has happened to her, but she did say that she spent some time in east London when she first arrived in England." She shivered before continuing. "It hardly bears thinking, my Mireille in that . . . that . . ."

"Hellhole," Berkeley supplied, temporarily discarding his usual fondness for well-turned phrases.

"Exactly. But, Rand . . . the situation is even more difficult, in light of what I'm about to tell you."

"I can scarcely wait to hear it."

"I think . . . that is, to all appearances . . . she has been Lord Sackville's mistress for the past two years. She hasn't exactly admitted to it, but—"

"Oh God," he muttered.

Rosalie drew herself up like a mother hen protecting her chick. "Rand Berkeley, I hope you're not about to offer a word of criticism!" she whispered rapidly. "She's only done what she's had to do. And you know very well that once upon a time you put me in that same position—don't forget that I was your mistress for three months before we were married!"

Rand winced, his hand rising as if to cover her mouth.

"It wasn't at all comparable with this," he said. "For one thing, I wasn't twice your age—"

"I don't see what age has to do with it."

"There are times, Rose, when your moral code is conveniently ambiguous."

"Please, my lord," Rosalie said with a frown, "—just for a minute try to understand what it might be like to be a woman, alone, without protection. I once had to contemplate such a prospect and it frightened me to death. Somehow Mireille has managed to survive it, but she has been hurt—"

"Hurt? How?" Despite his worldly demeanor, Berkeley was a compassionate man, and his voice softened with what Berkeley knew was concern.

"I don't really know yet. But it is clear that Mireille needs rest and attention. She was such a confident child—now she can hardly bear to meet my eyes. She seems so dispirited and hopeless that it disturbs me dreadfully. In fact, she is so upset that she refuses to go back into the manor. I don't know how we're going to get her things out of there—"

"Wait. Slow down. What do you mean, 'get her things out of there'?"

"Rand," she said, looking at him with pleading blue eyes, "she meant so much to me in France. She was my only friend at a time when I needed one. She took care of me when I was ill . . . I would like to return the favor now."

"You're asking if we can take her back to Warwickshire with us," he stated resignedly.

"You had no objection to the idea five years ago," Rosalie reminded him. "Remember when you said then that she could live with us?"

Berkeley lifted his eyes heavenward. "Dammit, you never forget anything . . . yes, the offer still stands."

She squeezed his hand tightly. "Oh, how I adore you—"

"Before you smother me with words of affection, be forewarned that I fully intend to question her about Guillaume."

"Of course, my dearest husband."

"I've been altogether too lenient with you lately," he grumbled, basking in the glowing smile she bestowed on him. "I wonder that you asked my permission at all."

"I must ask you one more favor: would you allow me to take her to Warwickshire now?"

"Now?" Rand repeated, giving her a genuine frown of displeasure. "And miss the hunt?"

"I don't know what else to do with Mireille. She will not spend one more night on the Sackville estate. You know I dislike hunting anyway, and I certainly dislike most of the women whose company I would have been forced to endure."

"Do you realize how it will appear if you turn around and return home, leaving me alone?"

"If you really cared what people thought, you

wouldn't have married me in the first place," Rosalie said softly, stroking her fingers along the back of his hand, soothing his ire as only she could. "And though I dread the idea of sleeping apart from you for a night or two, I am already looking forward to welcoming you back." She stood on her toes as she murmured into his ear, ". . . and I *promise* to make up for all of this on the eve of your return."

"How?" Berkeley inquired, characteristically concerned about specifics, and she smiled slowly before whispering a few well-chosen words to him. Her promise earned the guaranteed response, for he offered no further argument.

7

Surrounded by green grottoes and thick woods, Berkeley Hall presented the picture of a well-ordered fantasy. It graced Warwickshire like a perfectly cut diamond, poised between the land and the sky with vaulted arches and neatly finished crenellation that formed the base for pinnacles that seemed to pierce the clouds overhead. Trefoil-shaped windows and fluted pillars lent the house an air of lighthearted grace. As Rosalie and Mira were helped out of the carriage and escorted into the hall by two footmen, Mira discovered that the interior of the house was even more beautiful than the exterior, adorned with imported yellow Siena marble, shining mahogany, bronze railings, and richly framed portraits.

"Lady Berkeley!" came a pleased exclamation, and a stout woman who appeared to be the housekeeper approached them. She was followed by two maids, one of whom looked to be considerably chastened. "You've returned home earlier than expected."

"Yes, Mrs. Grayson," Rosalie replied. "There were some unforseen difficulties . . ." She stopped and frowned as she noticed the tear-streaked face of one of the maids. "My goodness, Nell, why are you crying?"

"We're having a problem of discipline," Mrs. Grayson said grimly. "Nell would rather gossip and chatter all day than do her work."

Despite the fact that she had her own problems to worry about, Mira looked at the slumped shoulders of the maid and nearly smiled with sympathy. Apparently Rosalie felt the same twinge of pity, for her voice was gentle as she addressed the girl. "I had hoped that the last time we discussed your gossiping would have done more good, Nell. I would like to speak with you as soon as I see to the comfort of my guest."

"Yes, mum," the girl replied, shooting a baleful glance at the triumphant housekeeper.

Mira was to learn later that although Mrs. Grayson was a militant and effective housekeeper, Rosalie played a significant role in the running of Berkeley Hall. She attended to countless problems and decisions, used all the wiles of a seasoned diplomat to keep the servants in harmony with each other, and never lost her temper . . . she was active in charity projects, maintained close friendships with neighbors and relatives, spent a considerable amount of time each day with her child, and above all, she saw to the needs of her husband. And though her days were sometimes long and trying, her voice was never loud or sharp, her manner was always gentle and kind. How did she manage to make it all seem so effortless?

Most of the servants and tenants who lived on the Berkeley estate usually attempted to approach Rosalie first with their problems, since it was well known that not only would she be sympathetic and understanding but also she had the power to influence her husband as no one else was able to do. The guests and relatives who spent time with the Berkeleys also besieged her for time and attention, basking in her company and endeavoring to monopolize her for as long as possible. All of this was done behind Rand Berkeley's back, as discreetly as possible, for it was common knowledge that he was a fiercely protective and jealous husband, and the demands made upon his wife by others never failed to irritate him. He made it very clear that *he* was Rosalie's first responsibility, and he seldom tolerated anyone daring to interfere with their time together.

A footman and two other maids hovered around Rosalie now, all attempting to speak at once. "Mireille, I know you are exhausted," Rosalie said, apparently unruffled by the small crowd in front of them. "I apologize for the disturbance"—she sent a meaningful look to the group, whose clamoring subsided somewhat—"but there are a few matters I must take care of. Would you care for a hot cup of tea while I attend to them?"

Rosalie directed one of the plump, pretty maids to bring a tea tray to them, and led Mira to a small room while pointing out the winged sphinxes and griffins which grinned and scowled down at them from the ceiling moldings.

"This is all very lovely," Mira said, following Rosalie into a beautiful room filled with delicate stuccowork and rose-colored marble. Soft brocaded chairs were set before a pilastered fireplace, while gold-framed engravings adorned the walls. Rosalie beamed at the compliment.

"Thank you. Shortly after we were married the house was designed by an acquaintance of ours, the Duke of Stafford."

"Alec F-Falkner?" Mira managed to stammer, suddenly feeling trapped by the house that had seemed so charming just a minute ago.

"You've heard of him?" Rosalie inquired, walking to the window and straightening the drapery sash.

"Yes . . ." Mira said faintly. "Do you often . . . that is, is he a close acquaintance of yours?"

"Not really," Rosalie replied, her blue eyes becoming thoughtful, her forehead furrowing slightly as she pondered the question. "I suppose we should be closer . . . after all, not only did he design this house, but we are on good terms with the Falkner family in general. On the few occasions that I've met Lord Falkner, I've found him to be pleasant and polite, and Rand likes him well enough, but . . . he is a rather unsettling man. I don't quite know how to explain it, since he is always very courteous, but still . . ." She frowned quickly and then dropped the subject, throwing Mira a pleased smile. "Oh well, it's not likely that you'll meet him here."

Mira nodded uncertainly. "My lady—"

"I would prefer it if you called me by my first name."

"Rosalie, then. I would like to thank you for the invitation to stay here with you. I am grateful for it, and I would like to accept your hospitality for a short while. But I am afraid that I will not be able to stay for long."

"Mireille, don't even think of leaving yet," Rosalie began in a small rush, then smiled and continued more calmly. "You will discover in a few weeks that as winter approaches, half of the extended Berkeley family moves in with us. As you see, it is a very big house, and the heating is excellent—so a large number of friends and relatives come to visit during the months of harshest weather. They provide interesting company, if not always the most restful, and I can promise you a most entertaining stay with us. You will not inconvenience anyone a bit, since one guest more or less will make little difference . . . and I want you to stay here. You once extended your hand to me when I was ill and needed friendship—don't deprive me of the opportunity to repay your kindness."

"I don't consider," Mira said slowly, her dark brown eyes downcast, "—that you owe me anything. I don't think I'll ever be able to forget what happened in France. I . . . I betrayed you—"

"Not consciously. Not willingly," Rosalie insisted, and then bit her lip as she cast a perturbed glance at the door. "Let's talk about this later when you have rested and I am not pressed for time. For now I am simply glad that you're here. Here is Mary with the tea—I'll be back soon." With a rustle of silk skirts Rosalie left, the soft scent of her perfume lingering in the air.

Mira sat down in a brocaded chair and picked up a cup of tea, her eyes lingering on the well-tended landscaping visible through the spotless windows. Though the sunlight would eventually fade the rich colors of the carpet and furniture, Rosalie insisted on letting the sun into every room she frequented. It was a habit of hers that Mira remembered from their days in the château in France. Most people preferred the restful dimness of heavily draped windows, yet Rosalie was not one who would allow her tastes to be dictated by others.

So Alec had designed Berkeley Hall, Mira mused, intensely curious to see the rest of it. Knowing him, she was not surprised at the touches of whimsy that graced the little that she had seen of the house . . . like the griffins in the main hall, and the concealed closets in this room, decorated with Chinese birds, and the bits of mirror glass lining the edges of the windows. She smiled slightly at the irony of the situation. In trying to escape him, she had managed to find refuge in a place that he had created.

She knew exactly why Alec made Rosalie uneasy, even if Rosalie herself could not explain it. Rosalie was used to straightforward men like Rand Berkeley, not ones who were adept at saying one thing while meaning another. Alec would be too much a man of extremes to make Rosalie feel at ease in his company . . . he was too handsome, too unpredictable, too perceptive. Any woman who loved him would be an absolute idiot, Mira thought. As she berated herself silently, a tear rolled down her cheek and dropped into her tea, and as another followed, she set the cup down and hunted for a handkerchief.

"No more tears allowed after today," a voice came

from the door, and Mira looked up to see Rosalie's eyes warm with sympathy.

"You're finished so soon?" she asked huskily, leaving off her search for a handkerchief.

"I managed to postpone the minor problems for later. I explained to the servants that we have a very special guest who will be staying here indefinitely—and that she must be treated like royalty."

"I am the last person in England who should be treated like royalty," Mira said bitterly, spooning more sugar into her tea and stirring nervously even after it was dissolved. "You don't know who I am, or what—"

"I do know," Rosalie said gently. Their eyes met and the agitated movement of Mira's spoon stopped abruptly. "Guillaume told Rand many things five years ago in France before . . . before we were separated. I know about your mother. I know about your upbringing, and your background."

"You do?" Mira froze in astonishment. "You know and yet you've asked me to stay with you?"

"Oh, Mireille . . ." Rosalie sat down in the chair close by, arranging her skirts automatically and folding her hands in her lap. Her expression was pitying and affectionate, and vaguely amused. "From the day I was born, I thought I was the daughter of a confectioner and a governess . . . I was a *housemaid*. Although I was educated, I had to work with my hands sometimes . . . I polished and scrubbed . . . I knew what it was like to have to pick up after someone else . . . I knew what it was like to want things that I thought I could never have. But when I was your age, I found out that I was the product of a secret love affair between a noblewoman and the most notorious dandy in the world—"

"Beau Brummell?"

"Yes, Brummell." Rosalie's smile became wistful. "He is my father. But I discovered that the dandy's daughter was no different, no better, than the confectioner's daughter. It made no difference who my parents were—I was still the same woman. Now people think of me as Lady Berkeley, and some of them scrape and bow, and some whisper about my shadowed past, but most of them would never believe that I had once run up and down the stairs lugging buckets of coal for the fire, afraid I would get my ears boxed for being slow. And if things could change so drastically for me, they can for you."

"But a confectioner's daughter is one thing . . . I am something else entirely. "I am"—Mira's face whitened as she forced out the words—"the daughter of a prostitute." She had never said the word out loud before. "That makes me lower than—"

"Don't." Rosalie's blue eyes flashed, and suddenly her face seemed chiseled out of brittle ivory. She spoke with a meaningful slowness. "I don't want you to say that ever again. Not to me, not to Rand, not to anyone. Your future depends on it, do you understand?"

Mira shook her head, transfixed by the sternness that had transformed Rosalie's expression. "No, I'm afraid I don't understand. I don't have the kind of future that—"

"You have a wonderful future," Rosalie corrected determinedly. "I intend to make it so." She continued in a softer tone as she witnessed Mira's increasing bewilderment. "I will take care of everything. We'll be very clever . . . we'll be very discreet. Believe me, I am England's foremost authority on how to survive a scandal. For the first two years that Rand and I were married . . . well, that's a story in itself. The next several months you will rest here quietly while the gossip about you and Sackville recedes—"

"It won't."

"It will. Gossip is only enjoyable when it's new. It will fade eventually. And when it does, and you have been forgotten about, I will bring you out as a different woman."

"*Sang de Dieu*, what are you saying?" Mira demanded, horrified. "You can't do that!"

"I certainly can. We will make you Rand's ward. Mireille Germain . . . a timid young woman brought up by a fine, very old, very respectable French family, transferred to the Berkeleys' safekeeping along with her very attractive dowry."

"I have no dowry."

"Of course you do—I'll supply it."

"I won't accept it. And besides, there are hundreds—*thousands*—of ways that people will poke holes in my story."

"But I still remember what a superb actress you are. You'll be so convincing that most people won't think of disbelieving what's in front of their eyes."

"What about everyone who saw me at Sackville Manor?" Mira asked desperately. "They'll remember me, and they all know I'm not from some respectable French family."

"That *is* a slight problem—"

"It's a tremendous problem!"

"—but Rand will help us think of some good lies. And he'll convince Sackville to support whatever story we come up with. Rand is *very* persuasive."

"There is another problem," Mira said hoarsely, thinking of Alec, his eyes smiling into hers, his lips seeking hers tenderly. She did not want any other man but him, and the thought of belonging to someone else was unbearable. "I don't want a husband, be it a chimney sweep, the King of England, or anyone in between. So it's not worth the effort, the lies, the stories, and everything else necessary to get me a husband. I don't want one."

"What?" Rosalie asked, astounded. "Of course you do! You don't want to be alone, do you?"

"Yes, I do. I want to be alone."

"No, you don't. You may think you do, but you don't," Rosalie insisted. She was about to lecture the younger woman about the benefits of matrimony as opposed to the problems of being alone, but as she saw the signs of stubbornness on Mira's face, she gave up the debate temporarily. "Let's not talk about it anymore," she said with a smile. "While you rest here, I'll have several months to convince you that you need a husband—"

"I won't change my mind."

"You look tired. You must nap for an hour or two, and then I will take you to tour the grounds and to visit with Christian."

"I don't know if I can rest," Mira said agitatedly. "I have so much to think about."

"Think about only one thing," Rosalie said, standing up and regarding her fondly. "After a little time here, you will start to look at things the way you used to. Remember how eager and vivacious you were? I've never seen anyone plunge through life with that kind of energy."

"I remember that I was always getting into trouble," Mira said.

"That, at least, hasn't changed."

It was impossible to combat Rosalie's relentless optimism. Mira felt her spirits lighten as she was shown to a charming bedchamber decorated in shades of white and blue, filled with walnut and oak furniture. The gowns she had brought from Hampshire were already hanging in an armoire with fielded panels, while her accessories were placed neatly in a Charles II oak chest. Mira toyed absently with the brass-ring handles of the chest as she peered about the rest of the room. A set of ivory-handled brushes reposed on top of the Queen Anne dressing table, while pewter jars painted with Chinese figures perched on the mantel of the simple stone fireplace. It was not at all difficult to fall asleep in such pleasant surroundings, and Mira woke an hour or two later with a strange sense of peace and belonging. With the help of the shy, plump maid who had brought her tea before, she freshened her clothes and brushed her rumpled hair ruthlessly, confining the thick black-brown mass in her pearl-studded hairnet.

She walked with Rosalie and Christian through the immaculately tended grounds, enjoying the cool October air and the cavorting of Rosalie's young son. Christian was the most engaging child Mira had ever seen, blond and green-eyed, possessing a round face and sturdy-legged body. Dressed in a belted tunic and simple pantaloons, he raced back and forth as the two women walked along the garden paths, occasionally interrupting their conversation with questions and forth-right observations.

"He is unusually bright for a boy of three," Mira said after Christian recited the names of all the different kinds of leaves he was in the process of collecting, and Rosalie laughed with delight.

"His papa certainly believes so. And unfortunately Christian is all Berkeley, down to the eyeteeth."

"All Berkeley? Is that bad?"

"It forebodes a great deal of trouble," Rosalie said, lifting her graceful hand in a helpless gesture and smiling resignedly. "The Berkeleys are a reckless lot, with an ancestry of highwaymen, incendaries, and trou-blemakers . . . and I have no doubt that Christian will follow in the same tradition."

"But Lord Berkeley is a very responsible sort of man," Mira pointed out.

"Due solely to my influence."

"I can see that he has changed a great deal since your marriage," Mira said, thinking back to that long-ago summer in France. Berkeley had been younger, rougher, irritable whenever he and Rosalie were apart.

"Especially since Christian was born," Rosalie said, her eyes glowing as she looked at her scampering son. "This child has brought out the side of Rand that only

I was able to see before. He has become more approachable, gentle . . ." Rosalie grinned impishly. "He used to intimidate most people quite terribly."

As if he still didn't. "I remember," Mira said dryly.

"But now Rand and I are closer than I ever dreamed we could be. The kinds of doubts that I hear my friends speak of . . . their worries about their husbands' fidelity, their lack of trust . . . I will never have those kinds of fears."

"You're very fortunate," Mira commented softly, and as she looked at the small boy in front of them, she felt a pang of hunger for the kind of love, the kind of security that Rosalie had described.

"You will have that someday," Rosalie said.

Mira shrugged, concealing her emotions with a careless smile. "Perhaps," she said noncommittally, knowing that if she denied the statement another lecture would ensue.

"Has there ever been a man who . . . well, one you might have fallen in love with?"

Mira hesitated before replying. She would not lie to Rosalie, but there were some things that must never be revealed. The fact that Alec Falkner had been her lover would always be a secret. "Yes," she murmured.

"Lord Sackville," Rosalie said, her brow wrinkling with a perplexed frown.

"I can't confirm or deny that."

"Mireille, if it was Lord Sackville," Rosalie said tentatively, "it is my opinion that he was more like a father to you than . . ." She broke off uncomfortably and sighed. "I suppose I can't really offer an opinion on something I know so little about. But love . . . *real* love . . . only occurs between people who have a great deal more in common than you and Lord Sackville."

"I know what real love is," Mira replied quietly as memories flashed through her mind: Alec holding her against his broad naked chest, his eyes sparkling with wicked laughter, or glowing with anger, or quiet with thoughtfulness. The chinks of vulnerability he fought so hard to conceal from everyone. The trapped, hungry expression that he had sometimes worn as he looked at her. *Oh, Alec*, her heart whispered in despair, *why did you let me leave you?* "Although my feelings were not returned," she continued with effort, "I know what it is like to care so deeply that there is nothing left inside me to give. I won't love anyone that way again—it would be impossible."

"You are too young to be so certain of that," Rosalie said. "Do you know what the Gypsies believe? . . . that men and women are the halves of a single unity that has been split and separated . . . that we are each searching for our soulmate, the one for whom we have been destined. If you are truly meant to be with Sackville—"

"I didn't say that Sackville was the one—"

"The man you care for," Rosalie amended. "If you are meant to be with him, then fate will bring you together. And if he is not the right one, your soulmate is still out there somewhere looking for you."

"And waiting for the social season to begin?"

"Yes," Rosalie said, laughing. "Waiting for you to appear, after having spent a long and cold winter alone."

"Alone?" Mira repeated. "No, somehow I don't think he'll spend it alone." Through her anguish came a sudden flicker of anger, and she grasped at it tightly. Anger was a far healthier emotion than grief, and perhaps if she was fortunate, she could nurture it into indifference. She would never be able to completely overcome her feelings for Alec Falkner, but she would find some way to survive them.

"Would you like some breakfast, my lord?"

"Thank you, but no."

Georgiana Bradbourne, the recently widowed Countess of Helmsley, padded barefoot across the room to the small table on which a breakfast tray had been placed. The scent of strong coffee filled her bedchamber with an acrid aroma. She poured the beverage with practiced movements, her slim white hands alighting daintily on the silver and china cups. As Alec watched her, he reflected on the fact that she did everything with the same type of well-rehearsed precision, whether it was dancing, flirting, pouring coffee, or lovemaking. There were no surprises to Georgiana. Even her body, so clearly visible through the filmy wrap she wore, was smooth and regular, with no birthmarks or moles to mar its velvety surface. Her conversation was pleasant, for she seldom argued with him, preferring instead to align all of her opinions with his. Most men would count their blessings if they possessed the affection of Lady Bradbourne, a woman who was as close as possible to being perfect. Alec frowned slightly, realizing that Georgiana's endless perfection was beginning to bore him. He sat up and rested his shoulders against the paneled headboard of the bed, catching at the edge of the sheet to keep it from slipping down his hips.

"Don't pull the sheet up," Georgiana said, smiling and coming to sit on the edge of the bed as she sipped her coffee. "I like to look at you." She was a beautiful woman, voluptuous and blond, with pale coloring and aristocratic demeanor.

Knowing that it was expected of him, Alec took her free hand and lifted it to his lips, pressing a kiss to the center of her palm. "As always, I contemplate the prospect of leaving your bed with the greatest reluctance," he said, and she laughed lightly.

"As always, I don't want to let you go. You are an unprincipled scoundrel, which is why you are such a marvelous lover."

"As long as the performance matched your expectations," Alec murmured in a tone which caused Georgiana's feline smile to falter for a split second.

"It was more than a performance I hope," she said. "When we are together I feel close to you . . . in a way that I never did with my husband. You are able to touch my heart and spirit so easily. Each time we make love, I feel more and more as if I belong to you."

Alec's gray eyes narrowed as he looked at her. Georgiana delivered a convincing performance. She spoke with apparent sincerity, her expression smooth and guileless. But there was something else in her face, an expectancy, that betrayed her true thoughts. She had decided that she wanted to be Alec's wife, but not for reasons of love, as she would have him believe. It was well-known that her debts were beginning to mount up, the creditors knocking at the door. If she was waiting for him to propose, she was wasting more time than a woman in her position could afford. Though her face and figure were attractive, they would soon begin to fade from the rigors of the overindulgent way of life. She drank too much, she spent far too much time going to parties and gambling . . . both before and after the recent death of her elderly and harried husband.

"Georgia," he said softly, using a nickname that she would tolerate from no one else, "why don't you let me settle up with your creditors?"

"I . . ." She looked startled at his suggestion. "I . . . Whatever brought up such a subject, my lord?" She took a deep swallow of coffee, closing her eyes as it burned its way down her throat.

"Let's stop the game," Alec said gently. "You've been refusing gifts from me for the same reason that you refuse to allow me to pay your bills . . . because you like to pretend that you're more than just my mistress."

"I'm *not* your mistress!" Georgiana snapped, standing up from the bed. "I'm your lover."

"Georgia, I have no desire or need to marry anyone," he told her flatly. "Call yourself whatever you like, my lover, mistress, or friend, but facts being what they are, our association has developed to its fullest potential. In other words, things have gone as far as they're going—so you might as well take advantage of the situation and stop waiting for a proposal of marriage that you'll never receive. You're never going to be the Duchess of Stafford, but you will profit well enough from having been my mistress. I am willing to be generous with you—"

"Please. Please don't say such things to me," she said, a sparkling mist clouding her pale blue eyes. "I don't understand what you're—"

"It's useless to resort to tears," Alec said, a trace of derision coloring his voice. "I'm immune to them."

"Bastard." Georgiana's misty tears dried instantly, and she favored him with a cool glance as she went to her dressing table and sat down to brush her hair. Alec smiled slightly, meeting her gaze in the mirror.

"At last the genuine Georgia shows through," he commented. The solid shoulders flexed as he folded his arms in back of his head. "Suddenly I find you more appealing than ever before."

"That's because you are the kind of man who only wants a woman who despises him. You don't like anyone who dares to be nice to you."

"I like any kind of woman as long as she's genuine," Alec replied. His thick lashes lowered to conceal the expression of his eyes. "As long as she's honest. It's difficult to find a woman who doesn't play a role in bed."

"We all do," Georgiana informed him curtly, drawing a brush roughly through her long golden hair. "You poor stupid men don't like us as we are. You want a virgin every time."

Alec grinned. "Deliver me from women who like to pose as virgins when they're not—or worse, as ladies," he said, and then his amusement disappeared in a twinkling, as if an unpleasant memory had crossed his mind. "After the authentic experience, the imitations are difficult to bear."

"Whom are you thinking of? Was she an authentic virgin or an authentic lady?" Georgiana demanded, the sharpness of her voice jolting him back to considerations of the present moment.

"Both," Alec said, brushing a hand across his chest in an absentminded gesture. He had worn the Falkner medallion around his neck for so long that he had still not become accustomed to its absence. "You haven't yet answered my question. "Would you like me to settle your accounts or not?"

"Is paying a few paltry bills all you're offering?" she asked silkily, causing him to laugh.

"From what I've heard, they're far from paltry. But I'll throw in a gift for you as well—"

"Emeralds."

"Diamonds," Alec corrected lazily, stretching and standing up from the bed. "You're not worth emeralds, Georgia, though I'll admit you've been very entertaining this morning."

"Perhaps I can convince you of my worth," she said. Slowly she walked toward him, staring at the naked, powerful lines of his body. "In a few minutes I'll have you begging to give me emeralds. . . ." Enticingly Georgiana dropped her wrapper. Alec's gray eyes flickered over her nude form thoughtfully. Then he smiled with a peculiar bleakness and placed a kiss on her forehead with a casualness that infuriated her.

"It's over, Georgia. I won't be visiting any longer. But thanks for the invitation . . . it's nice to know that one is wanted."

"Bastard," she said for the second time, shrugging and turning away from him. "I'll take the diamonds, then."

The Berkeley grounds were covered with a sea of

tables, all laden with the most enormous amount of food Mira had ever seen. Roasts and hams were being brought from the kitchens as fast as they could be carved and served, while vast crowds gathered to partake of puddings, breads, and other dishes. After living a month with the Berkeleys, Mira was finally becoming accustomed to their grand style of doing things, yet she was awed by the size of the gathering that they hosted. The feast was an all-day event and would be concluded by a fireworks display when night had fallen. The affair was for the benefit of the tenants of the estate and the residents of the surrounding villages, but members of the local gentry also came to partake of the food, drink, and merriment.

"There must be more than a thousand people here," Mira breathed in awe, burrowing her hands deeper into her swansdown muff as a chilly breeze pinkened her cheeks. Rosalie smiled, nodding in greeting to the people they passed on their way across the lawn.

"Every year it seems to get bigger," Rosalie admitted. "But how could we turn anyone away? Most of these people are local villagers who work desperately hard every day of the year. I only wish we could give them move than this little bit of pleasure."

"I've heard many people talk about how generous you and Lord Berkeley are. Your tenants must number among the most well-fed and content in all of England."

"Rand would like to do more for the local people. He is considering asking King George for a summons to Parliament—either that or he will find an overlooked district to represent. Now that the shipping company practically runs itself, he must look for new challenges. And I will be glad when he becomes more involved in politics, for that will draw his attention away from uncovering my little secrets."

Mira cast a curious smile at Rosalie. "You have secrets from him? I thought neither of you made a step without the other."

"You did? Goodness, how boring that would be. No, Rand is not aware of all of my activities, and I make certain that he knows it. It would never do to let him think he has the upper hand over me."

"What exactly . . . ?" Mira began, and then stopped herself with a chuckle. "No, I won't ask."

"I'll tell you if you promise not to let a word out to anyone about it." Rosalie glanced around to make certain that no one was near enough to overhear their conversation, and then she lowered her voice a few degrees. "You know that Brummell, my father, has been in exile in France for the past few years. He had run up so many debts here, gambling and otherwise, that he couldn't possibly have paid them . . . and after his friendship with King George ended, he was bound to end up in debtor's prison. Even though he still has many rich and powerful friends in England, Brummell is terribly incompetent with money . . . no control whatsoever. He insists on buying only the best, and he is such a horrible spendthrift . . . and he won't take any money from me for reasons of pride."

"How awful to be unable to help someone when you want to."

"Yes . . . but a man's pride is easily bruised. In some ways men are so much more fragile than women." Rosalie sighed. "For numerous reasons, my husband and my father dislike each other intensely. The only thing they agree on is that we should never acknowledge my kinship to Brummell. But despite all the good reasons for ignoring it, he is my father! He is my only natural parent. I can't forget that, no matter how much Rand would like me to."

"Of course you couldn't," Mira murmured.

"So in secret I arrange for little ways to help Brummell, because he is in bad straits financially. I pay anonymously for as many of his bills as I can without arousing suspicion from either Brummell or Rand."

"What about Brummell's family? If he is in need of money, why don't they help him?"

Rosalie frowned, shaking her head in disgust.

"They tolerated him while he was rich and influential, but now he is nothing more than an embarrassment to them. They like to pretend he doesn't exist—for that matter, they pretend I don't exist! So they won't offer any help to him at all." A faint smile touched Rosalie's lips. "Mireille, no one knows about this, but twice my father has come to England to visit secretly, just for a few hours. I have met with him both times without my husband's knowledge. Rand would forbid it—"

"Surely not," Mira protested, knowing that Berkeley wouldn't refuse his wife anything she truly desired.

"Well, he might not forbid it," Rosalie conceded after a moment's thought, "but I do know that he would insist upon accompanying me, which would spoil things altogether. I can picture what it would be like to try to talk with Brummell, who is so easily upset anyway, with Rand in the background scowling at us both."

"I see what you mean," Mira said, and they exchanged a wry smile.

"The reason I'm telling you all of this," Rosalie continued, "is that I received word from Brummell yesterday morning that he is coming to England in a few days, and this will probably be his last visit. He is coming to speak to his attorney about some secret funds of his that still exist in London, and also to talk with a publisher about a book he has been writing on costume and dress. He is the acknowledged expert on the subject, and perhaps the proceeds of the book sale will help to cover his debts and expenses."

"How are you going to manage seeing him without Lord Berkeley's knowledge?"

"The same as the previous times—I'll tell Rand I'm visiting my mother, who lives in a terrace house in London. But this time, I'd rather not go alone. Would you consider—?"

"I would like to accompany you," Mira said.

Rosalie visibly glowed with pleasure. "I'm so glad! Thank you. You will enjoy meeting Brummell, I assure you." She closed her eyes briefly, as if trying to suppress an overwhelming tide of excitement. "I'm going to see my father soon," she whispered, as if trying to convince herself that it was true. "I could die of happiness. It's been so very, very long since I've seen him. You must think it's terribly odd of me to love someone I barely know," she said huskily.

"Not at all," Mira replied, looking away and biting her lip. "Not at all."

After a pleasant but unmemorable supper at Bedford House, the guests retired to the ballroom, which was flanked on either side by small orchestras. Now unencumbered by Lady Georgiana Bradbourne, Alec was officially considered to be the most eligible bachelor in London, and the inconvenience of such a position was forcibly brought home to him as the evening progressed. He could not look around without meeting the inviting glances of scores of women. He had not engaged in a single conversation that failed to include probing questions about his romantic life, his intentions toward this woman or that, his future plans for marriage. Fielding the barrage as best he could, Alec began to wonder if he would be hunted in this way for the rest of the winter.

"It will get even worse when the Season begins," a voice intruded on his thoughts, and Alec turned to meet the clear, intelligent eyes of Lord Melbourne.

"Explain, if you please," Alec said, allowing a faint smile to cross his mouth. He liked Melbourne for his frankness and easy laughter. Melbourne was a statesman who thought whatever he liked and said whatever he thought, but he was so engaging that even when his opinions were displeasing, he was still respected and regarded with affection. Tact and honesty were rarely so comfortably combined in one person.

"You're done for," Melbourne remarked laconically, waving his white hand gracefully. "Come spring, you won't last a week. They'll be after you like seamen around a harpooned whale. I would bet my fortune that you'll be married within a year."

"Risk your fortune on a worthier cause," Alec said, his eyes sparkling with laughter. "I have no intention of marrying anyone."

"Dear fellow, you'll have no choice. No man ever intends to marry, yet sooner or later most of us end up that way. Curse it. I didn't intend to marry anyone either, and yet one morning when I awakened I discovered that the woman sleeping next to me was my wife."

"And so ended the pleasant dream of bachelorhood with the rude awakening of matrimony?"

"Exactly," Melbourne said, about to continue when his eyes fastened onto a sight beyond Alec's back. His face froze. "Good God," he said softly, a small indentation of confusion appearing between his sandy eyebrows. "Who is that? I thought it was . . ."

Alec turned and cast a quick glance at the man who had just walked in. His fingers tightened around the glass of port he held, and then he returned his attention to Melbourne, who was rapidly recovering himself.

"That is Carr Falkner. Late as usual," Alec said lazily, his attitude relaxed although his eyes were hard. "Just returned from a long trip abroad. Holt's younger brother, about twenty-two or so."

Melbourne nodded, his handsome face flushed slightly. The likeness between Carr and Holt must have startled Melbourne to no small degree, since he was usually one to maintain his composure at all times. "I was acquainted with your late cousin," Melbourne said quietly, "but lamentably not with his immediate family. I had no idea that he had a younger brother who resembled him so closely."

"Carr has never cared for the London scene. He has always preferred to stay in the country and engage in scholarly pursuits," Alec said, frowning darkly. "Until now."

"Don't hold that against him," Melbourne advised mildly. "He has come to the age when all young men want to experience the temptations of life: women, gaming—"

"I think his reasons for moving to London are more complicated than that," Alec said, thinking of Carr's cold, shattered young face as Holt's body had been lowered into the grave, the trip aboard that paralleled the trip that Holt himself had taken at twenty-two, the gradual change in Carr's behavior from his natural quietness to an irrepressible recklessness. Holt's recklessness. "I'm afraid that Carr is trying to fill his brother's shoes."

"Consciously?"

"I don't know." Alec admitted, his shoulders tensing at the sound of Carr's laughter. Carr sounded too damned much like Holt. And when he cavorted and played pranks with that lopsided grin, he reminded Alec so much of a younger Holt that it caused a suffocating mixture of pain and anger to surge inside him.

As a boy, Carr had always been a sly creature, the darling of the family with his big green eyes and enchanting smile, a stealthy little prankster with the face of an angel. Many a time Holt and Alec had found their plans ruined and their secrets revealed because of Carr's habit of eavesdropping and telling tales. As they had all grown up, Carr had turned into something of a scholar—little surprise in that, considering his remarkable memory and his ability to repeat everything he overheard. Now they were boys no longer, but Alec remembered how devious, how untrustworthy

Holt's younger brother had been, and he doubted that Carr had changed much. And if there was one kind of man Alec hated, it was an untrustworthy one.

"He's coming this way—it's clear that he intends to speak to you," Melbourne said, and Alec's mouth quirked in a cryptic half-smile.

"I wonder why." God knew they'd had nothing to say to each other for years, not even at Holt's funeral.

"Hello, Alec," Carr said as he stopped in front of them, shaking hands with a sturdy grip.

After brief introductions were made, Melbourne took a step back and regarded them uneasily. "I must dance with my wife before I earn her disfavor with my inattention," he said, looking from one Falkner to the other with unconcealed amusement. "Good to have met you," he said to Carr, then turned to Alec with a wry smile and a nod. "My best wishes."

"My thanks," Alec said, his eyes resting thoughtfully on Melbourne as he left, knowing why that gentleman had been so perturbed. There were more than a few physical similarities between Alec and Carr, for they both possessed an abundance of Falkner traits. Like Alec, Carr had jet-black hair, strongly marked brows, a slight golden cast to his skin, brutally molded cheekbones, and an unyielding jaw. But Carr's eyes were dark green instead of wintry gray, and Carr was shorter and slighter. His appearance spoke more of graceful elegance than of Alec's solid power. "Dressed like a swell," Alec commented, his gaze missing no detail of his cousin's new and fashionably altered appearance. The unruly black locks had been shorn to a shining, immaculately trimmed crop, while his clothes of black, white, and buff were arranged to perfection. Quite different from the tumbled youth who had pored over piles of books.

"I should hope so," Carr drawled, affecting a dandyish accent. "But this deuced getup cost me a sweet fortune, don't you know."

"How was your journey?" Alec inquired flatly, and Carr sobered immediately.

"Pleasant. No, just tolerable." His dark green eyes met Alec's, and a brief flash of desperation illuminated Carr's gaze. "Bloody awful," he said. "I have to talk with you."

"Talk your problems out with someone else," Alec said softly. "You know as well as I that we don't get along well with each other . . . and furthermore, I'm not generally regarded as the compassionate one in the family—"

"No, you're not," Carr interrupted, his expression twisting in self-doubt, as if he wondered why he had approached his cousin in the first place. "But you're the only one who'll understand."

Conscious of the many pairs of eyes on them, Alec hesitated and then nodded slightly. "If you're willing to risk the possibility of eavesdroppers."

"No one is close enough to hear," Carr said, his glance flickering around the room and then returning to Alec's face.

"Go on, then."

"The trip was miserable. With all the sights and sounds of the Continent spread before me, I couldn't see anything. I couldn't hear anything. I couldn't sleep. Every night I thought about it, until I nearly tore my hair out in frustration. The unanswered questions are killing me, very slowly."

"Holt?" Alec asked softly, and Carr nodded.

"Yes . . . Holt. I could accept his death if there was a reason for it. But there was no reason, there was no explanation at all for what happened to him and why he was . . ." Carr stopped and forced himself to speak more calmly. "I've got to find out why, I've got to find . . . Why are you looking at me like that?"

"You're just a little too sincere about this. I'm wondering what you're really after, and what these theatrics are really about."

"Theatrics! Is it that difficult to believe that I cared for my own brother?"

"Yes. I know you, and I know how things were between you and Holt. You rarely had a word to say to each other."

"I couldn't talk to him," Carr said, his gaze round and sincere. "I was too awed by him. You don't understand how it really was . . . all my life everyone talked about how perfect he was . . . I tried to measure up to the standards he set . . . I failed every time. But I did care for him, and I've got to find out who killed him or I'll wonder about it for the rest of my life. If I don't at least try, I'll never find any peace. You don't know what the past months have been like—"

"I do," Alec interrupted. There was a raw note in his voice that momentarily silenced the younger man. "But there were no leads. No clues."

"We can search for them."

"Do you think," Alec inquired coolly, "that it is going to do either of us any damned good to dredge this over and over? It's taken long enough for me to accept what happened—"

"I haven't even been able to get that far," Carr said miserably. "Alec, you're the last one I thought I'd have to convince to help me look for Holt's killer. I thought you cared for him as much as—"

"Damn you," Alec said, his eyes suddenly flashing. "If you're going to fling words so foolhardily, you little pup, then we'll continue this conversation outside. Holt was more a brother to me than my own. Another comment like that and I'll thrash you damned cheerfully . . . or call you out, which is probably more what you deserve."

"I'm sorry," Carr said, hanging his black head. The sight brought him back so many memories of a penitent Holt that Alec looked away and gritted his teeth.

"Damn you," he said again.

"Forget about it for now," Carr said in a low voice. "I'm going to Goodman's Tavern. I'll be there for a while tonight, so if you'd care to join me later, I'll buy you a few drinks by way of apology. I shouldn't have approached you with this at such a time and in such a manner."

Alec did not reply, keeping his face averted as Carr walked away. Setting his port on a table, he scowled at the embroidered tablecloth as a brief flashback raced through his mind: Holt walking into Alec's terrace rooms unannounced, good-natured as he had always been when half-drunk.

"It is I, most responsible and hardworking cousin," Holt had announced, setting a gin bottle down in the center of Alec's paperwork. After staring at the ring of alcohol blurring into the ink, Alec had met Holt's twinkling eyes with a feigned scowl.

"If you've come for money, I don't have any."

"The devil you don't . . . but no, I haven't come for money," Holt had informed him loftily, shaking an unsteady finger in the manner of the stern tutor who had schooled both of them in mathematics. "I've come to rescue you from your labors before your mind wears out from all those parchment scratchings. I'm going to find you a woman." Picking up the gin bottle, Holt had taken a swallow of the clear distillation before adding, "You need a woman. One like my Leila. Come to think of it, maybe Leila has some friends who—"

"Damned if I need your help in finding a woman," Alec had said, grinning suddenly and setting down his pen. He had reached for the gin bottle and taken a swig himself. "I'll find my own woman tonight—one that will make Leila look like the display on a fishmonger's cart."

"Oh-ho!" Holt had chortled, making his way to the door and holding it open deferentially. "Just for Leila's honor, I'm going to call you out . . . when I'm sober." He had smiled crookedly, appraising his own condition. "Which puts you out of danger for a good while. . . ."

Alec sighed, bringing his thoughts back to the present as the orchestra began to play a polonaise. He realized that he was desperate for another drink. Or a woman. Or anything to take his mind off the memories. Guilt twined around him, squeezing until he was numb from the pressure of it. *You can't bring him back*, Alec told himself, and he was nearly overwhelmed by an abrupt pang of loneliness. He was alive, Holt was dead, and there was nothing to do but go on with his life. But knowing that didn't ease his pain.

Suddenly he thought of Mira, and he was unable to rid his mind of her . . . her brown eyes filled with a teasing light . . . her cool fingers stroking and kneading his shoulders, sliding over his skin with a sweet, arousing touch. Her mouth moving under his, their lips clinging, parting, and reuniting. The addictive feel of her body, the passion that only she had been able to rouse so high and satisfy so deeply. He needed to wrap his arms around her small form and bury his face in her hair. Mira could help him forget his pain. But Mira was not his. She had left him, and he had convinced himself at the time that it was better to let her go. He had not wanted to need her so badly . . . he still did not want to.

Perhaps, Alec reflected moodily, he should join Carr at the tavern. At the moment, a series of drinks seemed worth the effort of tolerating Carr's company. Squaring his shoulders and raking a hand through his raven hair, he began to make his way through the conglomerations of people along the edges of the ballroom.

Then he caught sight of something that set off an inner shock of recognition. A woman, turned away from him, her dark locks neatly confined by a jeweled hairnet that glittered and shone under the blazing lights of the chandelier. She stood alone, apparently waiting

for someone to bring her a glass of wine or punch.
Stopping in his tracks, Alec stared at her with a mixture of surprise and instant, raging hunger. Although
he could not see her face, he knew that it had to be
Mira. She was the only one who had ever adorned her
hair in such a way. She was thinner than he remembered, her figure less voluptuous. He felt such an
incredible rush of desire for her that it didn't matter,
nothing mattered except that she was here and that he
was going to hold her, talk to her, touch her again.
Perhaps he would pull her out to a concealed place in
the gardens nearby and hold her tightly, crush her lips
under his . . . Not even bothering to wonder why she
was there or whom she had come to the ball with, he
reached her in a few long strides.

"Excuse me . . ." he said, and as the woman turned
around, Alec's impatience dwindled instantly into dis-
illusionment. She was not Mira. Her face was thinner,
her features were more sharply drawn, her eyebrows
were more arched. Even through his disappointment
Alec realized that she was an attractive woman, with
soft blue eyes and an inviting smile . . . but she did
not have Mira's distinctive beauty. Her eyes did not
shine with Mira's lively intelligence, her mouth did
not curve with Mira's provocative smile. She was an
imperfect copy of the woman he wanted. "Please forgive my impetuousness," he said, the blaze in his eyes
fading rapidly. 'I'm afraid that I've mistaken you for
someone else."

"How dreadful," the woman said in a lightly ac-
cented voice as she smiled at him, obviously believing
that he had wanted to meet her but had not been able
to find someone to make the proper introductions.
"We women do not like to be mistaken for each other
. . . it wounds our vanity."

Alec smiled slightly as he placed her accent. French,
an aristocratic dialect. A small measure of his interest
was reawakened.

"It is a mistake I will never make again," he said, looking down at her with silvery gray eyes.

"And why not?" she parried, her long lashes flickering against her cheeks before she looked up at him.

"Because I would never forget a face as beautiful as yours," he said, causing her to simper prettily.

"I'm not certain I believe you."

"Don't believe me, then," Alec said, giving her a smile guaranteed to make her heart beat faster. "Just dance with me."

Not Mira, but close enough.

"How did you learn to drive a phaeton?" Mira asked, wedging herself more firmly against the cushions of the light high-seated vehicle. It was an open carriage, and the cool damp wind of October blew against her face as Rosalie urged the chestnut horse faster down the London streets. Rosalie held the ribbons with a firm, expert grip, leaning forward to better control the horse as the wheels seemed to fly over the road. Only reckless young bloods were supposed to drive themselves in high-flier phaetons, not well-bred gentlewomen like Rosalie.

"It's not that difficult," Rosalie replied, reaching up to free a strand of hair that had blown across her lips. "When Rand and I take drives through Warwickshire, he lets me take the ribbons if no one is looking. Needless to say, he never dreamed that I would ever dare to do this without him beside me."

"I'm still amazed that your mother said nothing about us taking this out without an escort or even a footman—"

"She knows that this has something to do with Brummell . . . she wouldn't dare interfere. Although she's not my natural mother, she raised me from infancy and has always known how much I wanted a father. Now that I have found out who he is, she will not prevent me from seeing him or doing anything I like about him."

"Is this her phaeton?" Mira inquired, pulling the hood of her cloak more tightly around her head to keep the wind from blowing it off. The heavy garment was made of camlet, a waterproof fabric of wool, silk, and camel.

"In a way. Actually, it belongs to Baron Winthrop, the man who . . . er, pays for my mother's wardrobe, lodging, and so on . . . you know."

"Oh." Mira reflected on the information for a few seconds. No wonder, she thought with a sense of irony, that Rosalie had not been revolted by Mira's reputation of being Lord Sackville's mistress. When one's own mother was in a similar position, it was difficult to cast stones.

"Here we are. The Savoy Stairs," Rosalie announced, pulling the horse to a halt. They were near the edge of the Thames River, which slapped gently at the banks and emitted a repugnant smell. Mira twisted her head around to look at the ruins of a castle beside them; the walls of it were three feet thick.

"Why did Brummell want to meet us here?" she asked in distaste, shivering slightly.

"I requested that we meet here. It's the most convenient for him, since this is where he'll pass through on his way to Threadneedle—"

"This seems like a very unsavory place," Mira observed uneasily. "Wasn't the street that we passed back there the Strand? Isn't that where all the prostitutes go to—?"

"Yes. But we're very close to the West End, and there are charleys around to protect us—and really, we're not far from my mother's terrace. We're meeting Brummell here because he is coming across the river in a tilt."

"One of those little blue boats?" Mira asked, unable to picture the famed Brummell huddled in one of the cramped little water taxis.

"Yes," Rosalie replied, staring at the dark blur of

the river water that stretched out before them. "Look over there—right there a ship called the *Folly* was anchored about fifty years ago. People would take the tilts out to visit it. It was a floating 'den of iniquity' —drink, music, harlots, curtained rooms—no decent women were allowed, but of course many young lords went slumming there." She smiled mischievously. "Rand said that many a Berkeley had been a guest on the *Folly*, but of course the rest of the family denies it."

Mira smiled also, about to ask another question, when a distant crack, like the firing of a gun, popped in the silence. The noise startled her, and she clutched her diamond-shaped reticule uneasily.

"What do you have in there?" Rosalie asked.

"Nothing I'd care to have to use tonight," Mira replied grimly. Unlike Rosalie, she had had personal acquaintance with some of the worst parts of London. Yes, they were near well-to-do streets lined with bow windows, lamps, and fancy colonnades, but they were also perilously near alleyways and rows of slums that oozed with several different kinds of vermin, including the human variety. Rosalie could afford to be nonchalant about the situation, having never known the kind of danger that Mira had been exposed to. Aside from a few brushes with adventure that had all turned out well, Rosalie had been sheltered and well-protected. In fact, Rosalie possessed a belief in her own invincibility which disturbed Mira more than a little. Confidence was sometimes helpful, but overconfidence was very hazardous indeed. "Presently I'm wondering if we haven't been rather foolhardy in refusing an escort," Mira confessed. "It's dangerous this close to the river. It's too dark to see well, and I don't care for all these shadowy places—"

"We're perfectly safe," Rosalie asserted spiritedly. "Besides, I don't know of anyone whom I would trust with knowledge of this. Sometimes the people you have the greatest confidence in might be the first to betray you."

"That's true enough," Mira said, her voice quiet. "I just hope Brummell will arrive soon, that's all."

"He will."

Goodman's Tavern was especially raucous tonight, filled with an intoxicating combination of saucy barmaids and undiluted liquor. Alec walked in, ignoring the way the soles of his boots stuck to the unwashed wooden floor. Goodman's was a popular place to go slumming, having just the right amount of atmosphere and yet located in a place that wasn't as rife with crime as other parts of the city. Carr was sitting alone at a table, surrounded by a slew of empty glasses and opened bottles. He looked up without surprise as Alec sat down and slouched in a comfortably worn chair.

"So you decided to join me," Carr said, carefully arranging the glasses before him into a wall, and Alec regarded him darkly.

"I came here primarily for a drink. Not your company."

"Here," Carr replied, handing him a glass. "I think this one is close to being clean. Or would you rather wait until a barmaid comes to serve you? There are some very nice-looking—"

"No. God, no more women tonight," Alec muttered, taking the glass and examining it dully. "Do you have any brandy in your collection?"

"The best brandy in Romeville." Carr squinted at the assortment of bottles in front of him and selected one. "Here." He poured the liquid liberally with one hand while bracing his head on the other. "I think I'm going to have a devil of a head tomorrow morning," he said mournfully, filling his own glass with the vintage. "I'm pretty well disguised. Drunk as David's sow."

"Don't you know better than to mix spirits when drinking this hard?"

"When you're drinking for the reasons I am, it doesn't matter."

"I suppose not." Alec grimaced as he tossed down the brandy and reached for the bottle.

They drank in silence for a few minutes, until Alec could feel the pleasant burn of alcohol deep inside. His mood lightened, and he relaxed more deeply into his chair.

"No luck tonight?" Carr asked eventually, his green eyes overbright with the effects of a surfeit of gin. "Just before I left I saw you conversing with that little brunette demirep."

"It was not good," Alec said, his voice muffled as he pressed the heels of his hands into his eye sockets. He had danced with her, flirted, enjoyed a kiss or two as well as the other preliminaries to a promising evening of lovemaking . . . useless. Boring. The easy conquest had robbed him of all anticipation. He had not accepted her invitation to go to a quieter, more private place to continue the dalliance. "I was using her to forget someone else," he muttered. "It didn't work. Don't ever become attached to one particular woman, not for any reason. It's madness." Alec would never have made the admission in his sober moment, but strong drink and undemanding companionship had a way of wringing the truth out of a man.

"I won'," Carr promised, his voice so slurred that he was beginning to drop the last letters of his words.

"I keep on thinking I saw her." Alec ran the tip of his finger over the rim of the glass as he brooded over this unprecedented problem. "Every time I look at someone else, her face is there. I didn't think I would be like this . . . I didn't think she would be a problem. I keep on asking myself: why do I want her? She's not my usual type—"

"No," Carr said, shaking his head in agreement.

"—she's no taller than a child, she swears like the very devil, she has no parents, no family . . . the little muff can be as abrasive as gravel, and I can't stand an argumentative woman."

"I hate them too." Carr lifted his head and looked at Alec, his expression rapidly turning a shade of green that complemented his eyes. "I think I'm goin' to step outside. My head is swimming and turning aroun'."

Alec sighed and beckoned to a barmaid. She smiled at him with flirtatious eyes as he thrust a handful of money into her palm.

"Usually they slips it into my bodice," the maid said, her eyes batting suggestively.

"Why not?" Carr mumbled, standing up and swaying as he looked for the way out. "There's more than enough room in there."

Keeping stern control over his features, Alec handed the girl another sovereign and followed his lurching cousin out of the tavern. The corners of his mouth lifted slightly as he observed Carr's unsteady exit.

Suddenly the loud clattering of a hard-driven phaeton filled the air outside, and Carr staggered backward to avoid being run over. As the horses thundered by, Alec stared at the driver of the vehicle, whose hood had blown back off her face.

"What the devil!" Carr exclaimed, squinting after the rapidly departing phaeton. "Rattling through the streets like a pair of demons out of hell. Alec . . . tell me, am I too foxed to see clearly, or was that a couple of women?"

"It was," Alec said, looking as if he had been struck. "And not only was it two women, but . . ." He hesitated and then cursed, his eyes glittering with self-disgust. "*I'm* the one who's seeing things."

"It's been a hell of a night. I'm going to go home," Carr said, pressing his fingers into the corners of his eyes and shaking his head.

"Did you get a look at either of them?" Alec pressed, staring down the empty street. "Did the one who was driving look familiar?"

"Like who?"

"Like Lady Rosalie Berkeley."

"I've seen her only once. I wouldn't really know. Does it matter?"

"It's just that I'm acquainted with her husband," Alec said absently. "Berkeley would never allow his wife to frequent this part of London at this hour, especially not without an escort. And if that was Rosalie Berkeley, her companion might have been . . ." He closed eyes, letting out an exasperated sigh. "It probably was. Damn, that woman *attracts* trouble. But I'm not going to make an ass of myself combing the streets of London . . . she's not worth it, no woman is worth a man's self-respect. I'm ignoring all of this." Turning to look behind him, he was met with his cousin's absence. Evidently Carr had decided to leave. Alec turned back to the sight of the empty street.

If that had indeed been Lady Berkeley driving the carriage, then her companion had to be Mira. If it was not Lady Berkeley, he was a first-prize fool, because he was already looking around for a horse or a phaeton to borrow. But he had an intense feeling that he was going to see Mira tonight, and his blood was hot at the prospect. "Mira, what the hell are you involved in now?" he muttered, suddenly consumed with anticipation.

8

As the blue tilt approached, Rosalie turned pale and began to tremble, as if she were prepared to face some terrible catastrophe. This reaction was so far removed from her previous anticipation that Mira was alarmed. "Do you feel faint?" she asked, looking at her closely.

Rosalie shook her head, her eyes shining with tears. "No . . . I . . . Don't worry. I'm a little overwrought, that's all."

Mira nodded, averting her gaze as Rosalie dabbed at her eyes, cleared her throat, and readjusted her composure until it was only slightly askew. The first man who stepped out of the tilt was only in his thirties, a solid fellow of middle height with a round, attractive face. He had a pleasant appearance and a gentle smile, his brown hair arranged in the conspicuous style of a practiced dandy, his dark eyes glowing warmly above an absurdly small nose.

"Lord Alvanley," Rosalie murmured, giving him her hand, which he raised gallantly to his lips. Later she told Mira that Alvanley was one of the most loyal friends Beau Brummell would ever have, interceding on his behalf again and again whenever Brummell most needed help.

"Lady Berkeley. Under any circumstances it is a pleasure to see you," Alvanley said.

"Thank you, my lord. It is certainly a pleasure for me also. I would like to introduce you to Miss Mireille

Germain, my fellow conspirator and Lord Berkeley's ward."

Alvanley took Mira's hand courteously, his smile increasing in warmth. "So you are the mysterious woman being kept so closely under wraps by the Berkeleys," he murmured. "A dear friend indeed, to be trusted with such a precious secret as this meeting. But I can see every reason why Lady Berkeley has placed such confidence in you."

Mira lowered her eyes in what she hoped was an appropriately shy manner. Since Alvanley was a leading social figure in London, his approval of her was crucial: his good opinion of her would open many doors and silence some of the rumors that might be circulated about her. "I am honored to make your acquaintance," she said, glancing at him with a mixture of modesty and admiration.

"But two women alone . . ." Alvanley continued, glancing around the area disapprovingly. "This is a bad business. I confess with shame that I was too preoccupied with arranging Brummell's schedule and transportation to give a thought to your safety. Forgive me, I should not have consented to our meeting in a dangerous place such as this."

"Have no fear as to our safety," Mira reassured him hastily. "Secrecy is the most important thing to consider. I know that it is dangerous for Mr. Brummell to be in England—he is the one we should save our concern for."

Alvanley looked at her with a warm smile. "How selfless you are."

"No, not at all."

"Lady Berkeley is to be congratulated on her taste in fellow conspirators."

"So is Mr. Brummell," Mira dared to say, causing Alvanley to laugh delightedly.

Rosalie had moved forward to assist the second man out of the boat. The third, a cockney lad who had rowed the tilt, sat down with a small bag of coins weighting the pocket of his coat. He pushed the craft away from the riverbank and began to row back across the water. "Mr. Brummell," Rosalie said, the small sound of her voice surprising Mira. Dauntless, determined Rosalie, looking and sounding almost frightened as she faced the man who had sired her.

"Madam Berkeley."

They did not touch hands. They did not embrace, nor voice any of the thoughts that must have besieged their minds. They merely stood there and looked at each other with wide, identically shaped eyes.

Brummell was the picture of elegance fallen on hard times, yet there was a presence about him that could never be matched by any other man. He had a charisma which stemmed not from anything he said or did, but from the mere fact of his existence. His clothes had once been staggeringly expensive, well-cut, and faultlessly clean. His cravat was a blindingly brilliant white that shone in the light of the tin-and-glass lamp that illuminated the scene. Hair a few shades lighter than Rosalie's was brushed back perfectly, while his complexion shone with the same pale, aristocratic luster as that of his daughter. His mouth was small and shaped in a bow, a stylish mouth that betrayed a great deal of wit and latent charm, but a lack of determination and will. And if Rosalie was regarding him with a full measure of uncertainty, he was looking at her with no less.

"I . . . I have brought you a small gift, sir." Rosalie handed him a simply wrapped package that Mira knew contained a dozen Indian silk handkerchiefs.

"How thoughtful of you, my dear," Brummell replied, appearing to relax as he found himself on more familiar ground. He had no experience at conversing with his daughter, but he had much experience at receiving presents and took great delight in them. "There was no need, I assure you."

"I am never certain . . . what is available to you."

"My life has become quite desultory," Brummell responded sadly. "I enjoy none of the small pleasures that I had come to take for granted in England. But I have faith that all of that will change after this visit."

"I hope so." Rosalie paused and then added with uncharacteristic timidity, "Mr. Brummell, you know that I have many means at my disposal to help you, and if you ever need—"

"No, no . . . please," he interrupted, his eyes widening with alarm. "I would not ask anything of you, save the privilege of seeing you when it is possible." He hesitated for a few seconds, and gave her a shy smile. "How is . . . your son?"

"Christian is very bright and sweet. I am told often that he is an uncommonly handsome little boy."

"He must resemble you."

"Actually, he is more like his father, blond and charming—and very willful."

"I am not surprised. The Berkeley strain is very strong."

"But there is Brummell in him too," Rosalie said. She exchanged a smile with her father, and then there was long silence, so long that Mira felt an almost palpable awkwardness surround all of them. Throwing Lord Alvanley a quick glance, she silently implored him to do something to break the tension. He stepped forward to touch the Beau's elbow.

"Brummell, there is much business we should be about tonight. I regret that we have so little time . . . but we should be off to Threadneedle Street now. Our business must be undertaken and concluded in only a matter of hours. Before we leave, however, I would like to present Miss Mireille Germain . . . a guest of Lady Berkeley's—who will be the toast of London this Season."

Mira flushed, shaking her head. "Lord Alvanley, you are very kind, but I doubt—"

"If Alvanley says you will be the toast of London," Brummell said, taking her hand and bowing over it gallantly, "have no doubt, you will be. His approval is all that is required."

"I would not think of contradicting anything you have to say, sir," Mira said in a respectful tone, and Brummell chuckled in a pleased manner.

"You are quite charming, my dear . . . you will indeed go far." He looked at her quizzically, missing no detail of her small face. As a breeze blew in a cool gust, a long black-brown lock of hair escaped from the hood of Mira's cape and curled gently over her shoulder. Brummell spoke to Rosalie in the manner of a man long accustomed to giving advice. "She is not a typical young miss . . . that will serve her in good stead. Make certain that when the Season opens you take her to a masquerade . . . dress her in something exotic. Simple, but exotic."

"I will," Rosalie promised. Her blue eyes glistened as she looked at him. "I am glad to have met with you again. The next time, I will come to France."

"I would prefer you didn't until my circumstances are better," Brummell said, almost whispering. "Then I will have you to tea and we will have a long conversation."

'Yes. I would like that," Rosalie replied with a tremor in her voice as he clasped her hand and pressed it lightly.

"Good." Brummell let go of Rosalie's hand and gave Mira a cordial nod before turning away to straighten his gloves and coat.

"My private carriage is waiting nearby," Alvanley said to Brummell. Quickly he whispered to Rosalie, "Have your husband speak to Canning in the Foreign Office about finding Brummell a post. Perhaps that of consul in Calais. He needs it badly."

Rosalie nodded, her eyes darting to the Beau, who was so busily engaged in neatening his appearance that he had not heard a word. Then the two men walked away slowly.

"Rosalie . . . ?" Mira asked when the pair had disappeared, resting a small hand on the other woman's fine-boned shoulder in a protective gesture.

"I'm not certain what I wanted him to say." Rosalie's eyes gleamed with tears of frustration. "But whatever it was, he didn't say it. We'll never be more than strangers to each other. He looks at me with such regret in his eyes . . . regret that he doesn't know me? Or regret that I was ever born?"

Mira noticed as she accompanied her friend back to the phaeton that they seemed to have switched roles temporarily. For once, she was soothing Rosalie, instead of the other way around. "*Of course* he is very glad that you were born—how could he help but be proud of a daughter like you? He just doesn't know what to say—you yourself told me that he is frightened of confrontations and emotional scenes."

"I know." Rosalie fished around in her reticule for a handkerchief and wiped her eyes.

Intuitively Mira sensed Rosalie's need to talk about her feelings with someone far better acquainted with the situation than herself. "Your mother will understand . . . you'll be able to talk to her about it soon."

"I wish Rand were here," Rosalie said in the midst of her watery sighs. "No one could understand like he would. But I can't tell him because he would be so angry that I came here in the first place." Her face crinkled as a fresh wave of emotion overcame her, and at the same time she chuckled tearfully at the pitiful picture she must have presented. It was one of Rosalie's most endearing qualities, the ability to laugh at herself.

Mira chuckled as well. "Of course you do. We'll be back in Warwick tomorrow. And perhaps you should tell him—he wouldn't be that angry, would he?"

"Perhaps not . . ."

As they neared the phaeton, a raspy voice singed the night air. "Stop!" The two women started and turned around in unison. Outside the dim pool of light shed by the streetlamp stood a young man, perhaps only a few years older than Mira. He was dirty, lean, and shaggy. There was something unbalanced and desperate in his expression, and his face was lined from years of want. Mira had known others like him before, whose eyes had been empty of everything but hunger. In his hand shone the dull steel blade of a knife. "Take off the ridge," he said harshly.

"God in heaven," Rosalie whispered, her face blanching.

"The ridge, the fambles," he repeated impatiently, and she shook her head in confusion.

"I don't know what that means."

"Your jewelry," Mira translated softly, having been acquainted long ago with the intricacies of cant, the language of the street.

Rosalie reached up with shaking fingers to pull off her sapphire earrings, while Mira regarded the stranger silently. Much earlier this evening she had had a premonition that something like this would happen. Why had she not paid more heed to that warning voice inside? Because, she thought numbly, for the past few weeks she had given up listening to the silent promptings of her heart.

The young man directed his next words to her. "Get moving, or I'll give y'a topper!" His voice was rough with a cockney accent.

"I don't have any jewelry."

"Clouts, then."

"I don't have any of those either," Mira said, surprised to hear how calm her voice sounded when her heart was pounding so hard.

It was obvious that he was not going to take her word for it. As he opened his mouth to answer, he was distracted by the clink of Rosalie's jewelry. She held her sapphire necklace and earrings in her palm, her hand visibly trembling as she faced the young man. He looked at her in a a peculiar manner, his eyes hot and insolent.

"What do you want me to—?" Rosalie began unsteadily.

"Put them in the reader and bring it to me."

"Put them in your reticule. But don't go near him," Mira said insistently. Once either of them was within striking distance of the knife, they would both be completely at the stranger's mercy . . . and she doubted that mercy was a quality he was familiar with. Rosalie cast Mira a frightened glance before bending and tossing the reticule toward the man's feet. It landed on the pavement close to him with a metallic sound.

"Pick it up and bring it to me," he said, his eyes fastened on Rosalie's pale face.

If it had been just the money and jewelry he wanted, Mira would have done nothing. The contents of Rosalie's purse were a small price for remaining unharmed, and the Berkeleys could well afford such a small loss. But Mira recognized the look in the stranger's eyes. She had seen it many times before, and she knew what it meant. He wanted to hurt Rosalie for what she was and what she had . . . he wanted to hurt someone for the feeling of control it would give him. Slowly Mira reached inside her own purse, moving her fingertips cautiously until she felt the cool, weighted handle of a small knife. It had been a gift from Guillaume several years ago, and he had taught her how to use it. She was no expert, but she had used it before with gratifying results.

"Please . . ." Rosalie faltered.

"Now!"

The lessons from Guillaume flashed through Mira's mind. *Don't throw by the handle, throw by the blade.* She would aim for a soft spot in the body that wasn't protected by bones. In a swift movement she pulled the tiny weapon from her reticule and flung it, aiming at the base of his throat and holding her breath as it flashed through the air. Rosalie gasped. The stranger reacted automatically, twisting and knocking the missile aside with his own knife, the speed of his reaction unexpected.

"Bloody *hell*," Mira swore without thinking, and the young man glared at her.

"Little bitch!" he exclaimed, starting to walk toward her determinedly. "I'll fag y'good!"

Even as Mira began to back away, a dark shadow distinguished itself from the other shapes among the castle ruins, moving with such silent swiftness that at first Mira thought it was an animal. The young man's wrist was grasped and slammed against a solid thigh. The knife fell uselessly from his hand and clattered against the pavement. Mira blinked in amazement, watching as their rescuer put a hard fist to good use. His arm hooked through the air, and there was a snapping blow as a sickening, cracking sound split the air. That noise along with Rosalie's frightened shriek spurred Mira into action. She grasped Rosalie's arm and began to pull her into the phaeton, swearing in her panic as they were both impeded by their heavy cloaks and skirts. She froze at the sound of the newcomer's voice.

"It's all right."

Mira gasped as she realized who it was. *No, how could it be him?* She spun around and looked at him and a shudder ran down her spine. Oh God, it *was* him, and she wanted him even more than she had remembered wanting him before . . . and she would do anything, *anything* to be held by him again. A frantic urge took hold of her, to run to him and burst into tears, to burrow into the shelter of his arms . . . and yet he was looking at her as if he didn't know her; there was no recognition in his eyes.

"It's all right," he repeated quietly, walking toward them. "Is either of you hurt?"

Rosalie shook her head, gasping for breath.

"We're fine," Mira said, her eyes locked on his face. Searching for words, she made an attempt to speak and found that her voice was a shadowy remnant of its usual self. "How . . . ?" was all that she could manage, and Alec seemed to understand the multitude of questions that were invested in that single word.

"You nearly flattened my younger cousin with your phaeton as we were coming out of a tavern." His smile flashed white in the darkness as he looked at Rosalie and added, "Remarkable driving." Rosalie turned red with a mixture of embarrassment and dismay. He nodded his head respectfully to her and handed the fallen reticule to her before adding, "Knowing a little about this section of the city, I was concerned for your well-being and took the liberty of following you."

"It is a happy circumstance for us that you did." Rosalie raised a gloved hand to her cheek as if to cool its burning.

"I assume your husband does not know of your activities tonight?"

"No," Rosalie replied, not daring to look at him. "Lord Falkner, you have my word that I was not—"

"I have neither the right nor the desire to demand an explanation from you," Alec interrupted gently. "I merely wish to know if you would prefer my silence concerning what happened tonight."

"Please," Rosalie said, and blushed. "I would be very grateful."

Mira watched Alec with more than a touch of confusion. She had never seen him act this way before. Certainly he had never treated *her* as he did Rosalie, as if she were some fragile and ethereal creature that could not tolerate harshness or censure. He was quiet and gentlemanly, his voice reassuring, as if he sensed that he made Rosalie uneasy and was doing his utmost to put her at ease. So that is how he treats a woman whom he respects, Mira thought, irritated that he had not yet even acknowledged her presence.

"Excuse me," she said in a low voice, and the other two looked at her. "While you are talking, I will retrieve my knife."

"Wait," Rosalie said, growing even more flustered. "I'm so sorry—I was so upset that I did not think of introductions. Lord Falkner, this is Miss Germain, a close friend and guest of mine. Mireille . . . may I present Lord Alec Falkner."

"Miss Germain," Alec acknowledged, his mouth curving in a lazy smile as Mira refused to give him her hand.

"I . . . think we both must be quite upset," Rosalie said, making a hasty effort to cover up Mira's silent snub. "Miss Germain is very grateful for what you've done—"

"Yes," Mira could not resist saying as she detected the warm scent of brandy that clung to him, "Grateful that you were not too sodden to be of assistance to us."

Rosalie's eyes widened at the calculated rudeness of the remark. "My lord," she said uncomfortably, "what Miss Germain means is that—"

"I believe I understand what she means," Alex said dryly.

"I must look for the knife," Mira murmured, turning and walking toward the area where the prone assailant still lay unconscious.

"Allow me to assist you." Alec fell into step beside her, his eyes fastened on her rather than the ground. He wanted to shake her for the anxiety that she had caused him. A thousand words were on the tip of his tongue, yet in his heightened state of emotion he dared not say anything for fear that she would guess how much he had missed her or how much he wanted her. Mira did not say a word as they walked farther away from Rosalie and the phaeton, until she saw the thin sliver of the blade.

"There it is."

"Damned little idiot," Alec said, unable to hold back any longer. He bent and picked up the knife. Glancing back at Rosalie, he softened his tone to ensure that she did not overhear. "What did you think you were doing?" he demanded in a searing whisper. "You have no business flinging this around like a second-rate Gypsy—"

"What was I supposed to do?" Mira responded heatedly. "Tremble and faint and hope that someone would rescue us? I had no idea that *you*, of all people, were lurking in the shadows."

"You shouldn't have been here in the first place."

"Rosalie asked if—"

"Lady Berkeley is naive and too impetuous for her own good. I've known the Berkeleys ever since their marriage, and this isn't the first time she's landed herself in a bad scrape. I don't envy her husband the job of keeping her out of trouble . . . but you! You know better than to get yourself involved in something like this!"

"Don't you dare try to lecture me. You have no right to tell me what to do."

"Dammit, you need a hand taken to your backside!" Alec raked his fingers through his black hair, disrupting its sealskin smoothness.

"Give me my knife—"

"Your toy, you mean." Alec regarded the tiny blade in his hand with disgust. "What exactly did you hope to accomplish with this excuse for a weapon?"

"I was going to sink it in the hollow of his throat. I have excellent aim."

"I have no doubt that you're a wonder if your target decides to hold still for you," Alec said grimly. "But it was so slow that he had time to do a jig before knocking it away. Your arm doesn't have the necessary strength to throw this hard enough. A child could evade your—"

"Give it to me!"

"You don't understand," Alec said patiently, ignoring her demand. "You are not capable of defending yourself with this . . . and you damn well should be staying away from situations in which you would need to use it. Do you have another one?"

"No!" Mira said, holding out her hand.

"Good." Alec pocketed the knife and smiled pleasantly into her flushed face.

It took Mira several seconds to find her voice. "You arrogant bastard! You *obnoxious*, self-righteous spawn of a dog—instead of sticking your nose into *my* affairs, why don't you stick it up your own—"

"My, my, Miss Germain," he murmured solicitously, his smile deepening, "I had no idea you were so familiar with such vulgar terms of address."

"Yes, you did. I've called you worse before."

"With less reason." He laughed softly. "What a quick study you are . . . a demure society miss one moment, a little caw-handed street urchin the next."

"I am *not* caw-handed," Mira hissed, resenting the implication that she was clumsy.

"No?" His eyes traveled over her with calculating slowness. Then he saw her hands, which were trembling roughly. Alec's mouth tightened, the muscles in his jaw flexing. When he spoke, there was a hard note in his voice that she had never heard before. It wasn't anger and it wasn't concern, yet it was undoubtedly born of strong sentiment. "Don't do this again, Mira."

"What?"

"Don't take chances. There might have been a time in your life when you could afford them. But you can't any longer. Don't gamble with your safety. Do you know how many women disappear from this area each week? Do you know what kinds of things happen to them?"

"There are charleys to protect us—"

"Oh, really?" He cast an eye around the empty street. "Well, I won't worry any longer about your safety, not with such an impressive source of protection—"

"I don't need a lecture from you," Mira interrupted indignantly. He did not own her . . . he did not have the right to tell her what to do. He had no vested interest in her safety, and by not coming after her when she had left Sackville Manor, he had made it clear that she had been nothing more than a night of entertainment for him.

"Yes, you do. You can't go on flirting with disaster anymore. You need to put yourself on a tight rein . . . or if you're incapable of that, you need to find someone who'll do it for you."

"Do you know what you need? You need someone to remind you that you aren't the authority on what other people should do . . . you need someone who isn't impressed by your conceit-ridden, high-handed attitude . . . and you need someone to take you down a step or two whenever you storm around like a . . . like a second-rate Napoleon!" she finished triumphantly.

Their eyes locked together, and they were furious not only with each other but also with themselves for wanting each other so desperately. Questions filled their minds, questions that they would never ask each other.

They wondered.

They still wanted.

"Mira?" came Rosalie's anxious voice from the phaeton, and Mira tore her gaze away, walking back quickly.

"We couldn't find it," she said, and the other woman shivered slightly.

"I'm glad. I never dreamed you were carrying around

something like that in your reticule. Promise me you won't again."

"I promise."

"Would you like me to take you to wherever you're staying, Lady Berkeley?" Alec asked, helping Rosalie into the carriage. "I could tie my horse to the back of the high-flier—"

"Thank you, but I think I can manage. We're staying the night at a terrace in Red Lion Square. I can certainly drive that short distance without mishap."

"Slower this time," Alec suggested, and Rosalie smiled reluctantly at him.

Mira took Alec's outstretched hand and climbed into the phaeton, letting go of him as soon as she was settled. Her fingers tingled from the touch of his.

"One more thing," Mira said, her eyes darting to his inscrutable face. "What about the man who . . . what is going to happen to him?"

"Lord Falkner," Rosalie inquired earnestly, "should we turn him over to one of those felons associations for prosecution?"

"If you wish," Alec replied, his expression blank, his tone polite. "Which one would you prefer? The Society for the Suppression of Mendicity, or the Society for the Reformation of Manners?" Only Mira was aware of the utter mockery behind his question, and she longed to tell him what he could do with his suggestions.

"What would happen if we did turn him over to either of them?" Rosalie asked.

"He'll probably end up dangling from the end of a rope."

"Could we let him go?" Rosalie entreated. "I don't think I could bear having his death on my conscience."

"Of course," Alec replied, handing her the ribbons. He glanced at Mira. "*Au revoir.*" He slapped the horse's haunch lightly as the phaeton pulled away from the bank of the Thames. Mira fought to keep from looking back at him. *Au revoir* . . . unlike the more formal *adieu*, it implied an expectation that they would see each other again.

"You stopped to speak with him out of my hearing," Rosalie observed, her hands white with tension as she grasped the ribbons and guided the horse through the street.

"Yes," Mira replied dazedly, wondering if the past two hours had somehow been a dream.

"You seemed to be arguing."

"We had a brief exchange of words."

"Tonight was not the first time you have met."

"No. He was . . . he was a guest at Sackville's hunt. Almost everyone at that hunt knew who I was and the pretext for my presence there."

"Those things you said to him just after he came to our aid . . . Mireille, I've never seen you act so rudely! It seems to me that your acquaintance with him must be more than superficial if you—"

"I was merely upset," Mira said instantly. "I hardly knew what I was saying." She knew exactly what she had been saying. But for her own peace of mind, her past relationship with Alec would have to remain in the past, and the only way to ensure that was to pretend that nothing had gone on between them. The question was, would Alec fall in so easily with this plan?

"That's a relief," Rosalie said, sounding vaguely unconvinced. "I certainly would not have been happy to find out that you had been involved with him in any way."

Mira frowned and peered at her curiously. "You sound as if you dislike him."

"To be dreadfully honest, I'm afraid that's true. I don't like him. I appreciate what he just did for us, and I won't deny that he is a charming man when he cares to be, but . . ." Rosalie's voice nearly sank into the wind, ". . . he is not a gentleman. I have heard many things about him. He has a bad temper. Furthermore, he is not in the least straightforward . . . he will say one thing when he means another, and he seems to be a most untrustworthy man. There have been tales of his involvement in shocking scandals, even though nothing is ever proven—"

"But it would be rather hypocritical of *me* to hold a scandal against someone, wouldn't it?" Mira pointed out. As Rosalie made no reply, she added, "Are you keeping something back? Has he ever done something objectionable to you?"

Rosalie sighed uncomfortably. "I don't like the way he treats people . . . especially women. One of my friends was in love with him once—she is married now but was unattached at the time—and he did not return her affection. He could have tolerated her attentions until she tired of pursuing him—as a gentleman would have—but no, he was cruel and cold to her, breaking her heart and severely injuring her self-confidence. So he can be as sweet as treacle to me, but I'll never forget how unkind he was to my friend. He treats women as if they are disposable objects. Everyone knows it. He has never kept a mistress for more than a week—and do you know why? Because women are as convenient and meaningless to him as cotton handkerchiefs."

"I see." Mira could think of no defense to offer on Alec's behalf. The story sounded too much like him. He was capable of being kind and gentle, but also of being brutal, and he did not often tolerate the company of those he disliked.

"I just hope he doesn't say anything about what he saw tonight," Rosalie said. "I wonder if he was here when we were speaking with Brummell and Alvanley. He did not mention their names, but I wonder . . ."

"I don't really know what he saw."

"Oh," Rosalie wailed softly, "I just hate the thought that a secret of mine depends on *his* sense of honor!"

"So do I."

As the days and weeks passed, Mira's fears about Alec were completely undone by the simple and disconcerting fact that she never heard from him, not even a short note. Apparently he had forgotten about her. Strange, that the relief she would have expected to feel was absent from her heart. In a moment of honesty, she admitted inwardly that she was far from relieved. She was frustrated, despondent, and terribly disappointed. She had thought during those weeks at the Sackville hunt that she had meant *something* to him—he had seemed to need her; it had even seemed as if he had cared for her a little . . . or had she merely been a fool, easily taken in by words and empty promises?

Taking out the Falkner medallion one afternoon, Mira wound the gold chain around her wrist and held the round disk in her palm. The design of the falcon in flight was familiar to her by now: she had held the medallion often and had thought of Alec as she stared at it; she had even worn it underneath her clothes a few times for ridiculously sentimental reasons. She still did not know why Alec had given it to her, especially since it was a family heirloom. Had he wanted to give her payment for what he might have considered to be "services rendered," he could have offered her money or a gaudy piece of jewelry, but the medallion—that had been a puzzling gift indeed.

Mira had been further puzzled when, the day before Christmas, a package was delivered to Berkeley Hall by a boy who had not revealed the identity of the sender. The package had been addressed to Miss Mireille Germain, in handwriting that no one recognized. *From an admirer.* The words were written with clean, neat strokes of ink on a simple white card with no other identification. The card had accompanied the most beautiful set of books Mira had ever seen, with red morocco covers and gilded pages. All during the holidays, the Berkeley relatives and guests had made a game of guessing the identity of Mira's admirer.

The Berkeleys, all thirty-plus that had decided to stay at Berkeley Hall during the worst months of winter, were a nosy, comical, pretentious lot. One always knew what to expect of a Berkeley; they respected only those with wealth or political influence, they were fiercely protective of their own but were not above gossiping about them, loved off-color jokes but felt that it was bad taste to laugh at them. Although their veneer was genteel, the men of the family—with the exception of Rand—had earned reputations as philanderers and adulterers, while the women were "fast" and led very active social lives. The Berkeleys were an attractive lot, most of them tall, fair-skinned, and golden-haired. In reference to the proliferation of blonds around the household, Rand had informed Mira sardonically that it had been necessary to marry a brunette in order to distinguish his wife from the other women in the family.

The family gatherings were often accompanied by petty squabbles that involved everyone but Rosalie, who was the only Berkeley considered by the rest as being generally tolerable. Perhaps their affection for her was regulated by the fact that pleasing her was the only way to gain Rand's approval . . . and Rand, after all, was the head of the family . . . or perhaps it was because Rosalie was the only one who was more willing to listen to other people's troubles than to complain about her own. Whatever the reason, there was a large measure of goodwill for her, and luckily this good feeling had been extended in some part to Mira.

Very slowly and carefully Rosalie had introduced Mira to the members of the family. After several afternoons of tea, needlework, music, and gossip, after long discussions during which Mira would politely evade a slew of sly, digging questions, she was tentatively accepted into the flock. As Rosalie had instructed her, Mira never said anything about Lord Sackville, save that she had been a guest of his during the hunt. "How, exactly, are we explaining *that* away?" Mira had asked Rosalie in private, and Rosalie had momentarily worn an uncomfortable expression.

"Don't bother with that, Mireille—I've taken care of it."

"But how? And why do you look so guilty whenever I mention his name?"

"I look guilty? . . . I don't know why I should—I haven't done anything so very wrong . . . but a few sacrifices had to be made in order for your reputation to be saved."

"Sacrifices?" Mira had repeated, so suspiciously that a light blush had swept across Rosalie's cheekbones and the bridge of her nose. "Whatever story you made up—it hasn't done anything to hurt Sackville's reputation, has it?"

"Now, don't be upset. I may have stretched the truth here and there about him, but only for your sake."

Horrified, Mira had stared at her with round eyes. "It's not like you to tell an untruth about anyone or anything."

"But I will," Rosalie had said quietly, "if it's necessary to protect someone I care about."

"But Sackville's good name is so important to him! If it has been damaged in any way, I would feel responsible—"

"He took terrible advantage of you," Rosalie had said flatly, all signs of apology disappearing from her face. "Rand told me that Sackville did some boasting about you to his close friends . . . I don't want to upset you, but it was the kind of boasting that no gentleman would do, even about his . . . You understand what I'm saying. He used you to enhance his own self-importance, and in my opinion there's nothing wrong about my tearing it down to help you.''

"In what way did you tear down his reputation?" Mira asked, but Rosalie did not answer. No matter how Mira persisted, she would not say another word about Sackville. The "tearing down" Rosalie had done, however, had been clever and incredibly subtle, for it was impossible to find out what she had said about Sackville, and it had resulted in ostracism. No one ever mentioned Sackville's name; he was seldom seen and seldom heard from. Mira felt guilty whenever she thought of him; indirectly or not, she had been the cause of his misfortune . . . and she felt even worse about Rosalie, who had, on Mira's account, found it necessary to compromise her own integrity.

As a light winter snow fell gently on the thick white blanket that already surrounded Berkeley Hall, the fireplace roared with a bright, warm blaze. Mira held one of the morocco leather books in her lap and leafed through it. The room was full of Berkeleys and their languid conversation, the younger ones gossiping while the older ones reposed, made drowsy by the heat of the fire. Rosalie sat nearby, holding Christian on her lap and nuzzling his hair occasionally while he drew pictures on a frost-coated window with his finger.

"Perhaps we can find out who sent the books by looking at the titles and the authors," Wilhelmina Berkeley said as she cast a blue-eyed glance at Mira. "Would it be some kind of code?"

"I don't think so," Mira replied, sighing inwardly as she realized that once more the conversation had turned toward the identity of her "admirer." It was a subject that wearied and exasperated her, since she knew already who had sent the collection of novels. They were all works of Jane Austen, and she remembered once having talked with Alec about that particular author. But why would he have sent her the gift, and why would he have signed it "From an admirer"? He had never professed any sort of admiration for her before. Despite the questions and the uncertainties, she could not help but find pleasure in the books, for they were beautiful and smelled delightfully new.

"Are you absolutely certain," Wilhelmina pressed, "that you have not met any young man who might have sent the books to you?"

"Absolutely," Mira said firmly. As she felt someone's eyes on her, she looked up and met Rosalie's gaze. From the way Rosalie looked, acutely perturbed, it was clear that she had little idea of who had sent the novels. So far she had not asked Mira a single question about them.

"Lady Berkeley," a maid's carefully modulated voice interceded respectfully, and Rosalie was presented with a silver tray littered with calling cards and notes. There was little to do in the winter except to attend parties and pay calls to one's neighbors, and so the arrival of this tray was regarded with a high degree of interest.

"Hmmnnn . . ." Rosalie said absently, scanning a pale blue card and smiling as the room quieted. "It seems that a sleighing party is being formed for this afternoon. Lord and Lady Stamford invite us to have hot punch at their estate afterward."

Several murmurs of "It sounds delightful" and "What a splendid notion" were heard throughout the room, while Mira looked at Rosalie questioningly. Aside from mixing with the Berkeley family, she had been isolated from society parties and gatherings while the rumors of her connection with Sackville died down. Rosalie read the silent inquiry in her eyes and nodded slightly.

"I think it is a good idea," Rosalie said aloud, and although she spoke in a general manner, Mira knew that the words were meant for her. She felt a flutter of excitement in her stomach. What kind of people would she meet? What would they say to her—would they ask her about Sackville . . . would they recognize her or know that she had reputedly been Sackville's mistress?

They all departed to their rooms to begin preparations for that afternoon, and Mira tossed her clothes to and fro in her search for something to wear. The scarlet wool gown trimmed with sable would be perfect . . . but would the color be appropriate? No . . . since there were more than a few shadows on her reputation, it would not do to wear such a bold shade of red. Her pale beige gown . . . no, that color made her skin look sallow. Perhaps the blue? No, the material was not heavy enough, and she had no desire to take a chill. Frowning, Mira decided on the scarlet, and she rang for a maid to help her dress.

After her attire was completed, she buried her hands in a small sable muff and went downstairs, where many of the Berkeleys were already gathered. Small groups of four and five formed as the sleighs were being readied. Her steps slowed as she reached the bottom of the stairs, for she became uncomfortably aware that many people were staring at her. She wondered if it was her attire. Unlike the other women, she was not wearing a pelisse and concealing poke bonnet; instead she had donned a dark fur-trimmed cape with a hood that flowed softly onto her shoulders and draped in a soft, romantic style. She had no way of knowing that excitement had lent a fresh glow to her cheeks, and that the scarlet gown turned her eyes a dark autumn brown, and that suddenly, instead of a quiet and vaguely defensive girl, she was a strikingly beautiful woman.

"How charming," Wilhelmina Berkeley said, her features pale with a touch of envy. "However, this is not a masquerade, Miss Germain. Your hood and cape are lovely, but do you really think you should wear that instead of more conventional attire? I've noticed your clothes before, many times, and they are very different from the proper—"

"I appreciate your concern," Mira interrupted quietly, "but I am quite content as I am."

"I am certain you are," Wilhelmina said, her blue eyes resolute, "but if you insist on wearing something so different from the rest of us, you will be thought of as trying to secure undue attention to yourself. It is a sign of vanity, and since you and your appearance reflect on all of us, I would wish for you to keep from embarrassing us by displaying yourself in outlandish fashions."

There was complete silence in the hall. Wilhelmina would not have dared to utter such criticism of any guest, especially Mira, had Rosalie been present. But since Rosalie and her husband were still upstairs, Mira found herself in the position of having to defend herself.

"I will wear what I please, Miss Berkeley," she replied evenly. "And I trust that I will not embarrrass you today, for I have always heard that in England one's manners are more highly regarded than one's appearance. *My* manners, therefore, will be faultless."

"Bravo," came a voice from the top of the stairs, and they all looked to see Rand Berkeley escorting Rosalie down the steps. They were a handsome pair, for everything that was dainty and beautiful about Rosalie was emphasized by the blunt attractiveness of her husband. An aura surrounded Rand Berkeley, the kind that instantly commanded respect, for he was a man on whom power sat comfortably, a man who could treat the most grave matters with suitable seriousness or razor-sharp irreverence. His approval was something that everyone wanted; his disapproval was something that everyone feared. No one in his or her right mind would ever cross Rand. "Well said, Miss Germain," he continued, his golden eyes gleaming. "I must apologize for my cousin. But, as any of us can tell you, when one is a Berkeley, he often finds himself in the position of apologizing for the caprices of his family."

Mira smiled gratefully at him, knowing that his words were a subtle warning to the rest of the Berkeleys. After this, none of them would dare say anything even remotely offensive to her. She rode in the sleigh with Rand and Rosalie, her manner becoming even more animated as the three of them exchanged quips, lingering on the subject of the Berkeley family until Mira laughed helplessly.

"You look just as you did when you were fifteen," Rosalie said approvingly as Mira rested her head against the back of the seat and sighed contentedly. "Full of high spirits and eagerness."

"I do?" Mira asked, beginning to chuckle again. "Only three months ago I couldn't talk to you without tears coming to my eyes. I felt very . . ." She paused, and her expression became more thoughtful. ". . . beaten and worn. Very old. Why has everything changed now, I wonder?"

"Because you're not alone any longer," Rosalie answered simply.

"Do you always have the perfect answer?" Mira asked, smiling.

"She does," Rand assured Mira, lifting his wife's hand to his lips and kissing the back of it. "Which is why I married her."

The driver stopped the sleigh in the midst of a large assemblage of similar vehicles. Some were constructed with a third seat for the driver, whereas some were smaller and made for the gentlemen to take hold of the reins themselves. Driving oneself instead of hiring a coachman was an activity of well-established and fast-growing popularity.

The buzz and hum of enthusiastic conversation filtered out to the arriving guests. Rand helped his wife and Mira out of the sleigh and escorted them inside an enormous Palladian mansion, where they were faced with a vast assortment of well-bundled individuals who waited for the sleighs to be lined up and readied for the long ride. As Rosalie had explained to Mira, they would all form a long line and drive through the countryside, singing, talking, and laughing.

Mira looked around the crowd and did not see one familiar face. That was good. Smiling gamely, she allowed Rosalie to introduce her to several people, all of whom were kind and very pleasant. Her spirits rose as several minutes of entertaining conversation ensued. Why, these people seemed to like her! It was not that difficult to fit in here, at least superficially. She had changed. She was no longer a clumsy village girl or the shy pretend-mistress of an aging bachelor. She was young and lively, a "charming creature," as someone had pronounced her not a minute ago, a woman who wore expensive clothes with ease and could carry on a conversation about many different subjects. Her newfound confidence increased with every minute, and she became less inclined to cling to Rosalie's side.

Mira's good mood was dampened slightly as Rosalie brought over someone for her to meet, a young man by the name of Edgar Onslow. Perhaps someday he would be an attractive man, but for now he was only a nervous boy who flushed as he was introduced to her and took her hand too tightly. His hair was red, a shade that presently formed an incongruous combination with his bright pink skin.

"Mr. Onslow is such a *nice* young man," Rosalie said, obviously delighted with the situation. "Of course, Miss Germain, I knew that I had to introduce the two of you."

There was a betraying note of satisfaction in her voice, and Mira smiled weakly as it became clear that this was what Rosalie considered to be a prime candidate for a meaningful courtship. Oh, Rosalie, Mira thought wryly, tamping down a sense of panic as Edgar Onslow stared at her with obvious fascination, I know you want me to marry a nice young man who will never hurt me. But I am not as fragile as you think. I need someone I can badger every now and then . . . someone who is strong enough to take care of me . . . someone who won't let me bully him. I don't want someone who is weaker than I am.

"Goodness, I must find my husband," Rosalie said, and disappeared before Mira could utter another word.

Onslow was sweet and sincere, and possibly the most boring man Mira had ever met. She tried to involve him in conversation, but all she received in return for her artful attempts at conversation were monosyllabic answers. Either Onslow was too smitten with her to talk or he had painfully little talent with words. When it became evident that Rosalie did not intend to return and rescue her, Mira acknowledged to herself that the exciting sleigh ride she had hoped for was going to be a dull journey indeed, for there was no prospective rescue from Onslow in sight. "Miss Germain, would you care for some punch?" Onslow inquired hopefully, apparently as tense as she was at the chore of having to make conversation, and she nodded with relief.

"Thank you, Mr. Onslow."

As soon as he left her, Rosalie appeared out of nowhere and rushed over to Mira. "Did he ask you to ride in his sleigh?" she demanded, her blue eyes glowing with enthusiasm.

"We hadn't gotten to that yet," Mira replied unenthusiastically.

"And you let him go?"

"He's fetching me some punch."

"*Sacrebleu*, I'm going to follow him to make certain that no one else gets him. I saw that little minx Letty Wheaton eyeing him from the corner."

Mira was about to point out that there was hardly a line forming to compete for the charms of Onslow, but she saw how determined Rosalie was to play matchmaker. Mira sighed as the other woman set off in pursuit of the escaping prey with the intention of dragging him back. "Letty Wheaton can have him," she murmured under her breath, and then she started as she heard a soft chuckle right at her ear.

"Previously I had assumed that Lady Berkeley had faultless taste. But then, we're all entitled to a mistake once in a while."

Mira whirled around and found herself staring up at Alec Falkner. He gave her a slow grin that made her heart skip a few beats.

"She has wonderful taste," Mira managed to say in response to his remark, and the corners of his well-shaped mouth twitched in amusement.

"A red-faced boy who is so nervous around you that he'll probably end up overturning your sleigh . . . no, for the sake of our past association, I cannot allow that to happen to you."

"We have no past association," Mira informed him curtly.

Alec hesitated before replying. As he looked down at her he felt a pang of hunger, and it was not a hunger similar to anything he had ever felt before. It could be relieved only by the sight of her, the feel of her, the sound of her voice, the scent of her. It was the last thing on earth he wanted to feel for her. Love was something he could have reasoned away, talked himself out of . . . but hunger was an inescapable reality. Love was something one could ignore, replace, mourn, forget. Hunger nagged and probed, and forced its way into a man's thoughts until it was appeased. "Forgive me," he said huskily. "I had assumed your memory would be as accurate as mine when it came to such matters. Not only do I recall having enjoyed a past association with you, I remember having shared a certain number of intimacies—"

"Hush. *Please!*" Mira begged, looking around in the fear that someone would overhear. "Don't be so ill-mannered as to bring that up. And you dare to criticize that Onslow boy—I suppose you think I'd be better off riding in a sleigh with someone like you."

"That is exactly what I think," Alec replied.

Shocked into silence, Mira looked into his gray eyes. There was no ridicule there, no mockery. She realized that he was asking her to ride with him, and that she had no idea how to answer.

She had more reason than ever not to trust him.

She was so desperately in love with him.

All it would take was a simple refusal. Falkner would not plead with her to accept, and she did not think that he would ask again. He grinned at her expression of indecision, and as she stared at him, Mira could not help smiling back. It was impossible for her to refuse the opportunity to be with him. You're mad, she told herself. You deserve everything you get from now on, because you're begging for trouble!

"I accept your invitation," she said to Alec, and her eyes danced with sudden laughter. "But if we don't hurry and leave, Rosalie will drag Onslow back, and then I'll have to go with him and listen to all of his schoolroom adventures."

"Poor brat," Alec murmured sympathetically, and grinned again as he held out an arm for her to take.

9

After Mira took Alec's arm, they crossed through the hall and walked to the doors. Within a few seconds Mira was aware that they had attracted an inordinate amount of attention. Although she was the subject of a few stares, it was mainly Alec that people were watching. There were few men like him, who could command the attention of the whole room so effortlessly; it was impossible not to notice him. It was exciting just to be near Alec . . . he was handsome, quick-witted, he had an audacious smile, his moods could change with dazzling speed. It was difficult to predict what things he would take seriously and what he would jeer at, but that only make him more attractive. As he escorted Mira outside, she wondered at his apparent indifference to the multitude of gazes.

"Do you attract this sort of interest wherever you go?" she asked wryly.

"Of course I do. Haven't you heard? I'm one of a limited selection of bachelors this year, indecently high on the list of preferred catches. They won't stop staring, or pursuing, until I'm trussed up and readied for marriage like a chicken for the pot."

"Perhaps I should free you so you can accompany someone more desirous of your company. I have no intention of trying to 'catch' anyone."

"How interesting. My impression was that you were here for precisely that reason. And with Lady Berkeley as your champion, you stand to do very well.

Edgar Onslow aside, it should be fascinating to see whom she finally maneuvers to the altar with you."

"She's not going to *maneuver* anyone . . ." Mira said, and made a wordless exclamation before adding. "I had forgotten how disagreeable you are!"

"I haven't forgotten a thing about you."

"Including my taste in reading material . . . or wasn't it you who sent the books?"

He made no reply as he helped her into the sleigh. A footman placed heated bricks on the floor of the vehicle for her to rest her feet on, and a thickly woven blanket was draped over her knees. Shivering a little in pleasure from the warmth and snugness of the sleigh, Mira buried her hands more deeply in her muff.

"Are you cold?" Alec inquired gently, and she shook her head.

"The books . . . ?" she reminded him.

"Do you like them?"

"Of course I like them. I just don't . . . I don't like feeling obligated to you."

"You're not obligated to me," he said casually. "Not for a few scraps of leather and paper."

"You wrote 'From an admirer' on the card," she commented, her eyes questioning, and he shrugged.

"I do admire you." He spoke so lightly that there seemed to be no real meaning behind the words at all. "No matter what happens, you're the kind who will land on your feet . . . and you have a talent for making friends with those who can help you the most."

"That doesn't sound very complimentary."

"Doesn't it?" he asked lazily. "I meant it to be."

The first few sleighs began to skim over the thick, well-packed snow, the bells on the horses' bridles providing a merry chorus to the thrashing hooves. Contrary to Mira's expectations, the sleighs did not travel in a single line; there were too many antics going on that prevented any sort of organization from imposing itself on the large group. A few of the young men made a game of passing each other despite the protests of their female passengers. Several sleighs tried to lag suspiciously far behind the others, leaving little doubt in anyone's mind about what the occupants intended. Stolen kisses and other quickly taken liberties were far from uncommon during a sleighing party.

Just in front of them, a young man with auburn hair caught a small clump of snow that had been kicked up by the horse's hooves and surreptitiously dropped it down the neck of the girl beside him, eliciting squeals of indignation. Mira chuckled and glanced at Alec.

"Who it that?"

"Spencer Whitebrook," he replied, his eyes twinkling. "A lad about your age . . . locally famed for his original approach to the art of courtship."

"Ah . . . now I am forewarned. I will tell Rosalie not to consider him as a good prospect."

"Before you start crossing names off the list, you should realize that you don't have a wide range of choice—now wait, let me finish before you give me that freezing stare. It's not because of you—God knows that you have enough of what it takes to attract a man—it's just that there's an unusually limited supply of marriageable young men this year."

"Which must explain why you're considered to be one of the prime catches."

Alec raised an eyebrow. "Are you implying, Miss Germain, that if there were more eligible bachelors around, I might not be so high on the list?"

"Definitely somewhere in the middle."

"You've wounded me deeply," Alec said, laughing softly. "Why such a poor opinion of me? I've been told occasionally that I'm quite tolerable."

"Sometimes you are. Sometimes you are a great deal more than tolerable . . . but sometimes you are a great deal *less* than tolerable."

"Wouldn't you say that averages out fairly?"

"No . . . because you are less than tolerable more than half the time."

"Before I decide that you're a great deal less than charming, why don't you tell me how living with the Berkeleys suits you?"

"It suits me very well, thank you."

"So demure . . . so ladylike . . . you've been spending too much time with Lady Berkeley. Tell me the truth—you've dared to before."

"Yes, I've told you the truth before . . . and you waited exactly twelve hours before betraying my confidence!"

Alec was not in the least disconcerted by her accusation. "There were extenuating circumstances. The fact that he was handling you like a Fleet Street doxy in front of me was one of them."

"Don't use that as an excuse for telling Sackville that you knew his secret! It wasn't your right to do so. You bullied it out of me in the first place, but I lacked enough common sense to realize that you would use it against Sackville when it suited you. It was dishonorable and—"

"Don't bring up the subject of honor in reference to any of it," he said softly, throwing her a swift warning glance. "I don't value honor lightly, my petite friend, and I regret the fact that so far it has had no place in any of my dealings with you. Of all the qualities you seem to inspire in men, honor is not one of them, nor honesty. I know exactly what I did, and what Sackville did, and the reasons why."

"You're looking at me as if I'm the one to blame for everything," she said, her brown eyes narrowing. He was as aggravating as ever—but what a relief it was to be able to talk to someone so freely! He was the one man in the world to whom she could say almost anything she liked. They had a common understanding, born of the intimacy they had shared, that enabled her to talk with him in a way she would never attempt with someone else, not even Rosalie. "It's convenient for you to blame me for the way you and Sackville behaved, but I would have expected more justice from you."

"Now why," Alec inquired dryly, "would you have expected that?"

"Because you wouldn't dare have the gall to judge me when you're so much more unscrupulous than I am."

Alec chuckled. "Point taken."

"Good. Then I would prefer not to talk about this any longer."

"You were the one who brought it up."

"We were talking about the Berkeleys," Mira said, making an effort to steer the conversation in another direction. She did not want to spend their time together exchanging recriminations.

"Yes, and you were telling me what you thought of them. Are they treating you well?"

She looked at him quickly, surprised at the tone of his voice. He almost sounded concerned . . . but his expression was bland as he met her eyes. "They're treating me well," she replied, "but aside from the earl and Lady Berkeley, I find them all very . . ."

"Judgmental?"

"Yes, that's exactly it. Whenever Rosalie's not around, they seem to go out of their way to find fault with me."

"If that's all, you're doing well. The Berkeleys are known for being that way. They don't reserve their criticism for anyone in particular, they hand it out to everyone."

"Well, it's comforting to know that I'm not alone. But it's difficult to live with them."

"Count your blessings. I belong to the Falkner

family—they're even worse than the Berkeleys. Falkners love to argue and harp on each other's faults, and they all have fearsome tempers."

"Like yours?"

"Much worse than mine. I'm the meek one of the family."

Mira laughed. "*Dieu*, you've actually managed to frighten me with that remark. Where do these formidable tempers come from?"

"My father. He was the hotheaded one, while my mother has always prided herself on being cold and practical. She's become slightly mellowed with age, but in her youth she was the most hard-hearted woman in England."

"Then how did it happen that she married a man like your father?"

"He wore her down with his persistence. She finally relented after a particular incident at the medieval tournament, which was held in Staffordshire about thirty years ago. It was a grand production sponsored by Edward Penrhyn, who had always shown a great interest in medieval history and fancied himself a modern-day knight. At the tournament there were to be jousting and mock skirmishes, authentic costumes and traditions . . ."

"Jousting? Wasn't that rather dangerous, even at a mock tournament?"

"It depends on how involved one became with the game, I suppose. Penrhyn was enthusiastic about the idea because of his interest in two things. History was one of them."

"And the other?"

"An elusive and strong-minded woman . . . my mother, Juliana Penrhyn."

"Penrhyn . . . they were related?"

"Cousins. After the death of her first husband, Juliana had decided to marry again, and she had set her sights on Edward. It would have been a perfect match. But John Falkner, a local youth, had decided that *he* wanted her, and he pursued her relentlessly. She would have nothing to do with him."

'Why not?"

"My father was four years younger than she was, and hot-tempered. My mother has an icy nature, and the mix was not what she considered to be a good one. And John was the duke's second son, which meant that he would never have a title or money."

"But which man did she love?"

"She loved my father," Alec considered after a thoughtful pause, "but she didn't intend to let that change her decision to marry Edward. She was not a romantic."

"Impossible," Mira said firmly. "I haven't yet seen a woman who isn't a romantic at heart, no matter how well she conceals it."

"You haven't met Juliana."

Mira shook her head and smiled. "Getting back to the tournament . . . ?"

"There was a crowd of seventy thousand people attending, including the king and the royal family. My father signed up on the list to compete in the jousting as the Knight of the White Rose. He would ride against the man who was most favored to win the tournament—the Knight of the Red Lion."

"Who must have been Juliana's cousin Edward."

"Exactly. Juliana sat in the covered grandstand to watch the jousting. She was elected Queen of Beauty, which meant that she would place a wreath on the winner's head. After several runs and a few well-placed hits with a blunt lance, Edward bested my father and won the tournament. So Penrhyn was the victor of the day, while my father lay on the field with a slightly injured arm and gravely wounded pride."

"Did Juliana go to him?" Mira inquired softly.

"As my aunts tell the tale, she knelt by him on the

ground and promised him heaven and earth. She thought he was badly hurt, you see, and perhaps even feared that the was going to meet an early demise on her account." Alec chuckled as he envisioned the scene. "Lord, I would have loved to see it."

"Playing sick seems to be a particular talent among the men in your family," Mira observed dryly.

"It worked," he pointed out. "Their engagement was announced at the ball and banquet that night."

Mira grinned. "I think that despite what you say, your mother is a romantic."

"Not as much as you are."

Though she tried to ignore his teasing smile, it sent a flicker of warmth through her. "There is one thing I don't understand," she said. "How did you receive the title if your father was only the second son?"

"My oldest uncle died before siring any children. My father was killed in a riding accident about ten years ago."

Mira nodded silently, and then she realized that during their conversation Alec had slowed the horse's pace until they were at the very end of the line of sleighs. "Why are we going so slowly? Is the horse tired?'

There was a devilish gleam in his eyes, a gleam that she mistrusted. "We're taking a shortcut."

"You haven't asked for my permission."

"I told you once—I don't like to ask for permission."

"What kind of shortcut?"

"Everyone is driving around the outskirts of the woods along the loop that leads back to the Stamford estates. We're going to cut through that path . . . right through there . . . and join up with them on the other side."

"Listen well, my lord. *You* may be willing to take chances with *your* reputation, but I—"

"I told you once to call me Alec—"

"Many things have changed since then."

"—and no one will notice our absence."

"Rosalie will!"

"Do you think she'll say anything about it if she does notice?" Alec asked, and clicked to the horse. "Not unless she's willing to risk having the story of her meeting with Brummell spread all over London."

"You'd actually blackmail her?" Mira demanded, clutching the edge of the sleigh as it coursed smoothly and quickly away from the others.

"I prefer to think of it as exchanging my silence for hers."

"You are a scoundrel! No wonder she said you . . ."

"I what?" Alec prompted, grinning as she sputtered into silence. The sleigh sped past pine trees glistening with icicles. "Never mind, I can guess. I make her uneasy, don't I? She doesn't trust me—"

"Obviously she has excellent instincts.'

"—and she doesn't want me around her poor lamb. Poor defenseless Mira, who carries such interesting toys in her reticule."

"I don't anymore."

"No daggers today?"

"No!"

"It makes no difference," he said, and stopped the sleigh at the edge of the woods. "You can wound with your words far more deeply." The stillness of the winter forest was broken by the crackling of ice and branches. It was a world suspended in time, brittle and beautiful.

"They can't wound you. My words merely glance off you like blunted arrows," she replied, her voice hushed in the quiet surroundings. Alec shook his head, his smile fading. Suddenly he was serious and tender, and he was staring at her as if he had just realized something he had not understood before.

"Not at all. They strike and sink in deep, and resist my efforts to pull them out."

"Alec," she whispered, "I'm afraid I don't believe you."

"Your voice is shaking. You aren't afraid, are you?"

"I'm cold."

"I won't hurt you." He leaned closer, tracing the curve of her jaw with a gloved fingertip.

Her eyelashes fluttered downward at the smooth, cool touch of leather on her skin, and anticipation held her motionless as he bent his dark head.

His mouth touched hers, and his lips were warm and slow . . . the sweetness of the kiss seared through her deeply. Their bodies were separated by layers of thick clothing, and all Mira could feel was that hot, intimate kiss burning into her mouth so gently, so persistently. It had been so long, so long since she had felt cherished. He made her feel special, he made her feel as if she were the only woman in the world he wanted. There was a sensual twisting inside of her, and a strong throbbing . . . her thoughts became confused, and everything faded except him as she responded to him blindly.

As she took a shivering breath, the bitter freshness of winter air filled her nostrils. Needing to be closer to him, she drew her hand from her muff and lifted her fingers to his cheek. The masculine abrasiveness of his skin was there against her fingertips, and her palm curved tenderly around the hard edge of his jaw as she savored the freedom of touching him. His arm tightened around her back . . . craving the taste of her, Alec slanted his mouth across hers and sought her tongue with his, their lips fused together tightly, until Mira was too overwhelmed to bear it any longer and turned her face away with a gasp.

"Why did you leave Hampshire without a word to me?" he murmured, his breath soft and warm in the fragile indentation behind her jaw. There was a trace of bewilderment in his tone, and something else she didn't understand. Mira closed her eyes as she remembered the pain of the day she had left Sackville Manor.

"You gave me no alternative," she said woodenly. "The Berkeleys were there, offering to take me with them. And Sackville had asked me a few days before that to leave."

"You didn't tell me that."

"Would it have made a difference if you had known? You made no promises to me, ever. You didn't offer me any way out of the situation I was in, not even after the night we . . ."

"You knew that all you had to do was ask me for help," Alec said quietly, pulling away from her and staring at her intently. "I would have given you a place of your own, if that was what you wanted—"

"—if I would have consented to be your mistress." Mira smiled bitterly. "And fool that I was, I probably would have accepted. But I wouldn't now, not for a palace, not for any amount of money at all. I've changed since then, and I've begun to see that I want more than you could ever offer me."

He gripped her upper arms, his gloved hands like steel vises covered with velvet. "What do you expect me to offer you?" he demanded with a sudden flare of anger, his voice hard with frustration. "You know what kind of position I'm in . . . you know about the responsibilities I have to shoulder. God . . . I still want you—you can't help but know that—but I'm a *Falkner*. I'm the firstborn son. I have to take care of the rest of the family, and someday I have to produce suitable heirs to carry my name. If you were someone different . . . if I were someone different . . ."

"I understand," Mira said quietly, feeling frozen inside. "I understand all of that."

"Then for God's sake, would you try to consider accepting what I *can* give you? I can give you everything, everything but my name. I could make you happy—"

"No, you couldn't," she interrupted swiftly. "You might have been able to once, but not now. It isn't your fault . . . it's just that everything's changed. I don't need beautiful clothes or spending money to make me happy. I don't need theater tickets and balls. I don't need passion. I don't want to be dazzled. All I want is a quiet life and a family of my own—I will do my best to get that, and maybe if God is willing I'll succeed. I don't understand why I came with you today. I know I shouldn't have. Rosalie was right: I would have been far better off with someone like Onslow." She felt him stiffen beside her as she continued. "After we join up with the others and arrive at the Stamford estate, I don't want to talk to you again. I don't want to see you again. Fortunately I won't be attending more than one or two more parties until the spring, so all I ask is that you make the same effort that I will to avoid being near each other."

"That would be for the best," Alec agreed with cold politeness, and flicked the reins neatly to join the passing convoy of horses and vehicles. Mira sat as far away from him as possible during the long, cold ride back. They did not exchange another word, not even as Alec helped her out of the sleigh and into the mansion with the other guests. When she was safely inside, he left her and did not even glance at her for the rest of the afternoon.

"I am sorry," Mira said to Rosalie as soon as they had an opportunity to speak to each other. Her voice rang with a sincerity that dissolved any reprimands that Rosalie might have intended to deliver. "I made a terrible mistake. I shouldn't have gone with him. You were right."

"It gives me no pleasure to be right," Rosalie replied, staring at her with searching blue eyes. "Not when you look so rueful about it."

The winter did not pass as slowly as Mira had feared

it might. She found more than enough activities to occupy her time, not the least of which was tending the various illnesses that cropped up among the guests and the tenants of the Berkeley estates. The cold air was infused with a damp that seemed to sink through clothes and skin down to the very bones, and even the hottest soup, the strongest spirits, and blazing fires did little to warm the body after being outside for more than a few hours. Luckily the kitchens were well-stocked with dried plants and herbs that Mira used to treat the rounds of colds, coughs, joint aches, sore throats, and earaches.

She made flax poultices and crushed eryngo plants to use their juice in a recipe for eardrops. She used gerardia and germander to make a lotion that eased the pain of arthritis, rheumatism, and gout. For swelling of the ears, throat, and neck, she made hot poultices of boiled barley, fleawort, honey, and oil of lilies. All of her recipes and remedies were in constant demand; the weather was relentless.

However, only one week of that frosty winter was truly unbearable for everyone situated near or on the Berkeley lands, and that was the week in March when Rosalie was ill. It was merely a bad cold and a touch of fever, and yet Rosalie's illness threw the entire schedule and organization of Berkeley Hall into disarray. The worst problem was Rand; when visiting his sniffling, feverish, red-nosed wife, he was tender and gentle, but when she was napping or out of hearing distance, he was so moody and irritable that no one dared approach him. Mira observed this with well-concealed sympathy and humor, knowing from past experience that Rand could not bear it when anything threatened Rosalie's health or happiness.

"You must get well very, very soon, Rosalie," she said late one afternoon, bringing a cup of hot liquid to the Berkeleys' bedchamber. Rosalie made a face as she stretched out a hand and received the cup.

"What is in here? More of your ghastly herbs?"

"Tea and honey."

"Oh, praise heaven . . ." Rosalie took a deep swallow of the sweet tea and sighed in pleasure. "Now, tell me why I must be up and about so soon. I've rather enjoyed the past day or two of leisure."

"Your husband is becoming unmanageable."

"Really? I thought he'd been extraordinarily sweet."

"To you," Mira said, and chuckled. "Don't pretend ignorance—you know how he's been to everyone else. The walls aren't *that* thick."

"My poor Randall," Rosalie said softly, giggling and sneezing. "He grumbles a little, but he really doesn't mean to make everyone—"

"Don't make excuses for him. Just get rid of your cold as soon as possible . . . He's terrifying the lot of us."

"Poor Mira." Rosalie looked at her speculatively, frowning. "You look a little thinner, and I don't like that at all. You have spent all of your time taking care of others, and that was not my purpose in bringing you here. You need to rest much more . . . and have you been eating?"

"The Season is still a month or two away—don't worry, I'll be in presentable condition by then."

"Don't joke about it. In another month we will start to pay calls and undergo the social rounds in earnest, and I don't want you to be tired or overextended. You look as though you've been pining for someone."

"Pining," Mira scoffed, soothing her hands over her bangs in a nervous gesture. "Over whom? Edgar Onslow?"

"I wish you were. Because *that* would be a problem easily solved."

"I'm not pining for anyone," Mira said gruffly.

"Something is bothering you."

"The same thing is bothering me—the same thing

that has bothered me for weeks." Mira sat on the foot of the bed and rubbed the side of her face against the velvet hangings absently, letting a gold-fringed tassel trail over the bridge of her nose. "The Season's going to begin soon, and finally I've come to the realization that I've run out of parts to play," she said softly, closing her eyes and sighing. "I've never played any one of them especially well . . . I've become more and more of an impostor, until I no longer feel comfortable doing *anything*. None of it feels right any longer. Where and how am I going to belong anywhere—?"

"But you belong somewhere already," Rosalie said anxiously. "You belong here."

"I am welcomed here. But this is your home and your family."

"You will have a home and family of your own someday," Rosalie insisted. "Then you won't have cause to worry about where you belong."

Mira smiled wistfully, opening her eyes and regarding Rosalie quizzically. "Do you really think marriage is the answer?" she asked. "I don't. It will merely be a new role for me to work on, and I'm terrified that I'm going to fail at it . . . but there's nothing else I can do." Marriage was simply a ceremony . . . and although it was intended to join two people in an everlasting bond, she knew that no ritual, pronouncement, or ceremony on earth could dispel the sense of apartness she felt. Marriage would not change her, nor would it change the inner certainty that she would not fit into any one kind of life.

"I don't understand your fixation with roles and parts," Rosalie said, bewildered. "You're not playing a part, you're living your own life."

"I've lived several lives so far, when all I wanted was just one." She rubbed her forehead tiredly. "Oh, how old, how *shopworn* I am going to feel next to those girls of seventeen and eighteen. They know nothing of the world, but still they know what their places are in it. They already know who they are and exactly what they are supposed to do. They're so wonderfully conventional . . . I envy them."

"I don't think that you can define yourself by conventional standards."

"But everyone else will judge me by conventional standards. Don't you see? This is all wrong—it's wrong to try to pretend that I belong in your world, it's wrong for me to sneak in through a side door and take a place next to someone who has been born to all of this. Can't we just find some kind of employment for me somewhere? Somewhere safe, somewhere quiet, where no one will notice."

"You wouldn't be any happier that way," Rosalie said stubbornly. "And if what you say is true, and you really don't belong anywhere, then you might as well fall in with my plans for you—you're just as suited to marry a baron as you are to marry a baker."

"Isn't that a slight exaggeration?"

"You're not a conventional person. You have your own rules and your own ways of thinking and feeling. You are far more beautiful than those girls you profess to envy, far more interesting and worthy of love than they are. You're . . ." Rosalie sighed and looked at her helplessly. "You're Mireille Germain . . . you're many different things . . . you're . . . a little bit of everything. And there's no way to change that."

Mira was silent for a long time, turning the words over and over until they made a peculiar kind of sense to her. With the innate practicality that had been bred in her through many generations of Frenchwomen, she began to see how useless it was to regret what she could never be. She was what she was, and as Rosalie had pointed out, there was nothing she could do to change it. Would it be so difficult to make the best of the situation? And was there really any other choice?

"So I am," she said to Rosalie with a tired smile.

"Yes, I am Mireille Germain . . . and I suppose there are worse things to be, aren't there?"

"So you've brought a summons from Juliana," Alec said, looking up from his desk. Carr walked into Alec's terrace rooms, straightening the jaunty knot of his cravat. The room in which Alec worked was simple and Spartan in design, decorated with the pleasant symmetry of an Egyptian motif. A wide mahogany desk was braced between two fretted windows. Alec had spent many hours working there, either on his architectural designs or the family bills, accounts, and interests both domestic and international. He had assumed such responsibilities ever since he had been eighteen and had grown accustomed to wielding complete control and power over the Falkner estates and properties.

"She's your mother," Carr said reasonably, daring to lean against the desk and fix Alec with an ingratiating smile. "She likes to see you every now and then . . . and especially after the last time you visited . . . what was it, three months ago?"

"Two months."

"Whenever it was, she wasn't pleased. She said you looked like a damned Frenchie, pale and thin—"

"'Have you finally been reduced to carrying my mother's messages back and forth for pocket money?'" Alec growled. "Don't you have anything better to—?"

"Come to think of it, you do look better. You've filled out again and your color's good."

"When I want a diagnosis, I'll send for a physician."

Alec knew that his appearance had been distinctly unhealthy the last time he had visited the Falkner estates. A few weeks of dissipation and unrestrained drinking tended to do that to a man. After the disturbing episode with Mira during the sleighing party, he had disappeared to London for a month, drinking heavily in order to drown the thoughts and the insatiable longing for her from his mind. He had spent each night at Brooks's, gambling with his cohorts until the early-morning hours, going to bed when daylight broke through the sky, rising in late afternoon. No matter how extreme his exhaustion was, he could never rid his sleep of the dreams he sought to escape. His face had become pale, his eyes glittery and unsmiling, his mouth harsh with discontent.

But as winter ended and spring began, he had taken a look at himself and been filled with self-disgust. He was no Byron, to moan and sigh over a woman who would not have him. He had never been given to prolonged fits of melancholy, nor the lazy dissipation of a dandy, and he had changed back into something approaching his old self. He had cut his drinking down to a small fraction of what it had been, and once again he had taken up frequent riding. He began to mix with a better crowd than the gamblers and dandies at Brooks's. When he went to the club, it was usually for dinner, not betting. Now he was hard and fit again, and the outer difference was noticeable. If only it were possible to work such a change within himself as well as without. He could not lie to himself by pretending that any other woman could substitute for her.

"You can tell Mother I'll come to the country and visit her this weekend."

"She'll be overjoyed," Carr said, and grinned cheekily, his green eyes glowing.

"Anything else?" Alec asked, picking up a clean quill and tracing an invisible design on his thumb with it.

Carr's smile changed, became guarded and more than a little defensive. "Yes. I wanted to ask you a question. I was talking to Jules Wyatt the other day— you know, the tall one who always followed Holt around and tried to imitate—"

"I remember."

"I've been asking questions here and there. Nothing specific, I'm just curious about a few things. I was talking to Wyatt about Holt . . . you know, remembering the old days . . . and Wyatt mentioned something that I never knew about Holt before."

Alec's silver gaze sharpened. "What did he say?"

"That before he died Holt had been seeing a young woman, a girl named Leila, who was very important to him. Wyatt said that Holt was wild about her. Holt never mentioned her to me, and usually he never failed to brag about his romantic conquests. But it sounded as if this girl had cast some sort of spell over him—Wyatt implied that Holt had even talked about marrying her."

"Yes," Alec said, shrugging carelessly. "But who gives a damn now?"

"I do. What was her last name? Do you know it? Did he ever tell you?"

"I don't remember. What is so important about her?"

"According to Wyatt, Leila disappeared a week before Holt died. I mean *disappeared*, as if she had been wiped off the face of the earth. As if she had never been born." Carr frowned, visibly perturbed by his train of thought. "If I could just find out what happened to her, I know it would explain why Holt was murdered. I feel it in the marrow of my bones!"

Alec stared at him transfixed. For once he found that he could not disregard his young cousin's words; he sensed that there was something important about Leila's supposed disappearance in connection with what had happened to Holt. "Leila Holburn," he said softly.

"Holburn. Are you . . . are you certain?" Carr asked, stuttering in excitement.

"Yes, I'm certain. I never saw or met her. But he talked about her to me incessantly."

"I've got to find her family . . . talk to them—maybe she's been found now, or perhaps they could tell me—"

"No." Alec settled back in his chair, propping his boots up on the desk and studying his feet thoughtfully. "I will." His authority had been established so firmly and for such a long time that no male in the Falkner family, not even Alec's own uncles, dared to question his decisions. But unexpectedly he raised his gray eyes to Carr's face and continued slowly, ". . . if you have no objections."

Carr blinked, obviously startled. Alec was inviting comment, disagreement, questions. Previously it had been a privilege granted only to Holt, and Carr was well aware of it. "No, I don't mind," he said, but was unable to resist adding, ". . . if you'll let me join you."

To Carr's relief, the other man laughed shortly. "Why not?" Alec found that he didn't mind his cousin's company as much as he once had. Carr was very different from Holt, but he had a kind of foolhardy courage that Alec was beginning to find quite likable.

"I had begun to wonder," Juliana said frostily, "what had become of you."

Alec smiled and bent to kiss her cheek. She turned her face away regally so that his lips merely brushed the air, but her coolness did not disturb him—it had been expected. There were some things about his mother that would never change. Although her metallic blue eyes had dimmed with age, they were still razor-sharp with intelligence and will. Juliana was the only person Alec had ever known who never worried about whether or not she was right: she *knew* she was right and that anyone who failed to agree with her was distinctly in the wrong. Juliana had admitted only once in her life that she had been wrong, and the admission had been dragged out of her by John Falkner when he convinced her to marry him instead of Edward Penrhyn. But even then she considered that she had been right to admit her mistake, which surely canceled out the original *faux pas*.

The greatest praise that she had ever given Alec was to admit that he favored her more than he did his father. Her younger son Douglas was much more like John Falkner had been—sweet-natured, friendly, perhaps even complacent . . . content and at times self-deprecatory. Although she had sincerely loved her husband, Juliana held none of these qualities in high esteem, for none of them had helped her to become one of the most powerful and influential women of her time. She forced people to compete for her approval, to work for her affection, to earn her regard. In her opinion, the most valuable weapon anyone could possess was the ability to make others want him or her. There was no one like bristly, vigorous Juliana, who could manufacture and engineer everything except motherly tenderness.

"Carr told me that you—"

"Carr," Juliana snorted, reaching for the cup of tea on the Sheraton tripod table next to her. "I'm surprised that he managed to deliver the message to you. Flighty boy, no substance to him. But that's only to be expected when a Falkner marries a Falkner." Alec's Uncle Hugh had married a distant Falkner cousin, a mixture which Juliana had always predicted would produce simpleminded children. After having observed Holt's recklessness in the past and Carr's budding irreverence, she concluded that the evidence supported her original conclusion. "Why are you standing so far away?" Juliana suddenly demanded, squinting at Alec and pointing to the elaborately adorned settee nearby. "Sit here so I can see you."

"I'm not standing far away," Alec said gently, sitting where she indicated. Juliana's eyesight was failing, a fact she refused to acknowledge. She inspected him gravely and then nodded in approval.

"I see you listened to my lecture the last time you visited."

"I listen to all of your lectures."

"Now you look like a son of mine again . . . healthy, strong—it's that good Penrhyn blood coming to the fore again."

"It must be," Alec agreed matter-of-factly, his eyes flickering with amusement.

"You may look like a Falkner, but your spirit comes from *my* family, and no matter what happens, it will always prevail." Juliana lowered her voice conspiratorially. "And though I've always contended that intermarrying is bad for the blood, I wouldn't mind adding a little more Penrhyn stock to the pot. Have you seen my niece's daughter Elizabeth lately? She has become quite an attractive—"

"I'm not going to marry a Penrhyn," Alec said firmly. "Nor a Falkner, for which I'm certain you will be thankful. In fact," he added dryly, "I'm considering the prospect of remaining a bachelor all of my life."

"Nonsense. I want you married, and what's more, married soon."

"Any particular reason?"

"You're twenty-eight, three years older than your father when he married me."

"But you didn't marry my father until you were twenty-nine," Alec said with silken innocence.

"Provoking boy—you won't succeed in diverting my attention this time, for I mean to have my say."

"I wouldn't dare attempt to dissuade you."

"For the past few years I've watched you sail through each Season without dropping anchor. I have seen for myself these giggling ninnies you've shown occasional interest in, and it would turn my stomach to call any of them my daughter-in-law."

Alec cleared his throat and looked faintly amused. "I see you've decided to speak frankly."

"You are too stubborn and too proud to court the kind of woman who would suit you best—a woman like me. These gilt-haired, simpering girls—all very popular, of course . . . and naturally you always skim them off the top. But a diet of cream and no milk is harmful to the digestion. I hope you understand what I am explaining to you."

"You object to my taste in women," Alec stated, and adopted an expression of polite interest as his mother responded spiritedly.

"I object most strenuously. All surface. No heart, no spirit, no strength. You would crush any one of them without intending to, and then she would be of no use to you."

"I appreciate your maternal concern," he said, smiling at her with warm gray eyes. "But somehow I doubt that you will ever be satisfied—"

"I'll be satisfied," Juliana interrupted, "when you choose your women with the same discretion that you choose your horses and liquor."

Alec laughed, throwing his dark head back and then regarding her with the remnant of a smile playing carelessly on his mouth. "I'll make you a promise. This Season, I give you leave to find someone whom you consider suitable for me. If for no other reason than to satisfy my curiosity about what kind of feminine baggage you would approve of. And I will give your candidate due consideration. My only condition is that she be neither Penrhyn nor Falkner . . . and keep in mind that I prefer blonds."

"Blonds," Juliana muttered. "Egad, men are loathsome creatures. Every last one of them, including my own sons."

Brighton Pavilion looked like a temple erected solely for the purpose of pursuing and celebrating all the different kinds of pleasure that the senses could experience. It was a multiheaded monster, a conglomeration of exotic architectural styles that bewildered the eye. Part of the building was Greek, part of it Egyptian, part Chinese, while the huge central dome was Turkish. It had been designed by John Nash and constructed at an exorbitant price, all to suit the whim of King George. Adorned with palm trees, dragons, and strange inverted funnels, the Pavilion gave Mira a sense of wonder and unease. She felt as if they were entering some sort of palatial harem.

"You will adore this place," Rosalie said, her face radiant with excitement as they walked through the Chinese gallery and looked up at the green-and-gold dragons that leered down at them from the ceiling.

"Yes," Rand Berkeley added, his golden eyes gleaming wickedly as he escorted the two women past a row of Oriental colonnades. "Tasteless but amusing."

"There is always something going on," Rosalie continued animatedly. "Water parties, auctions, suppers and banquets, concerts, balls, theatricals . . ."

"I'm already exhausted," Mira said, but she smiled as she spoke, anticipating all the new sights and sounds she would experience at the Pavilion during the next few days. They stopped to admire a wall painted with delicately scrawled Oriental designs.

"And there is always music playing, for the king is passionate about it and has a private band that performs every morning and evening."

"I can scarcely wait to see him," Mira confessed, having heard so many tales about King George that she knew not what to believe about him. Stout and brilliantly attired, he was reputed to have the most perfect deportment and the most elegant bow in all of England. During their conversation on the long ride from Warwick to Brighton, Rand had explained that George IV invited to Brighton only those who could be of use to him. There was a huge number of social and political figures staying here. Mira knew that this fact held a secret significance for Rosalie, who was hoping that George Canning, head of the Foreign Office, would be at the Pavilion. Rosalie was determined to speak to Canning secretly about finding a post for Brummell in France, and Mira was prepared to do anything necessary to help her in this mission.

"I would prefer that both of you watch your step very carefully for the next few days," Rand said.

Rosalie and Mira looked at each other guiltily. Rand still did not know about their secret meeting with Brummell or Rosalie's plan to talk with Canning alone, and it was nerve-racking to keep a secret from him. Rosalie's husband was no fool, and few things escaped his notice.

"Whatever do you mean, my lord?" Rosalie asked with a halfhearted smile.

Rand subjected his wife to a slow, searching look before replying, "Only that the king's taste for older women has changed. Now it appears that he is drawn to young, attractive women of lively disposition. He would easily be encouraged by the smallest word or smile from either of you . . . and I would rather not have to extricate you from such a situation, since his pride is easily damaged, and he is not a particularly forgiving man."

"I know that." Rosalie was instantly agitated. "And it would probably amuse him to see *me* in an awkward situation, since he has heard the rumors about me and Brummell. He never forgave my father after their falling-out, even though Brummell sent him his best snuffbox and made every effort to win back his friendship. The king could easily see to it that my father is allowed back into England, but he won't, because he's too ungrateful and jealous of Brummell to—"

"Shhhh . . ." Rand whispered gently, sliding a hand to the back of Rosalie's neck and stroking his thumb along her rapidly throbbing pulse. "I know, *fleur*." He understood more than any other person alive what Brummell meant to Rosalie, and how easily upset she could become when the subject of her father was mentioned. Taking a deep breath and calming at his touch, Rosalie raised her blue eyes to his.

Mira averted her gaze from the strangely intimate gesture, at once flustered and touched by the revealing scene. At times Rand and Rosalie could shut themselves away from the entire world. In a few seconds they could read each other's thoughts and sense each other's needs in a completely private communication, no matter who was with them or what their surroundings were. At the moment Mira was merely a self-conscious outsider.

As she turned her eyes away from the pair, Mira heard the sound of footsteps at the end of the hall, firm footsteps coupled with a long stride. She looked at the approaching figure . . . and suddenly her heart beat in a staccato rhythm. Alec. She put a hand to the base of her throat, feeling all the color drain from her face. It had to be Alec. She had missed him so much that her whole being ached with the painful joy of seeing him again. It was Alec . . . or was it? His hair was coal-black, his form was tall and broad-shouldered, his features were severely perfect and graced with a raffish white smile . . . but as he came closer, Mira realized with utter bewilderment that the newcomer was not Alec. He was too young, and somehow he seemed less polished, his manner speaking more of cockiness than Alec's self-assurance. And his eyes . . . they were not silver-gray but deep green.

He stopped upon seeing her, blinking a few times and then smiling anew. "I seem to have lost my way," he said, staring at Mira with rapt attention. She made no reply, her eyes dark with confusion.

"Well . . . Carr Falkner," Rosalie said, and came to stand by Mira. "How pleasant it is to find you here."

"Lady Berkeley," the man answered, his eyes still on Mira, "it seems to be a day for pleasant discoveries."

Nudging Mira imperceptibly, Rosalie made the proper introductions, and Mira allowed the stranger to take her small cold hand in his warm one. *Carr* Falkner, she thought, recovering very slowly from her surprise. If there were any other Falkners here at the Pavilion, she prayed that she would receive more advance warning, for coming face-to-face with someone resembling Alec so closely was almost more than she could bear. No matter how darkly attractive any of the Falkners were, none of them would be anything but a disappointing imitation of Alec.

"He is a cousin of the Duke of Stafford," Rosalie whispered to Mira. "Perhaps you recall the duke . . . ?"

You mean the one I accompanied during the sleighing party? Mira thought numbly. *The one I fell in love with during Sackville's hunt? The one who knows my deepest secrets, the one who took my virginity? Yes, I believe I can recall him. . . .*

10

"We must be careful," Rosalie said, looking in the full-length mirror and adjusting the magnificent lace-trimmed bodice of her velvet gown. Mary, the maid who had come with them from Berkeley Hall, knelt by her and made a few small repairs to the hem of her gown with needle and thread. "Tonight I am going to find a way to speak to Canning about Brummell—during the dancing, perhaps. But I'll need your help—and remember, this must be done in complete secrecy. Any sort of untoward or unusual behavior is going to be noticed tonight, since there is always a great deal of scheming going on at affairs like this—this is the perfect environment in which to breed scandals."

"That isn't surprising," Mira replied, pinning a small green velvet hat on her head and angling it at a coquettish tilt. "It's a masquerade, and everyone feels quite daring in a disguise, all of us supposing that we can look out at the world while no one else can look in"

"Wrong," Rosalie said flatly. "I can see through even the best disguises—there are always telling clues. For example, the king will be the one with the enormous belly, and the blond by his side will be Lady Conyngham."

Mira winced at the venom in Rosalie's tone. It was not like Rosalie to say an unkind or undiplomatic word about anyone, but it seemed that not only the king but also all of his close associates bore the brunt of her contempt. "Who is Lady Conyngham?"

"His latest mistress. He has given her the title of 'Lady Steward,' and the two pretend that she is merely the mistress of his household, while it's commonly known, even to her husband, that she shares his bed." Rosalie shook her head disgustedly. "What men see in women like her escapes me. She is vain, silly, greedy, and she encourages the king in all of his worst habits. He is killing himself from overeating and then over-dosing himself with opium and bark brandy to cure his indigestion—"

"Opium and bark brandy!" Mira exclaimed, wrinkling her nose. "A dram of powdered galanga would help a great deal more than that to—"

"I hope he consumes all the brandy he wants," Rosalie said, shrugging carelessly. "I hope he becomes so fat and indolent that he cannot move. Because of him, my father is in exile in France and will likely starve to death. Did you see how thin Brummell was? He used to weigh thirteen or fourteen stone, and I don't think he was over nine or ten stone when we saw him!"

"Rosalie . . ." Mira said cautiously, "I would advise keeping your voice lowered when you speak either of Brummell or of the king."

Suddenly Rosalie laughed. "Are you afraid I'll be hanged for treason, Mira?"

"Worse. I'm afraid Lord Berkeley will overhear you talking about our misadventure."

At the mention of her husband, Rosalie's eyes widened. "Heavens, the time has slipped away from me! Let me finish telling you about my plan before Rand gets here. When I contrive to have a few minutes alone with Canning, I'm going to ask him about finding a position for Brummell in Calais, just as Lord Alvanley suggested. Or perhaps Caen—"

"But how are you going to accomplish that without

your husband noticing, and what about all of those who might see you and Canning sneak away, and put the wrong construction on the situation—"

"That's where I need your help—" Rosalie began, and just then a light, decisive rap vibrated the door. "It's Rand," she whispered in frustration, raising her eyes heavenward. "Let him in, Mary,'" she said to the maid, and Mira turned to the mirror in consternation.

"We're already fashionably late," Rand said by way of greeting, striding into the room and stopping to take note of his wife's appearance. A slow smile stole over his golden, blunt-featured face. "Lady Berkeley . . . as usual, you are breathtaking," he said softly. Mira could not help smiling as she beheld the Berkeleys, who were a perfectly matched pair.

Rosalie was dressed as Marguerite de Valois, the wife of Henry IV of France. Her gown was a magnificent creation of red velvet trimmed with gold and jewels, nipped in tightly to reveal a tiny waist and spreading outward in a huge bell of glittering skirts. The bodice was low and pointed, trimmed with the same pattern of gems that carried down the front of the gown, while her shoulders rose in elegant majesty from sharp, fragile points of lace. Her sleeves were long and puffed, ending in bands of gold. Rosalie smiled flirtatiously and flicked open a golden feathered fan. Her hair was piled high on her head, gleaming sable curls arranged carefully to balance the tiny jeweled crown on her head.

"I shall be accompanied by the most handsome man in England tonight," Rosalie said as her gaze moved appreciatively over her husband. Rand, of course, was masquerading as Henry IV, and his impressive masculine form was resplendent in sixteenth-century garb, including a scarlet robe, a jacket of gold cloth, spurs on his boots, a blue garter on his left leg, and three bars of ermine on the left arm. His tawny eyes, hair, and skin were emphasized by the richness of the costume. "All you need is a white courser," Rosalie continued softly, and Berkeley gave her a self-mocking smile.

"All I need is my queen," he replied, holding out his arm. "Now, let us venture down to the ball before I begin to feel like a prancing fool."

"Wait—aren't you going to admire Mireille's costume?"

Mira blushed slightly as Berkeley's eyes alighted on her. At Rosalie's prompting, she held out her skirts and turned around to display her outfit.

"Maid Marion," Rand said, and grinned in approval. "Perfect. I could think of no better costume for a wood sprite."

"We were concerned about the length of the skirt—it is rather daring," Rosalie said critically, and Berkeley shook his head.

"It is perfect," he repeated.

Mira's Maid Marion costume was tempered with a saucy charm that suited her well. Her dress was made of velvet, dyed in rich forest shades of green and brown, while a small bow and quiver of arrows were slung over her back. The skirt and bustline were bordered with dark fur, and her small hat was a smaller version of Robin Hood's, complete with a sprightly feather stuck in the brim. The skirt was only calf-length, coming to the top of a pair of soft brown boots. She looked exotic and elfin, especially with her black-brown curls pulled away from her face and left to fall down her back.

Mira fussed nervously with her costume as they went downstairs, where the mock altars to Bacchus, Apollo, Venus, Minerva, and Mars were burning with incense that filled the air with a spicy scent. Music rang through the Pavilion as the orchestra played with determined gaiety. The king had not appeared yet, but there were rumors of a very large Turk wearing a satin turban having been seen in one of the small alcoves adjoining the ballroom. Mira looked from left to right with delight and wonder, amazed at the creativity, color, and often the brevity of the costumes that people wore. As the elderly women, dowagers, and widows sat on the sides of the room to monitor the activities of their charges, young women were whirled about on the dance floor by wizards, beasts, long-dead heroes of legends, villains, and mythological figures.

Almost as soon as they entered the ballroom, a fifteenth-century knight approached Mira. It was Carr Falkner, clad in chain mail, black hose, and rough boots. His dark green eyes, framed with black lashes, sparkled down at her merrily. Mira smiled back at him, finding his rough-and tumble charm attractive. It was obvious that he had been waiting for her to arrive.

"Miss Germain," he said, giving her a half-smile that reminded her of Alec, and she caught her breath involuntarily, "either my memory is faulty or you are even more ravishing tonight than you were this afternoon."

Mira smiled at him and shot a quick glance at Rosalie, who appeared to be vastly pleased with Carr Falkner's evident interest in her charge. Carr also looked at Rosalie, lifting his eyebrows entreatingly. "Since introductions have already been made, with your permission I would like to claim the first dance with Miss Germain."

"Only one," Rosalie replied, her blue eyes laughing. "Miss Germain may not be aware of the fact that more than one dance with the same man will place her in a most compromising position."

"Surely you wouldn't count *our* dances," Carr protested to Mira.

"I certainly will," Mira said. "I will not allow myself to be compromised at the first ball of the Season."

He grinned and offered his arm in a gallant gesture. Mira handed her bow and quiver of arrows to Rosalie, and she allowed Carr to lead her to the crowded middle of the ballroom. As he whirled her amid the glittering couples, Mira found that he was an adept dancer and that her steps were well-matched to his. After a minute of silence, Mira threw him a teasing glance. "Have I said something to rob you of speech?"

"No . . . no . . ." he said hastily, "I was just . . . thinking of something."

Mira looked at him through her lashes and smiled. Although Carr had no way of knowing it, his similarity to Alec was enormously intriguing to her. It was possible, she mused, that this was what Alec might have been like when he was younger . . . a little vulnerable, his manner both cheerful and slightly awkward, his handsome face touched with the innocence of youth. Was Carr an accurate picture of what Alec had been several years ago?

"Thinking of something?" she repeated, forcing herself back to the conversation at hand. "Of anything or anyone in particular?" Carr merely shook his head slowly. "How disappointing," she said coquettishly. "I had expected you to say that you were thinking of me."

He laughed, his hair falling in a coal-black spill over his forehead as he looked down at her. For all his youth, he was still taller than most of the other men in the room and dwarfed her considerably. "If I thought only of you, Miss Germain, my feet would stumble to a halt, my chin would drop to the floor, and all I would be able to do is stare at your beauty in stupefied amazement."

"You would be the first to do so," she assured him.

"With all respect, I doubt that."

It was with difficulty that Carr kept from complimenting her so lavishly that he would appear foolishly smitten. He managed to conduct himself with commendable restraint. This was his second Season in London, and by now he considered himself to be more than proficient in the art of flirtation. He had even thought of himself as becoming rather cynical, though not quite as impressively jaded as his cousin Alec. Women, all women, had once possessed the power to make Carr feel awkward and tongue-tied . . . and just when he had congratulated himself on overcoming such an affliction, this small woman in his arms had brought it back in less than a minute. He was bewitched by her, and moreover, he could feel the jealous stares of his comrades as they watched him dance with her. A night like this was the stuff of a young man's fantasies. Carr gave up all attempts to make conversation and simply concentrated on memorizing each detail of her face.

Content to dance in silence, Mira followed him easily, her fingers resting lightly on the metallic fibers of Carr's costume. It was with great reluctance that she realized the waltz was ending. She walked back very slowly with Carr to the Berkeleys, who were conversing with Helen of Troy, Shakespeare, Delilah, and Henry VIII.

"He is perfect for you," Rosalie whispered behind her fan to Mira. "Young and sweet, and very handsome. Play your cards wisely."

"I will," Mira whispered back, unable to think of any way to explain to Rosalie that Carr would have indeed been perfect, had he not been so young . . . had he not been Alec's cousin. Aside from the fact that she would inevitably find herself making comparisons between the two of them, she knew that Alec would not tolerate any involvement of hers with a member of his family. What would he do if Carr became seriously interested in her? The thought was both amusing and horrifying.

As she turned her attention to the conversation and laughed at a quip Carr had made, she felt a sudden prickling sensation along the back of her neck, as if someone's eyes were on her. Glancing over her shoulder, she saw Alec in the midst of a large group . . . and he gave her a long, measured glance before turning away. His gray eyes had been smoky with jealousy. A quiver of excitement raced through her. That doesn't change anything, she told herself sternly. It doesn't matter that he still might want you, and you're a fool to care. . . . But she couldn't deny that it had felt good to have him stare like that . . . yes, it felt very good. And even though she had disclaimed any tie with him, she couldn't repress a twinge of pride as she looked at him; he was very handsome tonight, even more than usual.

There was something unspeakably potent about his darkness, a virility that few men possessed in such abundance. He was not a man who brought to mind thoughts of fairy-tale princes and knights on white chargers. When a woman looked at him, she thought of forbidden pleasures and clandestine meetings. He was the kind of man who seemed to have been created expressly to bring women heartache, yet even knowing that, how could she help but be drawn to him? To possess a man like him, even for a short time, was every woman's private dream.

Apparently Rosalie had noticed Alec as well, for her slim brows had lifted slightly, lending her an expression of thoughtful disgruntlement. "I've seen that costume before," she said in a low voice, making certain that Rand and Carr were engaged in conversation before she continued: "but I'll admit that no man has ever been able to carry it off so well. I'm afraid it's far too suitable for him."

Alec's tall, broad-shouldered form was clad in black breeches, a crimson damask waistcoat, fringed gauntlets, and high-topped boots of spur leather. His black hair, uncovered by any hat, shone with the gleam of pure obsidian. Around his neck hung a gold cross, and a sword was strapped to his lean waist. "What costume is it?" Mira whispered, moving her gaze back to Rosalie's face with an effort.

"Captain Bartholomew Roberts—you can always tell by the cross. A pirate, quite swarthy from what the legends say, who was killed in battle during the sixteenth century. A heroic figure, though reputedly not a very kind man."

"I'm going to dance with him if it takes me all night to get an invitation," Helen of Troy said, following Rosalie's eyes and sighing as she stared at Alec.

"Bonne chance," Mira murmured, staring down at the floor as a secret smile forced its way to her lips, no matter how she tried to prevent it. Tonight it would not bother her if every woman at the Pavilion plied her wares on Alec Falkner . . . for just now he had been staring at *her*, only her, and the knowledge made her heart sing.

As the ball continued, Mira was buffeted with a large number of introductions and invitations to dance. Rosalie was clearly delighted by Mira's popularity, and even more so by the fact that Carr made every effort to monopolize Mira's attention. The ball was interrupted for a few minutes while the assemblage received the news that the king was indisposed and would not be able to attend the festivities that night. A few people seemed regretful at the announcement, but none seemed surprised, attesting to the truth of what Rosalie had said earlier about the king's indolence.

Standing near one of the tables of refreshments and sipping punch, Mira stood by Carr's side and conversed idly with a small group of people. Nothing more than mundane comments were exchanged, which caused Mira to relax in their company. She listened to the latest gossip and laughed in all the appropriate places until her attention was occupied by a minor catastrophe. Miss Henrietta Lester, a flirtatious and empty-headed girl, had accidentally dropped her glass of punch, shattering the crystal and splashing brightly colored liquid everywhere. Miss Lester's face flamed red with utter humiliation, and after endeavoring to make an apology while servants rushed to clear the mess, she burst into becoming tears. Carr and the other men in the group rushed to comfort her, while Mira retreated to the corner of the room to survey the damage done to her dress. The hem of it and her boots were splattered with the punch, which had probably created permanent stains.

"Nom de Dieu," she said as she dabbed at her clothing with a napkin, never dreaming that anyone was within hearing distance. She heard another of Miss Lester's heartrending wails over the music and scowled in disgust. "Oh, don't be such a shallow-pate," she muttered. "Much good your crying's going to do anyone—"

Just then Mira's grumbling was interrupted by an amused cackle. "My sentiments exactly."

Mira spun around to observe an elderly woman sitting in a small chair with a tiny table set in front of her. There was no one else nearby, and Mira wondered why no one was there to keep company with the woman, who wore a sharp, assessing expression on her aristocratically boned face. She was small and thin, with slate-shaded hair and a vital, fierce personality stamped on every line of her skin.

"Excuse me—I had no idea anyone would overhear me," Mira managed to say. "You must think that I am extremely uncharitable—"

"I think you might be somewhat sensible," the woman replied, gesturing to Mira's dress. "Go on with what you were doing. You might be able to soak up enough of that . . . whatever it is—"

"Punch," Mira said, bending over her task again as she smiled ruefully. "I had considered it to be first-rate punch until it was splashed on my costume."

"Do you need my handkerchief?" the elderly woman inquired, fishing out a small white square and holding it out to her. The handkerchief fluttered out of the woman's pale, well-veined hand to the floor. "I've dropped the damned thing," she said, and Mira smiled, finding a certain delight in the discovery of another woman besides herself who knew how to swear effectively. "Where the deuce is it?" The woman leaned forward slightly, squinting at the floor until she located the patch of white and pointed to it. "There. Drat, my companion has taken leave for a few minutes and isn't here to fetch it. That confounded girl is never here when I need her."

Mira bent over and picked up the small lace article slowly, looking at the woman's face closely before standing up. There was what appeared to be a thin, light film covering her eyes, and Mira's heart softened with compassion as she realized that she could not see very well.

"Madam," she said, placing the handkerchief on the woman's lap carefully, "may I ask you a question?"

"I suppose so," she replied sharply, as if being asked questions were a bother she would have liked to do without.

"You are not the kind of woman who would be easily offended, I can see that . . ."

"Of course I'm not!" came the indignant reply.

"Then," Mira continued, "I could not help noticing that you . . . well, it seemed to be a strain for you to look down at the—"

"Impertinent chit. There is nothing wrong with my eyes. Now, be off with you, and go on dancing and prattling with your—"

"I am glad there is nothing wrong with them," Mira said, dabbing hurriedly at the punch stains again, which had all but disappeared. "I just thought that if they were blurry, I could make a suggestion that might help."

"You? By all appearances, you left the cradle last week. Now, run along with you."

"Yes, madam. Thank you for your offer of the . . ." Mira's voice faded as the woman waved her away impatiently.

Shrugging lightly, she walked back to where the punch had been spilled and found that Carr had finally consoled Henrietta Lester by asking her to dance. He stared at Mira as he turned the girl around the floor sedately, and he made a brief, anguished grimace that caused Mira to laugh softly. Her attention was caught by the sight of Rand waltzing with one of the Berkeley cousins and wearing that polite, attentive expression that could only mean he was bored to distraction. Mira's smile changed to a thoughtful frown. If Rand wasn't dancing with his wife, then where was Rosalie?

It was not difficult to spot Rosalie's red-and-gold gown amidst the throng of costumes. She was dancing with a man that Mira did not recognize. From the satisfied expression on her face, it was likely that her partner was George Canning.

"I'd lay a quart of heavy wet on it," Mira said out loud, using an expression that was popular in certain districts of London, and she crossed her fingers. If it was indeed Canning, he appeared to be far more approachable than she had expected. Dressed plainly in the costume of a Greek philosopher, he was handsome, compactly built, and rather short. There was an aura of innate assurance and confidence around him . . . but would he dare grant Rosalie a favor if it risked the displeasure of the king?

The dance ended, and among the rain of applause, Rosalie's partner left the room discreetly. It took Mira less than half a minute to reach Rosalie's side, and they walked to the punch table, talking rapidly.

"Canning," Rosalie said breathlessly. "He's agreed to speak with me—he's going to wait in one of the rooms nearby. We can't let anyone find out—"

"Shhh—your husband is coming," Mira whispered,

and pasted a look of solicitous concern on her face as Rand walked up to them with a few long strides.

"Rose?" Rand inquired, his hazel eyes darkening to deep olive as he regarded his wife with concern.

"She is not feeling well," Mira said smoothly, her expression guileless and sincere. "Too much wine and dancing, probably."

"Yes, that's it," Rosalie said, not daring to look at Rand, who could always tell when she was lying. She kept her panicked blue eyes on Mira's face.

"I'm going to take you upstairs to rest—" Rand began, settling a square brown hand on his wife's arm.

"I'll accompany her upstairs," Mira interrupted, taking hold of Rosalie's other arm.

"Yes, Mira will go with me," Rosalie chimed in, giving her husband an agitated smile. "You stay here for a little longer—remember, you still haven't danced with your cousin Thalia, and I don't want her to feel like a wallflower."

"I'm not going to dance with Thalia," Rand said, his tawny brows lowering over his eyes. "Not when you're feeling ill, and certainly not when her habit of stepping on her partners' feet is still fresh in my memory."

"Poor Thalia," Rosalie said sadly, wrinkling her forehead. "Couldn't you ask one of your friends to dance with her, darling? As a favor to me?"

Berkeley stared at her for a minute and then whispered an oath, loosing her arm. "Go with her upstairs," he said to Mira, and shook his head as he left them, muttering under his breath.

"He is concerned for you," Mira said.

Rosalie smiled wryly. "Don't attempt to explain my husband to me," she said, patting Mira on the arm and then pressing her temples to restrain a headache. "I know him very well—he knows that something is going on, and he doesn't like the fact that I won't tell

him about it." She sighed. "I can't think about that
now. I must speak with Canning about my father."

They made their way through the crowded ballroom, and Mira became mildly disturbed as she realized that Rosalie's paleness had increased. "You really
aren't feeling well," she said, wondering why Rosalie's
expression was so weary . . . was it a result of tension
or actual illness?

"The air was so thick with incense I could hardly
breathe!"

"It's better out here," Mira replied, and they paused
as they turned right to face a long hallway and rows of
small rooms.

"Second door on the left. He said he would wait in
here for a few minutes." Rosalie hesitated before the
elaborately carved doorknob. "Suddenly I feel so guilty
. . . but I'm not doing anything wrong! It's not as if
this is some sort of tryst. I'm trying to help my father."

"Would you like me to go in with you?"

"No. . . please don't. I told Canning that this is a
private matter."

"Well, then, what should I do? I can't go back into
the ballroom—I'm supposed to be with you."

"Could you manage to stay out of sight for a while?"

"Of course."

"I'll meet you here at eleven o'clock."

"Good luck," Mira said, watching as Rosalie slipped
inside the room. Venturing down the hallway, she
tried a few of the doors until she found one that
opened. Peering inside, she discovered that it was a
small portrait gallery filled with scarlet-cushioned furniture and heavily ornamented frames. The dull gleam
of gold was apparent even through the murky dimness
of the room. It would be a perfect place to hide until
Rosalie's meeting with Canning was over. She stepped
inside and started to close the door, but abruptly it
trembled on its hinges and stopped. The tip of a spur-

leather boot was wedged firmly against the bottom of the door.

"Alec," she whispered without even looking at his face. He shouldered his way in without answering, closing the door with the back of his heel. The paneled portal squeaked slightly in protest as he propped his broad back against it and bent one knee in a relaxed posture.

"What the hell is going on?" Though his pose was careless, his voice was rough.

"I . . . You . . . Rosalie is going to . . . You're spying on me!"

"I don't give a damn about the little plots that Rosalie Berkeley is hatching, or your involvement in them," Alec said with barely leashed violence. "I'm talking about Carr."

"Carr?" she questioned stupidly. "Your cousin?"

"Yes, my cousin. Stay away from him."

"Why? Is he so corruptible that a few minutes in my company would prove harmful to his character?"

"You're using him."

"You may think that I'm not good enough for him," she said, feeling a blaze of anger spreading through her body, "but you can't always have everything your way. Unfortunately, Lord Falkner, I enjoy your cousin's company, and he seems to enjoy mine, and I intend to spend *much* more time with him, and there's not a thing you can do about it."

"The next time I see you with him, I'll wring your neck," he promised savagely.

"You couldn't. I'm Berkeley's ward," she said triumphantly. "I'm not some helpless nobody who—"

"Berkeley can go to hell. I'm warning you away from a boy who isn't capable of defending himself from you."

'You're *defending* him from me? Just how do you think I could hurt him?"

"By using him as a substitute for the man you really want."

She stared at him with disbelief, and then a dry laugh broke from her throat as she started to walk away from him. "What unbelievable arrogance."

Alec's control snapped as she turned her back toward him. He moved too swiftly for her to react, pinning her to the wall and jerking her wrists over her head.

"It's the truth," he said, his voice rasping as he stifled her struggles with the pressure of his body and crushed her against the wall. His entire being was focused on the small slim form in his arms. "You knew what would happen if you started encouraging him while I was there to watch. You knew how I'd feel—"

"I don't give a damn how you feel," she gasped, writhing against him in the darkness.

"Liar. You knew what you were doing."

"Let me *go*—"

"—holding yourself just out of reach," he said unsteadily. "You can play your games . . . but I won't let him have you . . . I won't let anyone—"

"You're mad," she choked, and then as she realized the extent of his wrath, she changed her tactics abruptly, trying to plead with him, trying to soothe him. "Alec . . . please, have you forgotten where we are? Remember . . . what we said to each other . . ." Her frantic struggles slowed as she felt his muscled thighs press against hers, his powerful arms subdue her. "I wasn't playing a game," she said, fighting to stifle a moan as she felt the fiery heat of his masculinity pulsing between her legs, burning between their clothes. "Alec, you've got to stop . . ." Her face was almost pressed into the strong column of his throat, and she was light-headed with the scent of his skin. "I can't think, and you don't know what you're doing—"

"Nothing has changed," he said hoarsely, pressing every inch of his body against hers, his hands tightening around her wrists. "I knew I could forget about you . . . I knew it would only take time . . . but it's only worse now, it's *worse* than before . . . and some nights I want you so badly I can taste you, I can feel you, even though it's someone else I'm holding—"

"Oh, stop . . . don't say anything else," Mira groaned, tears welling in her eyes. The thought of him holding someone else, making love to someone else, made her want to die. "I don't want to know. I don't want to care. You've got to let me go—"

"I need you. I've needed you for months . . . and what we had—"

"We're never going to have that again."

"I damn well am . . . I'm going to have you *now*." He crushed his mouth over hers, his body pressing her back against the wall even as she tried to shrink away, and he forced her lips open, plundering her hungrily. She refused to respond, tearing her mouth away from his and gasping frantically. "You're mine," he muttered, his lips hot against her throat. "How can you deny it, when even I can't? . . . Don't lie to me . . . dammit, don't turn away from me."

She fought him until his mouth found hers once more, and then suddenly she couldn't move as she was flooded with warmth, and she gave a helpless sob . . . she was born for this, for him . . . it would be a lie to deny it. Weakly she tilted her head and yielded herself to him, her lips parting as his tongue feathered against hers. He felt her response and groaned with relief, easing the crushing pressure on her body. Breathing heavily, he lifted his mouth from hers and stared at her clenched fists, which were trapped in his own.

Something in his expression changed, and a curious shock went through Mira as she felt his lips brush against her hands. He nipped at the fragile skin over her knuckles, and his tongue flickered in the crevices between her fingers. She made a shuddering sound, her heart slamming inside her chest, her fingers slowly uncurling. The warmth of his mouth moved over her throbbing palms, and he freed her wrists to gather her against him. She was stiff against him for a few seconds, knowing she should refuse him, knowing that she would regret what was about to happen. But as Alec looked down at her, she saw the desperation in his gaze, and she was lost. Slowly she slid her arms around his neck, pulling his dark head down to hers.

"Mira . . ." he whispered, and their mouths opened and fused together, tasting, moving, stroking ardently in a physical expression of love. Blindly Alec sank his hands into her hair, pulling out the pins, clenching his fingers in the mane of thick skeins. Every other reality, every other passion, was gone, as if there had never been anyone else but her. Mira wrapped her arms around his neck, allowing him total access to her mouth, her body. Perhaps she did not deserve the rapture of this, but she needed it, she could have it, if only for the next few minutes, and she would take it without hesitation. They kissed and touched with blistering ferocity, taking and receiving, melding together urgently. She felt his hands tugging at her clothes so roughly that they were in danger of tearing, and she didn't care.

He freed her shoulders from the bodice of her dress and pressed his mouth into the vulnerable shallows near the slope of her neck, flaming, greedy, probing. Mira froze in a state of bewildered pleasure, and then she turned her face into the ebony silk of his hair as his head bent over her. There were no longer any pretenses, no questions, nothing except honesty: they wanted each other, neither of them could resist it . . . neither of them wanted to.

He scooped her up in his arms and carried her to the low, flat sofa, spreading her along the length of it and covering her body with his. Moaning, Mira lifted her breasts against the cupping warmth of his hands, impatient to be rid of the barriers of cloth that separated them.

"The laces . . ." she gasped against his mouth, fumbling with the cords that held the front of her bodice together. He brushed her hands away and yanked at the laces, his expression harsh with desire. They both sighed as the cords gave way and her dress opened, the edges of it spreading apart like the petals of a disheveled flower. His palms curved under her breasts and lifted them upward, his teeth grazing the dainty peaks. Mira's fingertips dug into the brocaded upholstery of the sofa as the damp velvet of his tongue feathered across her nipples, as he drew the tip of her breast into his mouth and held it there possessively. His hands slid under her bare back and he shifted her higher.

"Pull up your skirt." His whisper tickled in the gentle valley between her breasts. Mira felt a blush stain her cheeks, even in the darkness, but she obeyed him with clumsy haste, feeling cool air touch the places that the velvet material had covered. Alec rewarded her with a long, deep kiss, tasting the inside of her mouth and sliding his arms more tightly around her back. "Now your pantaloons . . ." he said thickly. She hesitated and then unfastened the dainty white garment with trembling fingers, pulling it down over her hips and down to her ankles. He said nothing then, the ragged sound of his breathing becoming more pronounced in the quietness, and Mira touched the fastening of his breeches, shivering as she felt the thrusting hardness beyond the cloth. One by one, she undid the buttons, releasing his hot, full maleness, and her delicate fingertips brushed over him, caressing him lightly. Alec groaned deep in his throat, lowering his naked hips to hers. He muffled her thin cry with his mouth as he entered her, taut, heavy, hard with arousal. Despite the urges of his raging desire, he pushed into her slowly, giving her body enough time to accept him completely. Mira quivered, burning with desire, and she opened her thighs hungrily, feeling him press inside her until there was no more he could give her, no more she could take.

They entwined in a damp tumble, and Mira felt the violent power of his thrusts all through her body. Helplessly she fumbled with his clothes, trying to slip her hands underneath them to his skin . . . but then her overcharged nerves focused only on the pounding force of him within her, and she was not capable of doing anything but cling to him. Her arms wrapped around his neck, her knees flexed as she pushed against him strongly. Feverishly she answered his driving movements, faster and harder, until she was seized with an upheaval frightening in its intensity. She arched upward, making a sharp, broken sound. Alec murmured something tender in her ear, cradling her quaking body in his arms, moving within her in a way that stretched out her pleasure as long as possible. He kissed her bared throat . . . he denied the fulfillment of his own release in order to thrust into her with slow, purposeful strokes. "Let it last . . ." he whispered to her, glorying in the feel of her, suspended and paralyzed beneath him. And then, as he allowed himself to follow her into that arena of savage pleasure, Mira felt a hot burst of warmth inside her. His big body tightened against hers, the muscles of his sturdy shoulders bunching under her palms.

Unconsciously she murmured his name, a trail of wetness slipping from the outside corners of her eyes down to her temples. The taste of her tears was on his tongue, and Alec cupped her head in both of his hands as his lips skimmed over her face. Pleasure sifted through her in silky ripples, like light moving through water. His hands stroked her body, his fingers and knuckles lingered in the warm, damp crevices of her, and she found herself floating in a dream world . . . she was part of the silence and the darkness, writhing underneath the slow, knowing movements of Alec's hands. The tip of his tongue traced the silkiness of her inner cheeks, delving repeatedly . . . his fingertips drifted over the softness of her abdomen, massaging gently until the hunger began to stir inside her once more. "Oh . . ." she breathed, pulling her mouth from his, ". . . you can't, we just . . ."

"What have you done to me? Damn you, it's like this with no one else. No one. Do you understand that you're the only one I want? After that night, I couldn't forget you—I can't leave you alone, and I'll be damned if I'm going to give you up again." His middle finger traced a path through the downy curls between her legs to a small secret place that was painfully oversensitive. She flinched and tried to jerk away. "Don't!" she gasped in protest, and the stroke of his fingertip became so light that she could barely feel it. Sucking in her breath, she relaxed and accepted the gentle, tickling touch, concentrating on that tiny circling of his finger . . . she groaned and shifted underneath him, and he stifled her restless sounds with his mouth, continuing to knead her with that same teasing slowness until there was a hot, satiny wetness between her legs.

Mira looked up at him with eyes that had darkened to black. "Alec?" she gasped, starting to struggle beneath him.

"Don't fight it," he whispered. "I want to watch you." He lowered his mouth to hers, muffling her cry of pleasure, and her body convulsed violently, straining to accept the flood of ecstasy that suffused her. He held her securely, his arms strong and secure around her, and she collapsed against him, her limbs slack and trembling. Burying her face in his neck, Mira was racked with such a confusing mixture of emotions that tears came unbidden to her eyes, and she wept softly for a reason that she didn't understand, pressing her face against his warm skin. "Mira . . . sweet . . . don't cry." Alec reached underneath her disheveled clothes and stroked her back gently.

"Before tonight I thought . . . I thought I finally had control over everything—"

"So did I . . . God, don't cry, I can stand anything but your tears."

"Why did I let it happen?" she asked, sniffling ungracefully. "I should never have—"

"There was no way to avoid it," Alec said against her temple, and he dug in his vest pocket for a handkerchief. She accepted the white linen square and blew her nose, her forehead wrinkling in misery as she realized that except for his unfastened breeches, Alec was still fully dressed.

"You . . . you didn't even take your boots off," she said in a watery voice, wiping her eyes with a corner of the handkerchief. "Oh, how awful—"

"Mira . . ." Suddenly a tremor of laughter laced through his voice. "Would you feel better about this if I had removed my clothes?"

She did not know what he found so amusing about the situation. "Of course I would have. I think . . . I don't know . . ."

"My precious brat, I wasn't thinking about boots or clothes . . . except for how to remove the ones that were in the way."

"Oh, stop sounding so *damned* pleased with yourself, and . . . and let me up—I've got to think of what to do . . ." She covered her eyes with her hand and let out a shuddering sigh. "Name of God, what have I done?" Had she ever been in a predicament this dire? She was a disheveled, tumbled mess, and in only a few minutes she would have to meet Rosalie, whose eye for detail was able to detect the disarrangement of one lock of hair . . . and after this she would have to attend a ball filled with people who would surely know what she had been doing.

"I know that you're accustomed to thinking for yourself," Alec said, sitting up and calming her struggles as she attempted to twist out of his lap, "but for once you're going to let me help. Be still." Too tired to fight him, Mira allowed him to cradle her against his broad chest. He spoke to her with calm assurance, as if he were supremely accustomed to being in this sort of dilemma. He probably was, Mira thought woefully, and rested her head on his shoulder. "It will take only a few minutes to reassemble your costume, and then it will be time for you to meet Lady Berkeley. If I heard correctly, she has been meeting with Canning—"

"You are a terrible eavesdropper," she said gruffly.

"I'm a very good eavesdropper," Alec corrected equably. "After you meet Lady Berkeley again, tell her that you wish to retire to your room early. Tell her that your head aches—"

"I can't tell her that, she's the one who is supposed to have the headache."

"Then tell her your monthly time has—"

"I'll tell her that my head aches," Mira interrupted hastily. "But no matter what excuse I offer, she'll know after looking at me that something has happened, and I don't know what sort of explanation will—"

"You don't owe her an explanation."

"I most certainly—"

"You do not."

"I see. The only person I owe explanations to is you, is that correct?"

"That's right," Alec replied, his fingers going to the laces of her dress.

"You are the most arrogant—"

"And now, seeing that you have recovered your breath and your capability for sarcasm, it is time to send you out to the lions again. May they all beware."

He was more efficient than any lady-in-waiting could ever hope to be, lacing and straightening her clothes in almost as short a time as it had taken to disrobe her.

Mira turned away from him as she pinned the hat on her head once more, her eyes focused on the closed door. "Thank you for a most interesting evening," she said huskily, stabbing her scalp accidentally with a pin and almost welcoming the pain. Anything to take her mind off the thought that once more she had lost the battle. Was her life destined to be shaped around these brief, draining clashes with him, which would become more and more defeating until she expired from the hell of wanting and not having?

"You're welcome," came Alec's voice right next to her ear, and she jumped as his hands settled at her waist. "There's no more time for us tonight. But there are several things we have to discuss. No longer will I lust and scheme after you like a demented, oft-thwarted Don Juan. We'll talk tomorrow, during the boating and water festivities in the afternoon."

"I think we should try to forget about tonight."

"You know that's impossible. Don't be difficult, sweet—just agree with me for now."

She sighed and leaned back against him. "Where should we meet?"

"I'll find you." He turned her around and kissed her deeply, and she was unable to hold back her response. As her mouth clung to his, a fresh fire flickered between them, and Alec cast a vaguely wistful glance at the sofa where they had lain. "Oh yes . . . I'll find you easily," he murmured, bending his head to nip at her bottom lip very gently with his teeth. He doubted that the sum total of all the satisfaction he had felt in his life could equal this moment. She was his, and finally she knew it as well as he, and somehow, some way, he would find a way to keep her.

11

"Will there be anythin' else you need, miss?" Mary asked, and Rosalie shook her head. "Thank you, that will be all." She sat at the dressing table, picking up the ivory-handled brush that the maid had just put down, drawing it through her hair in a distracted gesture. She was reluctant for Mary to leave, since the maid had provided an effective barrier between her and Rand ever since they had retired from the ball. He had been watching her with a sharp and exasperated gaze all evening, and though she knew him well, there was no way of predicting how he was going to react to her obvious attempt at subterfuge. Sometimes Rand would confront a problem between them with disconcerting directness, while at other times he would merely watch and wait until he had enough information to corner her.

She looked into the mirror, watching him walk up behind her. His rich blue robe gleamed in the muted lamplight. Her eyes, darkened to violet-blue, met his tawny ones in the mirror.

"What did he say?" Rand inquired, noting the pulse that beat so agitatedly at the base of her throat.

"What did who say?" Rosalie asked faintly.

"Ah . . . now, that's an interesting question. Would you mind answering it?"

It was fast becoming obvious to Rosalie that she could keep up the pretense no longer. "You know about . . . tonight?" She moistened her dry lips with the tip of her tongue.

"Unlike your little friend Mira, you are a poor actress, my love. I admit that I would not have you any other way, but it is more than I can tolerate to see you trying to hide something from me. Yes, I know about Canning. Five minutes after you danced with him, you both slipped out of the room. God help England if Canning isn't more subtle than that on his missions of foreign diplomacy."

"Rand, you certainly don't think I was meeting him in order to—"

"I have no doubt of your fidelity to me," Rand interrupted dryly, and she breathed a sigh of relief. "Since you have no vested interest in foreign policy, I assume you spoke to Canning about one particular resident of France."

"Yes . . . I had to ask him about finding a post for Brummell as consul at Calais. My father is in desperate straits, and since neither you nor he will allow me to support him emotionally or financially, I had to think of *something* to do."

Rand's dark, blunt-featured face looked as if it was carved out of mahogany. "Who came up with the idea of Brummell serving as a consul?" he asked with ominous gentleness. Rosalie's shoulders drooped slightly, and she looked away from his reflection.

"Alvanley. When Mira and I went to visit my mother in London, we had arranged to meet Brummell and Alvanley that night."

A quiet growl of displeasure came from Berkeley's throat, and then an annoyed sigh. "Saints' blood . . . you're not telling me that you were cavorting around London with only Mira for companionship that night? Good Lord, woman, with all the crime that . . . No, you wouldn't put yourself in that kind of danger. You wouldn't."

"I did," Rosalie admitted in a small voice, and he put a hand over his eyes, rubbing them tiredly. Then he looked at her, not with anger as she had feared, but with a disturbed frown that wrenched at her heart.

"Do you think there is anything more important to me than your happiness?" He sighed, his hazel eyes dark and troubled. "The subject of your father has always been a point of contention between us, Rose, and it's time we resolved it. I will not prevent your seeing him, and I will not interfere in your relationship with him. It is your right to handle that relationship in any manner you desire. But I will not allow him to compromise your safety, nor will I allow him to take advantage of you—"

"He has never done either of those things—"

"Hasn't he?" After exchanging a long look with him, Rosalie's eyes fell. There was no need for Rand to voice his opinion of Brummell, for he had stated before that he considered Brummell to be a vain, selfish, shallow leech. And even Rosalie had to admit that Brummell had played a minor part in the long-ago plot hatched by Guillaume Germain to kidnap her. But to her, blood and family overrode every other consideration, and no matter what her father had done, she would forgive him anything. She was completely aware of her own vulnerability on this point, and she also knew that Rand's protectiveness of her was what motivated his real dislike for Brummell. Ah, what complicated situations people wove for themselves.

"I won't do something like this again without talking to you first," she offered.

"No, you won't," he agreed curtly.

"Besides, I don't think I had a great deal of influence on Canning tonight—he said he would consider finding something for Brummell, but he said that we had to consider Britain's political welfare in its entirety, and not just the needs of one man."

"In political cant, that means no."

"I was afraid of that." Rosalie stood up and approached him hesitantly. "You're still angry."

He frowned at her, his burnished hair, eyes, and skin all disappearing into the shadows as he turned down the lamp. "Only because I love you, headstrong wench that you are, and the thought of anything happening to you drives me insane."

"Forgive me for not telling you, Rand . . . it's not that I don't trust you, but I know how you—"

He quieted her by touching his forefinger to her lips, and then his hands went to the ribbons of her filmy white gown. His hazel eyes flickered from her face to the curves and shadows of her body, barely discernible through the folds of the garment. Suddenly his hands were rough with impatience, breaking the knotted ribbons with a flick of his fingers, shredding the delicate material carelessly. She took in a quick breath as the garment dropped from her body like a web tattered by a strong breeze, and she felt the caress of his eyes on her bare skin. He lifted her naked body into his arms and murmured, "Don't tell me how sorry you are. Show me." Her mouth clung to his, and she was swept with a dizzying torrent of passion as he carried her to bed.

"Mon Dieu." Mira stirred as the sunlight poured over her bed with knifelike intensity. She squinted at Mary, who had come in with the breakfast tray and was engaged in pulling back the draperies. The maid paused at Mira's audible discomfort and cast a sympathetic glance in her direction.

"You told me last night to wake you at ten o'clock," Mary said. "Would you like for me to close the sun out and return in another two hours or so?"

"No, no. I smell coffee." Mira struggled up to a sitting position. She felt sore, disheveled, and wretched. What had happened to that sense of well-being she had felt after that first night with Alec so long ago? Why did she feel so anxious and guilty now? She rested her head against a pillow and slitted her eyes. "Mary . . . ?" she asked carefully. "This morning I would like some hot water for tea. My herbs are in the bag in that armoire—"

"You are ill?"

"My head aches."

"I will bring water right away."

Mira wondered why the maid looked at her so speculatively before leaving the room. It was a general rule that the servants knew all of the secrets of the people they attended. Having once been a maid herself, Mira could attest to that fact with certainty. She wondered if Mary had suspected anything last night upon seeing Mira's wrinkled undergarments and flushed face . . . ah, and there were those tiny marks on her neck and the highest curves of her bosom, left by the scrape of a man's bristled face. Mary had to suspect, Mira thought, and made a small uncomfortable noise in her throat. Rosalie also suspected that something had happened to Mira while she was speaking with Canning. Although Rosalie was preoccupied with her own problems, there was no mistaking the thorough appraisal she had given Mira when they had met near the ballroom.

Mary returned with a small silver teapot and a tiny tray arranged with Sèvres porcelain and a silver spoon.

"Thank you." Mira opened her bag of herbs carefully, hesitating as she regarded the variety of dried plants, powders, barks, and roots. What she needed was turnsole, a crooked plant with threadlike roots, but although it grew plentifully in France, she had never found it in England. "What else . . . what else?" she muttered, holding a hand to her temple and staring at the herbs. Of all the cures she knew how to prepare, of all the potions and elixirs, she had never paid close attention to any of the remedies that were reputed to prevent conception. Until now, she had had no need of such a recipe. Perhaps it is already too late, she thought, and bit her lip while touching her abdomen lightly. The thought of having a child, *Alec's* child, filled her with a curious yearning . . . yet she could not, unless *le bon Dieu* had already decided for her. Slowly she dropped the pale red blossoms of garden thyme into the water, as well as rue and the fibrous strands of creeping tormentil. She added violets, rose hips, and fennel to improve the taste of the brew, which had begun to smell decidedly bitter.

"More rue," Mary said, busying herself with small tasks around the room.

"More . . ." Mira started to repeat, flushing guiltily.

The maid's expression was perfectly calm and frank as she looked at her. "I learned that recipe before I knew how to mix bread dough. More rue."

Mira ducked her head and put more of the strong-scented root into the mixture, poking at it with a spoon and then taking an experimental sip. "Ugh." The taste seemed to cling to the back of her throat, and she nearly gagged on it. "This is *terrible*."

"Every morning," Mary said, and Mira pulled a face as the maid left. Closing her eyes and pinching her nose shut, she swallowed more of the tea.

The day was sultry and humid as the races, parties, and festivities progressed along the river and around the Brighton grounds. Mira and Rosalie exchanged friendly but guarded conversation, making no reference to anything that had happened during the masquerade. It was the best quality of their friendship, the mutual respect that caused them not to pry or make demands of each other. Rand escorted them to one of the many gardens near the Pavilion, and Mira gradually drifted several yards away from the Berkeleys, who seemed especially close to each other today and were deeply involved in conversation. As she examined some of the plants that grew along the hedges, Mira heard a vaguely familiar voice.

"Ah, the little chit with the punch stains." Turning sharply, Mira saw the elderly woman she had encountered last night, sitting in the small courtyard adjoining the garden. Her iron-gray eyes narrowed as a shrewd expression settled on her face. "Come over here, child . . . I can barely make you out through all this sun." Casting a dubious look at the hazy sky, Mira made her way over to the shady tree and the chairs where the woman and her stern-faced companion were seated. "Who is chaperoning you? Why do I always see you wandering about alone?"

"I dislike being supervised." Mira said, and smiled slowly as the woman's lips twitched in amusement.

"By Lucifer's wig, so do I. Sit down here and talk to me."

Mira obeyed immediately. "My chaperon is Lady Berkeley."

"Lady Berkeley . . ." the old matriarch mused. "Egad, you're the one. I've heard many rumors about you, my gel."

"You don't believe them, I hope."

"I believe there's a grain of truth in every rumor. Very few people have the imagination to create one that is entirely false, you know. Of course, when I was younger, some of the rumors about me were indeed outright lies, but they were manifestly more complimentary to me than the truth would have been."

"And what was the truth about you?"

The woman looked at her approvingly. "It's rare that anyone dares to ask me that. I'm certainly not going to answer, but it speaks well for you that you asked." The graying, elaborately dressed head tilted to one side. "I heard that you were toasted many times last night while the men were liquoring . . . it seems that the gossip has done nothing to harm your popularity."

"How flattering."

"Don't be too pleased. A man will drink to a woman much more readily than he'll choose her to wive."

"I'm not overly concerned with finding a husband."

"How delightfully unconventional. But are you not afraid of becoming an ape leader?"

"A . . . a what?" Mira asked, beginning to smile at the odd phrase. "I'm afraid I'm not familiar with the expression."

"It is an old maid's punishment for refusing to 'be fruitful and multiply.' She will go to hell, of course, and her duty will be to lead apes around." The matriarch eyed her wickedly, apparently hoping to shock her. Undaunted, Mira grinned at her.

"It was, I assume, an unmarried man who devised this punishment?"

The question caused the old woman to laugh and the companion to choke behind a lace handkerchief. "Go find my son," the woman said to her sour-faced companion. "He should be down by the river with the rest of the family."

"Your son?" Mira inquired politely.

"Yes. I intend to introduce you to him."

Another one. Mira suppressed an inner sigh as the companion rose from her chair and left. Briefly she contemplated the idea of telling this sharp, aggressive little woman that she did not care to meet anyone. She wondered what the son of such a mother would be like—crushed and submissive, or gruff and surly?

"You're not English."

"No, madam," Mira answered docilely.

"French?"

"Yes, madam."

"French," the old woman repeated dourly. "Well, I suppose you can't help it."

"No," Mira agreed gravely, smiling slightly at the typically English attitude. What was it that caused the Britons to consider themselves so superior to the rest of the world? In France, Englishmen were regarded as cultural barbarians for their lackluster manners and tasteless food, for their lack of grace and crude commercialism.

"I have never heard of the Germains of France."

Mira raised her eyebrows in a surprised manner,

then shrugged. "I can understand why you have not," she said kindly. "The Germains are very conservative, very discreet. We have never allowed the family name to be publicized or associated with scandal."

"Until you?"

"Ah, you have a point, madam. But one cannot pay attention to unkind rumors, one must rise above them."

The grilling seemed to continue for several minutes, while Mira began to enjoy the thrust-and-parry conversation. Evidently the other woman did as well, for her interest in Mira increased with each minute. Where in France had Mira originally come from? Which young men had paid court to her so far, and whom was she interested in? How had her family come to be acquainted with the Berkeleys? Mira spun dramatic and intricately detailed answers to the prying questions. The conversation must have entertained the woman to a great degree, because she frowned as she saw her companion returning.

"The devil. We'll have to continue our talk some other time. They've arrived."

"Madam, before you introduce me to anyone, I must remind you that I don't know your name."

"You don't? You don't know who I am? I thought everyone did. Help me up, child."

"Of course. No, I do not know who—" Mira began, helping the elderly woman out of the chair. She stopped in mid-sentence as she saw whom the companion had brought back, and she blinked in surprise as she stared up into clear gray eyes.

"Alec," the elderly woman said briskly, "this is the one."

And with that she bade the companion to lead her away, leaving the two of them to stare after her in stunned silence. Juliana's notion of an introduction had never been very complicated.

"Was that . . . is that . . . your mother?" Mira felt her cheeks turn crimson.

"Unfortunately, yes."

"Oh, the things I said to her," Mira groaned, covering her mouth with her hand. "Oh, the things I *told* her!"

"She *would* pick you." Alec's voice was threaded with dry resignation. "I should have expected it."

"Pick me for what?"

"Pick you for me."

"Me for . . ." Mira stammered, now regarding him with such complete confusion that Alec laughed.

"Mira, *ma chère*, don't ask me to explain what is going on. I'm not at all certain that I know. Or care."

She looked at him in confusion, and as the sun shone on his hair and glowed in his eyes, she thought that she had imagined last night. In the light of day it seemed impossible that she had loved him, touched him, known him in the most intimate way possible. Yet he had given her that freedom last night, hadn't he? Hadn't he encouraged her to want him and respond to him?

"What was your first thought this morning?" he asked, smiling slowly.

"What a ghastly night it was. And you?"

"I was besieged by a number of important questions."

"The most pressing one being . . . ?"

"What it would feel like to wake up with you in my arms," he answered reflectively. "And I wondered if you kick in your sleep, if you make any noise, if you pull the covers onto your side of the bed or—"

"I don't do any of those things."

His eyes glowed warmly. "I would like to have the opportunity to find out."

Just then Rosalie's voice broke into the conversation. "Mireille?"

"The Berkeleys . . ." Mira turned her head to watch Rand and Rosalie strolling toward them.

"Don't look so guilty." Alec grinned at her unsettled expression. "Keeping company with me is not a crime."

"In Rosalie's opinion it is," she assured him, and for the next few minutes she could not look at any of them . . . not Alec and Rand, who exchanged polite and cordial greetings, not Rosalie, who was eyeing her with vigilant interest.

"I was hoping for the opportunity of speaking to Miss Germain in private," Alec finally said, directing the gentle request to Rosalie. "Perhaps you will permit me to walk with her through the garden in order to gain a few moments of secluded conversation. Of course, I realize that it might be looked upon as an imprudent demand—"

"Yes, her reputation—" Rosalie began.

"I have not the slightest inclination to leave so much as a bruise on her reputation," Alec continued firmly. "However, my intentions are nothing but honorable in making this request, and after the discussion is done, I trust you will understand my desire for unhindered and uninterrupted—"

"Enough, Falkner," Rand said, his hazel eyes twinkling with a smile. "I am certain that my wife gives her consent."

"Yes," Rosalie murmured, her blue eyes round with surprise at the words "honorable" and "intentions." Everyone knew what was implied when those two words were used in conjunction with each other. Overcome with curiosity, she threw a sharp look at Mira's downbent head.

"Thank you." Alec held out an arm for Mira to take. "Miss Germain?" he prompted, and as her fingers curved around the top of his forearm, they walked along the garden path at a leisurely pace.

"I thought you said that you never ask for permission." Mira concentrated intently on the path in front of them.

"I did not say that I wouldn't if necessary."

"So formal, so amiable . . . I am trying to remember if you've ever begged me so prettily for anything—"

"Miss Germain, have I ever told you that you have the makings of a fine shrew?"

"I don't recall that, no."

They stopped in a secluded spot, and Mira sat down on a small marble bench while Alec leaned his shoulder against a sturdy tree. "Then have I told you," he continued more softly, "that your eyes are like two dark stars and that your hair is softer than silk?"

"Not often enough." Mira felt an unfamiliar shyness cover her like a diaphanous veil.

"Mira . . ." Alec opened his mouth and then closed it, looking as if he did not know how to continue. It was the first time Mira had ever seen him look so indecisive . . . almost uneasy . . . and she sat there staring at him silently, having no idea what he intended to say to her. "It is time to be honest with each other," he finally said. "There has been enough game-playing between us, enough secrecy, enough . . . emotional subterfuge. It's time now to look at things honestly . . . and you must be honest with yourself as well as with me."

"I'll try . . . but perhaps you'd better tell me what it is that we are talking about."

"First of all, some things are obvious. You know how I feel about you—"

"No, I don't," Mira said, finding that her heart was pounding with nervousness. "I don't know that at all."

"I've wanted you from the first moment I saw you. There have always been many practical reasons not to, but nothing I can do would change the fact that I want you more than I've ever wanted another woman. It has been an unending invasion, relentless, tireless—something that I don't seem to have control over. I've told you before that you suit me . . . but it is more than that. You are the only woman I've ever known who can swear like a dockyard lumper. You are also the only one who has somehow managed to win the approval of my mother, though I am not certain if that counts for you or against you."

"I would consider it a mark in my favor."

Alec smiled, looking more at ease. "Do you remember the morning I was thrown from Sovereign? After what I has said to you before, I expected you to run up and kick me . . . and you should have . . . but you were compassionate. I suppose it all began at that moment."

"Yes, I remember."

"And then, that first time . . . it meant more than I had expected, to discover that I was the only man ever to have you. I was the first man you voluntarily gave yourself to, without any feelings of obligation, without anything to gain, without any bargain struck between us." His gaze was bright and intent as it held hers captive, all traces of humor fleeing his expression. "I want you," he said quietly, "to be my wife. In spite of all I said before, it seems to be the only way to make sense out of what's between us."

Mira stared at him in mute amazement. "Well?" he pressed after a few moments of silence. "What is your answer?"

Gradually she found her voice. "Answer to what?" she asked, stalling for time that she desperately needed in order to think. "I wasn't aware that you had asked me a question."

"What is your reaction to the idea?"

"I . . . I'm not certain." Mira stood up, too agitated to remain sitting. This moment was something she had not even dared to fantasize about. He had just asked her to be his wife! But something was wrong, all of it felt wrong to her, and she didn't know how to explain it, either to him or to herself. "I'm more than surprised . . . I'm astounded that you asked me to marry you."

"Yes," he said impatiently. "Now give me your answer."

"I can't . . . not right away, not without first telling you how I feel," she said. "You asked me to be honest . . . I owe that to you, at least."

"What do you mean, 'at least'?"

"Alec . . ." she said, and it was painful to continue, because suddenly she understood the truth for the first time and she wished that she could just ignore it. "My first impulse would be to accept your proposal—it would be easy to say yes. I want to say that word, more than anything I've ever wanted."

"Then say it."

"I can't. Not when I know what a disaster it would be. You haven't thought about what it would mean, I know you haven't."

"Of course I have," he said roughly. "I'm not a fool—I know it will be difficult, and I realize what we'll have to face—"

"I doubt that," Mira said, fumbling for the right words. "You don't fully realize how different we are. It would be impossible for you to understand just how different my background is from yours. You've said that you want me, and . . . I feel the same about you. But I'm not the kind of person you really want for a wife."

"Would you let me be the judge of my own feelings?"

"Your feelings about me are going to change," she said, with such utter conviction that Alec was temporarily surprised into silence. "And if you made me your wife, you would wake up one morning and see what a tragic mistake you had made, and that you should have married one of your own kind—"

"Mira," he interrupted, and his expression had changed, as though he had sensed that his anger would only make her more obstinate. His voice was soft and very persuasive. "You *are* my own kind . . . and you know I'm not an impetuous boy who doesn't know what he wants. I've thought about everything, including your past, and I still want to marry you. You're afraid that your past will come between us. That's not for you to worry about. My feelings about your past are my problem, not yours, and I'll deal with them—"

"I don't think you'll be able to. Almost any other barrier between us might be surmountable . . . but there are things about me that I can never change, just as there are things about you that never will. We don't belong together, and you don't know how much I wish we did . . . but I can't marry you. The answer is no. *I can't.*"

"Just like that. After all that's happened between us, you can refuse me so quickly? . . . Name of God, do you think I made this proposal lightly? It hasn't been easy for me to make this decision! I've had the choice of the best blood in Europe and I've just proposed instead to a woman with no title, no name of any consequence, no family—a woman who won't tell me much about herself or her past."

"That's exactly what I've been trying to explain."

"My point is that I know all of that about you, and I've decided to accept it. Do you think I'd propose to you without making certain that it's what I want?"

"My past—"

"Your past," he repeated with disgust. "I'm damn well sick of this past that I know so little about—what is so horrifying about it? What are you hiding? Why don't you tell me about it and let me decide if it's something I can't deal with?"

Mira's cheeks burned, and she could not meet his eyes. She couldn't tell him. She did not want to see the revulsion in his eyes when she told him that she was a whore's daughter. It would be more honest of her to tell him . . . but if he knew of her childhood and where she had spent it, he would not be able to stand the sight of her. He would regret every time he had ever touched her, and *that* would be too much for her to bear. And if she did what her heart was crying out for her to do—if she married him and kept the past to herself—the constant fear of his finding out would be impossible to live with.

"No," she whispered. "I'm sorry.'

Alec raked a hand through his hair and cursed. "You're leaving me with no options," he said curtly. "You've made it clear before that you don't want to be my mistress. You wanted more than that. Fine— I've offered to marry you. But you don't want that, because you think we're too different to mix well together. That happens to be a matter of opinion. You're afraid of what your past might do to us . . . but you won't explain anything about it to me. The obvious conclusion is that that you don't want *anything* from me . . . and that, my dear Miss Germain, is something you'll never make me believe."

"It's true. I don't want anything from—"

"Stop." Alec's voice was oddly flat, as if it were necessary to command such control over himself that he could allow no emotion to show through. "No more. It's obvious that we both need time to think."

"It's over."

"*No.* We're going to talk about this later, when I've had time to figure out what the hell is going on."

"It's over," she repeated gently.

"Before I take you back to the Berkeleys," he said, his gray eyes turning silver with their chilling intensity, "I am going to say one more thing. In the past few years I have either lost or thrown away almost everything of personal value to me. But I am not going to lose you."

12

*R*osalie simultaneously struggled with the window of the private salon and fanned herself, her cheeks flushed with agitation. "Lord, it's so closed and dark everywhere at Brighton—why doesn't anyone like to let sunlight in here?"

"Fades the furniture." Mira sat down in a chair, inhaling gratefully as a cool, merciful breeze swept through the room.

"Mireille, you look so white—"

"I feel ill."

"You should feel relieved and very proud of yourself—"

"Proud?" Mira's voice cracked with a combination of laughter and despair. She lifted a hand to her forehead and closed her eyes in a helpless gesture. "I'm burning with misery. I know I did the right thing . . . I used my head, I made a sensible decision . . . but my heart keeps saying 'Look at who you are—how can you refuse such an offer? You should thank God for his mercy, and then accept Lord Falkner's proposal immediately.' But I know I'm not good enough for him, and when he comes to realize that as well, he'll—"

"Mireille, stop it." Rosalie paused in her vigorous fanning and nearly glared at her. "Of course you're good enough for him. That's not the issue at all. You were right to refuse him because of the kind of man he is. There is something every marriage must have, and it is more essential than love or passion. Respect. It is more important than anything else, and he's not capable of respecting *any* woman."

"I don't think you're right about him," Mira blurted out in confusion. "He would never harm anyone who couldn't defend himself . . . he's really very gentle and kind . . . he is hotheaded but not cruel. And he respects anyone who isn't afraid to stand up to him. I . . ." Her voice faltered and she said more softly, "Deep inside I know he's worthy of trust, even though I'm afraid to give it to him."

"Are we speaking of Lord Falkner?" Rosalie demanded. "Mireille, you barely know anything about him! Gentle? Trustworthy? Everything I have heard about him is to the contrary. Do you know how heartless he can be, have you heard anything about how callous he is? The Falkners are much feared and respected, but each and every one of them is abominably arrogant, self-inflated, uncaring, and Alec Falkner is the worst—"

"Whatever else he is, he is not heartless." Mira rubbed her forehead absently. "I am beginning to think that he is often misunderstood."

"Misunderstood! Mireille, listen to yourself!"

"You think I have no rational perspective on the situation. But I do."

"If all that I have heard about him has been wrong, if all of London and I have misunderstood him, and you *really think* that he could be a good husband, then why did you refuse him?"

"I told you before. He . . . he does not want to love someone who is not perfect . . . and I am certainly far from perfect. And furthermore, I don't want to be the wife of a man in his position. It's not something that I am suited for."

"Mireille, it wasn't easy for me," Rosalie said rapidly, in a different voice than before. "I was not prepared in any way to be the wife of an earl, much less the wife of a Berkeley! It is wonderful in some ways, and dreadful in others, but I would endure twice as much in order to be married to Rand."

"*Sang de Dieu*, I shouldn't have refused Lord Falkner." Mira drew her knees up on the chair and buried her head in her arms, unmindful of the position's lack of dignity. "I should have said yes, but all I could think of were all the reasons why I shouldn't. Maybe I should have accepted him. Maybe I should have said yes and ignored everything else. I wish someone else could make the decision for me."

"You'll forget about him soon enough. There are so many other men who will want you—"

"No, no other men. I couldn't. Another man even touching me . . . I won't even think about it." Mira looked up with eyes as dark as a midnight sky, the pupils dilated. She was beyond tears. "Without him, I will be alone," she whispered. "Even if I became another man's wife, even if I had children and a family . . . I would still be alone. He is the only escape from it."

Startled, Rosalie stared at her and shook her head, her mouth falling open. "How on earth can you feel this way about him? You hardly know him!"

"I do know him. He is the one who . . ."

Even though Mira did not finish the sentence, Rosalie understood what she had started to say, and she was stunned. "Mireille . . . what an idiot I've been. I didn't understand how this could have happened so quickly. As far as I knew, the only time you had seen Lord Falkner was at Sackville's hunt and the night we met with Brummell . . . but that's wrong, isn't it? You've seen him many more times than that . . . you must have . . . oh, how mutton-headed I've been! It was never Sackville. Lord Falkner was the one you loved in Hampshire, wasn't he?"

"Yes," Mira hid her face again, drawing herself into a tight ball.

"Why didn't you tell me?"

"You were so much against him . . . and besides, I wanted to forget about him. I tried to, with all my strength."

"I'm not against him if he's the only one who'll make you happy," Rosalie said hesitantly. "I know you're not a bad judge of character . . . you wouldn't love someone who didn't have *some* redeeming qualities. It's not too late for you to change things. We're leaving Brighton in a few hours. Perhaps you should go to him now . . . tell him you've thought about what he said and—"

"I can't. I've got to leave things as they are. He was right: we both need time to think. And if he still wants me, he will know where I am."

"You should have heard her bid me farewell," Carr said, filled with the boisterous spirits of a young and infatuated man. "Desolate. Those big dark eyes looking up at me, and that little bit of an accent in her voice as she told me that she hoped that she would see me again—"

"Are you certain that you're not mistaking common politeness for a declaration of affection?" Alec crossed his long legs, one over the other, and rested them on the carriage seat opposite his. Carr regarded the muddied buckskins with disdain and edged a few inches away from them in order to preserve the immaculate condition of his coat.

"Very certain. Her heart was in her face."

"How convenient for you."

Ignoring Alec's chilling responses to his rapture-tinged descriptions of Mireille Germain, Carr sighed happily and rested his dark head against the blue upholstery of the carriage. "You don't understand how I feel about her . . . you don't understand how *different* she is from any other woman I've ever met. Shy and flirtatious, and witty—without being cattish like all the others—and she's the sweetest, dearest—"

"How far did it go between you two?" Alec asked, suddenly tense.

"I'm *serious* about her, Alec! With any other woman I might have tried something, but I plan to take time with this one. I want her to know that I respect her."

Alec leaned back in his seat. "I hope that it will not be too much of a strain on your amorous sensibilities to engage with that maid at the Rummer this afternoon."

"No," Carr replied with the air of a man resigned to his duty. "I'm going to flirt and grapple with Jane in order to find out more about Holt . . . because I must, not because I want to." Slowly Carr smiled. "Her big pitchers don't mean a thing to me."

"The effort will not have been in vain if she'll make you into less of a greenhead," Alec said, grinning suddenly. Holt had also entertained a great fascination with big pitchers, an interest which had provided the material for many jokes and quips among their circle of friends.

"Actually, I do hope to get some useful information out of her," Carr said, his tone more serious. "I think that Holt started seeing her after Leila disappeared. Maybe Jane could provide a clue about what he was doing, or what kind of enemies he might have had." He sighed, his green eyes losing their mischievous sparkle. "Though it's hard to believe he had any enemies. Everyone liked him."

"No. Not everyone liked him." Alec studied his young cousin, feeling a twinge of compassion . . . he had not realized before now just how much Carr had idealized Holt. "Holt wasn't perfect. He was a good man, but you know just as well as anyone that he had his share of faults. He was a bastard sometimes, just like all the rest of us." There was no reaction from Carr except for a quickly indrawn breath, but Alec knew how much the remark had angered him. "I'd rather disabuse you of your idealism than have you make him into a damned martyr," he continued quietly. "He wouldn't have wanted that."

"I don't want to talk about this."

"You're not giving yourself a fair chance by trying to live up to his memory, especially when you seem to remember him as a saint instead of an ordinary—"

"All right," Carr snapped, his temper flaring.

"Just as long as you understand—"

"I understand," Carr said savagely, and for several minutes there was nothing but silence between them. Eventually the closed carriage shuddered to a halt. Alec paused and looked at his cousin as the footman opened the door.

"Still want to take a hackney from here on?"

"I couldn't take this to the Rummer."

"Be careful. Hackney drivers are known for their ability to strip a Rum Ned like you clean in five minutes. Keep your wits sharp, and have a care for what you drink."

"I've been to the Rummer before," Carr said with affronted dignity. "And despite your opinion of me, I am occasionally capable of thinking with my head and not my thomas."

Alec grinned reluctantly. "My confidence in you is greatly restored. *Bonne chance*, cousin."

Both men got out of the carriage, and Alec waited until Carr procured a hackney of disreputable appearance, its floor covered with straw that did little to camouflage the vermin it was intended to conceal. Sighing, Alec walked to the nearby bakery and peered through the diamond-shaped panes of the window before going in.

A fine mist of flour hung in the air, coating the windows, the floors, the tables and walls. The scents of yeast and butter rose thickly to Alec's nostrils, causing him to sniff appreciatively. The shop was well-lit, comfortable, and bustling with several towheaded children of varying sizes, all clearly members of the same family.

"Sir?" A round-faced, buxom woman approached him with a smile. Her appearance was warm and motherly; she had soft cheeks and twinkly brown eyes, and such a gentle manner that no one could help but be charmed by her. Alec mentally contrasted her to the sharp, iron-willed Juliana and smiled slightly.

"Are you Mrs. Holburn?"

"Falkner," she said with a start, her hands going up to her throat, her eyes gleaming with fear. "I thought you were dead . . . I heard that you had been found in . . . Oh, dear God . . ."

"Mrs. Holburn, I'm not Holt," Alec said swiftly, taking the liberty of holding her elbow as he saw how violently she was shaking. "I am his cousin, Lord Falkner. I did not mean to shock you. Would you like to sit—?"

"Mother?" a young voice interrupted. A flaxen-haired girl with round, pretty features ran up to them and brushed Alec's hand away. She slid an arm around Mrs. Holburn's waist and threw Alec a guarded look. Her skin lost its healthy pink color as she looked at him. "What's happened to Leila?" she asked sharply.

"It's not him," Mrs. Holburn said, staring at Alec with a mixture of fear and grief. Twisting her hands in her apron, she made an effort to calm herself. "I knew Holt Falkner was dead . . . but for a second I hoped that I had been wrong . . . and then I thought you were his ghost."

"No. He is gone. And I'm certainly not a ghost." Alec made an attempt to smile reassuringly, but his effort was met with little success. "I have come here in the hope that you would help me with the answers to a few questions. Would it distress you unduly to talk about him?"

She did not answer him directly, biting her lip at first, then asking a question with such hesitance that it seemed she was afraid of the answer.

"Lord Falkner . . . have you also come here to discuss my daughter? Do you know anything about Leila? Have you found out where she is? Do you know who might have . . . ?"

Alec shook his head, his expression gentling with pity. "I don't know anything about her. I'm sorry."

"There is a table in the back," Mrs. Holburn said, her eyes glassy with unshed tears. "My husband is away, but I will talk to you." A large part of the family crowded around the table, leaving Alec a respectful distance of two feet on either side. The oldest girls attended to the customers that wandered into the front part of the shop, and took a few minutes here and there to run back and listen to the conversation.

Half an hour later Alec began to understand why Holt had kept this part of his life secret. It had been his private haven, untainted by the slick and sophisticated manners of the people he had usually associated with. Most of their friends would have jeered at the revelation that Holt had been in love with a baker's daughter and had spent so many hours in the kitchen of a solidly middle-class family. Yet this family, this shop, this home, were filled with warmth and irresistible simplicity that were foreign to the Falkners. Alec could easily imagine Holt sitting here dandling a child on his knee and smiling crookedly at the girl who had caught his affections.

"I warned Leila about him every day," Mrs. Holburn said, a smile flitting across her features. "I said he intended to play the devil with her—Mr. Holburn agreed, but there was nothing we could do to stop her from seeing him. And then he began to charm Mr. Holburn and me as much as he had the rest of the family, and we started to understand that he did care for Leila. I did not see what good would come of it, though. Leila was a good girl, and I knew that she would probably refuse if he offered to . . . to keep her. I never expected that he'd ask her to marry him, but he stood here in this exact spot and asked Mr. Holburn for her hand."

"I never knew that." Alec cast his mind back for some clue, some sign that Holt might have given about his feelings for Leila . . . yes, there had been a few weeks of utter contentment and peace . . . but during the last two months of his life Holt had been wilder than ever before, drinking and capering, immersed in a mood that encompassed extreme highs and lows.

"He did. And he was sincere, Lord Falkner. I believe that he would have married her. But the next day I sent Leila on an errand—she usually went on errands alone, since it was never very far. And she . . . she . . ."

"She never came back," one of the children said simply.

Alec's gray eyes widened. He listened alertly as Mrs. Holburn cleared her throat and continued. "There was no sign of her. No trace at all. We were all in shock, especially your cousin. He told me that he would find her. If he spent the rest of his . . ."

"If he spent the rest of his life looking for her," Alec said impassively, nodding for her to continue. Her eyes became wet with renewed grief.

"We heard from him often. Until a week had gone by without a word . . . and we sent a message to him, which was not answered. I thought that he had decided to forget about her, or that he had lost interest in her . . . we kept trying to reach him, and finally received word of what had happened to him." She sighed softly. "A terrible pity. He was a young and very handsome lad. When I first saw you today, I thought it was him, come back to tell me—"

"I am sorry."

"Are you going to try to find out what happened to him?"

"Yes."

"Would you—?"

"If I discover what happened to Leila, I will tell you."

They looked at each other and smiled faintly, saying nothing more. There was no need, no use, for thanks.

Carr met Alec at his London terrace rooms a few hours later, smelling abominably of rum but remaining surprisingly lucid. As Alec's valet brought a large silver tray loaded with strong coffee and scones, the Falkners exchanged information. "He asked her to marry him?" Carr asked, and shook his head in wonder, raking his hands through rumpled black hair. "Poor Holt—to propose and have her disappear the next day. Think she ran?"

"No reason to. She was nothing but a baker's daughter. He was rich . . . he was a Falkner. She would have been a fool to refuse him if he proposed." Alec stared moodily into the dark, steaming coffee. "No, she didn't run. In fact, it's possible that he didn't ask her to marry him, though I wouldn't take Mrs. Holburn for a liar."

"Why do you think he might not have proposed to her?"

"He didn't tell me about it. And Holt kept few secrets from me."

"Good God, of course he wouldn't have told you!" Carr exclaimed tactlessly, biting into a thick scone.

Alec frowned. "About something as important as an engagement, he damn well would have."

"If I had been Holt, *I* wouldn't have! Marrying a baker's daughter? You would have talked him out of it, Alec—you know you would have. You would have said that he could do better . . . and that it was a Falkner's responsibility to marry into a good bloodline, and you would have pointed out all of her faults so accurately that Holt could only have seen her as a flawed creature after that. You would have done your best to split them apart."

"The devil I would have!" Alec snapped, standing up abruptly and pacing over to the extinct fireplace. Bracing his elbows on the mantel, he rested his forehead on his hands. "Dammit . . . does the entire world view me as some insensitive snob?" he asked in a muffled voice.

"We all understand that you were brought up that way."

"Bloody hell," Alec muttered.

"Wouldn't you have looked down on her?"

"I don't know." Alec refused to admit aloud that a year ago he probably would not have approved of Holt's marrying Leila Holburn. He *definitely* wouldn't have approved of it. But everything had changed. Everything was different now.

Or was it?

He thought of all that he had said to Mira, and her words seemed to catch hold of something in his heart. Suddenly he was stunned at the realization of what he had done . . . and more important, what he had not done. There were many things he had not told her, and silently she had begged him to give her the reassurance that he had been too blind, too stubborn to provide. *It did not matter* about her past, and the things that she lacked paled in importance beside all that she had. Was anyone else capable of giving him what she could? Would he ever be happy knowing that she was not completely his? No. Another chance, he thought, his mind clicking with the frenzied efficiency that desperation had inspired . . . I've got to have another chance.

"Well, I talked with Jane this afternoon, and there's no doubt she's a rum doxy," Carr was saying, and Alec forced himself to listen.

"What did you find out?"

"She knows something. I plied her with damned good-quality nantz and got her to talk about Holt. She implied that she had some names that might interest me. But she won't tell me yet. . . . I'm going to go back and find out tomorrow."

"Good. You do that. I'm heading back to Staffordshire."

"Tonight?"

"Yes, tonight." Alec raised his voice a few degrees and called to his valet. "Do you hear that, Walter? Pry your ear away from the keyhole and start packing."

"Yes, my lord," came a muffled voice from behind the door.

For other men, love was a gift, a blessing, a source of joy, a miracle. For Alec it was a calamity. He knew that Mira was only a few miles away in Warwick, a distance that he could have traversed quickly and easily. But he remained at the Falkner estate, searching for the right words to say to her, knowing that they would be the most important words he would ever speak. Perhaps it would have been easier had he been a man who possessed more humility . . . yet humility did not sit well on his shoulders. He was not accustomed to asking for something that had always been granted to him automatically, and so a woman's favor had never held much value for him until it had been withheld. Alternately he cursed Mira and wanted Mira, damned her in waking moments and held her in his dreams. His torment would not last forever, yet it was bound to last a good deal longer, and would have if not for the intervention of Juliana.

She ventured downstairs late one night, still fully dressed, her slate-gray hair neatly pinned in a coronet. Juliana's face changed from its usual grim self-assurance to a softer, kinder expression as she looked at her son, who had fallen asleep on a sofa with a bottle of brandy clutched to his midriff. His dark features, stamped for the past few days with frustration and obstinacy, were relaxed in sleep. His broad mouth, customarily quirked with skeptical smiles, was touched with a vulnerability that he would never have revealed voluntarily.

"My boy," Juliana murmured, looking down at the handsome stranger who was her son, "much easier for you, had you been more like your father. But you resemble me far too well, which is your downfall, and your strength, and the reason why you're presently too intoxicated to hear me."

She knew him more than anyone, and less than anyone. Reaching for the bottle clasped between his large hands, Juliana pulled it away from him. Alec stirred, a sleepy sound escaping his lips.

"Mira . . ." Slowly his eyes flickered open, drowsy and silver. He focused on Juliana, and blinked, and sat up without a sound, still looking at her.

"We have some things to discuss, Alec," she said briskly in a voice that would brook no refusal. "I will not require you to tell me everything. I do not wish to know more about you than is necessary. But I will insist on having the answers to a few questions."

"Mireille . . ." Rosalie appeared at the doorway of Mira's bedchamber, fidgeting in a manner that was completely unlike her. "A visitor is waiting for you downstairs."

Mira looked up from the book she had been reading, her fingers crinkling the pages as she gripped the edges. Ordinarily one of the maids would have been sent with the message. The fact that Rosalie had brought it to her indicated the importance of the caller. "Who?"

"Lady Falkner. She never pays calls on anyone, never, and she is downstairs in my home demanding to see you."

"Don't panic. I'll just need a moment to compose myself—"

"Hurry. Please. I have always been considered a skillful hostess, but she defies my every attempt to make idle conversation. No, don't do your hair over, just comb the sides . . . hurry!" Disappearing around the corner, Rosalie fled back to the stairs and descended with light, pattering feet. Mira inspected her appearance in the mirror, mentally blessing the fact that this morning she had chosen to wear a prim, conventional gown of pale yellow. Jerking the puffed sleeves firmly over each shoulder, she stared at her reflection in attentive panic. His mother, she thought, her fingertips flying to her mouth in a flustered gesture, and then she forced herself to relax. I liked her well enough before I found out that she was his mother, she reminded herself. Her dark, finely winged brows rose a quarter of an inch as a sudden thought struck her. Without hesitation, Mira went to the armoire and pulled out a soft cloth bag, taking it with her as she left to greet her caller.

Mira was met with two smiles as she entered the rose-colored salon: one from Rosalie, which could only be described as relieved; and one from Juliana . . . a vaguely calculating smile. Mira recalled having seen it on Alec's face once or twice.

"Lady Falkner, what a delightful surprise this is."

"You and I seem to have made a habit of surprising each other," the matriarch replied, settling back into the corner of the sleekly upholstered sofa and pointing to a chair nearby. "I came here to discuss the fact that we have been the victims of a rather interesting coincidence." She pinned Rosalie with a commanding stare. "Child, I came here without my companion because I wish for this conversation to be private. Would you—?"

"Certainly," Rosalie said equably, and sent Mira an encouraging glance before leaving the salon and closing the door quietly.

"Lady Falkner, may I ask if your son knows that you are here?" Mira inquired, seating herself with straight-backed grace and settling the cloth bag in her lap.

"He does not. At the moment I imagine that he is still abed, having last night drunk himself into the happy oblivion commonly experienced by mudlarks after a fresh rain." Mira frowned, both at the knowledge that Alec had been drinking and at the critical note in Lady Falkner's voice as she spoke of her son. Was there no one to offer him sympathy or comfort? Why did everyone, including his mother, seem to persist in regarding him as self-sufficient and amoral? "You needn't rise to his defense, child . . . I am here on his behalf," Juliana pointed out, and Mira lifted her chin slightly.

"I do not intend to rise to his defense. In fact, I do not wish to speak about Lord Falkner at all."

Juliana tilted her head inquiringly, responding favorably to the inexorable note in Mira's voice. "You have spirit and backbone, Miss Germain. I saw it from the very first, and that was the reason I introduced you to my son. However, I did not know that the two of you were already well-acquainted. I did not know who you were."

"I did not know who *you* were."

"No matter. Now, there are other things we must discuss."

"Lady Falkner, I was sincere in saying that I do not wish to discuss your son."

"Then why the devil are you here?"

Mira looked at her steadily, opening the bag and holding up a dried blackish-green stalk with pointed leaves and small white-and-purple flowers.

"Eyebright." Next she held up a generous handful of dried petals. "Celandine. Rue. Roses and—"

"Enough, enough." Although a betraying glint of

interest had crossed her face, Juliana frowned blackly.
"You're a well-meaning little chit. But I am too old to
bother with nonsense—"

"It is not nonsense. Many people's eyes dim with
age, and I know this will help you. I have seen it work
many times. If you just apply this every now and
then—"

"If I let you put some noxious concoction on my
eyes . . . and may God witness that if you cause me
any pain, I will leave here at once . . . if I allow this,
you will hear what I have come here to say."

"That seems to be a fair exchange." Mira folded the
mixture of herbs in a handkerchief with an air of
satisfaction.

"It does not. You have nothing to lose by the arrangement, whereas I am risking what little sight I do
have in order to pamper your inexplicable obsession to
doctor me."

"You were saying about Lord Falkner . . ." Mira
prompted, carrying the handkerchief to the untouched
tea tray on the Sheraton pier table.

"What precipitated my decision to call on you was
my discovery last night about the medallion."

Mira paused in the act of moistening the handkerchief with warm water. "The medallion . . ." She
flushed and turned her face away, feeling Juliana's
intent eyes resting on her averted profile.

"After many roundabout questions and astute guesses,
I wrung some reluctant admissions out of my son. I
had previously noticed the medallion's absence, you
see, and I began to suspect what he had done with it.
Alec admitted that he had given it to you."

"You would like it back?" Mira questioned fiercely,
pulling at the gold chain concealed underneath her
gown and fishing the medallion out of her bodice.
"Take it. I don't want it." The gesture was a grave
tactical error. Juliana pounced on the revelation with a

smile that was both pleased and mocking at the same time.

"You're wearing it, I see. No, leave it on. But kindly remove your scowl." Murmuring something under her breath, Mira finished dampening the handkerchief and brought it over to the elderly woman. With a martyred attitude, Juliana rested her neck against the back of the sofa and allowed the handkerchief to be placed over her closed eyes. "It stings," she observed mildly.

"Only for the first few minutes," Mira replied, sitting down and eyeing her cautiously. After a minute of silence had passed, she could not resist asking, "If you don't want it returned, then why have you mentioned the medallion?"

Juliana lifted a fragile hand to the cloth over her eyes, patting it into place carefully. "My dear, I am too old to be embarrassed by most things. But even I must acknowledge that the situation reeks of an appalling excess of melodrama—due entirely to my son, I admit freely. He is a Falkner, and you'll discover that they are proud, stubborn, and very sentimental people with a developed sense of the dramatic. When he gave you that medallion, I am certain that you thought it a very pretty ornament. What you were not aware of was that Alec's gift to you possessed a rather . . . symbolic significance."

"Symbolic of what?"

"That medallion has been passed between members of the family for years as a sign of an unbreakable bond. After receiving it from his father, my husband gave it to me in gratitude for the first son I bore him. I gave it to Alec when he was sixteen, to mark his coming of age. When Alec gave the medallion to you, he marked you as his. It was not a trifling gesture . . . and this I know about my son: he will never allow it to stray far from his reach."

Agitatedly Mira plucked at the gleaming medallion around her neck. "I must give it back to him."

"I gather he has proposed to you."

"Yes . . ."

"And you refused him?"

"Yes."

"Why?"

"Lady Falkner . . . I would feel very uncomfortable complaining about your elder son to your face."

"I am perfectly aware that he has faults, child, and I would not consider your complaints an aspersion on my capabilities as a mother. I have been quite proficient as a parent. His faults are not due to anything I may or may not have done, but are derived from the Falkner side of the family. So tell me, if you please, why you refused him."

"I feel that . . . that he is interested in me despite what he knows is best for himself. I am well aware of his family and his heritage . . . I am also aware that there is a certain kind of woman who would better suit him as a wife than I would. He would not *choose* to want me—frankly, he has made that clear to me—and I know that marriage between us would be a mistake. I would not want him ever to regret having made me his wife . . . but I'm afraid that someday he would."

"If my son's behavior has been what I expect it has," Juliana said, "then it is fortunate for you that I am here to explain it to you. He is a Falkner, through and through, and Falkner men are jealous, brutish creatures—"

"I wouldn't put it that way."

"Don't contradict me, child. I know what I am talking about. I married one, and raised two, and have been surrounded by the rest of the pack for years. Alec is the one most in need of reforming. But he has endured and thrived under special circumstances. You must be aware that his father died when Alec was not yet a man?"

"Yes."

"My son was forced to be a man too soon, and that has made him unique, and very hard, and inclined to demand too much, not only from himself but also from others. He is at once excessively cynical and excessively idealistic. I will tell you the reason why he is still unmarried: he has always wanted the perfect woman while believing in his heart that she does not exist. Of course, that is not so unusual, my dear . . . every man dreams of marrying a golden-haired angel, and in his folly, my Alec was no different. And then he met you. You are neither golden-haired nor, I suspect, an angel . . . and the discovery that he wants you has bitten deeply into his former convictions. It goes against the grain, it upsets his sense of rightness and order."

"I understand that." Mira's smile was strange and bewildered. "But, my lady, I do not understand why you are . . . why you have . . ."

"Why my allegiance is with you? Because my son wants and needs you . . . and I want what is best for him. I do not mind the rumors I hear about you . . . not because I don't believe them, mind you. After having become acquainted with you, I am certain that there are many more scandals you have been involved in that have not yet been discovered. I do not condemn you, however, because at your age I was far more of a hoyden than you could ever be. Do you think that I was born with lily-white hands or that I was sheltered and petted all of my life? Think again! There is a likeness between you and me . . . except that there is a softness about you that I was fortunate enough to lose long ago, while you will probably never lose it. Yes, there is a likeness . . . though at your age I was made of tougher material, and while my face was not so comely as yours, my figure was better. Has this blasted mixture soaked into my eyes long enough?"

Jarred by the abrupt change of subject, Mira remained stupefied and silent until Juliana repeated the question. "Yes . . . yes," she said, jumping up and going to the elderly woman. "Keep your eyes closed for a moment—they will be sensitive to the light. They are watering, but that is good." Slowly she lifted off the handkerchief and took it to the pier table, setting it down on the silver tray. Giving Juliana a dry square of clean linen, Mira sat down on the sofa with her hands clasped tightly in her lap. Very gradually the paper-thin eyelids lifted, and Mira found herself staring into a pair of eyes that approached the silvery shade of Alec's. They were reddened slightly from the acid of the plants, but much clearer and brighter than before.

"Yes," Juliana said, sounding faintly breathless. "Yes, it has worked. My sight is improved." She blinked and looked around the room slowly, her canny sharpness replaced temporarily by an expression of wonder. Then she dabbed once more at the rivulets running down her cheeks, saying gruffly, "My eyes are still watering from those deuced weeds."

"It will stop soon," Mira said gravely, respectfully.

After Lady Falkner had left, Mira did not know how to answer Rosalie's impatient questions. Although Alec's mother had left with a satisfied smile on her face, nothing had been resolved . . . had it? Juliana had indicated that she would not tell Alec about the visit, nor would she approach her son on Mira's behalf. What had the meeting actually accomplished? Very little . . . but somehow Mira was reassured by the knowledge that in Juliana Falkner she had a strong ally.

Another day passed by, and Rosalie began to make alarming hints about possible solutions to the dilemma. Perhaps, she suggested, they could go riding and stop at the Falkner estate on the pretext that Mira's horse had lost a shoe. Perhaps they could call on Lady

Falkner at a time when Alec was there. Horrified at the prospect of her friend's well-intentioned meddling, Mira refused all of Rosalie's ideas vehemently. Unexpectedly Rand lent his support to Mira's side, telling his wife that Alec was not a man to be taken in by such transparent tricks.

"Mira has a right to her pride," he said to Rosalie in private, sitting on the edge of the massive bed they shared and pulling her close to him.

"Pride! This has nothing to do with pride. One has only to look at her to see how unhappy she is—"

"*Fleur*, I understand that your motives are the best—"

"I just want her to be as happy as we are. It's true that I would not have chosen a man like Lord Falkner for her, but she seems to think that he is the only one . . . I wish I could convince her that somewhere there is a man capable of giving her his whole heart—"

"Why can't Falkner?"

"Because he *is* a Falkner."

"Perhaps she sees him with different eyes than you do."

"She doesn't see him at all. She's blind where he is concerned. Rand, do you think there is a chance that he really might love her?"

He smiled and pressed his lips against her forehead, closing his eyes in contentment. "You cannot force love," he murmured, kissing her neck and then the softness of her earlobe, "or create it when it isn't meant to be, or destroy it when it is destined to survive. Don't you"—his lips touched hers gently— "agree?"

Her arms crept around his neck. "No," she said softly. Rand chuckled as he looked into her deep blue eyes.

"My love . . . you would smother a flower by giving it too much care, too much water and light. Let this one take root on its own. Agreed?"

Reluctantly she nodded, smiling at him and lifting her face for another kiss.

The message was signed with the scrawling initial A. Mira examined the note, delivered into her hands early that morning by Mary. The letters were precise and strongly marked. She was not familiar with Alec's handwriting, but this looked like a valid sample. He had asked her to meet with him at the northwest corner of the Berkeley estate at three o'clock. Why had he chosen to meet her this way—wouldn't it have been easier to pay a simple call? Privacy. He wanted privacy, she thought. Her whole body felt as tightly drawn as a bow as she imagined what he might say.

"Rosalie," she said casually during the midafternoon meal, "I am going out walking after luncheon—"

"Splendid. I will join you."

"Actually," Mira said, giving her a placating smile, "I would like to go alone." Oh, why hadn't she just kept quiet and *sneaked* out later on?

"Alone?" Rosalie turned to her husband. "Rand, do you think it is safe for her to go out walking alone?"

"Mira, do you intend to stray far from the Hall?" Rand inquired carelessly.

"No, no . . ." she said hurriedly. "There is no reason for me to go far. Really, I should not have mentioned it, it is so insignificant."

"Then I have no objection," he replied, causing her to relax with an inward sigh of relief.

"Now, what were you saying before about the docks?" Rosalie asked Rand, and he launched into a grim description of the increase in crime that had started to affect his shipping business. Recently the Bow Street runners that he had hired to protect his various cargoes had caught a number of thieves on the docks, some of whom had confessed to being members of Stop Hole Abbey, an extensive criminal organiza-

tion. Ratcatchers, employed to catch the rodents in
the holds of the ships, had carried the same rats from
ship to ship, using them to climb on board and steal
liberally. And scufflehunters had been found as well.
"What are scufflehunters?" Rosalie asked, and Rand
replied that they were women and children who stood
in the mud beneath docked ships and caught the stolen
objects thrown down to them.

Mira listened with only halfhearted attention to what
Rand was saying, just as she swallowed and chewed
without noticing what she was eating. It seemed that
the meal would never end. Usually she enjoyed the
leisurely discussions held at the Berkeley table, but
today the word "hurry" drove her every thought and
action. *Hurry*, she thought as the clock ticked slowly,
its hands moving toward the numbers with the greatest
reluctance. *Hurry!*

The northwest corner of the estate was not far from
Berkeley Hall. Mira reached the small clearing at exactly three o'clock. Lifting the hem of her pale green
gown, she took care not to step on a bright burst of
red blossoms. Alec was already there, half-sitting, half-
leaning on a large angular boulder that had caused a
nearby tree to bend in a graceful arc. His arms were
folded across his chest, his face unreadable as he
watched her arrive. Mira paused several feet away
from him and stood there silently. She blended into
the stillness of the forest so perfectly that Alec was
almost tempted to pull her into his arms and find out if
she was real. Tilting her head at the sound of a horse's
nicker, Mira peered into the forest and caught a glimpse
of bright chestnut.

"Sovereign?" she asked.

Alec nodded. "The scenery brings a few memories
to mind, doesn't it?"

"Yes, it does." She remembered every word of their
conversations at the Sackville estate, those brief meetings in the forest, the wary circling of questions and

answers, the irrepressible curiosity, the insistent attraction when their eyes had met. "Is that why you wanted to meet here?"

"What?" Alec's dark brows drew closer together.

"Is that why you—?"

"I came here because of your note."

"Note?" she repeated in bewilderment. "I didn't send a note, *you* did."

"You think I did?"

"Well, yes, you . . . you didn't?" Mira stared at him in rapidly growing dismay. She flushed. "No, of course you wouldn't have." She had never felt so foolish, so embarrassed. "Oh, *damn*. Damn Rosalie. I'll strangle her for this!"

"It could very well have been my mother," Alec pointed out, his mouth twisting sardonically. "She's fond of meddling—"

"No amount of meddling could solve our problems."

"Not problems . . . problem. There's only one obstacle in our way, and that's you."

"Me?" she demanded, finding that in one sentence he had managed to send her into a blind rage. After her tears, her agony, her heartache, he stood before her and accused her of creating problems, as if . . . as if she had refused him merely out of a petty desire to annoy him! "I'm glad everything's so simple for you! How wonderful it must be to know that you're completely in the right and I'm wrong—your conscience must be *wonderfully* clear, you . . . you . . ."

"I asked you to marry me," he pointed out, his voice cutting. "You turned down the offer. It's that simple . . . but you've been trying to complicate it with talk, empty worries, fears of—"

"It's clear that you haven't heard anything I've said. You haven't listened to me at all. My worries are *real*. You haven't . . ." To her horror, Mira felt tears of frustration welling up in her eyes, and she bent her head, trying to suppress them. Once again she had lost her control in front of him, but this time her anger and misery were too strong to hold back, and her shoulders trembled with an escaping sob. She heard him say her name, sensed that he was walking toward her . . . but she turned away blindly, wanting to escape him and run back to Berkeley Hall. After the first step, her toe caught in a curling root and she fell to the ground with a cry born more of fury than pain.

The destruction of her pride was complete, she thought numbly, wrenching herself to a sitting position. There was a throbbing of pain in her ankle. "If you have one shred of kind feeling for me, you'll leave," she said hoarsely. Her hair, falling free of the pins that had confined it in a precarious chignon, concealed her face with a dark, shining curtain as she bent her head. Taking her slipper off, she concentrated fiercely on her ankle. Alec walked over to her slowly, his steps unusually light for such a tall man. She could feel his gaze raking over her, and she felt a renewed blaze of anger. "Go away and leave me alone . . . go back to your laystall, you brandy-faced—"

"Yes, I know, I know . . . name of God, any sailor would be proud to have such an extensive vocabulary. Is your ankle sprained?"

"No," she said reluctantly.

"Here, take my hand. I'll help you up."

"I don't want your help."

"Mira," he warned, "I don't have much patience right now." He extended a commanding hand to her, and she turned her face away, refusing to accept it. Suddenly she gasped as he bent and scooped her up swiftly, holding her stiff body against his chest and carrying her to the sloping boulder.

"I don't . . ." she began in feeble protest, but he silenced her with a burning stare, his arms tightening to let her know that he had had more than enough of her comments. "You're going to crush my . . ." she started once more, and his grip tightened even more, causing Mira to fall silent with an indignant sound of discomfort. Alec, she reflected inwardly, was not presently in a mood to be argued with. "Please . . ." she dared meekly, and his arms loosened at once. So this was how he wished to play it, she thought, and decided to keep quiet, suddenly interested in what more her temporary submissiveness might bring.

Alec sat down on the boulder, cradling her in pleasantly hard arms and looking down at her with those silvery black-lashed eyes. She had never felt the ache of longing so acutely. God help her, there was nothing that would ever feel as good as this . . . being held by him, being near him. Unable to meet his penetrating gaze, she lowered her head to his shoulder, pressing her face into the warm golden skin of his neck. The minutes drifted by at a lazy pace while Alec waited. The color returned to Mira's face in a pink glow and her body conformed to his.

A cooling breeze swept through the woods, rustling leaves together and producing the sound of waves. Slowly Mira lifted her face from Alec's shoulder, sensing his intent before he had even begun to move. Her lashes fluttered upward, and she saw his mouth descending to hers . . . she closed her eyes and her lips parted, eagerly accepting the warmth, the promise of his kiss. His hand slid to her hip and clasped her lightly, his finger resting on the curve of her buttock. Alec shivered slightly, and his mouth slanted more firmly over hers, his jaw flexing as he kissed her with the hunger that only she could assuage. Dimly Mira realized how easily the fire between them had been struck, how little effort it took for him to bend her to his will. Somehow she managed to tear her lips from his, her lungs contracting and expanding in an unsteady rhythm.

"Not again . . . not again . . ." she murmured brokenly, her hands clenching in the loose folds of his shirt. "I can't live through having you and losing you again. Don't you see how you're hurting me?"

He looked down at the naked emotion in her face, and something inside him seemed to break. "I've never wanted to hurt you."

"I know that. But I'm afraid you will, in the future—"

"I won't change. Nothing between us will change, except to get better. Dammit, don't look at me like that! What do you need me to do? How can I convince you that everything's going to be all right? How can I make you trust me? . . . I've shown you how I feel, I've given you all the promises . . . all that I've held back are the words."

Her heart seemed to stop beating, and she listened to her own desperate plea as if it had come from someone else. "Say them. Please—"

"Mira, I love you," he said huskily. "You're my other half. It makes no difference if you feel the same or not, because I love you damned well enough for the both of us. It doesn't matter where you came from, or who you are, or what you've done." Alec buried his face in her hair, then nuzzled past it to find her neck. He whispered against her frantic pulse. "I couldn't live through the rest of my days knowing every moment that you were somewhere else, living apart from me . . . I would always be wondering . . . I would always be afraid that you might need me and I wouldn't be there for you. I want you to belong to me completely . . . I want you to be my wife, not my mistress, not a memory, not—"

"But about my past . . ."

Alec heard the fear in her voice, and he gave her a little shake. "From this moment on we'll never talk about the past. Not yours, not mine. It doesn't matter to me anymore. I'll never judge you . . . and no matter what you do, I'll always take your side. Always."

"Even if I'm wrong?"

"Especially if you're wrong," he vowed, and she

chuckled tearfully. "Now tell me that you'll marry me."

"What if I'm not any good at being Lady Falkner?"

"You won't have to learn everything at once. And I won't ask anything of you that you can't give."

"We are bound to quarrel often. Will you still feel the same about me if—?"

"In between the times that we quarrel, I will worship you. And I will love you as no man has ever loved his wife. Now give me an answer."

"Your family . . . will they like me?"

"My sweet, they don't even like me."

"Will you promise . . . to give me many children?"

Alec smiled at the shy glance she gave him. "Yes."

"Several?"

"My exasperating brat . . . if you'll give me an answer, we can start on the children right now."

"Alec, no."

"What?"

"Yes, I will marry you . . . but no, we can't do that . . . not *here*." As she spoke, she felt the back of her gown loosen . . . he had unfastened it while they had been talking. He pulled it down until her shoulders were bare and her breath caught in her throat. "Alec . . ."

"Say 'husband,'" he said, easing her bodice down until her breasts were exposed and her arms were trapped. Uneasily Mira looked around at the still forest, feeling as if hundreds of eyes were watching them.

"Husband," she whispered, her heart hammering madly as his ebony head bent over her breasts, his mouth seeking and finding the most delicate nerves, teasing them into tingling arousal.

"Now tell me how you feel about me."

"I love you . . ." Her neck arched back as pleasure threaded through her in ever-thickening skeins. Somehow she managed to yank her arms out of the confining sleeves, and she twined them around his shoulders. "I love you so much . . . and I want you . . . Alec . . ."

Pulling one of her legs up, he cupped his hands over her buttocks and raised her hips to straddle his. She felt him through their clothes, the large, powerful shape of him straining up against her, and her fingers curled against his back as desire shot through her.

"Now tell me," he said hoarsely, urging his loins against the beckoning softness of her in a slow, deceptively patient movement, "that you'll let me have you anywhere I please."

She quivered, holding on to him more tightly.

"Anywhere."

Despite his overpowering hunger, Alec grinned, reaching down to help her unfasten his breeches. "Oh, how I'm going to enjoy being married to you, Miss Germain."

13

Alec accompanied Mira back to Berkeley Hall and informed Rand and Rosalie of the engagement with a matter-of-factness that amused Mira. Now that the agreement had been made and Mira's objections had been quenched, Alec's attitude toward the marriage seemed to be one of relief.

"He behaves," Mira grumbled to Rosalie later, "as if a minor but annoying problem has been solved! I would have thought that his feelings for me would have been a little more transparent."

"Perhaps Lord Falkner is a man who only wants the unattainable and loses interest after the conquest. Are you certain that you have no doubts about him as a husband?"

"Not as many as others seem to have," Mira rejoined defensively. Instantly Rosalie's expression became contrite.

"Mireille . . . please, let's not argue about him. Just try to understand that it's difficult for me to think of someone in a certain way for so long, and then to have to change my opinion so quickly—"

"I do understand. But you'll see how wrong you've been about him."

"If you feel so strongly about him, I know that he must be worthy of it."

Mira nodded, giving Rosalie a smile and turning to look through the window at the brilliant blue sky. I must continue to trust him, she thought, chewing gently on the inside of her lower lip. There was no predicting what kind of husband Alec would be, or what kind of marriage they would have. Perhaps Rosalie was right, but what shield did Mira have against such doubts? Only her faith in him.

After Mira had related the story of the mysteriously arranged meeting in the forest, Rosalie swore repeatedly that she had had nothing to do with the forged notes. Knowing what an unskilled liar her friend was, Mira was rather inclined to believe her. Juliana must have been the one to send the notes, though Alec had assured Mira that she would never admit to it. In view of the end result, however, it was not important to know who had contrived the meeting, and soon Mira's attention was diverted to other, more disturbing matters.

The morning after Alec proposed, he arrived at the doors of Berkeley Hall looking every bit like the kind of properly respectful fiancé that everyone knew he was not. He asked for the opportunity to speak with Mira in private, a request which Rosalie allowed very reluctantly. Rosalie had decided beforehand that until the wedding she was going to be a zealous chaperon—after all, the activities of engaged couples were scrutinized far more than were those of couples who were merely courting. After Rosalie led the caller to the salon where Mira waited, the betrothed couple exchanged polite nods.

"Lord Falkner," Mira said demurely.

"Miss Germain."

"I know that all this exaggerated restraint is for my benefit," Rosalie said, lifting her eyes as if in appeal to heaven. "However, I know *exactly* what goes on between engaged couples, and that is why I'm allowing you only fifteen minutes alone. After that, I will insist upon rejoining you." Throwing Alec a timid and suspicious glance, she left the room and closed the door. Immediately Alec's control vanished, and he leveled a hungry stare at Mira.

"A quarter of an hour," he said, leaning his back against the closed door and folding his arms across his chest.

"She knows that there's not much we can do in fifteen minutes," Mira explained, a soft smile drawing across her mouth as she remained seated on an embroidered chair and stared back at him.

"She doesn't know how fast I can be."

Insolently she looked up and down the rangy elegance of his body. "Yes, but I do."

Alec laughed softly, his eyes sparkling with the promise of retaliation. "Saucy wench. Come here. We've already wasted fifty seconds and I haven't even kissed you yet."

"Do you intend to kiss me or turn me over your knee?" she questioned, making no move to rise.

"One or the other. Perhaps both. Come here and find out."

Slowly Mira smiled and walked over to him, stopping in front of him and slipping her arms around his neck. His hands settled at her waist to steady her as she stood on her toes slightly, leaning into him. "Is this close enough?" she whispered.

Alec stared into her upturned face, so familiar and still so startlingly beautiful to him, and his arms drew around her possessively. Sometimes she looked like a mere girl, and yet the emotions of a woman shone in her eyes. He bent his head to kiss her so lightly that their lips barely met.

"What was your first thought when you woke up this morning?" she murmured, echoing a question that he had asked her once. As her breath mingled warmly with his, he smiled, briefly rubbing his nose against hers.

"That I don't care if there's a heaven or not, so long as I have a whole lifetime with you. What was yours?"

"I had too many thoughts all at once. I don't remember a single one of them."

"I assume they were all about me," he said with his usual flawless arrogance.

"Most definitely. About how handsome you are when you smile . . . and how wonderful your kisses are—"

"Just my kisses?" He parted her lips with his and savored the taste of her, his mouth moving deliberately over hers. Their bodies seemed to fuse together wherever they touched, and no matter how they strained to be closer, they could not get close enough. Mira broke the kiss with a small sound, flushing with arousal as Alec's manhood stirred against her.

"More than your kisses," she said breathlessly, and when their lips met again, it was her tongue that intruded into the searing dampness of his mouth. He groaned and pulled her closer, enduring the kiss as long as possible before it became necessary to stop.

"God . . . how soon is the wedding?" he asked, closing his eyes and holding her at arm's length as he strove to regain control over himself. "Did we even discuss the date?"

"No . . . but Rosalie said that although the proper waiting time would be six months—"

"*Six months*?" he repeated, scowling immediately. "You tell her—no, I'll tell her—I'm not waiting even six weeks to—"

"—*but* she said that she thought it should be very soon, perhaps even one month from now, in order to satisfy everyone's sense of propriety."

"I didn't know we had offended everyone's sense of propriety. Is Lady Berkeley afraid that we might have anticipated our wedding night?"

"Actually, she said that any fiancée of yours might as well walk around with the word 'deflowered' stamped on her forehead."

Alec chuckled, pressing a hard kiss on her brow. "And a man who could resist you would either be a saint or a eunuch."

"We'll just have to work on changing her opinion of you," Mira said thoughtfully.

"I don't see why. So far it's been accurate."

"She intends to chaperon us very closely—too closely. She feels that it is her responsibility."

"Poor brat . . ." He pulled her close again and smiled against her hair. "But do you think that any man or woman alive could stop me from finding a way to be with you?"

Mira brightened immediately. "Then you'll—"

"Actually, in this matter I happen to agree with your vigilant little friend. We're going to wait until we're married."

"You're joking. Why? Why do you agree with her? Merely to annoy me, or is there some deeper reason, such as disinterest—"

He stopped her words with a kiss that seemed to last for hours. "Does *that* feel like disinterest to you?" he asked when they were both gasping and light-headed. "God help me if I become any more interested in you. I'm barely sane most of the time as it is. And no, I have not decided to wait until our wedding night merely for the purpose of annoying you. The next time I make love to you, I intend to be your husband." Mira frowned at him. Juliana had been right. The Falkners were indeed stubborn and sentimental creatures. "And there is another reason," he added more gently. "I am going to be away for a little while—not long, but—"

"Where?"

"I'll be in London. You'll be busy enough here while I'm gone, making the wedding plans with Rosalie and Juliana."

Mira fell silent, her forehead creasing as she restrained herself from asking all of the questions that raced through her mind. She would not let him see how anxious she was not to let him out of her sight, nor would she smother him with possessiveness. Alec had fallen in love with a woman who had strength and independence. She would not turn into a spineless creature who was constantly in need of reassurance.

"That's true," she said quietly. "I will be quite busy."

"There are some things I have to do."

"Yes. I imagine there are quite a few farewells you have to make." The comment was out before she could stop it. Mira cursed herself silently. She sounded like a jealous shrew . . . *Dieu*, what love did to a woman's temperament!

"What is that supposed to mean?" Alec demanded, letting go of her.

"Nothing—nothing at all," she muttered.

"Do you think I'm planning to make the rounds one last time before committing myself solely to your bed?"

"It's not an unheard-of thing for an engaged man to do."

His expression of disbelief dissolved into full-fledged exasperation. "Dammit, Mira, what the hell do you think I . . . For God's sake, would you mind simply asking *why* I'm going to London instead of convicting, sentencing, and hanging me without evidence?"

She looked at him mutinously. "Why are you going to London?" she asked, by now indifferent to the answer.

Alec did not reply but continued to stare at her with unfathomable eyes, and Mira became contrite as she realized what she had wrought with her careless words. She was supposed to have more faith in him than anyone else, and instantly she had assumed the worst about him. He had promised yesterday never to judge her, but she had just judged him without reason, like so many others did. What kind of faith is that? she berated herself.

"Alec," she said gently, stepping close to him once again and laying a small hand on his upper arm. She could feel the bunched hardness of the muscle underneath her palm, betraying the tenseness that came from deep inside him. "I spoke without thinking. Of course I don't believe that you would be unfaithful to me. But where you're concerned I become jealous very easily . . . and you must remember that this is all as new for me as it is for you. I've never been in love before, and there are many things I am in the midst of learning." As she spoke, she inched closer and let her breasts press against him. "We have so little time together . . . don't be cross because of my thoughtlessness." She sought a sensitive nerve on the side of his neck and gave it a lingering caress with her mouth. "Tell me," she murmured softly, "why you're going to London and leaving me here to long for you."

Alec stood there under her beguiling ministrations, the tender caresses and coaxing words, succumbing to her spell even as he marveled at her ability to pull all the anger out of him. It was a talent of hers that would continue to develop as she came to understand him better; she could charm him as no one else could, and she could make up after an argument so sweetly that he was almost grateful for whatever had caused it in the first place. It was, he reflected wryly, almost worth going out of his way to disagree with her.

"It's about Holt," he said, draping his arms over her shoulders and pulling her closer. "There's a slight chance that Carr and I might be able to find out who killed him, or at least some of the reasons why—"

"No." A chilling premonition crawled through her at his words. Perhaps it was wrong of her to be so afraid of the future, but she knew how it felt to have happiness wrenched away from her. It had happened before, and there was no certainty in her heart that it would not happen again. "Alec, no. You're seeking revenge for something that should be left in the past."

"I'm not looking for revenge. Just answers. That's all I want."

"You can't bring Holt back. The answers won't change anything. Name of God, it is selfish of me to say this . . . but I need you now, and he doesn't. I know you and he were close, but—"

"We were like brothers," Alec said quietly. "You wouldn't understand how it was, what it was like when he was murdered. And you don't know what it feels like to have someone that close to you die . . . without dignity, without warning."

Mira's face was white, her eyes glittering. A strange feeling took hold of her, tightening around her throat, a combination of fear and dread and helpless anger. Yes, she did know what it felt like. Her own mother had died with far less dignity than Holt Falkner . . . for that matter, lived with far less dignity.

"No, I suppose I don't know how it feels," she said tonelessly, pulling away from Alec and walking to the other side of the room. "But I do know that I haven't the right or the ability to keep you from doing this. All I am going to ask is that you keep from putting yourself in danger unnecessarily."

His eyes flickered over her assessingly, but for once he could read neither her mood nor her thoughts. "Of course I won't take unnecessary risks. All I'm going to do is talk to a few people, pay a few calls, ask a few questions."

She nodded slowly, her face set and perfectly serious, as if she were aware that he was telling her something less than the truth. Alec did not smile again, wondering briefly what she would say if she knew where he was actually going. The sound of Rosalie's footsteps alerted both of them to the fact that their fifteen minutes were over. Alec threw an aggravated glance at the door.

"I'm going to tell her we need more time alone," he said, and Mira shook her head.

"We don't, really."

"The hell we don't. I'm not going to leave without settling this first."

"There's nothing to settle. You're leaving . . . I'm staying here . . . and I'll be here when you return."

The words should have eased the nagging sensation in Alec's gut. Why, then, did he feel as if she had just slipped far away from him? Was she the one in need of reassurance, or was he? "Mira . . ." he said, gritting his teeth and starting across the room toward her.

The door opened. "I hope you've had an enjoyable chat," Rosalie said cheerfully.

Her comment was greeted with a heavy pause.

"Let's just say a typical one," Alec muttered.

Sensing the explosive tension in the room, Rosalie cleared her throat lightly, her eyes darting from Mira's distant expression to Alec's grim one. "Would you like me to come back in another few minutes?"

"No, thank you," Alec said, trying to conceal his frustration as he took his gaze from Mira. "It appears that our conversation is through. Lady Berkeley, you may as well know that I am leaving immediately for London. Before I go, however, I would like to speak with your husband."

Rosalie looked startled. "I . . . oh . . . yes, of course. He is in the library. I will take you to him, if you wish."

"I would like to remain here undisturbed for a while," Mira said, her voice steady and even with artificial composure.

"Of course," Rosalie murmured. Uncertainly she preceded Alec out of the room. He paused at the doorway, his gaze locking with Mira's.

"Good-bye," he said. She looked directly at him but did not answer. The word would not leave her throat, even if she had tried to force it. With a smile that vaguely echoed his sarcasm of old, he left and closed the door.

Staring at nothing in particular, Mira leaned back on the settee. She held an embroidered pillow to her chest and rested her chin on it, curling her legs up so that her body was only a small lump amid the cushions. A circle of words turned through her mind, over and over again.

". . . you don't know what it feels like . . . to have someone that close to you die . . . without dignity, without warning . . ."

Indignity. Alec did not know the meaning of it quite as well as Mira did. Dignity was far more elusive for women than it was for men; women were far more easily robbed of it. She still remembered every detail of the brothel in France where her mother had worked. The procuress of the place had been fat and ill-tempered . . . "Madame" was what she had been called to her face, while behind her back everyone referred to her simply as "the abbess" or "the bawd." Madame had allowed Mireille to sleep in an undisturbed corner at night, so long as she was out of sight. Quiet and still, Mireille had slept near the warm stove in the kitchen, listening to the comings and goings, the creaking of the floorboards overhead, the sultry voices, the curious sounds and odd, muffled groans from upstairs.

She had rarely seen her mother, for during the day Mireille wandered through the village and the sleepy fields, far away from the brothel, and at night she slept while Maman worked. Some years, especially the early ones, she had been sent to the village school, where she had learned to read. As she had grown older, her education had become a patchwork of many different experiences. She had never thought of leaving Maman, the brothel, and the village; she hadn't known that a different world existed.

But one morning her mother was not there, and that was when Madame came to talk to Mireille, her plump throat quivering as she shook her finger angrily. It was wartime, and Maman had been arrested during a surprise attack on an enemy encampment of English soldiers, and she had been executed along with the other whores. According to Madame, it was very bad that

Mireille's mother had been so unpatriotic, and worse that now there were fewer women to take care of the customers, and worst of all that Maman had been servicing men on the sly without paying a percentage of her earnings to the brothel.

Soon Madame had told her that she would have to start working upstairs. Mireille rebelled violently, for she had no desire to do what Maman had done. She was afraid of upstairs, the dark honeycomb of rooms filled with strange smells and heavy grunts, and the absorbent blackness of the hallway. And then in the middle of her longest and loudest wail, she saw a lean, brown-eyed, black-haired stranger walk into the room, just as if he owned it. He looked exactly like her. He had scowled at Madame, saying, "Get some other blood for your pushing-school. You won't have any more Germains whoring for you." And then he had turned to Mireille. Although she had never seen him before, his eyes were filled with affection, a fact which caused Mireille to fall silent in wonder and confusion. "*Sang de Dieu*, you're small for a twelve-year-old, aren't you?" he had asked, catching her under the arms and lifting her into the air. Her feet had dangled as he looked at her critically. Then he had given her a dazzling smile. "Too small for a name like Mireille. I'm going to call you Mira until you're taller. Do you know I'm your half-brother, Mira?"

Even now she puzzled over the possible reasons why Guillaume had cared for her so immediately, so strongly. By all standards, his affection had been genuine. But she had never seen him care for anyone else, not even to show momentary compassion or kindness. Perhaps his feelings for her did indeed stem from the fact that she was the only family he had. Perhaps it was because they had been partners in so many underhanded schemes. Perhaps it was because until she became older, she had to depend completely on him, for food and water, for her very survival.

Maman had died without dignity. And a few years later, Guillaume had turned into a stranger, without warning. Both of them had left her, and as she reflected on that, Mira discovered something about herself: she was terrified of being left again.

He had received the message from Carr that morning: *Alec, Finally a name to start with. Tom Memmery, a little fence that Holt was seen with several times at the Rummer. Presently believed to be attending boarding school.* . . . Despite the serious nature of the information, Alec smiled at that, knowing that "boarding school" was cant for "prison." *But which one?* the note continued. *And if we can find him, how do we make the canary cackle? C.F.*

Of all the connections that Alec had assiduously acquired and maintained, he did not know anyone who was serving on prison commissions or in the magistrature. Lawyers he knew aplenty, for in the past the Falkners had found ample use for them . . . but no lawyer would be able to help him obtain the particular information he needed now. Rand Berkeley, however, might very well be able to provide assistance. Alec dimly recalled having heard once of a magistrate who went by the name of Berkeley. After engaging in a relaxed and friendly conversation with Rand, Alec finally broached the question.

"Yes," Rand said in response to the carefully worded query, his hazel eyes alight with curiosity, his mouth broadening in a comfortable smile. "My great-uncle Horace is a magistrate, as well as being involved in all manner of reformation societies. He would most likely have access to the right records . . . and would be willing to do a little work for us, with the proper inducement. Berkeleys are always open to the right kinds of persuasion, you know."

Alec laughed. "Memmery," he said, handing Rand a slip of paper with the name written on it. "A fence, and one that I would like to talk to. One that I might possibly decide to . . . bargain with. Would your uncle turn a blind eye to that?"

"I know he would. He has before. I'll warn you, though, he'll probably expect a favor in return."

"I would hardly expect otherwise."

Rand smiled again, glancing at the closed door before speaking a bit more softly. "I can't imagine that Mireille has taken the news of your imminent departure well."

"She hasn't," Alec replied flatly, "even though I wouldn't be of much practical use here anyway—the women take over the planning of the wedding, discussing ribbons and matrimonial fripperies to their hearts' content, whereas there's not too damned much a man has to do except appear at the altar."

Rand laughed heartily. "I agree. However, I can tell you from my own experience that women like the prospective bridegroom to maintain at least a semblance of interest in whether the trimmings are pink or yellow. God help me, I don't know why. Perhaps I can offer you a scrap of advice . . . ?"

"Only if I'm not obligated to heed it."

"In the weeks just before we were married, my wife was very . . . emotional. Tears, outbursts, that sort of thing. She felt certain pressures very keenly and needed a great deal of support. I am told that every bride does. Perhaps you should . . ."

"Should what?"

As pale gray eyes met hazel, Rand checked himself and backed away from the subject. Alec Falkner, Rand decided thoughtfully, was not the kind of man to whom he would offer advice unless it had been asked for. "You're an obstinate young strapper, Falkner," Rand murmured, tapping his fingertips together. It was clear that Alec would be resentful of any interference in his relationship with Mira, no matter how well-meant. If a solid friendship was to develop between the Berkeleys and Falkners, as Rand hoped, better now to keep silent and let Alec work out his problems alone. "Perhaps you should be leaving for London now. You've got distasteful work ahead of you; God knows I don't envy you."

If a place called hell existed, then Newgate was its earthly counterpart. It stank of human misery and wretchedness. Crowded in its maze of wards and passages were the immoral dregs of society . . . filthy criminals who had been born in streets and gutters and would die in a place far more obscene. Perhaps among them there were some men who still possessed a few remnants of humanity, but it was doubtful. After a month or two in Newgate, or "the stone jug," as they called it, the most honorable man would have come out either a rabid maniac or a cold-blooded killer. All the prisoners were thrown together: the first offenders with seasoned murderers, those who awaited trial with those who had already been sentenced, the strong with the weak, the old with the young. They were all crammed into buildings that were dark and crawling with insects and squeaking rodents. Even Alec could not help coughing slightly as he and Carr were led into Newgate, for the stench of human excrement and urine had sunk into the pores of brick and stone so deeply that no amount of washing could ever remove it.

"We'll both stink for a week after we leave," Carr murmured, looking almost overcome by the foul air that surrounded them.

Alec nodded, wiping the distaste from his own face with effort. "I must be insane," he muttered. "No one walks into Newgate of his own will."

For once Carr did not have a cocky reply or a wiseacre remark to make. He kept his eyes on the burly figure of the guard who led them by a row of wards. They passed the noisy, clamoring cells, filled with men who demanded drink and meat . . . men who called out to the passersby and threatened with thick cockney accents . . . thick-chested men who came out the victors in the daily squabbles for food . . . starving, bony men who were fast losing the strength necessary to survive. Carr's face became cold and shuttered, masking the unease he must have been feeling as they walked deeper into the prison. The thought crossed Alec's mind that perhaps he should not have allowed Carr to accompany him. Less than two years ago, Carr's world had been a safe and innocent one, full of the quiet pleasure of life in the country, full of books, history, and scholarly learning. Now he was learning far different lessons.

"Memmery." The guard stood at the door of one ward and called through the iron bars. A shuffling noise was heard, and little catcalls were made as the unfortunate Memmery made his way to the portal.

"Tonight, 'e'll piss when 'e can't whistle!"

"Mem, you'll stretch stoutly in an hour—"

"Poor Memmy, a wry mouth and a pissin' pair o' breeches—"

"Hurry now, Jack Ketch is waitin' fer ya!"

Noting Carr's confused look at the thick cant phrases, Alec translated softly. "They think we've come to take him out and hang him."

"A sentimental lot, aren't they?" Disgust flickered in Carr's olive-green eyes.

After receiving a nod from Alec, the guard fished a thin, sallow fellow of seedy appearance out of the cell and ushered him roughly to an unoccupied room. It was a barren little closet with four walls, a few handfuls of straw on the floor, and a heavily barred door. Memmery was shoved in there, and then the guard stood aside and allowed Alec and Carr to enter.

"Leave us alone with him for five minutes. Don't lock the door," Alec said, his tone low, flat, and utterly commanding. Though it was against prison regulations, the door was left unbolted. Nevertheless,

Carr jumped slightly when they were shut in the room. He glanced at Alec with a mute plea in his eyes to make the interview fast.

"Your name," Alec said to the pale-haired, pale-skinned prisoner, who could not have been more than thirty.

"Memmery, sir," the man mumbled. "Tom Memmery." Something in Alec's voice seemed to awaken his interest, for slowly Memmery looked up at him. The pale skin whitened to the shade of a fish belly. "Holy Jesus," he swore, his face contracting with fear.

"Do I look familiar to you?" Alec asked quietly. "I should. I gather you and my cousin were acquaintances of a sort."

"That's a rapper."

"Is it? I've heard differently."

Silence.

Alec's face contained all the warmth and animation of a slab of granite. Carr fidgeted uneasily, glancing at the door with an expression of longing. "Ever hear the name Leila Holburn?" Alec inquired, his voice a low rumble in the bandbox-size room.

Memmery studied the floor with absorption.

"Alec, he's not going to talk—" Carr began, simmering with impatience.

"Oh, he will," Alec said, sending his young cousin a silencing glance. "In fact, he's going to become the most talkative inmate in Newgate—"

"Go swive yourself," Memmery said politely.

"—because if he doesn't," Alec continued as if there had been no interruption, "I'm going to make certain that every slasher and shanker in this hellhole knows that Memmery whiddled the whole scrap on Stop Hole Abbey. In other words, Carr, they're going to think he told everything he knows, including names, dates, and places."

"Bleedin' cur!" Memmery snapped, suddenly shaking with a mixture of hate and horror.

"Do you know what will happen to him then, Carr?" Alec said conversationally. "He'll be ripped apart, limb from flabby limb, after enduring several hours of ingenious torture. His cellmates aren't the type who appreciate being discussed with the likes of us by a loose-tongued fellow like Memmery. Do you know why some of them are in here? . . . they're chalkers, men who amuse themselves at night by leaping out of dark alleys to slash the faces of innocent passersby with knives. What great fun they would have with a companion who had snitched on them. In fact, just being in here with us right now casts him in rather a suspicious light—wouldn't you agree, Tom?"

"What if I blab? It won't save my 'ide, now, will it?" Memmery asked darkly, his face taking on the resignation of a doomed man.

"It might. If your information proves to be useful to me, you'll be smuggled immediately to the Berkeley shipping docks and taken aboard a packet bound for Australia. There at least you'll have a chance to enjoy a few more years of your miserable life—you're young enough still to want that. However, if you don't tell me what I want to hear, you'll be taken back to your ward and cast upon the infinite mercy of your companions."

" 'Ow do I know you're not shavin' me?"

"You'll have to trust me."

Evidently deciding that the risk was worthwhile, Memmery nodded briefly. "What do you want to know?"

"You're a member of Stop Hole Abbey," Alec said.

"Aye."

"You were acquainted in the past with my cousin Holt Falkner."

" 'E didn't give 'is name. But 'e looked like you."

"And he paid you for information."

"Aye."

"What did you talk to him about?"

" 'E was lookin' for that dell . . . that girl you mentioned."

"Leila Holburn?"

"Aye."

"And what did you tell him?"

"I wadn't in on that part o' Stop 'Ole. But after 'e told me 'ow she disappeared, I told 'im I thought she'd been christened."

"Christened? What does that mean?" Carr asked sharply.

"White slavery," Alec replied, his lip curling in a faint sneer. "A lucrative business, currently in greater vogue than ever before. The youngest and comeliest of the women they kidnap are shipped off to the West Indies and certain parts of Asia. I'm afraid Holt's fiancée is probably located in some exotic bordello . . . or if she's lucky, a harem."

"How do we know where?" Carr inquired through clenched teeth.

"That's what y'r cousin was tryin' to find out," Memmery said. "I told 'im to look for a tall Frenchie by the name o' Tilter—'e knew about that part o' Stop 'Ole more than most."

"What is Tilter's real name? And where do we find him?"

"I don't know." Memmery leaned against the wall, looking curiously gray. "I don't know."

"Not good enough," Alec said heartlessly. "Unless you can give me something else, I'm afraid your voyage to Australia is in danger of being canceled."

"Wait. Wait, I can tell you 'ow to find 'im." The convict pulled a few ragged playing cards out of his shirt and handed them to Alec. "You got to look for 'im in the flash 'ouses . . . Tilter will be in one of 'em. Show the seven; it lets y' in anywhere you want to go. Show the jack, it means y're lookin' for information. The king . . . y' want to talk to one o' the 'igher-ups."

"Call the guard," Alec told Carr, who obeyed with

alacrity. The door was opened, and Alec handed a hefty pouch to the guard. "Get him to the west docks," he said quietly. "If I hear from the Berkeley officials that Memmery didn't make it on board tonight, I'll have your hide nailed to the wall and left to dry in the sun."

"Yes, sir."

Carr followed Alec out of Newgate, and when they were out, they both took deep, reviving breaths of clean air. "I never knew it smelled so sweet out here," Carr said, forcing a smile to his face, though his green eyes looked curiously stricken.

"Yes."

"How did Holt do it?" Carr suddenly burst out. "How did he bring himself to associate with scum like that and not tell anyone?" Facing the prisoners at Newgate had given him a sense of what kind of people Holt had been bargaining and dealing with in order to find Leila. For the first time, he realized what type of men had murdered his brother. Any one of the wretches he had just walked past could have done it, *would* have done it had they seen something to gain by it.

As Alec looked at the young man, who was losing his idealism so fast, the frightening coldness left his gray gaze, to be replaced by a subtle glow of sympathy. "He did what he had to do. He did it because he was capable of great loyalty to those he loved. And he would have done anything to get Leila back."

"It wasn't worth it. Trying to get her back wasn't worth his life," Carr said in a raw voice.

Alec thought of Mira. He would go to the same lengths to find her that Holt had gone to in order to find Leila. There was no doubt, no question of that in his mind. Had Holt really loved Leila Holburn in such a way, that he would rather die than forget her or try to live without her?

Before Mira, he would not have understood any of this. Like Carr, he would have been confused and resentful of the emotion that had indirectly led Holt to his death. But how could he make Carr understand that having a few months of that kind of love was worth a lifetime? His cousin was too young to regard such a statement as anything but banal. Alec lifted his shoulders and let them drop in a slight shrug. "To Holt, Leila was worth it," he said matter-of-factly.

"What are we going to do?"

"Find Tilter."

"Why? We're not looking for Leila, we want to know what happened to Holt."

"By following in Holt's tracks and making inquiries about Leila, we'll find out what happened to him." Alec smiled bleakly. "Though preferably not through firsthand experience."

Mira stirred drowsily, her eyes squinting against the brilliant sun, which had warmed her skin and filled her with languor. After reading in the garden for the better part of an hour, she had shifted from her seat on the giant sundial to the thick grass that bordered one of the many garden paths that wound around Berkeley Hall. Nearby, birds fluttered around a small stone pool filled with star-shaped flowers. Smiling sleepily at the sounds of tiny flapping wings, trickling water, and indignant chirps, Mira slipped an arm behind her head and sprawled more comfortably on the grass, drifting in and out of a light sleep. But then there was an abrupt flapping and a chorus of cries from the birds as they flew away. Although she had heard no other sound, Mira knew that someone or something had approached, and she opened her eyes quizzically. Alec was there, his hair shining as sleek and black as a raven's wing, a slow smile pulling at his mouth. He was back, she thought, and it brought her a sense of wholeness. He was so carelessly handsome as he stood there that Mira felt her heart clench in an instant of pure pleasure. Though she would love him equally even if he were far less agreeable to the eye, she could not deny that his attractiveness was something she took a certain measure of pride in.

"How unfair it is," she said softly, and Alec lowered himself beside her in a lithe movement.

"What is unfair?" He braced an elbow on either side of her head and looked down at her intently.

"That you received such an overabundance of handsomeness, and left all others only a little bit to share among themselves."

"Mira . . ." he whispered, his eyes caressing her. "How are the wedding plans progressing?"

"Marvelously. I have ordered the most wonderful gown to be made—chartreuse, black, and purple—and we are going to decorate the church with lovely green weeds, and you won't mind at all that you weren't here to help me decide everyth—"

He smothered the rest of her statement with an ardent kiss, a deep purr vibrating in his throat. When he lifted his head, they stared into each other's eyes with a new understanding. The separation of the past week had been different from the other separations which had preceded it, and they both knew why.

"I'm sorry for the way I sent you off," Mira said softly.

"I shouldn't have left like that. I should have made certain that you understood—"

"I did understand, I was just being selfish."

"I don't mind your being selfish about me."

"I am, terribly. If I could, I would just keep you in a room all to myself and never let you out."

"Just so long as it's the bedroom."

"Have we ever made love in a bedroom, like other people do?" Mira asked dreamily. "Wouldn't it be wonderful?"

"We did, once. And yes, it was wonderful." Gently his teeth caught at her lower lip. "Unspeakably wonderful."

They filled the remaining time they had together with low, soft murmurs, slow kisses, and stolen caresses. Mira did not ask about the week in London, nor about what Alec had discovered about Holt. Perhaps later. But for now, Alec did not mention it either.

The night before the wedding, Mira was unable to sleep. Lighting a candle, she made her way downstairs with the intention of heating some water for a soothing herbal tea. On the way to the kitchen, soft light shining from the library attracted her attention, and she went to investigate its source. Gently she tapped on the half-closed door.

"Come in," came Rosalie's voice, and Mira entered the room hesitantly, discovering that her friend was sitting in a leather chair with an open book in her lap and a glass of wine in her hand. "I couldn't sleep," Rosalie confessed sheepishly, closing the book. "Heaven knows why, since it's *your* wedding . . . but I came down here to read, thinking that it would help to take my mind off tomorrow."

"I can't seem to relax enough even to lie still," Mira said. Her glance moved to the wine bottle and the neatly polished glasses that were poised on a silver tray. "I was going to take some tea. I think your idea is much better."

"By all means," Rosalie said, and they both laughed softly. As Mira settled into a corner of the low-backed sofa, Rosalie's expression sobered somewhat. "Mireille, I've been lending some thought to the fact that this is the night before your wedding, and traditionally . . . you know that certain things should be discussed so that the expectations of a bride are not too . . . too . . . different from what is actually going to . . . happen. I know that you . . . well, we've never talked about your past relationships with men, so I don't know what you may or may not have done with . . ." She cleared her throat and forced herself to meet Mira's eyes directly. "But . . . what I'm trying so ineptly to say is that there might be questions that you have about tomorrow night. So if you would like me to—"

"Rosalie," Mira interrupted, smiling slightly, "I don't have any questions to ask about tomorrow night."

"I was afraid you didn't," Rosalie said, and suddenly they both chuckled. Taking a sip of the sweet, fruity wine, Rosalie relaxed and sighed. "Still, I wanted to be certain that you were not *un*certain about the wedding night. I was always told quite dreadful things about such matters—about a wife's responsibilities and duties in the marriage bed. The 'proper' thing for decent women to do, and all that."

"What is the 'proper' thing to do in the marriage bed?"

"I was told by my mother that a lady just lies back and thinks of England."

Mira giggled.

"Fortunately," Rosalie continued, "by the time she told me that, Rand and I had already been together. It would shock many people to know that we had been so intimate before the wedding."

"I knew how it was between you two when we were all in Anjou," Mira said, swirling her wine in the glass and sampling it with the air of a connoisseur.

"You did? How?"

"It was the way he looked at you. And the way you looked back at him."

"Oh . . ." Rosalie smiled. "I didn't know it had been so obvious." Tentatively she added, "Mireille, I believe I have changed my mind to some degree about Lord Falkner. I've noticed during the past few visits that he is different from what I thought him to be. At least, around you he is different, and that is enough to reassure me that he truly does care for you."

"I'm so glad that you feel that way."

"I hope that he makes you happy. I hope that he

regards your happiness, your comfort, your . . . pleasure as highly as he does his own."

"Yes. Oh yes, he does," Mira hastened to reassure her, and blushed. "I meant that he *will*—"

"I know what you meant," Rosalie said wryly.

The marriage took place the next morning in a small church in Warwickshire. It was a private and exclusive ceremony, attended by the Falkners, the Berkeleys, and a few carefully selected guests of special rank and significance. It was important to Mira, who already had trepidations about her social responsibilities as Alec's wife, to keep the ceremony small and to avoid the theatrical aspects of the situation as much as possible. Already society gossip and several London publications were treating her marriage into the Falkner family as a sensational drama . . . the unofficial headlines were widespread and very popular. There was an element of mystery about Mireille Germain, since no one knew exactly who she was or where she was from. There were rumors that she was originally from a well-to-do French family, and rumors about her involvement with Sackville, and controversy about where and when she had first been "discovered" in England . . . but nothing was ever proven or disproven. For the most part, she was an intriguing figure who had been brought into prominence by her association with the Berkeleys . . . and now with the Falkners.

In private, Alec had unequivocally refused the offer of a dowry from Rand and Rosalie. However, Alec did make provision for Mira to receive a number of dower lands and a castle somewhere in southern England. "In case anything ever happens," he had told her gravely, "this is yours, and no one will ever be able to take it from you. So no matter what the Falkners or anyone else may threaten you with, know that—"

"I don't want lands or a castle," she had said, suddenly shuddering at the thought of losing him. "I just want you with me always."

"I'm not going anywhere, wench." And despite the teasing way he had said it, Alec had taken her into his arms tenderly, trying to reassure her with the strength of his grip that the last thing he intended was to be apart from her.

Mira thought about that conversation now as she and Alec stood at the front of the church. Though a thousand thoughts ran through her mind in an endless stream, she was conscious of the smallest details of the ceremony . . . the brightness of the candle flames against dark mahogany, the mellow, aged scent of the wooden pews, the rustle of her ivory satin wedding gown, the powdery fragrance of roses. Her hands felt cold and frail as she stood with them clasped together, for despite the certainty that all of this was right, she was still nervous. At the proper time in the ceremony, Alec took her fingers in his strong, warm ones, and Mira watched as the Geminal ring was lifted from the pages of the Bible on which it had been placed. The Geminal was made of two gold bands that twisted together and interlocked into one. Because her hands were so much smaller and daintier than Alec's, her half of the ring had been altered to fit her more snugly. Slowly and deliberately he slid the band on her finger and repeated the vows. "I, Alexander Reeve Falkner, take thee, Mireille Germain . . ." She stared up at him, drowning in his crystalline gaze, unable to believe that all of this was really happening. After the next few minutes were over, she would belong to him, and she would be able to claim him in a way that no other woman would ever be able to do.

The vows were made and the rings were in place, the prayers said and the Bible closed. When the groom was given permission to kiss the bride, Mira blushed as she became aware of all the expectant eyes fastened upon them. Alec smiled slightly, hesitating before framing her small face with his hands and brushing his lips lightly against hers. As he felt the warmth and the yielding of her mouth, he kissed her longer than he had intended, taking advantage of her parted lips with more hunger than was proper to demonstrate in public. He heard a few gasps from outraged biddies who would later whisper among themselves disapprovingly about his demonstration, and there were also a few chuckles from others in the congregation. Their lips parted slowly, similarly moist from the kiss, and Alec thought of the endless day ahead of them with a flare of exasperated impatience. Mira smiled at him as if she knew what he was thinking, her eyes gleaming with private amusement as he reluctantly let go of her.

14

Mira's bridal anxieties were increased greatly by the sight of the Falkner estate. The thick, clustering forest that surrounded it contained kinds of trees and plants that she had never seen before, brought from faraway places. The private road took a wide, gentle turn, and then Mira was presented with a vision that took her breath away, a castle that rose majestically from a broad hill. Pale gray towers threatened to break through the clouds that wafted lazily overhead. A pair of ornamental lakes framed the east and west sides of the castle, their glassy surfaces reflecting the vaulted arches and mullioned windows that formed a pattern of granite-block on the walls. Mira was convinced that hundreds of people could live there comfortably, and suddenly she wanted to beg Alec to take her to some small, unassuming cottage and stay there with her forever. What was going to be expected of her? How was she going to adapt to this kind of life?

Since it would take days to explore the castle thoroughly, Mira was given only a cursory tour by Juliana, while several other Falkners followed and observed her reactions. Alec's wife was an object of fascination for them all, since they had debated hotly for the past few years about what kind of woman he would eventually choose to wed. There was no sign in their blank, curious faces as to whether she had fulfilled or contradicted their expectations.

Although Mira managed to take note of the most

impressive features of her new home, more of her
attention was focused on the members of the Falkner
family. They were as dark as the Berkeleys were blond,
most of them black-haired and green-eyed. Mira found
them to be an intriguing lot, for although they appeared to be as well-mannered, refined, and haughty
as the Berkeleys, a striking air of robustness surrounded
them. Though she had hardly been exposed to them
long enough to make any judgments, they seemed to
be volatile and quick-tempered. After meeting this
brood, Mira suddenly understood how her husband
had developed his icy, inflexible stare, his manner of
authority, and his ability to sense other people's
weaknesses and strengths. In order to manage the
Falkners and the vast complex of responsibilities that
being the head of the family entailed, it was necessary
for Alec to bully, persuade, and cajole by turns.

It was a source of interest and amusement to Mira
to watch Alec deal with the different people who
approached him, and she discovered over the next few
days that he had the makings of an excellent politi-
cian. To the caretaker, the servants, and the various
professional people who came to the estate to speak
with him, Alec was quiet and businesslike. With Juliana, his uncle Hugh, and his assorted cousins, he was
courteous and unyielding. With Juliana's two gray-
haired spinster sisters, Letitia and Jessamine Penrhyn,
Alec was gentle. He treated his eighteen-year-old
brother, Douglas, who was shy and rather bookish,
with an almost fatherly protectiveness. And with his
cousin Carr, Alec was sarcastic, frank, and devilishly
amusing. He sensed all of their needs, and he managed them with a velvet-clad touch, guiding firmly and
yet allowing more than enough freedom when it was
needed. Mira was the only one whom he could not
manipulate and did not even attempt to. She was not a
responsibility but a necessity. She was his essential
luxury. And in the privacy of the keep, a suite of

several rooms in the castle that were theirs alone to frequent, Alec indulged in her, loved her, and cherished her.

On their wedding night, Alec allowed her private time to prepare for bed, and he lingered downstairs while she dressed slowly in a lacy white gown. The bedroom was resplendent with the same dignity as the rest of the castle, with an intricate plaster-molded ceiling, Louis XIV furniture, a French tapestry, and an Aubusson carpet. Mary, a maid who had left the Berkeleys' employ in order to attend her, arranged Mira's hair in long, perfect curls and brought her a crystal flask filled with perfume. The scent was a fresh, clean distillation of sandalwood and roses, and Mira sniffed it approvingly before applying it sparingly to her throat and wrists.

"Would you like me to stay wi' you until—" Mary began kindly, noticing the trembling of the flask that Mira held.

"No, thank you." Mira smiled at her faintly. "I think I would like to be alone for a little while, Mary."

The maid curtsied and left quietly. Sprawling on the bed and propping her chin in her hands, Mira stared into the crackling fire that lit the fireplace. It was not a cold night, but she was glad of the small, cheerful blaze. It lent a companionable warmth to the room, casting its light on the walls and softening what could have been a harsh silence with the sound of its burning. In a few minutes she heard the steps of booted feet outside the door. There was a brief hesitation before a few light taps descended on the wood paneling.

"Come in," Mira said, surprised at the thin sound of her own voice. She jumped up, folding her arms protectively across her chest as Alec entered the room.

His eyes drank in the sight of her, and a smile shaped his mouth as he closed the door. "I couldn't wait any longer," he said softly. Silently she watched as he shrugged out of his coat, and she wondered if she should offer to help. What was the wifely thing to do? Should she ask about whatever it was that had been necessary for him to take care of? Should she turn back the covers and get into bed, or go over to him and—

"Mira, are you nervous?" Alec asked, his gray eyes smiling down at her as he dropped his coat into a chair and pulled his boots off.

"No, no, of course not. Why would I be—?"

"There's no reason to be. You know already how good it will be between us."

"It's just that . . . it's been a long time," she offered lamely, and he chuckled, padding barefoot to a small brass-inlaid table and uncorking the bottle of wine that had been left there with two elaborate goblets. The jeweled and gold-encrusted goblets were part of a set that had been given to them by Rand and Rosalie.

"Yes, it has been a long time," he said, filling a goblet and handing it to her. "A good month, at least. Perhaps you've a right to worry . . . God knows what could have changed in a month's time . . . What are you smiling at? This is a solemn occasion, Lady Falkner. A terribly serious business, marriage is. Now that you're my wife, you must learn to be dour and sensible."

"I will," she promised him, taking a sip of wine and feeling it trickle silkily down her throat. "Tomorrow."

"Good," he approved firmly. "I am told that it is a terrible burden to be the wife of a Falkner, but I will try to provide what few compensations I can. Do you like the wine?"

"It is lovely. But I deserve more compensation than a mere glass of wine for what I've gone through today."

He grinned and began to unbutton his shirt. "Don't worry. Tonight you're going to get everything you deserve."

"I can only hope so." Covertly she glanced at him, and a tiny blaze of anticipation flickered like fire within her. They had never had the privacy or leisure to look at each other in detail, and he was a beautifully made man. His body was large and sparely fleshed, his waist and abdomen well-tapered with tightly roped muscles, while the broad lines of shoulders and back were formed with an incomparable symmetry. Dark fur was spread lavishly over his chest, and Mira was tempted to go to him and splay her fingers through the textured hair, rub her face in it like a small cat craving affection. Instead, she looked at him over the rim of the goblet and finished the wine. Aware of her curiosity, Alec stripped the shirt off slowly and dropped it into the chair. Slowly his hands moved to the fastening of his pantaloons; then he stopped as her eyes flickered away immediately.

Crooking a slanted eyebrow, he strode to where she was standing, taking the goblet from her nerveless fingers and setting it on the table. Mira's mouth opened in surprise as her husband reached toward the bed and deftly whipped off the counterpane with a flourish. "What are you doing?" she asked.

He spread the thick, beautifully worked material on the floor in front of the fireplace. "I'm changing our venue."

"Alec," she murmured, casting an appalled look at his handiwork. "That expensive counterpane on that Aubusson carpet—it's going to get—"

"Mira," he interrupted softly, "they're not holy relics. They're just things . . . objects . . . articles meant for our use."

"They're expensive objects. I can't be careless with such things. I won't ever be able to." She pressed her palms to her forehead in a sudden gesture of anxiety and closed her eyes tightly. "*Dieu*, how am I going to live here? I don't want to live in a castle! I have been so afraid ever since we arrived that I would break something, or spill something—how am I going to live here?"

His powerful hands closed carefully over her wrists,

mindful of their fragility, and he pulled her hands away from her face. "This is not a castle. It's a home, yours as well as mine. There is nothing in it that can't be replaced if you break it. In fact, we can afford to rebuild and refurnish this whole damned place several times over. Does that make you feel better?"

"No. It is a palace, and it is too big, and it unnerves me. I would rather live in a cottage."

"My sweet love, picture a cottage. Four walls and a door. Our home is merely a variation on the same theme, except that there are more walls and more doors. I am reasonably well-versed in the principles of architecture—trust me."

She eyed him suspiciously. "You would say anything in order to make me more resigned to all of this."

"Anything," he agreed readily.

"But my perspective of these walls and doors is very different from yours. You are a duke, and you are accustomed to this, having been brought up to—"

"Don't think of me as a duke. Think of me as your husband." He sent her a beguiling smile. "Now, don't you want to sit by the fire with the man who loves you?"

"On that expensive counterpane—"

"Bedspread," he corrected. She smiled reluctantly, her mild panic subsiding, and she allowed him to pull her down onto the soft, cushiony counterpane. Leaning her back against his chest, she stared dreamily into the fire, comfort seeping into every pore of her skin. He was right. Names and objects did not matter. Only this mattered. Only him. "I thought every woman wanted to be carried away to a castle," Alec said, ducking his head to kiss the soft place where her neck joined her shoulder. "And kept safe and sheltered—"

"While you're away?"

"Yes, fighting the dragons."

"No. I intend to keep close by your side, fighting them with you."

"But how unfair for the dragons."

She twisted around with a smothered laugh, intending to pummel him playfully. Her gown became tangled around her legs, and her breasts brushed against his chest, and the veil of silk that covered her bosom did nothing to muffle the sensation of her flesh pressing into his. His body was warm, vital, hard against hers. Motionless, Mira absorbed the abrupt plunging sensation inside her abdomen, the quick throb between her legs. She took a slack, unsteady breath. "No mercy for dragons," she said, mesmerized by his lazy smile.

"Nor for husbands, it seems." Alec rolled her onto her back, looking down at her with eyes that shone like quicksilver. He hooked his fingers in the bodice of her gown and pulled it down her body, tugging briefly as it caught at her hips. Then the silk was thrust aside, and Mira quivered as his naked chest lowered over hers. He kissed her unhurriedly.

So sweet, this closeness.

Her body, tender and supple underneath him.

And his, racked with alternate drafts of hunger and relief.

The remainder of his clothes were cast aside.

"I love you," she whispered, saying the words without expectation, without demand, without fear. The way that they were meant to be said, as a gift of emotion, a declaration that to him was unequaled in value. He answered her with the same words, and with his body, and with a heart that had once scorned love as something that did not exist. His reason fled, and just as the times that had gone before this, sex became an act without calculation, without thought. Blinding excitement poured through and between them, around them with white heat. All of his senses were focused on her . . . Mira in the firelight, her hair entangling him in lengths of dark silk, her delicate hands slipping over his tensile strength.

Her skin was as soft as down. His hands moved over her, his touch bold, then excruciatingly light, slipping from the full swell of her hips to her finely boned shoulders. A muted whisper fell from her lips as his palm curved over the gentle rise of her breasts, brushing over the tips of them in a teasing caress. Alec pressed his mouth to the hollow of her throat, and the touch of his tongue awakened her nerves into trembling awareness. Another damp stroke between her breasts . . . eagerly she arched up to him, groaning his name as his mouth dragged slowly up the warm slope . . . so damned slowly, making her wait even though he knew what he was doing to her. Finally his lips reached her nipple, and she purred with pleasure. His tongue feathered over her artfully, tracing around the outline of the aroused peak.

Weakly she abandoned herself to him and the torment that he wrought so expertly on her body. The light of the flames struck off the ebony filaments of his hair, and her fingers sank into the thickness of it before slipping down to his powerful shoulders. At her touch they flexed involuntarily. Alec lifted his head, closing his eyes as her fingertips wandered along his spine, pressing lightly into the hollows. His mouth returned to her flesh, endlessly craving the taste of her.

"So beautiful . . ." he muttered, his voice low and ragged. "I want to know you better than any human being has ever known another."

"You do. You have."

He looked at her, his eyes shining hotly, and the merest intimation of a smile touched his lips as he read the sincerity in her expression. "Have I?" he asked, and as if to prove her wrong, he touched her in ways that he never had before, discarding more of his restraint. His hands curved around her buttocks, massaging and cupping . . . and suddenly his fingers dipped into the crevice between them, causing her to flush scarlet and writhe away from him. "Alec," she choked in protest, startled by the intimacy, and he laughed softly, withdrawing his hands to a less disturbing place. Effortlessly his knees spread hers.

"Don't move," he whispered, stroking her hips. "Don't move at all."

"Why?" Mira breathed, but he gave no answer. His mouth brushed over her skin down to her abdomen. Every muscle in her body tightened as his tongue invaded her navel, and she tensed in response to the strange sensation. His hands tightened around her hips, keeping her still, and gradually she felt an unfamiliar pulsing pleasure as he licked and tasted the tiny orifice. "Alec, please love me," she said shakily, wanting him to stop and raise his body back over hers, and thrust into her. She was damp with perspiration, trembling with need.

"I do," he said, deliberately misunderstanding her, his heart drumming with excitement.

She swallowed hard with relief as his tongue left her navel, knowing that now she would have him, now he would join his hips to hers and quench the agonizing emptiness inside her. But instead of moving up along her body, his head went even lower, and suddenly his mouth was playing gently between her legs. She made a small surprised sound, frozen in confusion, flooded with pleasure. Blindly she reached down to the large hands that clasped her hips, and his fingers tangled with hers, and the devouring sweetness went on until she thought she would faint. Painfully aroused, shocked into silence, she made no move, no sound, no protest when the caress ended and he let his mouth drift back up her body to her throat. Her eyes met his, her gaze so dark that it looked black. Slowly she slid her arms around his neck.

"Let me take you to bed," he whispered.

She nodded, hiding her face against his neck as he lifted her up easily. The mattress gave slightly underneath them, and he pressed her onto her back, his taut thighs wedging between hers. He took her mouth with a slow, hungry kiss, his passion honed and sharpened by her eager response. With a low, heavy thrust, he filled her until she gasped. "Mira?" he murmured, holding himself still within the throbbing snugness that surrounded him, and then he groaned as she lifted her hips against his and tried to urge him more deeply still. The scalding heat of his flesh surged into her, their bodies knitting together with stunning perfection. Urgently they moved and touched, learning the secrets that only lovers could know.

He discovered that she loved to sift her fingers through the hair on his chest, and that her legs were the perfect length to wrap around his hips. She found out that he shivered in pleasure when she scraped her nails very delicately across his back. And Alec, who never lost control, heard someone sobbing hoarsely, and realized that the abraded sounds came from his own throat. Burying his face in her hair, he felt her contract around him. She shuddered roughly, and drew a quick breath, and shuddered again, her body racked with brutal pleasure. Then he allowed himself to feel it also, the ecstasy submerging him in violent flood.

For a long time he held her without speaking, pulling her head to the hollow of his shoulder and sighing with satisfaction as she threw a slender arm over his wide brown chest. Contentedly Mira occupied herself with tracing idle patterns over his skin with her fingertips and then arranging long streamers of her hair over his chest in a silken net. Alec took her hand, kissing each fingertip before raising himself on one elbow and looking down at her. They smiled into each other's eyes. But slowly the amusement left Alec's expression, his gaze becoming grave and searching.

"How can I have lived so long without you?" he asked huskily. "How could I have ever thought that I was content? I didn't know. I didn't know that I needed you."

"I couldn't live without you," she said, her eyes suddenly glittering with tears. "Not after tonight."

He touched her lips with his fingertips, silencing her. "Don't say that. Don't be afraid of the future any longer. You're mine now, and nothing could change what I feel for you. Not even you could change it, even if you tried."

She nodded and tried to blink the tears away. In that second she was overwhelmingly tempted to unburden herself to him. More than anything, she wanted to tell him every detail, every secret of her past. It seemed perfectly natural that only now, in this moment of closeness, could they share their very deepest thoughts. The words hovered on her lips, struggling to escape the tight rein of silence.

No. She would not tell him now. She could never tell him. "Don't ever leave me," she whispered.

"No, I won't." Tenderly he kissed the dampness from her cheeks.

"I'm afraid for you. I don't want you to become more involved in looking for Holt's murderer with Carr—"

"I have to."

Her gaze was wet and bittersweet as she looked at him. "I won't let you go easily, Alec."

"I'm not going anywhere for several days."

"I will make a dreadful scene when you do leave."

He chuckled at her threat, dropping several kisses on her face and throat. "Just as long as you take me back when I return."

"I'll take you right now," she said in a muffled tone, and he grinned. His lips lingered on hers leisurely; his hands wandered over her body and pulled her further beneath him.

Mira had assumed that after their marriage she would come to know and understand her husband thoroughly. After all, living together as man and wife would engender complete familiarity between them, and she would be able to learn almost everything about him. However, she soon found that he was a more complicated and multifaceted man than she had guessed. She never knew which Alec she would climb into bed with at night—the tender lover or the earthy, lusty one . . . the flirtatious rogue from London or the seductive scamp who would not let any part of her body remain secret from him.

Most of the time he was given to spoiling her outrageously. He covered her with jewels, silks, and satins, took her dancing and kept her up until the sun rose, whispered nonsensical bits of poetry and extravagant flattery in her ear. At other times, he would encourage her to ride with him and romp through the woods like a hoyden, and she would tease him with glimpses of her bare legs as she waded in the bubbling current of a brook and scampered through sunny forest clearings.

One evening after her bath was readied, she sank down into the steaming water and immediately fought to evade his questing hands, for bathing her was one of Alec's favorite activities. "Let me alone—you nearly *drowned* me the last time," she accused, splashing him playfully. In response he plied his slick hands to her body lustily, at first drawing forth giggles and squirming struggles from her. But after a few minutes of such play, she leaned her head back against the rim of the porcelain tub and said his name, her breath coming fast between her lips. His soap-lubricated hand slid up along the inside of her thigh, and her legs parted underneath the water as he caressed the softest part of her. Kissing her warmly, he smothered her tremulous sounds and delighted in the tumult of her passion.

As she was learning quickly, making love with Alec was always pleasurable . . . but not always undertaken seriously. In bed he could be ardent and eloquent, but sometimes he was playful and surprisingly earthy. He was a supremely unself-conscious lover, and he tore down her inhibitions one by one, making her aware that the act of love was an art as well as an expression of emotion.

In turn, Mira plied the lessons she learned with a skill that never failed to surprise Alec. When they were in the company of others she played the high-born lady flawlessly, quiet and demure, with just the right amount of shy wit. But when they were alone, she was free and open with him, capable of brazen seduction or radiant tenderness, capricious one moment, cool and sharp-witted the next. They argued about politics and traded insights in a way that neither had experienced before with a member of the opposite sex. One of the topics that they discussed frequently was the growing amount of crime in London, not only because several popular debates about crime were currently taking place in the houses of Parliament but also because each of them had his own personal and unspoken reasons for having an interest in the subject.

"Did you read the article in the *Times* this morning about the hulks?" Mira inquired as they played cards after supper in the zodiac room. Evening shadows collected in the corners of the octagonal room and darkened the fanciful astrological signs carved into the woodwork. The table was flooded with light from a brass chandelier.

"No, I didn't." Thoughtfully Alec studied his cards.

"Is it true that almost five thousand prisoners are kept in just ten ships that are all moored in the Thames?"

"Yes. There isn't enough room in the regular prisons to keep them."

"But the article said that they are all packed on those ships, and every night the hatches are screwed down—how can those men even breathe? And what about disease and sickness, and what if a fire starts?"

"Only the strongest survive. There are many deaths

in the hulks." Alec shook his head slightly, losing interest in the cards and putting them facedown on the table. "And in the cases of the boys who end up there, it's better to die than to become what they are forced to become. The only activities for them are gambling and bullying or slaying each other. Some of the larger ones are put to word dredging and cleaning the river, while others make convict uniforms."

"And then they are set free," Mira said, greatly perturbed at the thought.

"It's just like Newgate—the hell of being imprisoned in such a place makes every man who is released determined to take revenge on the system and the society that put him there."

"And that is why they all band together in these crime organizations? To take revenge on society?"

Alec nodded, and Mira suddenly thought of Guillaume with a stab of sadness. She prayed that after they had parted company, her brother had not become a member of such a group. Although Guillaume had done many immoral and illegal things in his life, she hoped that there had been enough decency in him to help him avoid such a fate.

"What are you remembering?" Alec asked quietly.

"Nothing," she replied with forced lightness, sending him a smile that he did not return. Alec's expression was carefully blank as he tamped down an unexpected surge of frustration. When, he wondered bleakly, was she going to trust him? Would she ever? "I'm . . . I'm going to ring for some tea," Mira said, standing up and pushing her chair back. As she moved by the table, the draping material of her sleeve brushed a large portion of the deck of cards to the floor. They fluttered downward like a flock of descending birds.

Alec stared at the cascade of fallen cards. A closed door in his mind was abruptly battered down. For a second Mira saw a flash of something like fear or horror darkening his eyes, and she was at his side immediately. He did not look at her but continued to stare at the floor.

"Alec? What is it?" she demanded, kneeling by his chair and looking up at him. He closed his eyes and turned his face away.

"God. I hadn't remembered." His voice was rough and very low.

"Remembered what? Why did you look at the playing cards like that?" Turning her attention to the offending objects, Mira scowled at them, scooped them up quickly, and shoved them out of sight.

"I was the one . . . I was the one who found Holt's body," Alec muttered. She gazed at him compassionately and stroked his arm in a gesture of comfort. "It was late at night, in a dark alley. I didn't notice any details about it then . . . I was half-drunk to begin with. I just realized all at once what had happened, and . . . there were signs of a fight, a vicious one. The bruises on him . . ." He stopped suddenly and then resumed more calmly. "Just now I remembered that there were playing cards scattered on the ground."

Mira did not understand why the fact was significant to him. "Perhaps Holt was carrying them," she suggested, and he looked at her seriously.

"Perhaps he was."

Again she had the feeling that the observation held a meaning for him that escaped her. "How did you find him there?"

"I was supposed to meet him at the Rummer, which isn't far away from the spot. He had sent me a message saying that he had something important to discuss with me."

"What about?"

"About a girl named Leila. He loved her . . . she disappeared, and he was looking for her." Alec seemed to look right through her as he added distantly, "I think he had found out what had happened to her, who had taken her."

Mira stroked his arm once more and sighed. "It's so very late . . . let's go to bed."

"Why don't you go on? I'll join you soon." Picking up a card, Alec stared at it absently, seeming to forget her in his preoccupation. Mira smiled uncertainly at him and left the room.

He came to bed much later. Mira stirred groggily as he unfolded his long body beside hers and forced himself to relax. Willing himself to sleep, he shoved aside the thoughts that riddled his mind and shut his eyes tightly, but in sleep there was no escape from the questions and the memories. Restlessly he fought to escape the disturbing dreams, kicking the covers off and moving his head from side to side. He woke up from the middle of a nightmare with a muffled curse, his whole body jerking awake. Overheated and uncomfortable, he drew a forearm across his perspiring forehead, brushing aside the hair that clung to his skin.

Mira, who had been elbowed, kicked, and tossed for hours as a result of *his* bad night, lifted her head and regarded him exasperatedly. "You'll be cooler if you try to keep still," she said.

"I'll be cooler if you'll stop pulling the damned sheet up!" he snapped.

"A nightmare about Holt?" she asked, ignoring his bad temper, and he sighed heavily, dropping back against the pillows.

"Partly."

Since he had no desire to talk about the dream, she repositioned herself on her side of the bed and drifted back to sleep. Several minutes later, she was again awakened by his restless tossing. Yawning and grumbling to herself, she crawled over to him. At the sight of the small indentation of worry that had worked itself between his brows, her irritation fled. She brushed his tousled black hair away from his forehead in a soothing motion, waking him up with a whisper.

His spiky lashes lifted. "What?" he murmured.

"You were moving around again."

"I'm sorry," he said wearily, closing his eyes again. The apology was her undoing.

"Here, move to the middle of the bed. The sheets are cooler."

"There's nothing you can do to—"

"And let me rearrange the pillows. Better?"

"A little," he admitted ungraciously, the aggravated male in him placated by her soothing. She smiled as he settled his back more deeply into the mattress.

"You should try to stop thinking about it for a little while," she said softly, and he made a sarcastic sound, turning his face into the pillow.

"It's not that easy."

Leaning over him, Mira touched his lips lightly with her own. Her mouth was cool and sweet, and the tender, patient feel of it robbed him of his former annoyance. She brushed each corner of his lips with the tip of her tongue, then delved further inside his mouth to savor the warm, intoxicating taste of him. Alec's head shifted on the pillow, his mouth turning up to hers with growing interest. Her hands trailed across his chest, then traveled down to his flat midriff, and her fingertips drew across the muscle-strapped flesh. "It's very easy," she whispered, kissing the strong clean-cut line of his jaw, breathing in the fresh sandalwood scent of his skin. "Just turn all of your thoughts to me . . ." As she moved closer to him, the soft peak of her breast grazed his side, and Alec caught his breath sharply. Grasping her elbows, he hauled her halfway across his chest and pulled her head down to his. She gave him a deep kiss, and every sane thought, every question and problem that had been plaguing Alec the entire night disappeared in a single moment.

The locks of her hair trailed like flossy fire over his body as her small, sensitive hands swept over him. Though he urged and murmured to her impatiently, she took her time. The cool touch of her fingers drifted to his manhood, encircling leisurely, and Alec bit his lip as she aroused him to forceful readiness. Mira's lashes lowered as she felt the driving power of him under her palm. She wanted nothing more than to have him inside her, but somehow she managed to resist his efforts to pull her on top of him. Like a butterfly playing with a swiping cat, Mira eluded his grip and continued to torment him with light caresses. The stillness of the night was broken by their harsh gasps, and the pleasure was prolonged until finally Mira made no demur as his hands grasped her hips and urged them over his loins. Her head fell back weakly as she felt the thick, hot sliding of him in her body, as he drove into her with heavy, grinding strokes. She was soaring too high to breathe, paralyzed in a hurtling flight, her mind going black in those few seconds of rapture.

Gradually her limbs unclenched, and she recovered her thoughts slowly, moving off him and collapsing against his side with an exhausted sigh. Alec did not stir. Peering at his face in the dimness, she saw that he was already asleep, deeply asleep in a state that rivaled unconsciousness. One arm was outflung, the fingers slightly curled in complete relaxation. There would be no more tossing and turning tonight. She smiled slightly and snuggled against his still form.

"And yet another den of iniquity—is this our forty-second or forty-third?" Carr grumbled, his green eyes sullen as the hackney ambled along the small dilapidated streets. "Damn, but I'm getting tired of this. For the past few days we've been in nearly every flash house in London, consorting with every type of scum imaginable. I've been buying drinks for murderers and cutthroats, gambling with professional cheats and thieves, been mauled by the most ragged whores I've ever seen—none of whom would be harmed by a good washing, I might add—and no sign of Tilter. No one seems to have even heard of the bastard. Do you realize how many of these places we've been to? I've been inside so much that I've forgotten what the sun looks like, and I've inhaled more smoke and foul air than clean—"

"Don't complain," Alec said, his expression thoughtful and unsmiling. "We're both acquiring a nice prison pallor."

Carr scowled at him even though the point was well-taken. A decided pallor did not hurt their cause at all, since they could only fit into the scenery of the flash houses by blending in with the criminals that frequented them. In order to complete the impression, Alec and Carr were clad in old and rather worn attire that had once been of good quality—"malpreserved elegance" was what Carr had dubbed the look, and so far it had served them quite well.

During the past few days, the pair of Falkners had indeed learned a great deal about the flash houses in London. A flash house served as a place for criminals to hide from law enforcers. Often it was used as the headquarters for a particular gang, and it provided information and aid for a man who had just been released from prison, whether he was a loafer, semicriminal, or mass murderer. Stolen goods were taken there and given to fences, and anyone could go to a flash house to hire someone to steal for him or provide false testimony at a trial. It was the meeting-place for felons; it was their source of companionship and entertainment.

The particular place that they were approaching now was reputed to be a favorite of Stop Hole Abbey members. Hopefully it would yield some information about Tilter, some useful scrap about his identity or whereabouts that they could go on. The carriage passed through a web of yards and buildings that reminded Alec of a rabbit warren. It was a favorite design of flash house districts, since the area could be evacuated quickly during a raid, men and women scrambling and scattering as quickly as panicked rodents.

"God, this looks like one of the worst we've seen so far."

"Not one more word," Alec snapped suddenly, turning in a fluid movement and pinning Carr with an icy stare. "Not another whine. If you don't want to go in there, then have the hackney take you back to your nursery. No, you haven't seen the sun for days, and you haven't gotten a decent sleep, and you're understandably revolted by our current drinking companions. But neither have I—and I haven't seen my wife in three days! Do you think I would rather be here wading through the gutters with you than heading back home to her?"

"No." Carr averted his gaze and stared abashedly at the straw-littered floor of the hackney. "I apologize," he muttered. "I haven't bothered to consider the fact that this is all a hardship for you as much as it is for me."

Alec looked at him in vague surprise, not having expected such an admission from his cousin. Carr was not a humble sort, but he approached life with a brash sort of candor that was unusual for a young rake. "Such honesty," Alec said, his tone less sharp. "I've meant to ask you before about your habit of telling the truth. Where did you get it from? . . . not the Falkner side of the family, God knows."

"Holt was always forthright," Carr said, mildly flustered, wondering if he were being praised or rebuked.

"Ah yes, your brother the saint." The carriage stopped, and Alec tossed some money to the driver before preceding Carr into the flash house. They had to pass through two inner doors before reaching the main one, which was opened a few inches. Cautiously a grubby and misshapen face peered through.

"Bring yer own books?"

Alec pulled out one of the cards that Memmery had given him, the seven of diamonds, holding it between his first two fingers. The door was opened and they were admitted entrance. The air was thick with the scents of fish and drink, the noise of conversation and drinking songs. Instantly the two men split up, following the pattern of a routine that had been developed during the last two days. With the two of them working a room, there was a far greater chance of getting information. As Carr headed off for a drink, Alec was waylaid by a heavyset whore who possessed coarse features but good skin and an impressive bosom. He forced a smile, concealing the repugnance he felt at the invitation in her eyes.

"Aye, yer an 'andsome cove. Belly timber?" the whore suggested, her voice soft and scratchy at the same time, like a cat's tongue.

"Thanks, love, I'm not hungry."

"Taplash?"

"Later."

"Then 'ow 'bout a tip o' the velvet? Free."

To refuse the offer of her body would be an insult. To accept was unthinkable. Alec smiled and slid his arm around her thick waist, pulling her closer and slipping a few pound notes into her bodice. The touch of her jiggling flesh made him feel completely dead inside. "Later," he said, giving her waist a slight squeeze and watching thankfully as she left him with swinging hips.

The hours passed slowly. In accord with a previous agreement, Alec and Carr never completely left each other's sight. Carr threw himself into his role, drinking and spouting forth foul language and ribald curses, exchanging colorful stories with those closest to his own age, flirting cheekily with the women. He kept his ears and eyes open, latching on to certain fragments of conversation here and there, asking casual questions. Halfway through the evening, Carr glanced across the room and noticed that something was different from usual. Instead of carrying on in a similar manner, drinking and carousing, Alec had struck up a quiet conversation in the corner, propping his feet up on the table in a relaxed attitude. Next to him sat a grizzled older man whose face had the green-white tinge of someone who rarely ventured out-of-doors.

As Carr watched covertly, Alec slipped a leather pouch to his table companion and bent his dark head low to hear a short whisper. Even from a vantage point so far away, Carr could see the sudden absence of color in Alec's face. Carr's ears roared as his blood rushed in excitement.

He got something. Alec must have found out something, he thought, and carefully managed to extricate himself from the drunken group he had been talking with. Affecting an intoxicated stagger, Carr sauntered over to the table and braced his hand on it as he stared down at Alec. Their gazes locked, and Carr saw with a start of unease that the pale gray eyes were blank with shock. "I'm gettin' awful boozy, cuz," Carr announced. "Well into my altitudes." His voice seemed to snap Alec out of his frozen trance.

"We're leaving," Alec said curtly.

Eagerly Carr followed him out of the place.

The open air seemed unnaturally quiet after the suffocating din they had just left. Alec glanced up and down the empty street. "We need a hackney," he said emotionlessly.

"Alec, are you ill?"

"No."

"You talked to that bounder about Tilter?"

Alec laughed softly, and it was not a pleasant sound. "Yes."

"Was *he* Tilter?"

"No. But he confirmed what Memmery said, and more."

"More? What more? What else?" Carr demanded in excitement.

"Tilter is a member of Stop Hole Abbey," Alec said stiffly. "He has a high position in their white-slavery racket. He also has the responsibility of taking care of anyone who finds out too much about it—which means that he was probably the one who killed Holt."

"The bastard!" Carr exclaimed. "I can't wait to find him and tear out his . . . Wait a minute—why do you look so strange?"

Alec walked over to the wall of the building and braced his forearm against it. Slowly he leaned his forehead against his arm and sighed tiredly.

"Well, how can we find him?" Carr continued. "Did you manage to get his real name? If we can find out who he really is, then—"

There was something like a gasping laugh, and then Alec turned around with a pale face, his eyes gleaming oddly. "Do you want to know who Fate is, Carr? He's a malevolent little jester sitting up there in the heavens and pondering over how ridiculous we humans are."

"What does that have to do with—?"

"—and he does his best to make fools out of all of us. And sooner or later he succeeds."

Carr was annoyed and bewildered by the obscure comment. "Alec, I don't give a damn about fate. I just want to know who Tilter is, so I can find him and make him pay for what he did to—"

"His name," Alec said softly, "is Guillaume Germain."

"Germain . . ."

"Yes. The name should sound familiar. He's my brother-in-law."

15

*A*s the carriage headed back to Staffordshire, the silence inside was crushing. Alec was barely aware of Carr's presence, so intent was he on sorting through the questions in his mind. Mira and the nameless ghosts of her past—whatever they were, they had almost prevented her from marrying him. The past was so frightening to her that she would not tell him anything about it. Did she know that her brother had killed Holt? Had she known it all along?

He closed his eyes tightly, shaking his head as if to deny everything he had found out. He could see Mira's face as if she were there in front of him, her cheeks glistening with tears, her eyes haunted . . . she had tried to keep him from going to London, had seemed afraid when he told her that he was searching for Holt's killer. Had she been afraid that he would discover it was her own brother? He was appalled at his own thoughts but couldn't suppress them, and his ears rang with echoes of things she had said to him.

"You're seeking revenge for something that should be left in the past."

"Your feelings about me are going to change."

"Not again . . . I can't live through having you and losing you again."

"Do you think there's a chance that Mireille knows?" Carr asked hesitantly, and Alec kept his eyes closed to hide the pain the question had caused.

"God, I don't know. I don't know."

Alec tried to remember Holt, tried to recall the picture of Holt he had carried in his mind ever since the murder . . . the darkness, the alley, the blood . . . but no, it wasn't very clear . . . it was indistinct now. Holt was gone and the past was over—he was free of it, and nothing was as important to him as what he had with Mira, the future they would share, the children they would have, the memories they would make together. And if she had known about what Guillaume had done to Holt? . . . she had loved Alec enough to gamble that he would never find out. Alec hoped that Mira knew nothing about Guillaume. If she did, she was undoubtedly afraid, and it was something that he could never reassure her about; she would never approach him with it.

"The important thing to worry about now," Carr said, "is how to find Guillaume. It shouldn't be that hard, if we—"

"No," Alec said, opening his eyes and breathing easier, relief flowing through him as he realized what his only choice was. "There is something more important than Guillaume for me to worry about. You can look for Guillaume . . . and I wish you luck. But you'll have to do it alone. I can't help you."

"But . . . but he's Holt's killer!" Carr said, stupefied.

"Yes, and his sister is my wife . . . and I'm not fool enough to lose her. If I decided to hunt down her brother, if I did anything to make her afraid that I blamed her, if by chance she didn't know anything about this and found out about it from me, she might run."

"Run where?"

"Where I could never find her," Alec replied, realizing as he said it that the thought terrified him. Mira had run from her problems in the past, and he had no guarantee that she wouldn't do it again. It was still too early in their marriage; not enough time had passed by for her to be secure in his love and her place in his heart. The beginning they had made was still too tender, too fragile to withstand such a test.

"She wouldn't leave you," Carr argued. "It's obvious that she loves you."

"She might decide it's her only option." Mira was young and hardy, but she was also a war-scarred veteran who had faced too many battles alone. She hadn't yet become accustomed to the fact that she could rely on someone else for protection. "I won't risk her finding out, Carr," he said firmly. "She is to know nothing of today, do you understand?"

"But how can you discount the possibility that she knew about Guillaume and just didn't tell you?"

"I can't. But it doesn't matter to me."

"I don't understand why not."

"You will. You'll understand when you fall in love . . ." Alec paused and then smiled wryly. "There are a hell of a lot of things you'll understand then."

"Not this, I won't. Not giving up when you finally have the chance for revenge."

"Revenge is sweet," Alec acknowledged ruefully, "and I've had a taste for it in the past."

"But?"

"But as you'll discover, there's not much of a future in it."

The innocuous sight of a small white note should not have disturbed Mira so greatly. It was delivered early in the morning by a small village boy, according to Mary. Mira received it on her breakfast tray, tucked beside the latest issue of the *Times*. She picked it up curiously, noticing the rough quality of the paper and the burned candle-wax seal. For a reason that she did not care to examine, Mira delayed the opening of the note for as long as possible, finishing her breakfast, washing her face, choosing her clothes for the day, and dressing. While she busied herself with inconsequential tasks, the message lay unopened on the bed, its dark wax seal a malevolent eye that watched her every movement. Finally she picked it up and opened it.

Her first thought was about how odd it was, that although she rarely spoke French and had lost most of her accent, though she even dreamed in English, the sight of her native language was still more instantly comprehensible to her. It was more deeply familiar to her than the sight of her own face in the mirror . . . so familiar that she had read the note and understood its meaning before she had even realized that it had been written in French.

I will be in the woods at the edge of the garden all morning. I will wait for you as long as I must. Please come alone. I need your help.

It was not signed. A signature was not necessary, since he had known that she would recognize who had sent it.

She had never been so cold in her life. As her teeth chattered, Mira crumpled the note and wadded it up. Her heart beat in deep, violent throbs that hurt her chest and made her knees feel weak. She huddled in the corner of the room like a trapped animal, backing up against the wall, clasping her arms over her chest. "Please, God, don't take it all away," she choked, and tears squeezed out from underneath her eyelids. "Don't let him do it again."

A gust of wind shook the trees, causing the first few brown leaves of autumn to fall in a dry shower around her. Slowly they approached each other, dark eyes fastened on another pair of identical darkness. The breeze disarranged his black-brown hair, the same color as hers.

"Mira, ma soeur . . . c'est tu, vraiment?"

"Guillaume . . . *Qu'est-ce que tu veux?*" she asked unsteadily, stopping and backing away a few steps as he attempted to come closer to her. I'm a Falkner now, she thought, clinging to the knowledge as if it could save her from certain doom. She forced herself to speak English to him, though it would have been easier in French. "What do you want?"

"I knew that you would come to help me," he said, his eyes devouring the sight of her. "Mira . . . *c'est impossible*, Mira . . . I couldn't believe it when I found out what had become of you. Look at you! You're a woman—and you were a only little girl when you left me."

"When you drove me away." She wondered if she were more afraid of him than sorry for him. Guillaume had been handsome five years ago, fierce with a hunger for life, his face alert with ambition and desire . . . desire for women, for luxury, for money . . . yes, above all, for money. Now he was too thin, and he seemed far older than in his late twenties. She knew just by looking at him that he had gone far down the path he had begun to travel five years ago. It hasn't been entirely his fault, she thought heavily. Circumstances had played a part in making him what he was, just as they had made her what she was. Feeling a softening in her heart toward him, Mira hardened herself against it. Five years ago Rand and Rosalie had offered both of the Germains a new life in England, a life in which they would no longer have to steal what they needed and prey on those who were unable to defend themselves. Mira had wanted that chance desperately. Guillaume had destroyed it for both of them.

"What is it, Guillaume?" she asked quietly. "You're here because you want something from me."

"I . . . I don't know how to start."

Somehow they had switched roles. It seemed as if she were the older one and he was the younger, dependent one. "Start by telling me what happened after we parted," Mira prompted. "You had become involved with a gang—"

"An organization—Stop Hole Abbey. I've been with them ever since you left me. Over the past five years I have become an important man. I started out by doing little things—"

"Ah, *little things*," she repeated coldly, "like trying to kidnap Rosalie five years ago? And using me to betray her and Lord Berkeley?" Guillaume seemed surprised by her hardness. What had he expected of her? Mira wondered angrily. That she would run to him with outflung arms and tears of gladness? Had he expected that kind of reunion after what he had done to her? He reminded her of a child who knew that he had misbehaved but felt no real remorse.

"I had to do that," he said. "*Dieu*, they promised me so much, Mira. I had to do it. They said I would be rich someday, and I was going to share it all with you."

"You don't seem to be very rich," she observed, looking up and down his lean, ill-clad form, and suddenly his dark brown eyes flashed with resentment.

"But you are. Married to a Falkner. How did you do it? What trick did you use, or was it luck? You were always very lucky . . . you were my charm. When you left me—"

"I didn't leave you because I wanted to. I was forced to make a choice between going and staying and sinking down with you."

"I didn't sink," he said indignantly. "Far from it. I'm an important man in Stop Hole Abbey now. I have special responsibilities—"

"What kind of responsibilities? Things as bad as what you and I did—tricking people, taking their money, hurting—"

"What we did were merely children's games," he said scornfully.

She nodded slowly. Children's games—that was a good way to put it. While other children had been playing jackstraws or looking at picture cards, she had been picking pockets. But she and Guillaume had always stopped at certain unspoken limits. How far would he have gone, she wondered despairingly, after crossing the threshold of those limits? She looked away from him, trying to swallow the ache in her throat. "Do you want to know what I do?" he asked, his expression taunting. "I'm in charge of a whole group of men. I became friends with the leader of Stop Hole. He makes all the decisions and knows everything that goes on. He can have anything he wants, and he put me in charge of his special project. My men and I collect girls, right off the streets . . . sometimes from their homes, sometimes we even whisk them right out of the shops they work in. Only pretty ones. And we sell them and send them away to—"

"Don't tell me!" she cried, shuddering. "Why are you here? Why are you telling me this—to frighten me? What do you *want*?"

"I have a problem. Only you can help me. I had a few debts . . . I skimmed off a little money from Stop Hole's profits to pay them off. But now a few men in the organization are suspicious, and it's only a matter of time before they find out that I took the money . . . and when they do, I won't have a chance. If you don't give me the money to replace what I took from Stop Hole, my death will be on your conscience."

"No. You'll find some other way to get the money, but you won't get it from me. It would never stop . . . you would come to me over and over again, always asking for more."

"So you've become greedy, *petite soeur*. You have more money than you could ever spend, and you're married to a powerful man, but you won't spare a cent to save my life. I'll just have to ask your husband for help."

"What?" she whispered.

"I've heard that the Falkners take care of their own . . . and since I'm your brother, surely I must have some claim . . . yes, I'll have to talk to Lord Falkner about everything . . . explain my troubles . . . explain about our background.''

"You think you can blackmail me,'' Mira said, feeling a burst of inner panic, panic that she could not let him see. "But why do you think I haven't already told him everything? Including the part about Maman.''

"You wouldn't have—I know that about you, if I know nothing else. But if you're telling the truth, then you'd have no objection to my discussing it with him, would you? You may expect me to call later on this evening. We'll laugh about it together . . . the biggest joke in England. With all the women he could have chosen, Alec Falkner married a French whore's daughter.''

"No.''

"Should I tell him that Maman took care of her customers right in front of you when you were a baby? That you and she lived in the same room until you were old enough to move to the corner in the kitchen—''

"Stop it!''

"—and then I'll tell him that if I hadn't taken you away after Maman died, you would have become a whore too—you would be in that brothel today, spreading your legs for anyone with a pocketful of francs.''

"No!'' Mira wailed, covering her face with her hands and bursting into tears. She wept uncontrollably, turning away from her brother and hiding the sight of her fear and guilt from him. After the storm had subsided to gulping sobs, she staggered to a slender tree and leaned against it, unmindful that its bark was digging into the side of her face. She did not look at Guillaume, but she knew that he was still standing there, patient, watchful, waiting. "I have some money,'' she whispered, "but I can't give you more than a few hundred pounds in cash.''

"Jewelry. Surely he's given you plenty of that.''

"Yes.''

"Then bring it out here tomorrow and show it to me. I'll only take what I need."

"He's coming back tonight. He'll probably be with me all day tomorrow."

"Then go and get it right now. I'll wait here."

She was in the middle of a nightmare. In a matter of seconds, years had dissolved into nothingness, and she was no longer Mira Falkner, she was Mireille Germain, helpless, frightened, afraid to stay, afraid to run. "Guillaume," she begged, "after today, you plan to come back . . . I know you do. And there'll never be an end, not until you've taken everything I have and destroyed my marriage . . . and that will kill me. Don't come back again. *Please.*"

"Go fetch your jewelry, Mira."

Guillaume had taken a large portion of her possessions, and she was already frantic with worry—how could the jewelry not be missed? Perhaps she could claim that it had been stolen—but no, then the blame might be unfairly cast upon one or more of the servants, and she could never allow that. She sat in the bedroom after returning from her meeting with Guillaume, and she refused to take supper, feeling ill and forlorn. As evening fell, faint sounds from outside attracted her attention, and she went to the window. They had returned. The door of a carriage opened, and Alec's black head appeared. Running swiftly out of the keep and down a long flight of stairs, Mira reached the front entrance just as Carr and Alec walked in. She had never been so glad to see him . . . she had never needed his arms around her more than at this moment.

"Alec!" she cried out with gladness, and he laughed as she flew to him. He caught her in his arms and whirled her around once before letting her down to the ground and covering her mouth with his. She wrapped her arms around his neck and molded her slim body to his, and the kiss might have lasted several minutes more had it not been for Juliana's harrumphing.

"Ridiculous, these public displays. Mira, it only encourages him to neglect you when you let him go and then welcome him back without a fuss. You should chide him for leaving you, not scream and run to him as if you—"

"She doesn't need to chide me for leaving her," Alec interrupted his mother, his arms tightening around Mira as he smiled down at her. "I've been chiding myself for it every minute."

"Did you have any luck concerning Holt's—?" Mira began to ask, and he silenced her with a quick kiss.

"No, love. But it doesn't matter . . . you were right, it's better left in the past. I'm not going to look for the answers any longer . . . the answer to every question of importance is right here in my arms."

Oh, how she loved him! Right in front of Juliana, Carr, and anyone else who might have been watching, Mira pulled Alec's head down to hers, her lips passionate and sweet. She touched the tip of her tongue to his in a secret promise, felt a slight tremor in his arms, and pulled away with a shy smile.

"Has either of you had any supper?" she asked Carr, who shook his head in an unusually bashful manner. "I'm going to tell the cook to prepare something for you this very moment," she said. "I know how long the journey must have—"

"Thank you, but I'm too tired to eat," Carr said, throwing her a grateful smile. "Several hours of sleep is what I need."

"The only thing you can do for me," Alec whispered in her ear, "is take me to bed—right now."

They all retired to their rooms, and Mira acted as valet for her husband, helping him off with his boots and laying his clothes neatly across the back of a chair. He complicated the process, however, by insisting on removing her clothes at the same time, which resulted in a few tangles of arms and legs, several muffled laughs, and even a few popped buttons. Finally the task was done, and Alec fell onto the bed in a magnificent sprawl, tugging at Mira's wrist until she collapsed on top of him with a giggle.

"I love you, Lady Falkner," he murmured, straining his fingers through her sable hair as it cascaded over his chest.

"I love you, my lord." Her lower lip curved into a smile as his thumb caressed it gently.

"Don't call me your lord . . . call me your love, your husband, your—"

"My life," she whispered, her eyes glowing. "My love . . . my joy . . ." She trailed kisses across his neck and shoulder. ". . .my heart . . . my strength . . ." She pressed a kiss to his chest and then rested her cheek against it. ". . . or perhaps I should simply call you *mine*."

"Call me a fool for having left you," he said huskily, turning onto his side and gathering her close. Her slender thighs intruded between his and her hips cradled the hot, pulsing length of his manhood. They were both aroused by the contact, but neither of them moved, merely remained in the intimate clasp until Mira shifted slightly, eager to hasten their joining. "Always so anxious," Alec murmured, making no move to enter her.

"Always," she admitted readily, urging her hips against his until she felt the hardness of him riding between her thighs, and she gasped with anticipation. Alec smiled and bent to kiss her breasts, cupping them with his hands. Though his touch was far from rough, Mira couldn't help wincing suddenly. Instantly Alec was aware of her discomfort, and his hands became so light on her skin that he was barely touching her.

"More sensitive than usual," he said, a question in his voice, and she nodded breathlessly, trembling as he caressed her with incredible gentleness. His mouth moved tenderly over the soft peaks of her breasts until they hardened into rosy points. She moaned, lifting up to him, drawing closer to the source of her pleasure, drifting among blossoms of feeling . . . but then one of his hands moved down to her abdomen, and his palm pressed against the slight swell of her stomach. His hand was exploratory and curiously protective. Mira froze at the gesture, her eyes widening as they locked with his. His gaze was warm and searching, and he was touching her as if he thought . . .

"Mira," he asked softly, "is it possible that you're—?"

"No."

"I know every inch of you . . . and there's something different."

"No, you're wrong."

"When was your last monthly flow? You should have had it by now if—"

"I missed it because of the wedding. I was tense and upset, and in a few days I'm sure I'll . . . I know my own body far better than you do, and there's nothing different, nothing at all—"

"All right . . ." he soothed, his hand moving up to her arm. "Of course you do. It was only a question."

"It's . . . it would be too soon," she said, trying to explain her sudden apprehension. A baby, on top of everything else she had to worry about . . . She sighed inwardly at the thought. "I need more time with you . . . *alone* . . . and I would be so helpless and clumsy, and you wouldn't want me for months. Besides, I don't know how to take care of a baby—"

"Mira . . . shhh, wait . . . I wouldn't *want* you? Where did you get such a ridiculous idea? There won't ever come a day when I'll stop wanting you."

"I'll be twice this size when I carry a child—"

"You'll be twice as beautiful in my eyes."

"—and I'll waddle like a duck."

"That will make it easier for me to catch you when you make me chase you around the—"

"Don't joke about it! It's just like a man to say something like that!"

"I'm merely attempting to put your concerns to rest. Yes, I'll still want you. I'll always consider you the most beautiful woman I've ever seen—waddle or no waddle. And about taking care of the baby . . . there will be so many people who will spend their time ogling, pampering, and monopolizing the child that we'll have to visit the nursery by appointment."

"I wouldn't know how to be a mother."

"All women do, instinctively."

"Whoever said that didn't know what *he* was talking about. I don't have any of those instincts."

"You damn well do. I've never seen anyone who likes to take care of other people more than you do—"

"Yes, but—"

"—and you have so much love to give, sweet. I don't know of anyone more fit to be a mother than you."

"It's not that I don't eventually want children," Mira said, her uneasiness fading gradually, "it's just that I wouldn't want a baby *now*."

"I'd prefer it to be later," he admitted, smoothing her hair and kissing her forehead, "but if it isn't, then we'll accept whatever lies in store for us and deal with it together. Agreed?"

"Agreed," she said, and his arms drew around her firmly. As he held her, she closed her eyes and nearly quivered with contentment, warm in the circle of his arms, secure in his strength. "I suppose you may be right about a few things," she murmured.

He nudged her legs apart and buried his mouth in the valley between her breasts. "Of course I am."

"We'd still have time alone together, even after the baby was born, wouldn't we?"

"Of course we would."

"I would like to have a little boy . . ."

"Or a little girl."

"Yes . . . either one would be nice."

"Very nice," he agreed huskily, smiling at her with such heart-stopping warmth that she had to reach up and kiss him. Their mouths blended together as he responded slowly, appreciatively, kissing her with such tender skill that Mira felt the glow of fire spread over her body and down to her toes. Alec lifted his head and regarded her with gleaming silver eyes. "My love," he whispered, "you are holding a man in your arms who hasn't made love to you for days, and is feeling rather desperate. May we postpone the rest of our conversation, just for a little while?"

"We may," she said, and wrapped her arms around his neck.

Alec did not mention the possibility of a baby again, but as each day passed, Mira became more aware of the subtle changes in her body and was certain that she was pregnant. She visited Rosalie at Berkeley Hall to confide the news. Rosalie was clearly delighted, revealed that she herself was in the family way and had been ever since Brighton, and she diplomatically omitted to ask how far along Mira was. Which was just as well, considering the fact that the baby had probably been conceived a good month before her marriage to Alec.

It might have been a happy time for Mira, filled with anticipation, filled with new beginnings, but much of what might have been was obscured by the shadow that Guillaume had cast. It was becoming difficult for Mira to bear up under the strain of wondering about him and when he would appear again. Now there was even more for her to lose, even more that he could take away from her. Some days she could hardly swallow a bite of food, or concentrate on a book or a conversation, or relax enough to sleep. Sometimes she caught Alec staring at her with an unfathomable expression, as if he suspected something but could not bring himself to ask her about it.

The only time that she did not think about Guillaume or allow herself to worry about him was when Alec made love to her . . . only then was she able to escape. She knew Alec sensed that something was troubling her, but for some reason he did not pressure her to talk about it. Every night he seemed bent on wringing delight out of every nerve in her body . . . he tormented, teased, loved her until she was senseless with the most spectacular pleasure she had ever known. The days that she worried the most were when Alec was gone, either to attend to family business or to oversee the management of the estate. As she had expected and dreaded, on one of these mornings of Alec's absence, she received another note from Guillaume. Though her heart was filled with dread, she slipped out unnoticed to meet him at the edge of the garden. She had no alternative, nothing to bargain with.

Guillaume was waiting for her with an odd smile on his thin face, his dark eyes trained on her alertly. Mira was torn between pain and hatred as she saw him . . . she could not believe that they had come to this, not when they had once been as close as a brother and sister could be. They had helped each other to survive, defended each other from the rest of the world. But still, inside she had always been aware of a small flicker of fear; she had seen what he had been capable of doing to other people, she had recognized that he always put his own interests first, before everyone else's, before hers.

"More debts to pay?" she asked dully. "I knew you would want more from me. But the truth is that I haven't much more to give."

"The rest of your jewelry would be a good start."

"I brought it, in this bag. But after you take this, I have no other resources."

"You're married to a bloody duke, Mira—you have other resources. Here, give me that." Opening the bag and surveying its contents, he sent her a glance snapping with disdain. "Trinkets. I need more than this."

"I don't *have* any more!"

"That's too bad. I don't relish the task of telling your husband about you, *petite*, but it looks as though—"

"Wait," she said, biting her lip as her eyes welled with tears. With shaking hands she plucked at the golden chain around her neck, pulling the Falkner medallion out of her bodice. In the shade of the trees, the medallion gleamed with an almost unearthly brightness, rich and heavy, glittering with perfectly faceted gems. It was warm from her body, retaining the heat of her skin long after she had removed it. It had been hers ever since her first night with Alec . . . for months it had been her only link with him . . . it was their bond. Clutching it in her fist, she held it for one moment longer before giving it to Guillaume, feeling almost a physical pain as its weight was taken away from her palm and relinquished to his.

"Yes . . . something like this is more what I was expecting," Guillaume said, staring down at it appreciatively. "This should do very well . . . for now."

"It's the last thing I can give you," Mira replied, nearly choking with resentment. "I won't ever come to meet you again, Guillaume, no matter what you threaten to tell my husband. You'll never take anything from me again."

"You're wrong about that," he contradicted in a soft, insolent voice. "You're going to find more to bring to me . . . and I'll be here tomorrow morning, waiting."

"I won't be here."

"If you're not, I'll tell him everything—"

"Tell him about Maman. I don't care. You just might be underestimating him and his capacity for understanding and forgiving those he loves—and he loves me."

"He might forgive you about Maman," Guillaume conceded. "It's possible."

"He will."

"And I'm certain that he loves you. But love always has its limits."

"For you, perhaps. But not for—"

"You're a lovable little creature, Mira—I've always thought so—I imagine he'd be able to forgive you almost anything. Anything but murder."

"What murder?" Mira asked sharply, feeling her face go white. "You're talking like a madman."

"The murder of his cousin," Guillaume replied, seeming to relish her stunned expression.

"But that . . . that happened before he met me. I had nothing to do with that. Why . . . why did you mention it? I have no connection with his cousin's murder."

"I do," Guillaume murmured. "I did it."

"You're lying," she said, her voice shaking.

"I'm not. His cousin was asking questions around the Stop Hole flash houses, looking for one of the girls we'd taken . . . he found the right people, asked a few lucky questions, he learned too much. Naturally we couldn't let it go on. It's my job to clean up bungles and . . . complications, and I was the one who took care of him. At the time I had no way of knowing that he would have been a relative of yours . . . not that it would have made any difference."

"You're lying. It's not the same man."

"His name was Holt Falkner. Tall, slim, black-haired . . . strong bugger, too—as I remember, it took three of us to hold him down long enough to—"

"Oh God," Mira said brokenly, sinking down to the ground and putting her head between her knees as a wave of nausea nearly overcame her. Guillaume's story was too awful, too improbable not to believe. "Oh God."

"Yes, you realize exactly what it means. If he finds out what I did, he'll think of it every time he looks at you, every time he climbs into your bed."

Yes. She knew what Holt had meant to Alec . . . she knew the depth of Alec's loyalty, she knew of the sleepless nights that Alec had spent wondering *why* and *who* . . . No, he could not forgive this, even if he wanted to.

"I was such a fool," she whispered, "thinking that I had a chance to be happy."

"You still do—if you can keep it a secret from him. And that means keeping *me* happy, little one. So . . . until tomorrow, I'll leave you to think of how you're going to get more to bring me. *Au revoir.*"

She did not look up as he left. She was too weak, too defeated to move. Where, she wondered wretchedly, do you go when your life is over?

"Alec . . ." she whispered. "I'm sorry . . . I'm so sorry."

It was the first time Mira had not met him at the door when he returned home. Alec scowled slightly, having become accustomed to his wife's habit of coming down from the keep when he arrived and greeting him at the front entrance. Carr, who had abandoned London in favor of a few days' rest at the castle, walked to the bottom of the stairs and lounged against the railing.

"Hello, Alec. I have some things to ask you—"

"Where's Mira?" Alec asked shortly.

Carr shrugged carelessly. "Haven't seen her all day. Not since this morning. She said something about a headache and that she was indisposed and didn't want to be disturbed."

"Did she seem ill this morning? Was she in reasonably good spirits, or—?"

"I wouldn't be too concerned. Most women are indisposed occasionally."

"You haven't seen her all day?"

"That's right. Now, what I wanted to ask you—"

"In a few minutes," Alex said absently, glancing up the stairs. "First I want to see my wife." There was something wrong . . . the silence, her absence . . . it didn't sit well with his intuition, it didn't feel right. Resisting the urge to race up to their room, he walked up the steps, his scowl deepening as he reached the door of their bedroom. Turning the knob and going in, he cast a quick glance around the room, seeing nothing but empty shadows. "Mira?" he said aloud, though some part of his mind already sensed that it was useless. Slowly he walked to the dresser and picked up the scrap of paper folded in half, his hand trembling slightly as he saw his name written on it.

> Alec,
>   If I stayed here any longer I would be lying to you every day, trying to hide things that should not be kept secret from you. You will agree that it is best for me to go. What I must tell you will cause your feelings for me to change, just as I told you they would . . .

There was more, but suddenly Alec's eyes watered, and he could not read. The sound of his voice shot through the room like the crack of a rifle. "Mira!"

A few seconds later, Carr appeared at the doorway, his eyes wide with anxiety. "What? What happened? Is she . . . ?" Quickly he took in the sight of the empty room and the note in Alec's hand. He met Alec's gaze, which was such a glittery, pale shade of gray that he was chilled by it.

"She's gone," Alec said hoarsely. "I have to leave right away."

"There's still time to find her," Carr replied rapidly, not bothering to waste time with unnecessary questions. "She can't have gotten far in a day . . . she didn't take a carriage—I've been here all day."

"I'll take the carriage to the nearest posting house and hire a saddle horse there. You're right, she can't be far from here. By tonight she'll have reached an inn somewhere."

"I'll go downstairs and see that everything's made ready for you to leave."

As Carr left, Alec lowered his gaze back to the note and read it in a daze. Regret, anguish, love, and fear threatened to overwhelm him, and then all of it was masked with a surge of anger that burned right to the surface. Did she have so little faith in him that she would turn and run once again? After all of the reassurances, the support, the declarations he had given to her, she had reacted once more like a frightened child, and the helplessness he felt only added to his anger. Striding downstairs, he snatched up his coat and thrust the brief letter at Carr with a grimace. Carr took it automatically, his eyes on Alec's grim face. "I'm going with you," he said.

Alec shook his head. "I'll do it alone."

"It might take a day or two, but if you can find out where she's headed—"

"It won't take more than a few hours. I'm going to find her before tonight is over, if I have to tear the region apart."

"Alec," Carr said hesitantly, looking more than a little concerned, "I know you're angry with her, but she's obviously having a difficult time of it. Be lenient with her—"

"I'll be lenient," Alec assured him curtly, "after I wring her little neck."

"You told me that she's run many times before. Old habits are hard to break, and she just needs—"

"This one is going to be broken," Alec said darkly. "Soon."

"I think I should go with you."

"I think you'd better stay here and read that note."

"Why?" Carr looked down at the letter he held.

"Call it my gift to you. Guillaume will be waiting to meet with Mira at the edge of the garden tomorrow morning. Since my errant wife won't be here to welcome him, I'm certain you'll want to take her place."

"I'll be *damned*!" Carr exclaimed, his concern for Mira temporarily forgotten as he gazed down at the note, his expression vibrant with a blaze of fierce satisfaction.

"Enjoy yourself," Alec said softly, closing the door behind him.

Mira drew close to the fire, shivering as thunder roared outside the inn and rain poured down in a ferocious torrent. It was black and cold outside; the night was wind-whipped and rough, and she was lucky to have found refuge a few hours before the storm had worsened to this degree. Her room was small and comfortable, complete with a tiny bed and clean sheets, a fireplace, a table, a chair, and a washstand. For the most part, however, the comforts of her surroundings were lost on her. She stared blindly into the fire, hugging her knees, thinking of all that had happened that day, running over it repeatedly . . . seeing Guillaume's face . . . wondering what Alec was doing at this moment. Only a shred of doubt remained about whether or not she had done what was right. She knew that Alec would not want her after he read her letter . . . still, she knew that she should have told him everything in person. She had owed that to him. She had run without facing him—but facing him and witnessing his contempt, his anger, his rejection, would have been more than she could have withstood. She knew her limits—she knew what she could survive and what would be too much to bear—and the sight of Alec's hatred would have been worse than a bullet through the heart.

Her tortured thoughts were interrupted by a knock on the door. Thinking that it was the chambermaid, Mira rose to her feet and went to the door, her fingers poised above the bolt. "Yes? What is it?" she asked, and was startled by the sound of a man's voice, muffled by the door.

"Open it, Mira."

Alec's voice. She was astounded that he had found her so quickly, so easily, and she stared at the door, unable to move. Suddenly it burst open with the sound of a tremendous blow, the flimsy bolt popping off and bouncing on the floor. She fled to the other side of the room with the swiftness of a startled rabbit, her pupils dilated until the bittersweet brown was swallowed up by black. Alec stood in the doorway, his raven hair plastered to his forehead, his clothes dripping water in a myriad of puddles. His pale gray eyes were red-rimmed, glimmering oddly in his dark face, a face so harshly set that she barely recognized it as her husband's. He had never seemed so large or frightening; suddenly she was afraid of him. No trace of the man she had known and loved could be found in this apparition. He was a stranger who stared at her and spoke so coldly that she flinched as if he had struck her.

"You gave your maid's name to the innkeeper," he said. "I would have expected something more original from you." His gaze was icy as he looked at her, noting the way the firelight shone through her white nightgown and illuminated the slender shadow of her body. Then he looked around the room. "Tea and a feather bed . . . a fire . . . a newspaper. Very cozy, especially on a stormy night."

"Your clothes . . ." she said, her voice faltering. "You're so wet, you'll catch—"

"Spare me the wifely concern."

There was a wall between them that had never been there before, and it seemed so impenetrable, so unyielding that Mira took a few steps back, shaking her head helplessly. Her movement spurred Alec into action. He strode over to the chair, picked it up, and wedged it underneath the doorknob, sealing them inside the firelit room. Standing several feet away from him, Mira bent her head.

"How did you find me?"

"It wasn't difficult to figure out that you walked to the village and found transportation there. I knew you couldn't have gotten very far. This is only the second inn I've checked. The innkeeper was very helpful, telling me about a small dark-haired woman named Mary Cobbett who had—"

"I paid him not to talk to anyone!"

"If a man can be bought once, he can be bought twice. I paid him more than you did."

She nodded, staring at the floor. "Did you read the letter?" she asked huskily.

"Yes, I read it. Very informative, your letter. It made everything quite clear to me."

"You understand why . . . after I found out about Guillaume—"

"Oh, I understand," he said silkily, taking off his coat and flinging it in the corner with such savage force that she quivered in reaction. "I understand exactly how much you trust me . . . and exactly what you think of me."

"Alec, I love you, but I couldn't stay after—"

"Love." He sneered. "Don't offer that as an excuse. If what you did today was out of love, then I don't want it. I don't need any part of it. I've known about your brother for weeks, Mira . . . and all about what he did to Holt."

"You couldn't have," she gasped, her mind reeling with confusion. "Not during all those nights that you . . . all the times that we . . ."

"I found out during that last trip to London with Carr. I wasn't certain if you knew what Guillaume had done or not. But that didn't seem to dampen my ardor for you, did it? You seem so surprised, Lady Falkner."

"You still wanted me after you knew? I don't understand . . . you have every right to despise me for what my brother did . . . and what my mother—"

"I have every right to horsewhip you for sneaking off like a coward, without giving me a chance to talk to you. Your faith in me is rather negligible, isn't it? You were so goddamned certain that I would blame you, so certain that I wasn't worthy of your trust—"

"It wasn't like that!" Mira cried. "I was doing it for you . . . of course I wouldn't expect that you would want me after reading that letter—"

"Then what the hell *do* you expect of me?" he demanded in a black rage. "What in God's name were you thinking of? You let your brother blackmail you, you left me, intending to deny me the opportunity of ever seeing my son or daughter . . . all because you think I can't love you unconditionally. What makes you think that your capacity for love is greater than mine? I told you once that I would never judge you. I told you that I would always take your side. I told you that I needed you, and you . . ." Suddenly his voice cracked, and he turned away from her with a curse, his broad shoulders rigid with tension, his black head bowed. "I was afraid I'd never find you," he said hoarsely.

Mira made her way to him slowly, her eyes wet, her face flushed with hope, and relief that was dizzy-sweet as it coursed through her, and love that was so intense it felt like pain. Suddenly she saw how much she had hurt him, she understood that he did need her, and she understood what a terrible mistake she had made. Any woman would sell her soul to be needed so much. "Alec," she said unsteadily, "it broke my heart to think that I would never see you again."

He kept his back to her, his fingers whitening as his

hands clenched into fists. "How could you have left like that?" he muttered.

"I didn't understand . . . I didn't realize how you'd feel. I want you to be happy. I thought you'd be happier without me. It was cowardly, but I didn't want to face up to what I'd lost . . . what I thought I'd lost. But from now on, everything will be different. You know all of my secrets, and there's nothing I'm afraid of anymore."

"Don't ever leave me again," he said roughly.

"I won't, I swear it."

"Next time there'll be hell to pay."

"There'll *never* be a next time."

"I'm going to hold you to your promises."

"I'll keep them," she promised tearfully, and suddenly he turned, and his mouth was on hers, and she was held so tightly that she could barely breathe. His arms were hard and crushing, shaking from the force of his passion. Her thin nightgown was soaked by the cold rainwater that saturated his clothes, her fingers were sliding through the wet obsidian of his hair . . . she didn't feel the cold, she was burning from inside. Welcoming the punishing kiss, she parted her lips and offered him the sweetness of her mouth, and he took it, not with appreciation or gratitude, but with a fierce demand for more. His lips parted from hers and slid down her neck, and she trembled underneath his plundering mouth, words escaping her lips in a fragile whisper. "Take me to bed," she sighed. "Alec . . . I need you . . . I need to feel you inside me."

Silently he lifted his head and stared down at her, his arms tightening around her slim body. In a lithe movement he picked her up and carried her to the bed. His eyes, blazing with desire, fastened on her as if he were afraid she might disappear, and his gaze did not waver from her as he shed his clothes. He dwarfed the small bed as he pulled her to the center of the mattress. She caught her breath as he ripped her delicate white gown down the center, too impatient to unfasten the tiny buttons that held it together. Brushing aside the remnants of the gown, Alec lowered his body over hers, and she felt hot and cold shivers run down her spine as his naked flesh covered hers. He was as sleek and strong as a panther, demanding that she satisfy his hunger, unaware that there was any other world outside the small room. His bare flesh was damp with rainwater, and soon her skin was moistened from it as well, and she pressed her open mouth against his skin. He tasted like rain, like the storm, and she licked at the dampness with delicate flutters of her tongue.

He groaned her name and bent his head to her breasts, his mouth flickering around the pale pink areola of her nipple, drawing it into his mouth, playing lightly with his tongue until the aroused flesh responded, contracting into hard buds. He seemed to savor the helpless sounds she made, and as he continued to tease her breasts with his mouth, his hands drifted over the rest of her body. His fingertips smoothed across her legs and hips, drew a pattern slowly across her stomach, wandered to the insides of her thighs and teased them further apart. Mira arched up to him hungrily, crooning encouragement, desperate for the relief his touch could give her, but his hand moved slowly, lazily, until she whimpered her need for him to end the torment. Moaning as she felt his finger slip inside her, she undulated her hips in response to his rhythm. Suddenly his finger was withdrawn, and the shock of emptiness seared through her. Her hands slid down to his hard buttocks, urging him to settle on top of her.

"I should make you wait longer," he whispered, desire shining in his eyes as he looked down at her. "For all I've suffered tonight, you should know a little of it too."

"Don't punish me." She arched up to him, pressing

a coaxing kiss against his throat. "Don't punish me for loving you too much."

"Oh God, Mira," he breathed, and entered her in one stroke, hard and swollen, filling her softness until she gasped and writhed in an effort to accommodate him. Thrusting heavily, he joined his body to hers with long, powerful drives. As he brought her closer and closer to a dizzying precipice, her shaking hands locked behind his flexing back. She buried her face in his throat and sobbed as she was overcome by an ecstasy more perfect, more complete than anything they had ever shared before. Her flesh tightened convulsively around his, and as the same tremors shook his body she held him tightly, whispering her love against the damp heat of his skin.

When he had recovered enough to move, Alec rolled over with her and sat up, cradling her against his chest as he leaned against the pillows. She rested her cheek on top of his shoulder, sighing in contentment. "I love you," he said thickly, unfastening her long braid and playing with the dark, silky locks. "Don't ever doubt it. If it takes a lifetime, I'll do whatever it takes to make you believe it."

"I believe it right now," Mira replied, pressing a warm kiss on his lips, her eyes soft and brilliant as she met his gaze. "But I'll still require frequent reminders."

"So will I."

"It's a good bargain," she murmured. "Your love for mine."

"That's not a bargain, sweet . . . it's a guarantee."

The sound of raised voices filtered from the sitting room into the great hall, where they echoed until everyone in Falkner castle could hear the debate. Not a soul could be found tiptoeing through the hallways; when Alec matched up against Juliana, it was time to take shelter and close the doors. The Penrhyn will of steel and the explosive Falkner temper—there was no telling who would win, but the combination was not a good one. While the argument progressed, Mira sat in the corner of the sofa, occupying herself with sorting through her bag of herbs in order to make an herbal compress for Juliana's eyes. Carr, the subject of the debate, sat nearby with a drink in his hand, having little success in interrupting and offering a word on his own behalf. Alec paced edgily around the room while Juliana spoke from her chair before the fire.

"I don't see that there's much you can do to stop Carr from leaving," the matriarch said. "And your bullish temper isn't going to convince him to change his mind either. He won't be talked out of it."

"Carr," Mira interceded, "are you certain that leaving England to search for Leila Holburn is what you want?"

"It's what I want," Carr said, his green eyes sincere. "I know everyone thinks that it's merely out of obligation to Holt, but it's more than that."

"I asked Juliana to help me talk him out of it," Alec said grimly, "thinking that she would take a practical view of it all. And instead—probably just to confuse me—she prattled to him for an hour about knights and quests and all sorts of chivalric balderd—"

Juliana interrupted with a derisive snort. "I never prattle, Alec. And I dislike your implication that my advice to him has been less than sound. Furthermore, he's not a boy any longer, and he has the right to make decisions unaided by you, or me, or anyone else."

"Not when he has no idea what kind of trouble he can bring on himself!" Alec said, scowling. "We're not talking about sending him on a tour abroad! He's going to a place where none of us will be able to help him out of his scrapes."

"I daresay it will be safer than London," Juliana said.

"Not for a greenhead like Carr, it won't!"

According to Guillaume, Leila had been kidnapped, sold by Stop Hole Abbey, and sent to Northern Africa. There was no way of knowing who had her or where she was now, but Carr had surprised them all with the announcement that he intended to find her. Perhaps it had been his recent visit to Leila's family that had sparked the idea . . . perhaps it *was* merely out of a feeling of obligation to Holt's memory . . . but whatever the reason, Carr seemed determined to search for her. Mira felt a wave of sympathy and understanding as she looked at Alec's young cousin. Over the past few days he seemed to have left his boyhood behind. He had dealt with Guillaume with unexpected maturity, deciding to spare his life, and he saw to it personally that Guillaume was put on a ship to Australia. There Guillaume would have a difficult life to face, filled with work and hardship—and maybe it would change him for the better. Mira would always be grateful to Carr for his mercy toward her brother.

"Alec is just being protective," she whispered to Carr while Juliana and Alec continued to argue. "He feels responsible for those he cares about—and though he won't admit it, he's become very fond of you."

"I know," Carr said, chuckling softly. "We'll all be glad when the baby's born—he'll be too involved with his son or daughter to give much thought to the rest of us."

"I wouldn't lay odds on that," Mira replied, and they smiled at each other.

"Are you against my going?" he asked.

Mira hesitated for a moment, then reached around her neck and took off the Falkner medallion discreetly. Wrapping the rope chain around the gleaming object, she held the solid weight of it in her palm. "You brought this back to me," she said, looking at him steadily. "It was once given to Alec as a sign of his coming of age. Take it with you on your journey, as a sign of my faith in you, mine and Alec's." She grinned at him. "And bring it back safely, or he'll have my head."

"Thank you," he said simply, taking the medallion and pocketing it, ducking his head to hide the emotion in his eyes.

Mira smiled and called across the room to her husband. "Alec, I believe I'll retire now. It's been a very long day."

"I'll accompany you upstairs," Alec replied automatically, throwing both Juliana and Carr a dark look. "We'll finish this conversation tomorrow."

Mira slipped her hand into his as they walked upstairs to the keep.

"Juliana's filling his head with nonsense," Alec grumbled. "Can you picture him prancing through Africa, looking for that girl? He doesn't even know what she looks like!"

"Perhaps he should go. Have you considered what there is for him to do now? His brother's death has been explained. His books no longer hold the interest for him that they used to. He seems to think that he has little in common with his friends now. He's anxious to exercise his newfound independence. Perhaps he needs a quest."

"There are more practical things for him to set his energies toward," Alec said, picking her up when they reached the landing and carrying her to the bedroom.

"I agree." She hooked her arms around his neck. "But none of your suggestions would be as romantic as the idea of rescuing a fair lady in distress, would they?"

Alec grinned down at her reluctantly, his eyes twinkling. "No, they wouldn't."

"There you have it," she said reasonably. "Now, are we going to continue talking about this for the next few hours, or do you have any other suggestions about how we should spend the rest of the night?"

"I have a few," he admitted, depositing her on the

bed and sitting down beside her. "There's only one problem."

"What is that?"

"Tonight's not long enough for everything I have in mind."

"We have more than just one night," Mira said, stretching lazily. "We have forever."

His blood stirred with increasing warmth as he looked at her. So beautiful, so special . . . so much his. She was the one thing he had never taken for granted, nor would he ever.

"Forever's not long enough."

"Oh, we'll get by on it," she said, and smiled as he leaned over and kissed her.